Spellscribed

PROVENANCE

By Kristopher Cruz

With special thanks to James, Lacey, Larry, Gina, Alec, and everyone else who helped me make this possible. You all really did make the difference when things were getting tough for me.

Table of Contents

Prologue

The fates are an indecipherable sort. Their plots and plays cross the destinies of all men, human or otherwise. To them, time and life are but threads they weave together. They hold the strings; they know when certain ones weave, and when all strings are cut.

Of those strings, there are the ones who are considered heroes. They are beacons of light to those who live in darkness. Where their threads travel, others weave around them to form powerful cords which alter the flow of the destinies of hundreds if not thousands of lives. These great heroes are whispered about even in the years before their coming, to those whose minds and hearts are closely attuned to fate…

The light of the moon weakly played across the elder man's face as he watched the newborn child quietly shift within the blanket he held in his arms. The night sky was overcast, with dark clouds murky and obscuring the stars. The moon had only the littlest sliver of space to shed her light. Most of that light was on the infant he held, and for all purposes he supposed that some obscurity would be good. If an accidental observer saw the exchange, he would not be able to do his job effectively.

He smiled as the child cooed softly and chuckled as the babe grabbed at the stubble of his closely shaven chin. Looking up, he spoke to the one he had brought the child to.

"This child is yours now." he stated, adjusting his arms so the child would be comfortable. "Valeria cannot care for him."

The younger of the two held up a hand, his dark hair and eyes almost black in the deep night. "So I was informed. Is she really gone?" he asked.

The elder passed the child to the younger, nodding in the dark. "Yes, though it took nearly all three of our lives to end it. We did not foresee this result in the slightest when we assisted her with the ritual." He replied, shaking his head. "I only narrowly survived. Even so, I fear the death she brought against us was only forestalled. Valeria is… was one of the best of the Holy Circle. Her death and revival have shaken the foundations of the order."

The younger looked at the child in the dark. He was beautiful, with large and inquisitive emerald eyes that were pools of luminous green in the dark. Fair skinned, the babe would have a flawless appearance if it weren't for the effects his mother had left him with. A small curl of stark silver hair stuck to the newborn's forehead. The worst of it was thousands of miniscule red lines that covered his tiny fragile body. They twisted and whorled across his fair skin, following arcane patterns of spell work. They flowed over his meridians, using them as a guide for the powers worked into the babe.

It must have been horribly painful for the child, yet the babe merely looked up at the younger man and cooed. Reaching up with a chubby arm to tug at his clothes, he seemed no more inconvenienced by the magic woven upon him as he was the night air or the sound of their talking. As he held the child into the moonlight, he glanced up at Valeria's assistant.

"What about these marks?" he asked.

The elder frowned. "The hair will always be such a color, nothing that can be done to change it save for dyes. The marks were gleaming gold when he was born, and have been fading since that moment. I believe that they should either fade away entirely or at least become less obvious as time passes."

The younger tilted his head. "What are they?"

The older man shrugged. "I am not sure. Wizard Markus performed the ritual to tattoo them upon the babe, but he is dead now and hadn't said what its purpose was." He scratched his chin. "Though Valeria did things in threes. Three reasons, three tasks, three assistants, three investitures of power. Whatever it was, she was more than certain it would work."

The young man nodded, and looked down as the baby started to cry. "He's hungry." He observed.

The elder man shrugged. "Then make sure he's fed. He is your son now."

The young man sighed as he turned to the house he dwelled in, the fire inside framing the front door in light. "It's very strange, being the father of a child born to my great-great aunt."

The elder turned away. "Wizards live long lives, my friend. I am going to keep an eye on the child, to observe his growth and lend a hand where needed. He does not need to know my involvement, understand?"

The man only waved a hand over his shoulder, and the older man vanished with a twist of his wrist and a carefully enunciated word. Looking down, he saw that the child had quieted, and was looking about curiously with brilliant emerald green eyes that seemed illuminated despite the darkness of the cloudy night. "Well, Endrance." The man began. "Let us see about getting you fed…"

Chapter 01

The young man sat quietly in one of the dark chambers of his master's keep. The cold radiated up his limbs from deep within the stone beneath his soft-shoed feet. It made him at least mildly uncomfortable and cold.

Endrance had stopped growing after a while, remaining five foot six for the last year or so. His face was just angular enough to be attractive, with soft edges and smooth cheeks. His eyes and ears bore very faint traces of elven heritage, an almost unnoticeable slant to his eyes and point to his ear tips. Being short, he was also very slender, and had slimly developed muscles, perhaps another throwback to there being an elf in his ancestry somewhere along the line a few generations ago. The cumulating effect being that he looked either a very beautiful man or a handsome woman.

He wore cotton pants and shirt, simple and unembellished. They were covered over with a simple, sturdy cut, dark gray robe that had a white sash around his waist.

The sash was cotton, just as the robe, but it was bleached white and the end of the sash dangled from the looped knot on his side. It had three golden-threaded Sigils on the end, each vaguely circular in nature. They represented the stages of his growth as a user of magic, just as much as the rest of his ensemble did. The plain gray robes indicated he was an apprentice, while the white sash showed he had mastered the basics all apprentices had been taught. The three Sigils were his degree of mastery. All formal sashes were cut so there was room for twelve Sigils once they were tied. The young man knew that each degree of mastery was orders of magnitude harder to obtain than the last.

It had taken him nearly nine years of dedicated training and study to get to the third. Learning since his early childhood, he had learned prodigiously, yet still he had so very much that he didn't know. Like any craft, or art, there was always room for improvement.

He looked at his master, who sat upon a simple wooden chair across the room from him. His face was illuminated by a single tallow candle that the master kept in a candelabrum on the small table next to him. Its light flickered and jumped, casting eerie shadows across his countenance. He rested with his head propped up on one hand and his elbow on the armrest of his chair.

His master wore robes of dark blue silk and silver thread. His sash was black silk, and upon it eleven gold Sigils gleamed in the faint candlelight. His aged visage still held some of the sharp edges he bore in youth, some of which only had been made sharper by age, others softened over the years. His jaw line and nose were evidence he had been at one point very handsome. His wrinkled, weather beaten skin composed an aged and experienced inflection upon his person. Clear, sharp, calculating brown eyes peered out from beneath bushy gray-white brows. He seemed surprisingly alert for a man in his eighth century. Almost an afterthought to his appearance, his bone white hair was cut very short, almost like he had shaved it once long ago and only recently had grown out.

Master Kaelob was a High Magus, one of perhaps a half dozen in the empire of Ironsoul. Endrance knew he had been lucky; High Magus Kaelob had once been apprentice to the legendary mage Valeria and through the years leading up to the mage's death had proven himself time and again for Ironsoul as an independent Wizard. Her mysterious death triggered him into going into retirement, though he would not say specifically why he did so. Being picked as an apprentice by someone of his stature was a great boon and a sign of status amidst the magical community.

Today he stood before his master in an official capacity. Normally during training and study days they dispensed with formal dress and garb and merely dressed comfortably; after all no ceremonies had to be observed on a day to day basis. Today was important however, and all rites were observed.

The elder magus coughed gently, clearing his throat, though no one was present to hear the conversation other than his apprentice. He fixed his eyes on the young man, who tensed up slightly as he spoke.

"Apprentice Endrance. You have proven your breadth of knowledge and your studious acquisition of the art." He began, his voice soft but carrying throughout the room. "Your voice has been trained to carry the proper words to the great magic, and you have been instilled with the techniques to maintain that voice." The corner of his mouth twitched, as he subtly subdued a smile. "You have shown mastery of the sensory arts, as well as mastery over moving your spiritual force and shaping it into existence." He finished. "Would you say that this is true?"

The young apprentice nodded. "Yes, master." He replied, his soft voice seemed to be swallowed up by the stone instead of amplified by it. "I have accomplished such things."

The master's chin dipped towards his chest momentarily. "You have met all the requirements for the holy Circle of Magi to sever your title of apprentice, and bequeath the title of practitioner, except for one." He replied. He sounded like he had repeated this statement more than once before, and was drawing more from rote than active memory.

He held a finger out, pointing to the young apprentice. "You must prove your cumulative experience in a trial. This will challenge you in all aspects of your mastery, and know that you will be in very real danger." He let the last word drag out ominously. "Do you understand the risks?"

Endrance nodded solemnly, though inside he was trying very hard not to laugh. He had spent hours studying the customary speeches he would have to listen to in order to increase in status with the Circle of Magi, so he knew that Kaelob was reciting the ceremony word for word. He was also making it seem overly dramatic, with the dark room and the ominous tones. Even after all this time, the master had a sense of humor that bordered on insanity. It was to be expected as an apprentice of the mad mage.

"I understand, master." Endrance responded, "I am ready to begin the trial when everything is ready."

The High Magus popped to his feet in a smooth lurch, striding up to his apprentice and tugging his sleeve as he blew past. "Excellent!" he exclaimed, completely out of protocol or character for the rite. "This way then, m'boy! Had the spot set up for a week now!"

The apprentice spun about and tried to keep up with his master. Kaelob was tall and scrawny, with long legs and an improbably long stride for Endrance to keep up with, being a whole foot shorter than the man. He hurried along behind the High Magus, whose sweeping steps took the two of them to the keep courtyard.

Endrance looked about as they came to a stop. He had crossed through the courtyard every morning for nearly ten years, and it didn't look any different than it usually did. Heavy stone laid in even squares. Hard reinforced walls stood resolutely against the open sky above them. Banners drifted in the breeze from posts Kaelob put up long before. The blue banners had crudely sewn images of a face sticking its tongue out in white thread. It looked absolutely awful, but Kaelob never changed them.

"I don't understand, master." He said, scratching his head. "It looks like it always has."

He turned to look at his master as the old man made the deliberate action of dropping a small glass sphere upon the stones. The delicate object cracked against the flagstones and shattered into tiny pieces, and from within the sphere came a great rush of wind, whipping around the two magi. Endrance shielded his face and closed his eyes against the wind, which had the bitter cut of winter, even though the last snows had fallen months before.

The winds died down, yet it got even colder. Crisp cold air pervaded his robes, and he looked around in surprise. They were not where they had stood moments before. Instead they found themselves upon a small stone rise near the top of the local mountain. Endrance rubbed his arms and tried to keep warm as he looked around. He thought he could see his home village in the distance, and Kaelob's keep was protruding from the forests nearby that.

High Magus Kaelob clapped his hands and gestured in the other direction. There was a small stone tower jutting up from the top of the mountain. The Watchstone Tower, Endrance realized. He'd never seen it up close, and it didn't look as impressive as he thought it would be.

The stone tower was barely forty feet wide at the base and thirty where the top was broken off maybe sixty feet up. The grand stones of the tower were covered in layers of snow and ice, crusted around its outside and through its window's bolt holes. It stood at the tip of the mountain, a task of construction beyond anyone Endrance could think of. The only way to reach the tower on foot was through the narrow climb to the front arch. Steep drops encircled it on all the other sides of the circle, and a fall from the top would be certain death.

It looked like someone had reached up with a giant hand and swatted the top of the tower down long ago. Several of the large stones that made its walls lay scattered around the area, most covered in snow and frost, others half buried in the dirt. It was broken at what Endrance could guess was the halfway point. Almost level with the end of the tower was one of the floors, almost swept clean by how close the walls had come down around it. It made for a great platform to get an unimpeded view of the surroundings.

Kaelob pointed to the top of the tower. "There." He exclaimed, seeming unimpressed or impacted by the cold. "The top of the tower is where our test will begin. There you will demonstrate your resolve, concentration, and ability to survive in the world."

With that, the old man rotated his right hand around at the wrist, his fingers clenched in an unnatural pattern while he jabbed at the top of the tower with the other hand's index finger. "*Ambularus.*" he muttered, leaning forward and taking a single step.

His foot landed on the top of the tower, and the rest of him followed immediately after. Endrance barely felt a trickle of power coming from his master. It was a quick and effective teleportation spell with marginal draw on the weave of magic. Endrance shook his head as he trotted over to the tower's entrance. His master had proven his expertise with even his most simple of spells.

He didn't think that he could pull off a spell similar to that. Even so, he would have to take much longer to cast and drain far more energy than he felt given off from the magic his master wove.

As he got closer he slowed to a walk, eventually needing to carefully pick his way over the rough terrain. He saw blocks of stone, broken shards of the tower, imbedded in the ground. He gauged one block to weigh easily a few hundred pounds, so them being half buried on impact was to be expected. As he got close to the tower he started seeing the wreckage of the tower's armaments.

The cold started to wear at him, and he shivered. The robes were an extra layer of heat trapping cloth, but the wind was cutting right through it. As a result he was getting cold very quickly, and could do little to help himself. He would have to pass this test quickly and get back where it was warm. He smirked as he considered using the flame spell he had seen his master using so many times, but decided against it. He wanted to save that for when it was needed. He wasn't supposed to have learned the workings of the spell from just watching master Kaelob, but he had managed to figure it out.

He passed by a ballista bolt, snapped in half and partially buried in earth and snow. The head of the weapon was made of three staggered rows of sharp hooked blades, and the back end of the bolt had the rusted remains of a chain attached to it. *What could they have been using those for?* He wondered, stepping into the building proper.

The entrance to the tower was an empty stone arch, the wood and iron door had succumbed to the weather and old age centuries ago. Inside had been picked clean by scavengers and animals, and the continuous winds and cold air made the place a stone icebox, the only sound the whistling of the wind through its drafty bones. It was only marginally warmer inside, as the wind was cut down greatly by the stone walls. He still wouldn't want to stay a night here without heavy repairs and a large fire. And bedding, blankets too. Perhaps with a departure of his sanity to top it all off.

Along the back wall a set of stone steps curled along the wall leading up. It was likely only one more floor between the floor and the top of the tower. He sighed, rubbing his hands together as he moved up the tower.

The young apprentice made his way up the stairs and started clearing his head along the way. His master may have a great many things in mind for his test. Though he did not relish the idea, he had spent many nights studying a wide variety of spells. He just hoped that he wouldn't have to fight up there. He shuddered, this time having nothing to do with the cold. Combat magic was not his strong suit. Top that with slippery stone and a long drop off all sides, he did not favor his chances up there if it came to a fight.

He reached the top, the last flight of stone stairs covered in snow and ice, so he had to pay careful attention to his step as he ascended. At the top his master waited for him, arms crossed, his foot tapping incessantly. He seemed entirely unaffected by the cold, and the wind whipped at his robes slowly, giving the impression he was standing in slow motion through high speed winds.

"About time you got up here, m'boy." He grumbled amiably. "Your test is simple. You must remain conscious for five minutes." He stated, taking an hourglass from out of his sleeve and setting it on the utmost highest remaining block. The sand started trickling down slowly.

Endrance frowned as he looked at the hourglass. "That can't be all there is to the test, is there?" he asked defensively. Already he brought several spells to mind, and started preparing himself to throw energy into a spell in a hurry. He already knew the answer his master would give, but he had to ask. A line like that just begs to be answered.

"Of course not!" Master Kaelob replied, rolling his shoulders and stretching his legs a little for show. "I get the pleasure of trying to render you unconscious."

Yep. Combat magic. Endrance sighed. "Of course."

Chapter 02

Master Kaelob lost no time and began his assault, flicking his left hand in a quick, up and down motion, and his right hand came up, his fingers in a claw. *"Ignatius!"* he hissed, and flames roared out of his hand from his palm, spraying out of his hand in a rolling, shrieking cone.

Endrance was prepared for combat to begin, but had no magic to directly counter it, so instead he dove to the side, his hands shuddering as he attempted to cast his spell. The cold had made his hands mostly numb, and the added confusion of trying to not die made him unsure if he could pull it off.

The fingers of his left hand rapidly twisted into a swift pair of mudras as his arm moved from right to left across himself. His right arm swept into a circle in front of him. *"Peltaeus!"* He responded, his shoulder hitting the ice slicked snow as the spell took the energy he imparted into it. The flames washed across the area he was still in, but drew a strong hiss of steam as an eggshell thin bubble of congealed frost swept up from the snowy ground around him.

Endrance scrambled to his feet as his hastily constructed ice shield diverted the bulk of the flames, leaving him standing unharmed behind a cloud of steam. Warmth had filled the air around him for but a moment, but was swept away by the freezing winds. The steam cleared as the wind howled by, and Kaelob had not moved since the attack began.

"Excellent!" He exclaimed. "Use your environment to bolster your magic, very good. Using fire in a place like this is a bad idea, with so much cold and wind around!"

He thrust his arm forward, his hand formed into a claw. *"Culare!"*

Endrance dove to the other side, receiving a matching bruise on his other shoulder for the effort. Unseen force rippled past. It was invisible, but the effects it left behind were not. For the split instant that the spell shot through the sky, the snow in its path got caught up by it, hurtling past Endrance's side and clear out off the side of the tower. A column of snow-less air as thick as his waist traveled on past Kaelob's hand and beyond, and in an instant it was filled in as more snow fell.

Endrance skidded to a stop and flinched as his arm fell into the stairs leading down. He rolled in the other direction, and came to his feet again. He knew he would never be able to defeat his master in combat, especially not in a place of his choosing or preparation. He could, however use his environment to his advantage. He thought quickly, and devised a plan he thought was at least somewhat clever.

He dropped to a knee as Kaelob prepared to launch another spell at him. Again he brought up his shield of ice, but this time made a conscious effort to put more power into the spell. This time, the frost congealed together and thickened, forming a half-dome of ice nearly an inch thick. It's sloped side deflected whatever it was that Kaelob had thrown at him, and Endrance smirked. He felt the tingle of his master pulling more energy into a spell, and quickly went to work.

He brought his almost entirely numb hands together and entwined them into the sign of the dreamer and quietly whispered *"Praestigius."* More

7

of his power drained into the spell, and he felt himself starting to feel the wear. Master Kaelob could also force him to knock himself unconscious from overusing his magic, if Endrance wasn't careful.

He then immediately rolled back on his heels, sliding onto the top most steps of the stairs down. A quick twist of his waist, and he slid down the stairs on his back, his feet held out before him and his arms out to either side for stability. His image remained behind the frost barrier, appearing to be holding his hands out to the ice with his eyes closed in concentration. He appeared to be muttering, and his voice could barely be heard over the wind. To all purposes he appeared to be maintaining the barrier.

Endrance came to a stop at the landing, popping to his feet and stepping aside the stairs. He intended on maintaining the illusion from down below, and keep Kaelob focused on fighting it while he took shelter from the cold, which would most assuredly bring him down. There he could figure out how to defend himself against the cold, and come back up when he was certain of achieving his goal.

He turned to find a safe niche in the room and immediately spotted Kaelob standing in the same room. He had his arms up and oddly bent as if he was controlling a puppet, and he looked at Endrance with wide eyes, and his lips pursed. He appeared as a kid caught in the middle of doing something he knew was wrong.

"Ah, well." The apprentice muttered, scratching at his cheek. "I guess… damn." There went his plans. *It looks like my master had the same idea. Now what?*

Kaelob cleared his throat and brought his arms down, smoothing the front of his robes. "Hmmm… yes. Awkward." he responded quietly, his eyes still wide.

A tense moment passed, the only sound the wind whistling through the stone structure. Then they both broke into action at the same time. Kaelob thrust a finger out at him and cried *"Gelare!"* A ray of icy white and blue light shot through the air at his apprentice, who yelped and scrambled up the stairs again. The ray met stone, and a layer of ice burst outwards along the sides of the stone, encasing it several feet across.

Endrance came up the stairs in a rush, and hopped over the shield he had left standing. He skidded on his heels and fell on his rear, narrowly avoiding a bolt of force that Kaelob's illusory double launched at him. He was unsure if the attack would have done any actual damage since it was an illusion, but considering the power his master had at his disposal he was fairly certain that it was best to just avoid it.

A second Kaelob came up the stairs just afterwards, throwing a duplicate bolt of force at Endrance's prone form. He rolled, and cried out in fear as the *whoomph* of the energy crashing into the floor sent him skidding several feet to the side. That one hurt. As he saw Kaelob step onto the roof, a third copy poked his head up and glared at him as he ascended the stairs.

This was bad. If he was keeping these illusions running, he could be any one of the three. He could subdue him as he tried to take on a copy. A frightening thought shivered through his spine. *What if all three of them are copies?*

Uncertain, he knew he had to avoid all of their attention long enough to save his hide. He forewent standing in exchange for getting a spell off. He held his hand up into the air and shouted aloud as the spell released. *"Inumbrae!"*

The air around him went black, wrapped in the deepest of magical shadows. It swelled out, encapsulating almost the entire top of the tower. He couldn't see anything within the dome of darkness around him, but Kaelob and his duplicates couldn't see either. He wasted no time; He pulled himself up to a knee, but stayed low. A low profile meant less likely to be hit by a blindly thrown spell.

He shivered again, and realized he could barely feel anything. His feet had gone numb long ago. The exertion of casting and running around had helped to keep him warm, but he was tiring quickly. He quickly rubbed his hands together and breathed on them to try to warm them. As he puffed into his hands he had a brilliant idea.

He channeled more energy, formed the correct signs in the darkness as he drew in an icy, chilling breath. It was the long style of casting, so he had to waste precious seconds composing the spell. He muttered a long incantation, pleading the magic to grant him what he desired, taking one last breath. He exhaled, his breath coming out hot. Instead of being swept away by the wind, the hot air spread and wrapped around his body. Heat started seeping into his aching limbs, and he could feel the tip of his nose again. The spell should greatly reduce the effects of the cold. It might even keep the wind chill at bay since it would continuously warm the air around him so long as he kept the spell active.

He waited quietly, listening. Though it didn't give him much advance notice as, say, watching a wizard form hand symbols, mudra, or weave patterns as they prepared to cast a spell, hearing the final word of power might give him a chance to avoid the spell or even counter it if he knew what the word of power meant.

His skin prickled, and he rolled to his left, quietly summoning up his frost shield as he came back to his feet. He hadn't heard a word, but the wind was whistling through the air enough to hide murmurs and whispered phrases. Something collided where he had once stood, and he felt his newly forming frost barrier shatter under the blow. The spillover force knocked him on his back, and his head rapped against the stone floor. Stars swam across his vision, and he couldn't concentrate on anything.

Master Kaelob must have started tearing his darkness spell to pieces, causing light to gleam in cracks along the outer boundaries before it fell apart entirely. One of him walked up to the stunned apprentice and looked down on him, his face full of disappointment. Endrance's vision started clearing up again, the pain of his knock to the head fading slightly.

He held a hand up, pointing a finger at Endrance. From under his arm, Endrance could see that though he had lasted a goodly amount of time, some time still remained in the hourglass. He had no chance of casting any useful spell before Kaelob would be able to hit him. His mind raced as he saw his master take a breath to incant something dangerous.

Desperate, he twisted his hip, kicking out with his foot at his master's leg. It barely connected, causing Kaelob to shift his weight to try to keep from falling. His other foot slipped on the ice, and the High Magus looked surprised for an instant before he dropped to the ground on his back. Endrance slapped his hand on the icy stone below him and shouted "*Deserpo!*"

More power siphoned out of him and into the ice, he felt momentarily light headed as the spell came into effect. The ice below and around Master Kaelob experienced an explosion of growth, spreading across his robes and over his form. It only took an instant to completely cover over his opponent, leaving him encased in ice. The frost glinted with the faint suns light that pierced the clouds above.

Endrance stood up, and carefully looked down at his master. The old man looked up at him through the ice, and grinned at him. He looked pleased.

"Most excellent, m'boy!" Kaelob exclaimed, walking up the steps onto the open floor. Endrance did a double take, and looked down at the ice cage, which was still occupied.. The other duplicate he had fought was gone. "Not afraid to mix up physical combat with magical. Good!" the elder mage assessed. "And you creatively use relatively simple words of power. I'm impressed!"

Endrance panted, his hands on his knees. "Well," he stated. "You know me. Use all of what you learn, I always say."

The High Magus bobbed his head, rubbing his hands together. "Of course. Is that a warmth spell I feel you using?"

Endrance stood up, and half shrugged. "More of a wrap of warm air. It's not the most efficient when there's a lot of wind, but it won't melt the ice around me like others would."

Kaelob smiled approvingly. "Good. Good. *Gelare!*" He suddenly thrust his finger out, throwing another ray of frost at him. Endrance didn't try to block the spell or dodge. He instead thrust both hands out in their complicated mudras and shouted "*Ignatius!*" with more force and power than he suspected his master had initially used on him. From his hands poured forth a literal flood of bright orange fire, roiling and boiling outwards as it easily absorbed the freezing ray with no apparent loss of momentum as it swept over more than half of the roof and into the sky beyond.

"Oh my." Kaelob managed to exclaim before the fire was upon him.

Endrance didn't wait for the spell to peter out on its own, knowing that his master would survive such a simple attack easily. It wasn't weak; those flames were more than powerful enough to sweep across forty feet of open terrain and burn anything flammable within, or wash through seventy or so feet of enclosed spaces. It was also unexpected. Kaelob had never taught him that spell. He was also certain he had estimated the amount of power Kaelob was putting into his spells and put enough into his own to defeat it.

It wasn't a sure thing though. There was a great deal of theoretical math that would go into perfectly defending against a spell. A wizard would have to know not only the full properties of the magic being opposed, but also be able to provide just enough energy to cancel it out once cast.

He dashed towards the edge of the building, leaping out and grasping for the one thing that would grant him victory. His body ached, and he felt he was pulling out the last dredges of his energy just to keep the spell keeping him warm active. His aura was likely dangerously close to empty. His fingertips had just barely touched it when unseen force caught him and slammed him to the ground. He struggled with all his might and barely managed to flip over onto his back. Whatever it was, he was pinned. He didn't even have the strength to pit his will against the bindings he was trapped in.

Kaelob who stood before the cage was gone. Nothing remained at all except scorched stone and a swiftly vanishing waft of smoke. The ice cage he had encased the double in shattered, shards of frozen ice flying everywhere. "That was close, m'boy." Kaelob muttered, pulling himself to his feet. "And here I thought I had you all figured out. Then you surprise me like that." This time he kept him held with magic as he approached.

"You have done admirably so far. You have even managed to learn some of my spells just by watching me use them a few times. Only two other people have ever pulled off such a trick, learning the short form of a spell just by observing it a few times. How did you do it?"

Endrance struggled against the barrier a moment, trying to catch his breath. He took a breath and tried to shrug, but was unable to move enough. "Well, you know." He began. "I could sense the shapes you formed your magic into whenever you cast spells. I just held my own energy in the same patterns and imitated your mudras and words of power."

"You could sense the patterns of the spell, inside of me, with all this cold, under stress, and in combat?" he asked.

The young man clamped his mouth shut for a moment to stop the involuntary chattering. When did his warmth spell fail? "I had to guess at a bunch of it, to be honest, and I think I used many times more energy than was needed for a properly made spell, but it was a good show, yeah?"

Kaelob shook his head. "More like dangerous, and not for me. You know what can happen if you channel too much energy, and you still did it anyways."

Kaelob held his finger out towards his apprentice one more time, this time Endrance was not so sure he was doing it for a spell.

"Any last words before I flunk you out of this test, and send you to scrub the floors for the rest of the week?" he asked.

The hourglass Endrance had bumped teetered over the edge, finally tipped over by the whirling snow. It tumbled down to land on Endrance's stomach. He looked at the empty top half and then back up at his master. "I win?" he said hopefully. Chill winds whistled through the silent tower. Kaelob looked at the glass and grimaced.

Chapter 03

Endrance awoke the next day, later in the morning than was usual for him and yawned as he sat up in bed. He had long since moved to the only other room in their cottage, and Endrance appreciated the privacy as he washed himself and got dressed in clothes he was comfortable in.

He wore rugged pants of thick cloth, threaded with leather down the seams. Like most of his clothes they were at one point someone else's, but given to him as a hand-down. His father neatly cut them down to fit his son, and fixed the wear and tear before giving them over. Endrance slipped a pale cotton shirt over his chest, long sleeved but light and airy. He pulled soft-soled deer hide boots onto his feet, a commonly found kind with no cuff around the ankles.

Splashing water from his small washbasin into his face to help clear the cobwebs of sleep from his mind, he opened his door and walked into the other room of his father's house. The room had an earthy feel to it, stone walls and thatched ceiling, with only two crossing rafters and one wooden pillar in the center of the room to support the whole thing. Aside from a pair of wooden chairs, some shelves and a table, the only furniture in the room was his father's bed near the hearth, which was already empty as Endrance could hear his father was outside the cottage. The floor was packed dirt covered in wooden planking, with a large tattered rug covering the majority of the floor. There was a small fire in the hearth, with a kettle hung over the flames.

The young man checked the kettle and was pleased to see that there was still water steaming inside. Picking over the contents of a shelf, he selected a small cup and set it on the table. Using a heavy leather glove he swung the kettle out from over the fire and gingerly poured hot water into his cup. After setting the kettle back on its hook, he carefully measured and dropped a pinch of tea leaves into the water. Soon the aroma of steeping tea drifted up from the cup, and he smiled. Stirring the tea absently, he pondered the dream he had that night. He had been taught that dreams - specifically the ones that he remembers- have meaning and the ones that stick out in his mind the most are meant to deliver a message.

He had dreamed that night that he was standing over a great precipice, and in front of him laid a large expanse of land. From this place he could see every kingdom in the world, even the ones he had only barely heard of and even some he did not know existed. Over each city was a great cloudy shadow that stretched over the entirety of it. It gathered over the center of each city with dark tendrils of blackened cloud that reached down into the cities, and from those cities Endrance could hear the sobbing of many and the cries of terror of the people below him.

He had felt great sadness for these people, so oppressed and tormented by darkness, but from up on the cliff, he could do nothing but watch. Casting his eyes about, he looked for any city that was not being tormented by the shadow cast over them. He could find none. He turned his eyes away, hoping to shield himself from the creeping sense of fear. He turned away from the scene before him only to discover that he was standing on the side of a grand mountain. A great city had been carved out of the side of it. This city was large, and its buildings crafted of strong stone. The city itself was also cast in the shadow of darkness above it, but the darkness had not reached into the city, and he could hear no suffering from its people.

He looked, and saw that there was a bright light coming from the city, bright enough to hold the darkness at bay. As he looked on he saw the light flare brighter, and the darkness above the city scattered. The light flared across the expanse, and looking back Endrance saw the light had also banished the darkness from the other cities as well, and he could hear the cheering of all the people of the earth. Endrance looked back at the light to see what it was, and through the brightness he could barely make out the shape of a man. He could not get any closer, for that was when he suddenly he woke up.

His tea had finished steeping; he swiftly scooped out the leaves with a spoon and took a sip. Finding the drink to his satisfaction, he tried to figure out what the dream meant. Was it because of his magic? Could it be a vision of the future? He thought about it, but could come up with no answers.

Perturbed, he finished his tea and set the cup back on the shelf. He would have to ask Kaelob about this one.

He stepped outside to find his father hammering in the last post for what would be his new fence. Endrance waited patiently for his father to finish as he soaked up the warmth of the sunlight. His father worked bare chested, and sweat dripped from hard muscle and tanned skin. Endrance looked at his own hands and wondered what kind of woman his mother had been that he had ended up so very slight compared to his father.

Years prior, Endrance had asked his father about his mother, but had been told that he unfortunately didn't know a whole lot. Joseph only had seen her rarely, and she had died sometime shortly after giving birth to him. It was an embarrassing subject for his father, and Endrance tried to leave it alone. No one liked to be reminded that they have an illegitimate child, though in communities with no social stratum it meant much less than in a kingdom's courts.

Endrance waited for Joseph to finish tapping on the post before he approached. His father smiled as he walked up and immediately embraced him. His father smelled of hay and sweat and hard work. "Good morning my son!" he exclaimed. "I let you sleep in; I hope that's alright, since I heard you got your new title! A fully recognized wizard!"

Endrance nodded slightly. "I don't know about fully recognized, father. But I am now accepted as a practitioner. I would have to build a name for myself in order to be recognized."

"Still, it is amazing that you have passed High Magus Kaelob's training so quickly!" he said. "He has never seen someone complete training and still be in their teenage years."

Endrance shrugged. "I didn't know he had that many students before. How did you know?" he asked.

His response was assuring. "I have visited and talked to him about you several times before, my son." He smiled. "And he was quite famous a few decades ago. People still remember him in some places."

The young man nodded, stretching in the suns light. "Okay. He said he wanted to see me after I had recovered from my tests." An involuntary shiver ran through him, thinking of the cold.

Joseph smiled at him, "Well, you better get on your way. I think I remember him saying something about having something to tell you." He waved and watched his son as he set off to visit his master's keep, a smile on his face as he couldn't help but feel excited for him.

Endrance set off, moving at his leisure. He no longer had to rush to lessons, or hurry to keep up with the Master's long strides. He had accomplished something dozens wash out of, and did so with more power and knowledge than would be needed to gain his title, not to mention at the age of fifteen. He felt incredible right then, almost like he could fly.

The path to the keep was a narrow one, and only had a path due to Endrance's constant use of the trail for the last several years. Surrounding the path was a fair amount of green grass, with the occasional weed and shrub dotting its landscape. The path meandered from the edge of town up to the keep. This area was far too rocky to farm properly, so for years the villagers had left this stretch of land alone. The path widened as it approached the keep's entry, until it was nearly wide enough for a pair of men to walk abreast of each other and not bump elbows as they did so.

The path terminated at the stone entryways that lead to the keep drawbridge. It was one of the oldest parts of the keep, and the wood of the drawbridge was old and weathered. Endrance never even considered walking over it barefoot, as the wood was splintered in several places, and it creaked threateningly whenever someone tread its length. The iron chains that would have withdrawn it had long since rusted into oblivion, and Endrance was certain that in a few more years, Kaelob would have to either repair the drawbridge or figure out an alternate means of entering his abode.

Endrance carefully made his way across, coming up to the relatively small courtyard inside the keep. It was barren, empty of anything that wasn't necessary for keeping the building upright. All over the courtyard were scorch and blast marks from numerous years of practicing magic. The walls had divots all over its surface, and black scarring revealed it was the scene of a great battle.

Kaelob was known throughout the magic using community as being one of the cleverest magicians in Ironsoul, using magic in ways that were unique and unexpected. This was from as much his training as apprentice to the Archmagus, as was his ingenuity. He could take a spell that wasn't effective as a battle spell, and he could still manage to defeat his enemies. He had spent countless hours teaching Endrance to be flexible and to use magic at its fullest capacity. Many of the blast and scorch marks on the keep wall were not from things like fireballs or magical attacks.

Kaelob met him halfway across the short courtyard. His hands outspread in greeting. He embraced Endrance briefly, and was grinning quite wildly as he released him. "Well Kaelob," Endrance started, "I hear you have something to tell me?" Endrance followed Kaelob as the two of them walked into the keep proper and sat down in a room Kaelob had converted into a lounge.

Heavy rugs covered the stone floors, and the chairs and couches were imported from some of the most prestigious craftsmen in Ironsoul. Many warm tapestries adorned the walls, and even the torch sconces were of great quality. Where his master skimped on the exterior, he spared no expense on quality living chambers. The armchairs were skillfully upholstered and thickly cushioned, their subtle patterned cloth blending excellently with the theme of the rest of his décor. Even the shelves had been carefully hand carved with the same style of design.

"Yes!" Kaelob sat unceremoniously into his chair, waving a hand at the other. A faint tingle washed across Endrance's face, a sensation much like a faint draft of air across one's arm. The other armchair slid out, taking a position where the young mage could easily sit in it. "Please, sit!" he exclaimed.

Endrance plopped down into his seat as well, adjusting his shirt as the thick cloth seat back pulled the shirt up his back. Kaelob flicked his wrist again while Endrance was getting comfortable, and a nearby overloaded table slid jerkily up to the side of them. Endrance looked up just in time to catch the teacup nearest to him before it toppled into his lap.

"Well, you sure had me going there, m'boy!" Kaelob started, holding his teacup and stirring the tea with a small spoon. "I thought you were going to fail the final test there."

Endrance frowned into his teacup as he took a sip. "What do you mean? I made it the designated time." He asked.

Kaelob shrugged. "That's not the real test. The real test is to put you under real, extreme duress."

"Huh…" Endrance responded skeptically.

"Let me clarify." Kaelob continued. "The test is to see if you have the will to handle your magic safely, intelligently, and effectively in a situation where you are under massive stress. Only then would we be able to tell if you are skilled and trained enough to be able to make it on your own. Someone who is only capable of casting magic in a lab or library just doesn't have what it takes yet."

He took a sip of tea before continuing. "Additionally, you showed me what you've learned in this near decade of education and training." He held up one finger. "You've learned enough about combat to survive a while." He held up another. "You have acceptable enough control over your magical energy not to empty the well before the fight is over. You have no idea how many apprentices try to throw everything they have in the opening gambit and fail because they had nothing left to get them through the rest." He held up a third. "You also know how to improvise, and use your environment to help you. This is not something necessary to learn right away, but you have a good start." He held up a fourth finger. "Lastly, you showed me you are determined not to give up. This is in some cases the most important thing you can have. Even in the face of an opponent who could squash you like a bug any time he pleased, you still struggled and tried to solve problems, not crack heads."

He finished the last of his tea. "Try to think of almost any engagement, whether it is a battle or a ballroom, as a problem that you can solve, if you are smart, clever enough, and prepared. To this end, I have a gift for you, to celebrate your success."

He went to set the teacup on the table but found no room except on top of the box he was trying to reach for. He struggled to try to find a place to set the cup, and after a moment just sighed and let go of the cup in the air as if he had set it on a shelf. It stayed. He pulled the box into his lap and gently nudged the cup onto the table.

It was of polished wood two feet long, a foot wide, and six inches deep. He lifted the lid to the box to reveal two objects. One was a black leather bound book, with gold inlay and a runic sigil in the bottom right corner. The book took up most of the space inside the box, but to the side was a silver bracer that looked crafted specifically to fit him. It was made of highly polished silver, deeply etched with arcane script along the edges of the outer arm plate and along the bands that cross the inner arm.

On the face of the bracer was set a square yellow-orange gem, beautifully cut, and ringed by three concentric rows of miniscule arcane script. The gem gleamed in the torch lit room, almost as if it had its own radiance. Endrance gaped at the two of them as Kaelob pulled the book out and handed it to him.

Upon closer inspection, he was able to tell the book had over a hundred blank pages, all high quality parchment paper, and each page had a silver rune in the bottom left corner. He recognized the rune to be the one for which he was named, 'Endurance'. The surface of his palms tingled faintly as he gently stroked the pages. Yes, they were empowered. The pages, or the cover for that matter, were probably as hard to destroy as if they were made of steel.

"This first gift is from me. It is a masterfully crafted blank spell book." He declared. "The pages have been enchanted to resist wear and tear, as well as time." He chuckled. "Damn near fireproof too, I should add. Some of my best work I must say. That book is for you to record any spells you wish to keep as reference." He held up a hand. "Though I know you have memorized many spell forms and internalized many of those, you may wish to copy them down into your book, just in case. It's never a bad thing to remember the basics."

He held up the bracer to show it to him. "This second gift is special." He held it out to Endrance but didn't let go when Endrance took hold of it. "When I was trained by Archmagus Valeria, she gave me an item of great power as well. She told me it was an item her master possessed before he died. I find it only fitting to give you an item of hers, in the spirit of tradition. This item was one of the few things she left behind, and its mate is missing. But make no mistake; it is powerful of its own accord." He shrugged, letting go of the bracer. "Besides, it was the only thing I could find that would fit you."

"Uh… thanks." Endrance responded, realizing exactly how light the bracer felt. He expected it to weigh a few pounds, but it seemed only a few ounces. The gem in the center grabbed his attention, and he found it hard to look away from its glimmering depths. "Hmm… what is this?" He asked. "I have no idea what kind of gem this is."

"That is a rare form of crystallized magic called Crystalphage. It is a beautiful stone, and has several properties that make it invaluable to any magic user, from Apprentice to Archmagus." He waggled his eyebrows at the boy. "The first and most prominent thing about it is that a skilled mage can push the energy in their aura into the Crystalphage, and it will retain it, giving them an extended reserve of power they can draw from."

"That is… that's incredibly useful." Endrance commented. "How much can it store?"

Kaelob shrugged. "That thing? You couldn't put much into it. No more than a simple rote spell."

Endrance sighed. "That doesn't seem very efficient."

"On the contrary." Kaelob replied. "It's already almost full. It was full when I received it from Valeria, and she had instructed me not to touch it until I gave it to my next apprentice."

"So it has a lot?" He asked.

"Potentially." Kaelob responded, nodding his head. "Though most Crystalphage requires the mage to get to know that particular gem's properties before you can draw from its power. It may take several weeks of study before you will be able to use it fully. I'm sure there are other things it can do, but you will have to figure it out for yourself."

Endrance held the bracer. It felt slightly cool in his hands, and his senses didn't simply tingle or notice the presence of magic in it, they buzzed like a nest of bees that had been kicked up. There was power in the bracer, and he would probably find its presence nagging on his senses until he got it figured out.

Kaelob dropped the box back on the table. A loud crunch made him wince. "Ah yes. Teacup." He admitted. Gently picking up the box and peeking under. "I'll just… take care of that later."

Endrance set the bracer on the book he was holding in his lap and smiled broadly. "Thank you master, I have never owned anything so amazing in my life!"

"Of course!" Kaelob replied. "You're only fourteen, aren't you? Besides, you will find that you could accumulate quite a large collection of impressive things as you pass the years. Many of them you might make yourself, should you feel the inclination."

"I have been thinking about the possibilities." Endrance admitted

"Oh yes!" Kaelob exclaimed. "I recently received a message from an old friend of mine up north. It looks like I may have a task for you, should you think you are ready to leave for your first act as a mage."

"A task?" Endrance asked. "Do you mean like a single quest, or a long term task?"

Kaelob smiled, tapping the armchair he was sitting in. "Long term!" he exclaimed. "It would only be long term for people who can't make plans hundreds of years in advance!" he seemed excited. "I think you would find this one a relatively brief challenge."

The spry old man hopped up out of his chair, his robes fluttering around him as he stepped over to a bookshelf, scratching his chin as he looked around for a particular tome. "Let's see… Balkesh, Balrog, Balator… Aha!" he plucked a rather thin gray leather bound book from his shelf and set it on Endrance's lap as he passed, plunking himself back into his armchair. "There it is! My personal notes on the place you would be working for!"

Endrance looked over the book's cover. It looked gray and scarred. It even was pebbled like a lizard's hide. "What is this made of?" He asked, running a hand over the cover.

Kaelob chuckled, waving his hand as if to say 'of course' "Why that's hydra hide!"

"Ah." Endrance replied. "Already this seems ominous."

"Nonsense!" Kaelob responded. "The likeliness of another hydra of that size getting through the walls is…" He glanced at the boy. "Ahem. Don't worry about hydra, m'boy, that's not your job in the slightest."

"Uh-huh." He said, opening the book. Inside was Kaelob's familiar handwriting. He included sketches of things he found and details of the Kingdom of Balator. "What is this city?" the young man asked, "I've never heard of Balator before."

Kaelob shrugged. "I am not surprised you haven't heard of it. It is the capitol of the barbarian kingdoms to the north."

Endrance sputtered as he looked incredulously at his mentor. "B-b-barbarians?" he stuttered, "You want me to work for barbarians?"

Kaelob seemed confused. "Well, that's the job I handed you, isn't it?"

"I thought you said that barbarians hate magic." Endrance said flatly. He wasn't sure if his old mentor was being genuinely serious or was trying to pull a prank on him again. He was certain that eccentricity came with the man's age, but hoped it wasn't getting worse.

Kaelob snapped the fingers of one hand, his face lightening. "Incorrect, the barbarians of Balator *fear* magic. Their superstitions and paranoia lead them to shun the use of magic."

Endrance shrugged. "Then why would they want to hire me?" he asked.

Kaelob grinned. "Because they fear magic, they need someone who can deal with magic. Somebody who is skilled in magical arts and can put their fears to rest when something unexplained happens. It's kind of a self propagating position, needing someone with magic so they can avoid it.

"I have done this exact same task when I was younger, and I'll tell you that it is indeed rewarding but also demanding. You would be taking a long term position in Balator, their capital. There you would spend most of your time clearing up the barbarian's superstitious beliefs. The rest would be advising the king and his generals in other matters."

"Wait," Endrance looked up from the book as something Kaelob said caught his attention. "You did this job before?"

"Yep!" the elder man agreed, leaning back in his chair, a satisfied look on his face. "I sure did. Was a long, long, long time ago and all I can tell you, is that it's an experience that can be frustrating at times, but also be incredibly…" His eyes seemed to be focused on earlier times. "Satisfying."

Endrance paged through the book and almost dropped it when he saw a sketch of the kingdom capitol. It was a series of bowls carved out of the side of a huge mountain. Each bowl was above the other and stepping up the side of the mountain like stairs. Just like in his dream.

Endrance looked up at Kaelob, and did not know if he should discuss his dream with him. The man obviously knew more about this place than he was letting on, but what if he was also unable to tell him anything? Would he, even if he could?

The young man shook his head, and closed the book. "May I keep the notes?" he asked.

Kaelob blinked as he came out of his memories, "Sure, sure." He said, waving a hand dismissively. "I can always pen another if I wanted to."

"The barbarians will be impressed and frightened by your littlest tricks, so don't worry about needing a great many of the more powerful ones." Kaelob explained. "There is also a large collection of old spellbooks at the place where you will be staying, so you can study quite a few more spells while you are there." He chuckled. "Consider it a perk of the job that they're free to study. Most anywhere in the world would charge an arm and a leg for you to even learn a minor spell." He chuckled. "Sometimes their superstitions can work for you, you know."

"If any women in white dresses try to give you a ring," he stated, his expression serious, "By the gods, take it. They will be your guardians and assistants during your task."

"These people have had for every generation someone they call a Spengur. The Spengur is their wise man who is skilled in magical arts. The Spengur is almost always an outsider and serves the people until a new Spengur is chosen. They apply their magical knowledge to answer the people's concerns and solve problems that would ordinarily be too costly for them to solve in a physical manner.

"You also will be needed to deal with the people's customs and superstitions and supervising special events that deal with them. It's a position where you will have to live in their kingdom among their people, and you will have to learn their ways and mannerisms.

"As the Spengur, your living costs will be taken care of, and you will be paid a small amount monthly as well. As an added benefit, you will also have most of the things required for you to do your job provided for you. If there are any extraordinarily expensive costs needed for a job related action, you will be assisted in raising the money to do so, but in that regard you may be on your own."

"Anything else I should know about?" the young mage asked.

"The place is going to be very cold during most of the year except for the few months of summer. I suggest you pack cold weather clothing," Kaelob finished, separating his hands and leaning back in his chair.

Endrance blinked a few times, thinking this task over. He knew it would be a tremendous change in his life, especially since he would be away from home for many years. He would have to travel a great distance to even get there, and he had hardly been to the neighboring villages. He had however an extensive education of other cities, and he was certain that he would be able to identify them if he had to.

He had some questions for his old master. Putting the book next to his spellbook, he thought to ask a different question. "What about spells? Are there any particular ones that will help me in this task?"

Kaelob replied, "You will have access to the spellbooks and journals of every Spengur that has passed before you, even mine. There are books dating back two thousand years that were so fragile I was afraid to open them lest they render to dust."

"And I will be paid as well as have all my needs taken care of?"

Kaelob smiled. "Yes. You will have every need taken care of," he responded, "…Every need."

Endrance was already thinking of his next question and missed Kaelob's muted chuckle. "What about my station in their people? You said they're a very superstitious lot; how will they treat me in their community?"

"The Spengur is a very well respected and feared position in their community. The Spengur is considered a separate entity from Balator, and he does not ultimately answer to anyone but the king and his royal family. The Spengur also has two groups which traditionally assist him in everything that he needs. The first is a family of personal bodyguards to the Spengur whose sole task is to ensure the Spengur's well being and safety. The second group is a group of the kingdom's historians who are called the Ergkinoa. They are all women born of a particular totem that are raised from birth to be 'sacrificed' to the Spengur. They will be the ones who educate you in the ways of the barbarian people, and they will be caretakers of a sort."

Kaelob waved his hand dismissively. "It's all much easier to comprehend when you are actually there, and it's happening around you. Don't worry, it's a good thing. You can also read more about them in the notes I prepared for you." he finished.

"When shall I start?" Endrance requested. "How would I get there? I've only been to the nearby villages and those are still within the Satrapy of Veridian, and your lessons didn't include more than cursory geography."

Kaelob shrugged. "Your education in that subject only really requires you to have a grasp of geomantically important locales. It's not like you're training to be a wood guide or something."

Endrance fixed Kaelob with a sarcastic look. "Maybe I was trying to get back to the same spot that time."

"With all seven attempts? That week?" Kaelob returned with a smirk on his face. "I'm sure you are quite adept at getting nowhere in the wilds; in fact, I think you'd graduate that class after the first day, should they have offered it."

Endrance shrugged. "I like roads." He muttered. "And cities. Roads and streets are so much easier to find your way in."

Kaelob sighed, rubbing his forehead with the fingers of one hand. "Anyways, if you accept this task, then I will send a message ahead to my friend in Balator, and one of the Spengur's bodyguards will meet you at the capitol city of Ironsoul. There he will guide you the rest of the way back to Balator."

"I see." Endrance said, scratching at his chin as he absorbed the information. He knew the route to Ironsoul proper, and could travel with one of the trade caravans there for safety. Having a guide for the rest of the way would be most helpful, and ensure he would get there in a reasonable amount of time. Reasonable meaning at all, whereas he was sure he'd never arrive if he left by himself. He was just no good when it came to traveling through forests or mountains.

Endrance nodded, his primary concerns answered, "Well then, I accept this task set before me. I can see that even if it is the only task I was to take on, it would still be respectable and could be a career."

"Yes," Kaelob nodded "Think of it as a career. Although with your talent at magic, you could have many full careers over the course of your lifetime." He gave a half shrug as he held up his pinky, ring, and middle finger of his right hand. "I suspect about three decades. They tend to develop some paranoia when their Spengur doesn't seem to age after forty years or so. By then I'm sure someone would have given you a much more appealing job offer."

With that they stood again. They clasped hands, and after a pause they embraced.

"I know you will do right by me Endrance," Kaelob said, releasing him. "You learned everything very fast and have proven to be quite clever with word and spell. I know you will not bring shame to my name." He quirked an eyebrow and stared at him fiercely. "Or you may find yourself at the wrong end of one of my *Substituo* spells."

The young man blanched. "But you said you hadn't finished figuring that spell out yet…" he said incredulously.

Kaelob frowned. "I know." He responded, a glimmer of madness in his eye. "I still haven't found that cat from my last test."

"Blech." Endrance responded. "I still have nightmares about that…"

"Yes, yes. Well, a good motivator for you then, I suppose." Kaelob responded. He waved a hand at the door. "Go on, get going m'boy. Now that I've trained you, I don't have to have you cluttering up my study anymore. The next time you come here, you are merely a guest."

Endrance smiled and began to walk to the exit. "Thank you Master Kaelob. I will check in with you periodically as events play out in this new life for me."

He waved as Endrance disappeared through the doorway. "Farewell! Don't forget to write!" he shouted just before Endrance turned out of view.

Kaelob sighed as he leaned his head against the back of his chair, shaking his head as he closed his eyes. "Poor boy," he said to himself. "No idea what he's getting into. No idea at all." He chuckled. "I just hope the Ergkinoa don't kill him."

Chapter 04

Upon returning home and consulting with his father, Endrance found that the next caravan heading up to Ironsoul wasn't due for a month. This gave him plenty of time to plan for his journey and pack some essentials in advance. It was for the best, as he quickly realized how poorly prepared he was for long journeys.

While he had been intending on taking at least one week off to relax and put some serious time into painting, he found he had to instead work twice as hard to procure the supplies he would need to take on the journey. First he had to acquire worthwhile travelling clothes. He also had to trade for a travelling pack so he could carry all the necessities. Joseph procured a hardened leather scroll case into which Endrance carefully placed several of his best paintings into. He opted to leave his paints here since he was certain he could get real quality paints once he made it to Balator, not to mention it was a few pounds less materials for him to carry on the trip. The paintings he hoped to sell while in Balator so he could afford to buy winter clothes. The traders who came through Wayrest had little in the area of cold weather gear.

By the time he had gathered everything he thought he would need, he found a few more things that were necessary for the journey. Bedroll, blanket, lantern, and other similar things he spent much of his day going about the town searching and trading for. He tried to find a small enough tent to take with him, but could not find one. It was just as well; Tents were heavy and he was unsure he could set one up correctly.

He ended up only having a scant four days to relax. Those four days he was up at suns-rise, and went to bed well after the suns set, save for the last day. He was not frustrated that he was only able to finish one painting in that time; in fact he was glad of it. He had been so used to working on a large painting in pieces as his daily duties as an apprentice would allow, that he found he could only sit before an easel for about an hour before his mind started to wander on to other pursuits.

He ended up taking breaks over the course of a day, working on other tasks and painting when inspiration struck him. The rest of the time he spent transcribing the most important of his spells into his new spell book. His name was inlayed into the spine, so that he could easily identify it should it be on a shelf somewhere. The silver runes on each page gleamed in the candlelight as he transcribed his spells, and every time he noticed them he couldn't help but grin wildly in excitement.

Each page he carefully inked the inscriptions, diagrams, and formula for each of the pertinent spells he had learned and developed on his own over the near decade of apprenticeship. Spell-slinging, a term some of the apprentices used in their own social circles seemed incredibly easy to an observer. The wizard could just flick his wrist, say an obscure word, and set a dozen men aflame from a safe distance.

In truth, that seeming simplicity was the fruit of countless hours of distilled effort learning every single possible connotation of a single work of magic. It went beyond the basic understanding of a spell; an apprentice with a newly taught spell could chant the correct words, form the images needed in their mind, and empower the symbols they formed with their bodies and hands with their will and energy. The time this would take to even release a working spell took at minimum several seconds, and could extend into minutes for the very complex magic.

A spell that was studied and extensively practiced could reduce that down to a few seconds. Only when a wizard had truly absorbed everything there is to know about a particular working of magic could they abbreviate the spell casting process so. To them, it was just as simple as an experienced juggler keeping seven balls in the air. It would seem impossible to the untrained, but eventually they don't even think about it. They just do. Excepting that a wizard had to do that same process with every spell he hoped to be able to sling out, and each one was different.

A tedious process to be sure, but in light of his last battle with his master, Endrance felt better that he had burned through so many candles studying up late at night. He meticulously kept his handwriting steady as he transcribed; for the slightest waver could cause a symbol to misrepresent something, or cause him to misinterpret a word later on, to disastrous results.

The spells he transcribed were ones he was not absolutely certain he memorized. A few of them he could probably cast without aid from the book, though he would be loathe trying if he had the book at hand. He would take the book with him so that he could practice and study with them enough to master them as well.

The caravan arrived, and Endrance knew that it was his last day in Wayrest. Though trade was brief, the caravan master wanted to rest their horses and drivers for a fresh start the next day. Its usual route passed out of Ironsoul, through three of the Satrapies until it came to the sunsken Tower, and then looped back to the capitol, an established trade route taking a season to complete. Though he had more than enough escorts for the route, he was delighted to meet with the young man.

A grizzled older man with far too many scars across his knuckles than the young mage would think was possible ran the caravan. Endrance had found him giving orders to a couple of the escort guard as he approached late in the afternoon. The setting suns glanced over the rooftop and cast an orange and reddish gleam to the top of the man's bald pate as he turned to acknowledge the young man's presence, occasionally scratching at his gut which stretched the cloth of his shirt over the buckle of his belt. The young wizard held up his hand in greeting, and stopped a few feet away as the caravan master finished instructing his people.

"Ah yes." The man stated in a gruff but friendly manner. "How can I help ye, miss?" he smiled at him as he waved his hand over to the large wagons half encircling the village square. "The other men here may have some fine cloths you would find appealing."

Endrance fought to keep his face from heating up. He cleared his throat and responded, deepening his voice as much as possible. "I am no lady, kind sir."

The caravan master blinked and looked him over again, noting that he wore men's clothes, albeit fairly small sized clothes. "Oh!" he exclaimed. "I do apologize, sir!" he exclaimed, wringing his hands as he bowed his head to the young mage slightly. "I am terribly sorry; it must be the long journey and the setting suns." He explained.

Endrance shrugged, letting out a held breath. "It's alright, happens to me more often than I'd like to admit."

The older man laughed. "Looks like you got a bit of the elf in you don't you?" he asked.

Endrance grinned and scratched at a faintly pointed ear tip. "Somewhere along the line, I think. Probably a great grandfather I suppose."

The caravan master shrugged. "Well, don't you be worrying about us discriminating on you jus' cause of something your grandpappy did." He winked. "Your coin's just about as good as anyone else here, barring the exchange rate, of course."

Endrance laughed with the man this time. The caravan master wiped at an eye and looked at the young man sternly. "My name's Ked. So what kind of goods are you interested in?" he asked. "I can tell you not only which of my merchants have the best, but who's got the best deals as of late."

The young wizard smiled, pointing at Ked. "Actually, I have a deal for you." He began. "I would like to come along with your caravan to Ironsoul."

"Oh?" the caravan master replied, raising an eyebrow. "And forgive me for asking, but why would you think there is room for us to, ahem, cart you along? You have no wares to sell, no profits to share." He made a show of looking him up and down. "And you certainly don't have the physique to march escort."

Endrance drew himself up, trying his best to look respectable. "I am a newly entitled wizard. I am travelling to Ironsoul to take up a new line of work in the area."

It was quiet for a moment. Endrance watched Ked stare him in the eye for a moment, trying to gauge if he was joking. He had to struggle inside, but he resisted the urge to smirk at him.

"Well." Ked responded after a minute's pause. "That would definitely be an asset to our caravan, if you are being honest with me."

Endrance opened the satchel slung across a shoulder and withdrew his spell book. Would you like me to do a demonstration?" he asked. Though he didn't see it, he could hear some of the townsfolk who saw him do so start moving away as impolitely as they dared. It wasn't that they hated him or anything, there was just a few times where one of his learning exercises ended up getting out of control and frightening the daylights out of some of the people there.

He scratched at his gut again as he thought. "Well, I seem to remember hearing there being a kid who was training to be a mage last time I came by. You seem about the right age; I suppose you can come along, provided you carry your weight, one way or the other."

Endrance smiled broadly at him. "Thank you, sir. I will be ready to depart tomorrow."

"Best be early in the morn." Ked replied. "We're setting out at suns-rise."

The final night before the caravan left was rough on the young wizard. He lay in his bed for the last time and he couldn't sleep. Though he lay comfortably and his body was relaxed, his mind kept racing off the moment he stopped paying attention to keeping it reigned in. He wasn't sure when he eventually passed out, but he must have lain in bed for hours before sleep finally came upon him.

He was awakened too few hours later to his father pounding on the door to his room. He washed and dressed himself quickly, and gathered his things up. The caravan was already hitched up, and he had a scant few minutes to throw his things in the back of the last wagon before they set off. He said a quick farewell to his father, and promised him that he'd write whenever he could afford to.

As the suns rose that dawn, the caravan set off at a steady pace. Endrance sat on the back bench on the last wagon for a while, watching until Wayrest had shrunk too far off in the horizon for him to see. He hadn't the time for a proper goodbye that day, but he had the time over the month leading up to that moment to let everyone he cared to know where he was going and that he would be gone for a long time. Once Wayrest was out of sight, he hopped off the wagon and walked alongside it, moving towards the lead wagon and taking in the caravan's formation.

It was as slow as a walk, but much safer than travelling alone. The five covered wagons travelled in a chain, each one following the one before it, and the caravan master's wagon in the lead. Thirty men guarded the caravan total, and were broken up into shifts of fifteen men on the ground at a time. The men on the ground walked alongside, in front, and behind the caravan, spread out in a loose sort of boundary that could react to an unexpected situation quickly.

The men on the ground would switch with the men sitting on the sides of the wagons every couple of hours it seemed, allowing them to rest in shifts and still maintain a march while encumbered with armor and weaponry. They wore light steel breastplates, helms and longswords, with shields bearing the clenched fist of Ironsoul's home guard.

Each wagon was as large as Endrance's old home, and rolled on spoked wheels as far across as a man stretched. The horses were of a large, sturdy kind, bred for endurance and not speed.

He eventually made his way to the front, smiling and greeting anyone who even looked at him as he walked ahead. On the third wagon a little girl peeked at him from behind the canvas flaps on the back, and poked her head out the front to watch him as he passed the wagon by. Everyone he greeted smiled back and waved, even if it were a cursory manner.

When he reached the foremost wagon, he looked up to see the caravan master sitting alongside his driver, a modestly attractive older woman, very likely his wife. She smiled at him, her flaxen hair lightened by the dawn's light. "Good morn, miss." She greeted him.

Ked had been looking ahead and glanced over when he heard his wife speak. His eyes widened when he heard her address him and reached out to touch her shoulder. "Oh, not a miss." He corrected her, smiling over her head at the young mage. "A sir. And a practitioner at that."

She frowned faintly, but it quickly returned to a pleasant smile. "Well, good morn to you, sir wizard. My name is Beatrice" She greeted. "Is there anything you need?"

Endrance shrugged, hopping over a rock in the road before he tripped on it. "My name is Endrance." He began. "I needed nothing in particular. I was merely seeking to find out how I can be of help to the caravan during our journey north."

"Oh that's easy." Beatrice replied, flicking the reins to keep the horses moving. "You just do your wizard thing and help the caravaners however you can." She sniffed, glancing at him out of the corner of her eye as she looked down the road. "You don't look like much of a wizard though."

Endrance smirked. "Well, I'm still relatively new at this, hasn't been time for the beard to grow in."

She frowned, glancing back at him. "I thought you looked young. Well, hopefully you can be of help." she blew air through her lips. "And if you know any of that flashy stuff, it wouldn't hurt either."

"Oh? Why is that?" Endrance asked, his curiosity perked up.

"Bandits are much less likely to attack us if they think we have a wizard travelling with us." She explained. "Lots of people don't like the idea of getting burned alive with magic."

"It's not like it makes you any more dead than if one of the soldiers here ran them through with a sword." The young wizard countered.

"Does it?" she asked, looking over at him.

"Well, mostly." Endrance shrugged. "A properly placed and prepared spell could take the place of a dozen swords in the right situation."

Beatrice nodded. "I once saw a magus at the high temple in Ironsoul. He struck down twenty of those feral wolf-men with a wave of his hand and a word." She shuddered. "They just… fell over, clutching at their chests, and this mist floated outta their bodies and into his mouth." Despite the warmth of the early morning suns, she pulled her clothes tighter around her. "I don't think anyone should die like that, never."

Endrance whistled. That was some serious magic. Spirit magic like that teetered on the verge of necromancy. That practice was pure heresy to the holy circle of magi. To be able to pull a complicated spell off like that without harming innocent bystanders, and to sling the spell on top of it all, was bordering on fantastic. He shook his head, amazed. He had so much yet to learn.

"I have a few spells that might help." He replied at last. "And while I can't do something that dangerous, I'm sure I can be of assistance against bandits." He remembered the gout of flame he threw against his master before with a tug of pride.

"That's a relief," Ked interjected. "Why don't you go on back and have a seat, we've got a long ways to go before we stop for the night."

Endrance nodded and slowed his pace, letting the wagons start pulling past him. He winked at the little girl watching from the third wagon, and she let out a small yelp and pulled her head back inside. He grinned as he hopped up onto the back bench of the last wagon and let his feet dangle off the end, kicking his legs as he watched the countryside slowly roll by.

The suns rose, and the world brightened and got warmer. He leaned back against the canvas of the wagon cover and closed his eyes a moment. Though the ride was too bumpy for him to completely drift off to sleep, the warmth suffused him and he drifted for quite some time. He opened his eyes some time later to see the suns had made it a ways closer to midday.

The soldier walking in the back was nearing the end of his shift, and when his replacement came he trotted up to the bench Endrance relaxed on and hopped without ceremony. The man was lean, but taller than

Endrance. His simple helmet left his face clear, except for the studded nose guard down the middle. His skin was dark, and eyes blue. He smiled an easy smile at the young mage and nodded his head to him.

"It must be hard." He said.

Endrance looked back at the man out of the corner of his eye. Was he going to get hit on again? "What's hard?"

"Being so fair skinned out in the suns." the soldier stated, drawing a waterskin from his belt and taking a pull. "If I were you I'd be worried about getting a burn."

Endrance shrugged. He hadn't thought about that, but nothing he could do about the suns now. "It doesn't look like something you have to worry about." He responded to the man with a smile. "You've been on the roads much?"

The man laughed, clapping a hand on his shoulder. "Yes, yes I have, I s'pose." He commented. "M'name's Ethan." He stated, holding out the skin. "Want a drink?"

Endrance reached out to take the skin, but paused with his hand on it. "What's in it?" he asked.

Ethan laughed again. "Jus' water," he replied. "Only a green recruit or a fool drinks anything different on a long march."

He accepted the water and took a swig, handing the skin back. "Thanks." He said.

"No worries." Ethan responded. "We pull fresh barrels of water at every town or village we stop at, and clean out the stale stuff, if there's any left." He gestured at him with the skin. "This here's some fresh Wayrest well water, I reckon." He looked back over at the young man. "I don't suppose you're going to miss being at home." He said. "You got the look of someone on their first journey."

"Oh? How was that obvious?" Endrance asked.

"You notice quite a few things about a man," he began, shrugging, "or a woman, if you just pay attention to the little details. Things about how they carry themselves, the way they look at the world around them. The way they talk to strangers, and dozens of other things."

"Really?" Endrance asked. "That's amazing that you could pick up on all those things."

The soldier shrugged. "It's not like it's that hard, once you've gotten used to it." He jerked his head towards the front of the caravan. "Also, the caravan master came by and told us to be nice to the new wizard."

"Oh." Endrance stated. "Well, that made it easy."

"Sure did." He said with a grin.

"So Ethan," Endrance began. "Tell me about this route. Is there anything I should be concerned about?'

Ethan shrugged, scratching his chin. "Nothing beyond the usual. Bandits and thieves mostly, though I heard there were goblins in the area." He stretched his arms out, and scratched under his breastplate before continuing. "Most of the time they leave us alone, unless they got themselves a new leader."

"A goblin king?" Endrance asked. "I was told that he was slain by the Celestial Knight a few years ago."

"Aye." Ethan confirmed. "Goblin King Grush, and over half of his horde fell when the Knight took to the field." He smiled. "I wasn't there, but the men who had seen him still talk about his battle prowess to this day. The stories are so inflated that it seems almost impossible for him to have fought so many on his own."

Endrance shrugged. "I wouldn't put much stock in tales told over ale, unless you saw it yourself."

"Truth." Ethan grunted. He nodded to the large book by Endrance's side. "Is that your spell book?" he asked.

Endrance picked it up and held it out to him. "Sure is. Want to take a look?" he asked, winking.

The soldier held up his hands, but not quite touching the leather cover. "Naw, I'll pass," he said. "Us experienced men at arms know better than to try reading a mage's books."

"Suit yourself." Endrance replied, flipping the book open and paging through to where he had planned on furthering his study.

The soldier watched him quietly for a moment.

"Say, I never did get your name." Ethan said after a minute or two of silence.

"Oh, my name's Endrance." He responded without looking up from the pages.

The soldier nodded, leaning back and stretching out his legs in silence.

Chapter 05

The caravan pulled off the road near sunset along a grassland that seemed more than safe enough. Endrance noticed signs that other wagons had been there before: shorter grass where the drivers tied off the horses after unhitching, parts of the field bore the dirt from the repeated churning of wagons rolling through the same spots. Other myriad little details seemed to magically appear once Endrance put a mind to looking for them.

He had gotten bored studying his spells, since he could only read through them and not practice any of them while the wagons were on the move. So instead he talked with Ethan and his comrades, learning how to keep his eyes and ears open. It seemed so simple, yet most people never did it. They just kept their head down and went about their business, missing many of the wonderful sights that were just over their heads.

He spent the last several hours trying to spot specific things that they requested him to find. At first it was simple, like to identify which man had the highest grass stains on his boots. The difficulty increased as they travelled, where eventually he was asked to spot and catch a single red pebble amidst a dozen gray ones that were tossed in the air at the same time.

His eyes were scratchy and tired, and his head hurt from staring too hard at everything they asked him to focus on, but it was an appealing change of pace from staring at books all day. He might as well exercise his eyes so he wouldn't wear them out so quickly in the future. There were also more short term benefits to learning these tricks, and he was glad to add them to his repertoire.

Endrance helped set up their camp as best as he could, but ended up on the sideline for most of it. So he just watched, and learned. One of the things he was really good at, he took to learning something like it was what he was meant to do. He didn't have a perfect memory; he forgot things on occasion. He did, however, have the ability to recall things he was specifically paying attention to.

He was certain that the next night he would be able to contribute to the setting up of camp. For tonight he would just get in the way, so he kept quiet and ate his dinner when it was handed to him by the kindly woman with the large cauldron making food for everyone.

That night he helped others out where he could, which was predominantly him taking local herbs and compounding a salve for foot blisters. The soldiers, who had to walk for several more days were grateful. Ethan in particular was glad, and insisted on showing him the massive blister that his salve helped heal, despite Endrance's attempts to passively decline.

He could tell the people of the caravan were happy, many laughed and joked with each other. The caravaners seemed to be less of travelling businessmen and more like a large family on a journey. That night alone he heard more names and had attached to them more faces than he could count, and ended that night crawling into his bedroll unsure if he was going to remember their names at all.

He awoke to a single deep, low drumbeat in a panic. His hand clutched at his chest and he broke out into a cold sweat instantly. He realized he was breathing hard, and forced himself to steady himself. He looked around frantically, and it seemed everyone had awoken in a similar way.

His skin tingled, an irritating, itchy sensation. Endrance ran his hands over his arms, but only felt smooth skin. No bugs of any kind, and his brain finally kicked the doors of confusion in. Magic, magic woke everyone up. It didn't even have the courtesy of being well composed. From as best he could sense from the aftereffects of the magic that washed over him, it only did its work because the magic was so poorly constructed it agitated anything with any sort of magical energy in it at all.

He pulled a shirt on over his chest and crawled out of his bedroll. The cool night air would normally feel pleasant, but in the wake of the drum it was just another agitation to his skin. He shook his head as he walked to the outer ring of the caravan circle to try to clear the lingering effects from his body. The opposing energy bled invisibly from his body, and by the time he reached the man on watch he felt no longer afraid, just tired.

The soldier turned his head to take in the young mage as he approached, his face concerned and not entirely without fear. "Oh it's you, sir mage." He responded.

"Yes. I was trying to figure out what that was, sir… Perd?" Endrance replied, trying to remember the young soldier's name through the list of others he had pushed on him the last day.

"Yes, I'm Perd." The man replied, looking back out over the dark night. "I never heard them before, but some of the men here have before. They're goblin drums, sir mage."

A chill ran down his spine. "Goblins?" he asked. "I thought they only used the drums when they went to war."

The man nodded grimly, gripping the handle of his sword at his hip tightly. "And they only go to war when they have a leader." He finished for the mage.

The shiver down his spine turned to dread as he considered this. The last time the goblins had been allowed to unite under their king, they stood on the verge of sweeping through both Ironsoul and Salthimere's kingdoms, destroying everything. Only the swift action of a small group of dedicated people was able to draw their attention long enough for the kingdoms to build up a defense. Even then, the Celestial Knight alone was the factor in the prior wars, having beheaded their king and scattering the goblins to the winds.

"Surely they are not back in force." Endrance posited. The soldier shrugged.

"Most likely not, sir wizard." He responded. "But it spells out trouble for us regardless. Even if only two dozen of them found something they would let lead them, one attack and they would overrun us before we could mount a defense."

Endrance was silent for a few moments. "Not so," he eventually replied. "If I remember my teachings correctly, goblins would not bother using the drums if they thought they could ambush us as we are now."

The soldier's face brightened a small amount. "That's true. If they could they would rather slit our throats as we slept. There must be a bigger target nearby." He turned to look at him. "The only two places I know of near here is a viridian kingdom outpost farther along the road about four days walk from here, or…"

"Wayrest." Endrance finished. "I have to get word to them."

"Whoa there, sir wizard." The soldier responded, lightly touching the mage's shoulder and quickly withdrawing his hand as the young man turned back to him suddenly. "Your town is most likely completely aware of them by now, given the drum. Don't they have your master to rely on?"

Endrance quietly fumed. Of course master Kaelob was there. He would be able to help them, right? With his power, the goblins were probably doomed before they started. Endrance shook his head though. "My master lives almost an hour's walk from the village. If they get attacked before they can get to him…"

"Well your master must have heard it too, right?" Perd asked.

Endrance shook his head. "No. His keep has simple protections worked into the stone. Simple effects like the drum wouldn't even cross his walls. All he'd hear was a drum beat, and we wizards are notorious for not paying attention when we're studying."

The soldier spat. "Well, you better hope someone has the wit to get him soon. We don't have the resources to send you back to them. If you leave to go back, you're on your own. And against goblins."

Endrance shook his head. "If I went, then I still wouldn't get there for a day if I walked, and running will leave me too tired to do anything."

Another man in armor approached, and Endrance couldn't see who it was until he stood next to them. Ethan adjusted his helmet and settled his gaze on the young wizard.

"Sir wizard." He greeted him, "I was hoping you would be able to do something to help protect us from the drums the goblins are using."

Endrance looked over the camp. The families of the caravaners were huddled together near the fire, which someone had stoked up and added wood to. Their frightened faces framed in light and darkness as they sought comfort and shelter in each other.

As if on cue, the drum sounded again. The deep basso *thump* echoed through the camp, and many of the people cried out in fear and huddled closer. Endrance felt the hairs rise up all over his body and his first instinct was to bolt out into the darkness and hide. His skin itched horribly and it was all he could do to hold himself and stay where he stood.

The two soldiers to their credit did not flinch but immediately turned to look over the camp, and made sure nobody fled in a panic. They turned back to the wizard, and he could tell they were very worried.

Ethan spoke up; sweat visibly dripping down his face. "I think we are incredibly close to the goblin camp. That drum didn't sound too far off."

Endrance suddenly got an idea. "Do you think you could send a scout to find where it is specifically?"

Ethan looked startled. "Why on earth would I want to send someone to the goblins?" he exclaimed. "Even if he could make it there unnoticed, what good would it do to tell us where the goblins are?"

Endrance took a breath and cleared his head. Everyone was reacting to the magically induced panic the goblin drums were causing. He would need to sound perfectly reasonable or else no one would do what he needed. If only…

"Well, if you were to find where the goblin drums were coming from, I would be able to mount a suitable defense against their power." He began explaining carefully. "If I know where it is coming from, I can create a barrier that will stop their magic from affecting us."

While true, it wasn't entirely the full reason he needed to find the drums. He could create a reasonably safe barrier that encircled the camp, but it wouldn't be as powerful as a directed defense. The other reason was that if the goblins were closer to him than to Wayrest, he might be able to do something to divert them from the town. If it's a small enough group, he might be able to stop them entirely, though he was highly doubtful of that.

Ethan grimaced. "The only soldier in our group with any kind of scout training is me." He admitted. "I… guess I could try and find them, and report back."

The young mage felt a moment of pain. It was his job to help these people and he was the only one who could, but would he have to do so by using others? Ethan could very likely die trying to get this information to him, and he could still protect the caravan moderately without it. Was it his right to send this man to his possible demise just so he could go and dance with his own?

No, he decided. *This was more than just the caravan. The entire village of Wayrest was in danger. Many more lives than just this was in danger.* If he had to send one man to his death in order to save a hundred, he would. *Isn't that better?* He thought. *Surely one life is not worth a hundred, or even twenty.*

Endrance eventually nodded at Ethan. "Try to get as close as you safely can. If you think you have been discovered get back here as quickly as possible. I will be waiting to help divert any pursuit." He held out a hand to stop Ethan before he stepped into the darkness. "Ethan… Thank you."

Ethan didn't look back, but nodded, adjusting his sword at his belt. "I just hope you're good, Endrance. I will probably be back with something chasing me, if I come back at all." And with that he vanished into the darkness.

Endrance looked down at the loose thread he had pulled off Ethan's sleeve as he passed by. In the dim distant firelight it seemed so unimportant, yet to him it had estimable value. "Don't worry Ethan." He whispered. "I'll bring you back, one way or another."

Chapter 06

Ethan crept through the waves of grass, the starless night shrouding him from sight. He had been moving steadily at a slow pace, crouched low in the dark and only orienting towards the sound of the goblin drums. Though each beat got worse as he neared the goblin camp, he was able to resist the effects of the drum's magic more effectively the more he felt it. He barely twitched now when it sent fear coursing down his spine.

He was pretty sure that was because he was insane. Only a crazy man would actually willingly go *towards* an enemy encampment. Or think they would survive long enough to report back about it. Insanity did have the small perk that fear seemed less of a prerogative after it set in.

He could see a flickering fire a few dozen yards away and carefully slunk his way towards it. He had to be getting close to the goblin camp. The sound of crushing grass froze him, and he held his breath as a dark shape passed by not a few feet in front of him. He couldn't get a good look at it until it moved far enough away that he could see the firelight illuminate it.

The creature was stunted, only four and a half to maybe five feet tall. Though short its body was composed of knotted, cordlike muscle wrapping around a bow-limbed skeleton and covered in calloused, green-gray skin. It was wearing some kind of hide armor, and held a jagged, wicked looking forward bending blade with a leather wrapped handle. It walked in an odd off balanced lope, but its demeanor belied its deformed stature. Ethan could see that he had narrowly avoided detection as it cast its eyes about warily, suspiciously examining everything as it passed. The thing held it's sword with the casual grip of someone who had been carrying it around for a very long time, and was probably not an inexperienced soldier.

Ethan gritted his teeth for a moment before looking around for more patrols. He eventually found two others, moving in a circular pattern. He must have found the outer perimeter of their camp. He knew he would be spotted if he remained there, so he moved with great caution along the outer edge of the patrol's perimeter.

He found a small rise in the plains, a lump too small to be called a hill, and he moved up it only after the spot was between two patrolling goblins. There he took off his helmet, and crawled on his stomach and elbows to where he could part the grass and look into the camp. The small fire in the goblins' camp was not for their use directly.

Inside the camp he counted twelve goblins, not adding the three on patrol. He also counted five humans. Three adults and two children all bound in ropes and tied to posts around the fire. The goblins were taking turns amusing themselves by leaning one of the posts over the fire until the person on it was screaming into the gags from fear and pain as they were burned by the fire's heat. They would then pull them back, put out any burning clothes, and do it again to a different one. Everyone there had scorch marks on their bodies, and the woman looked exceedingly battered.

He silently cursed, and slowly backed away. He righted his helmet on his head and started creeping directly away from the camp when he caught a glimpse of movement out of the corner of his eye. He jerked his head back and fell on his rear, but it saved his life as a jagged piece of metal shot past his face and disappeared into the darkness beyond him. He shot off into a sprint, erupting from the long grass.

One of the goblins on patrol had found the trail of trampled grass he had left behind and had nearly been on him when he had suddenly moved. The goblin brayed a warning in a tongue Ethan couldn't understand, and he heard more of them start moving in the camp.

Oh gods, help me! He prayed as he ran for all he was worth. He could maybe kill one or two of them in a straight fight, but there were fifteen, and goblins never fought in a straight fight. As if he needed any further goading, the goblin drums sounded a quick staccato of three beats, causing his heart to almost explode in his chest as he flew into a completely blind panic.

He could only hope he could make it back to the camp before the goblins caught up to him. A crude spear flew past his left shoulder in the dark, and his hope dwindled.

Chapter 07

As soon as Ethan had left, Endrance sat down onto his bedroll and prepared. He drew his spell book out from his satchel and started reading through the spells he had successfully transcribed. It took him only a little time to re-familiarize himself with several of his spells, and he separately worked through the motions and then the words needed to cast them. He was interrupted several times by the beat of the drum, which seemed to have no set time or interval, but he endured. He would be getting into a life or death situation here, and he needed to be prepared. If he could destroy the drums maybe that would be enough to break the raiding party and send them back to the badlands.

Or at the very least, he could cause enough damage that they would no longer be able to attack Wayrest, and have to move on. No matter what, things didn't look good for him. He was just one young man, and a newly accepted wizard at that. Even if Ethan came back alive and even if he had found the camp, he might not be able to do anything.

He shook his head and moved on to the next spell. He had to try. People's lives depended on him. People who raised him and helped him grow up. People he respected and people that he loved. His father was there. He just could not ride on tomorrow and leave them to their fate. He would do something, he *had* to do something.

He had finished practicing his fifth spell when he heard shouting from the edge of the camp. He shot to his feet and ran to the outer guard, who had his shield unbuckled and his sword drawn.

Coming towards the camp at great speed was the barely recognizable form of Ethan, the glint of firelight off his helmet and wide eyes giving him away. He was running full out, breathing hard, and a scream seemed to trail from his mouth as he ran towards the camp. Behind him were four goblins. An ugly creature, Endrance had seen sketches of them in his master's tomes in the keep and was prepared for their appearance. The four of them bounded after Ethan in an almost graceful uneven lope, swords drawn. Unlike their prey the goblins seemed hardly winded by their chase.

Endrance knew enough about goblin tactics to know they would shortly turn tail and retreat in the face of a larger community of foes. He didn't want to give them a chance to. Ethan was sixty feet from him when he began chanting and forming signs with his hands and posture. He called to the magic, drew it into him and shaped it to his need. Ethan just blazed past him as Endrance finished shaping his spell and stepped forward with his right foot and jabbed out with the index and middle finger of his right hand.

"Fulmineus!" he shouted, and from deep in his chest lightning crackled up his throat, out his mouth and down his arm. The night became day for an instant, illuminated by the power Endrance was barely keeping in check. It leapt out from his fingertips and struck the farthest back goblin square in the chest.

The creature tumbled in mid stride and its corpse jerked in the dark grass, electricity still arcing off its body. The other three goblins skidded to a stop and glared hatefully at him. Two turned to run while the closest drew a long jagged piece of metal and hurled it at him. Endrance saw it coming but couldn't respond to it as he was already channeling energy into his next spell.

The soldier still on watch, Perd leapt in between the mage and his foe, his shield flashing up and catching the blade. It sunk an inch into the metal but didn't pierce any farther. He stepped back as Endrance had not changed his pose, and kept his two fingers pointed at the goblin on the ground. His left hand formed the mudra of primal directions and he incanted the last word of the brief spell he had practiced not moments before.

"Obversus catenatus" he finished, and with a twitch he flicked his pointing fingers towards the two goblins fleeing.

The lightning he had struck the first goblin with seemed to come alive and burst up from the first corpse into the air in a long arc, striking the closest retreating goblin in the back. It didn't finish there, but arced again to the goblin beyond the second. Endrance flicked his hand and pointing fingers back to him, and the lightning jumped back to its final target. Moments later, four smoking goblin corpses twitched and jerked in the darkness.

Perd stood next to Endrance as men with torches went to check the bodies. He looked at the young man and whistled.

"Well, I'm sure glad you are on our side." He said appreciatively. "And you say you're new?"

Endrance didn't respond at first, his ears were ringing. "Huh?"

"You said you were a new wizard?" Perd repeated. Endrance rubbed his ears and nodded.

"Yes," he responded after opening his mouth wide and feeling his ears pop. "I passed my tests a month ago."

"Can… any wizard do that?" Perd asked. "Throw magic that jumps from enemy to enemy?"

Endrance shook his head. "No, that spell is beyond my abilities at the moment. What I did was more complicated to pull off but made the same effect."

"Right. Well, thanks." The soldier said. "You saved Ethan's hide, you did."

"Thank you, Perd." Endrance responded. "You saved my hide too."

He shrugged. "Jus' doing my job, sir."

"So am I, Perd. So am I." Endrance sighed. "I'll go check on Ethan."

As he walked away, he lifted his hand up so he could see it in the firelight. The first two fingers of his right hand that he used to direct the lightning against the goblins, were blackened and scorched. Thin black lines ran down his hand towards his wrist, tracing the lines of magic that had flowed through him. The fingers tingled and the rest of his hand felt too warm, but otherwise it didn't hurt yet.

He grimaced and dropped his hand to hang loosely at his side, and shifted the sleeve of his shirt to cover most of it. He was not going to be able to use his hand until it healed, if his hand healed at all. Many wizards had 'burned out' before from using magic beyond their capabilities. Lingering wounds, damaged meridians, and even permanent aura damage.

That was the price a mage paid when they over exerted their power. As a mage improved in ability and practiced the art, their bodies grow accustomed to handling larger portions of their aura channeling through them. If they needed, one could grab more power than they could safely handle, but like with any power, too much too fast can burn.

He thought about the burned and still crackling corpses he left behind. He had killed them. He reached out with magic and snuffed out four lives in the space of a breath, but he just felt numb to it. He had never killed anything before in his life, and he destroyed four with magic as if he had been an old hand at it. He didn't try to suppress the shudder that ran through him. Was it really that easy? Was this what power like magic was for?

He found Ethan surrounded by his fellow soldiers. He lay sprawled on the crushed down grass near his bedding. Some of his comrades had unbuckled and removed his breastplate and helmet. His chest heaved as he tried to catch his breath and calm his heart. Ethan stared up at the night sky, his mouth slack and eyes unfocused. In the light and grass, Endrance could barely make out a trickle of drying blood trailing out his ears and down his neck. Flecks of foam stuck to the sides of his mouth.

"Ethan…" Endrance said softly, shaking the man's shoulder gently with his left hand. The soldier's breathing was slowing, but he did not respond. He shook his shoulder harder, and called his name more forcefully. "Ethan!"

Ethan finally blinked, and his eyes focused on the mage. "I…" he began, swallowing with a dry throat. Endrance gestured to one of the soldiers, who were already kneeling to give him a mouthful of water. He swallowed and cleared his throat weakly. "I believe I found their camp, sir mage." He finally admitted, a faint smile touched his face. "Probably."

Endrance sighed and nodded. "It would seem so. You made it back alive on top of it."

Ethan's chest jumped for a moment, and he winced. "Oh, don't make me laugh. My chest already feels like it's going to burst open."

"Okay." Endrance said. "How many were there?" he asked.

"I'm not sure." Ethan responded. "Did you get the ones that were chasing me?"

Endrance felt a twinge of slowly mounting pain in his hand, but smiled at the exhausted soldier. "I did indeed, four of them."

"Then maybe twelve more. Didn't see them all but it's what their raiding parties have been known to travel in." he stated flatly, his eyes closing for a moment. "That drum will make wiping them out difficult."

"I'll manage." The young mage replied, standing.

"Wait." Ethan exclaimed as he looked up at him. "They had a family, three adults and two kids. They looked local."

Endrance frowned, concern crossing his face. "That might be the Mathers farmstead, but they had four children and a few hired hands." Endrance responded, using enough control to keep his voice from breaking.

"Sir." Another soldier interjected. "Goblins have been known to eat human flesh."

Endrance shook his head. "Then I need to get going. Where are they?" he asked. Inside he was utterly terrified, but now he knew he could not leave the goblins alive. He knew the Mathers family personally. They came into Wayrest once a month and had always brought a few extra sweet potatoes for his family. He could not stand to leave the family to be eaten. He just couldn't, even if it meant harm would come to him.

Ethan relayed directions to him shortly before passing out from exhaustion. Endrance returned to his bedroll and gathered what little he would need and was only a few yards out of camp when he heard someone calling his name.

He looked back to see five of the caravan soldiers trotting to catch up with him. Before he could speak, the lead one, Julius interrupted him.

"We know where you are going, sir mage." He stated in a tone that refused objections. "Perd said you would try something like this. We also can't sit by while some monsters eat our own kind." He clamped his fist to his chest. "We are going with you, sir mage."

Endrance stared at the five of them. Having five experienced soldiers made his goal less of a suicide mission. It was still two to one at best, but it was better by far than twelve to one.

The five men were clad in their armor, shields and swords. They had all also fitted a dagger on their side. They were as ready as they could be.

"They will be waiting for us, sir mage." Julius stated. "We best be accommodating them."

Chapter 08

The five soldiers moved in a semicircle in front of him as they advanced. The six of them moved with a purpose in silence. The goblin drum had been silent for a while now, but the young mage knew it was likely due to the goblin getting ready to intercept them.

Endrance didn't want the others to know, but he was not in top condition. Not only was his hand scorched and relatively useless, but the spells he used had drained a significant portion of his aura. He was also mentally exhausted from simultaneously maintaining a spell that wasn't supposed to be kept active and casting another spell with only one hand. That was difficult enough under controlled circumstances, much less when under attack by murderous goblins.

He would have to endure, and help out how he could. He had originally planned on sneaking as close as he could and attacking the drums before the goblins could respond. Now he had a family that he couldn't leave behind, and a handful of angry soldiers to help him mete out justice. With the five soldiers covering him, he felt better about his chances of survival.

The night was the blackest Endrance had ever seen it, but he could still make out shapes in the dark. The moon was covered in dark clouds, swollen with potential rain. He could barely make out the swaying grass and shifting branches from the sparse trees that grew erratically in the countryside near to Wayrest. His night vision wasn't too good. An elf would have been able to count the blades of grass for yards around him.

They had chosen to move in the dark approaching the camp because with torchlight the goblins would see them coming from a long ways away. Even though the darkness also worked against them, at least they could get close before the goblins caught on to them. From what Julius had informed him, they could be clever if given enough time or direction from a superior. If they saw them coming from a long distance, the goblins could be ready for them.

They knew the goblin camp was nearby when they could hear a woman sobbing. There was no fire or signs of their presence; they had already cleared out of the area. Pushing through the grass, Endrance saw human forms held up against some kind of posts in a rough circle in the moonlight. One of the figures was breathing with difficulty, and the source of sobbing was the woman next to it.

Endrance started to move to free them when Julius held out his shield, stopping him.

"Hold." he ordered quietly. His men came to a halt, lifting their swords and shields defensively. "I know bait when I hear it."

"But I can see them right there," Endrance responded "and I don't see any signs of camp."

"You can see in this dark?" Julius asked. "Your night vision is better than mine. But this is an ambush. I can almost smell it."

"Then how do we..." Endrance trailed off. He looked around nervously. The grass swayed in the dark, and things that might have seemed innocuous was more menacing than they should have appeared. The fact that there could be a dozen murderous monsters hiding nearby was unsettling; as far as he could tell, the six of them were alone.

"We can't do much without light." Julius' whisper prodded him. "Goblins are expert ambushers, and now we're at the disadvantage."

"Okay," Endrance acknowledged "cover me, and I'll illuminate the area."

He could barely make out the shapes of the soldiers slowly move around him. They formed a lose circle around him, their backs to the mage and their shields to the darkness around them.

He tried to flex the fingers on his right hand, and winced as electric pain shot up his arm through his shoulder. He would not be able to rely on his other hand yet. He worked carefully with his left, and slowly worked through the mudras required for the incredibly simple spell. It took far longer than he liked, several seconds more than normal because he had never thought that he would need to spell sling this basic spell and hadn't studied it.

The spell completed as he finished the final sign and whispered the last name of the words of power he called upon. He clenched his fist, and lifted it into the air above him while opening it. From his palm a brilliant pinpoint of light burst forth. It's pure white light rose into the air over his head by several feet and hung there, bobbing slightly in the faint breeze as a lantern on a string. It suddenly became brighter than the day for almost a dozen yards around him.

Like dirt being rinsed from a stone, the brilliant light peeled away the darkness. Within the shadows and banks of grass hunkered several goblins just a few feet farther into the thought to be abandoned camp ground. Wrapped in shadows, the goblins had been almost entirely invisible to the eye in the darkness. Illuminated, they shrieked in pain and fell away, covering their eyes as their naturally light sensitive eyes were blinded by the brilliant display.

The soldiers around the mage were ready, and waded into the dazzled opponents with great zeal, shouting an unfamiliar battle cry and hacking with their swords. Within seconds, the four closest to the men lay slain, having been unable to even raise a blade in their defense. The brilliant light gleamed off the smooth reflective surfaces of their armor plates, giving them the temporary advantage.

Endrance had enough time during the exchange to sweep his eyes across the field around him, searching for the rest of the goblins. Many sets of tiny, hateful eyes gleamed in the darkness around them, and he knew the battle was far from over. He could see the captives were isolated, away from any of the goblins, and was glad they didn't use them as shields at least.

He felt air blow past him, and barely registered a jagged-edged blade tumble past him, the attack likely fouled by the brilliant light over him. It was useful, but also was making him a target. He shouted to Julius over the din of combat.

"They're using throwing knives!" he cried out, and was relieved to see Julius respond with precision and skill befitting an experienced soldier. He shouted a command and the other four moved to cover the mage.

Weapons clattered against shields and glanced off their helmets and armor. He heard one of the men let out a grunt, but kept fighting despite a blade burying itself into his thigh. The five of them hunkered down around Endrance, and the mage half crouched in their midst. The soldiers were covering most of their bodies with their shields, crouched down as they were, but even so the young mage's slight frame and short stature ensured he was almost completely covered on all sides.

"Sir Mage!" Julius said, glancing at him as they guarded against an uneven assault of thrown projectiles. "We can't-" he was cut off as a blade skidded off his helmet. He rolled his eyes in irritation and continued. "We can't press forwards like this!"

"Well," Endrance began, "They have to run out of knives sometime, right?"

"I don't think we want to wait for that to happen." Julius replied.

"Right, let me think!" Endrance replied.

He just started working on a plan when he felt the entirety of his back erupt into a fierce tingling sensation. Someone was working magic nearby and whatever it was, it was at least as powerful as he was. He threw himself down onto the grass and shouted in alarm.

"Get down!" he cried out. The men dove to the earth, but one man was not fast enough. The soldier who had taken a hit to the thigh was a second too slow responding, and caught the edge of the spell that was likely aimed at Endrance. He felt the disturbance of something moving through the air above him. He heard a loud dull thud as the spell hit the poor soldier, and his scream was mercifully short as he sailed limply over Julius' head. He was dead before his body touched earth several yards away; the back of his breastplate had a blackened smoking scorch across it. His face permanently frozen in terror, the man's skin had already turned as gray as ash.

"Goblin Mage!" Julius shouted.

"You four worry about the rest of the goblins!" Endrance cried out as he picked himself off the ground. "I'll handle the mage!"

The men scrambled to their feet, and charged into the goblins as they were regrouping. Having expended most of their projectiles, they drew wickedly jagged swords and axes and grouped together to handle the soldier's charge. The four larger men crashed into the six smaller goblins, and the fight was on.

Endrance mentally prepared himself as he got to his feet. He would have to match not only magical force with this enemy caster, but also wits. He couldn't underestimate his opponent because he was a goblin; in fact, he should fight all the more cautiously because of it. The young mage immediately started the rote mental exercise Kaelob taught him, preparing his mind for the action-reaction duel that was about to commence.

The first step was to even the playing field as much as possible. He held up his left hand in the same last symbol he used for the light spell, and then flicked his wrist towards the skirmish nearby. The brilliant pinprick of light shot off to float in Julius' general area, providing light for the combatants but still being far enough away that any attacks on the light would miss the men.

He knew his opponent was lurking in the darkness, and had natural night vision, making hiding in the darkness a poor tactical decision. He took off at a run, moving away from both the enemy mage's last position and the men he was fighting with. If he remained where he was, they could get hit with whatever spells missed him.

He had barely moved a handful of paces when he sensed another swell of magic coming from his left side. He ducked as best he could while running; a kind of awkward bobbing lope that would have been funny to watch if it weren't for the danger. Whatever spell the enemy used passed him silently and invisibly again, a narrow miss that made the hair on the back of his neck stand up. He skidded to a stop in a thick stand of grass and crouched as low as possible.

He wrapped his hand around a fistful of grass and cast the only spell he could think to use there. The abbreviated word of power released the spell's energy into the grass and the roots below him. He started pulling on the grass as he released a steady trickle of power into the plants around him. Instead of uprooting the grass, the clump in his hand and the grass around him for a dozen feet sprang up. It grew wildly as the young mage stood and when he let go of the grass it was easily nine to ten feet tall.

He carefully backed out of the overgrowth, his tired mind trying to remember every particular detail of the next spell he needed to cast. The spell he had learned early on in his education when his village had been suffering a drought, a good natured attempt to help out the people around him. He learned then that the plants he caused to grow would not survive for very long, but they also swelled with the energy he invested in them. The constant pulse of magic coming from the grass should be enough to make pinpointing him with any kind of magical sense difficult.

The problem was it also made detecting his opponent more difficult. He knew a spell that would help, but he couldn't sling it like some of the others he knew. The pain in his right hand was getting worse, and his mind was getting fuzzy from the lack of sleep and the stress of combat spellcasting. He hoped he had bought enough time to finish the next spell. He prepared his spell as his senses in front of him prickled with a slow steady buzz from the magic that remained before him.

He finished his spell almost half a minute later, but he hadn't come under attack while he channeled his spell. He threw his hand out towards where the last attack came from and called out the final word of power. Something dark rushed along his arm, missing his hand by scant inches and past his shoulder. The grass had separated as if a strong wind had swept down in the middle of it, flattening it on either side. The spell had passed by his face close enough to see it in the poor lighting.

It was not a gout of fire, or a burst of wind, but something dark. An inky black cloud roughly the shape of a javelin, trailing black smoke as it hurtled past. The smoke flowed against the sleeve of his shirt, and where it touched the cloth turned black. The side of his hand went instantly numb in its passing, and the skin grayed.

Fortunately his spell was released before he lost sensation in his hand. Arcane power flowed from deep within his chest, down his arm, and through his outstretched hand. A pulse rolled out from his hand and across the newly grown grass, invisible but felt. The vibration caused the blackened part of his sleeve to crumble to dust. The light of Endrance's lantern spell gleamed off the silver and gold of the bracer on his left forearm.

The pulse rolled across the field beyond, and wherever it swept Endrance became acutely aware of what life occupied that space. Grass, insects, even the wildlife cowering in their burrows as they fought over their heads were known to him. The pulse rolled only fifty yards in the direction he pointed, but it was enough.

Near the limits of his search range he was aware of the goblin. The thing was crouched in a slight depression in the field, using the grass for cover. It seemed to recognize the effects of his detection spell and started moving when the effect ended, but Endrance now knew the general proximity of the enemy. He took off at a dash towards the area in a circular route, curving into the area.

He felt himself moving and reactive to the battle, doing what he needed to survive, but inside he was almost paralyzed in fear. He'd only been in sparring matches with his master before, and though his master was more powerful and frightening than the goblin by a large margin he had always known his master wasn't trying to *kill* him. Even if the goblin didn't have murder on the agenda for him, both of his hands were almost incapacitated. His left hand still flexed, but was too numb to try any traditional casting. He was limited to spell slinging, with his left hand, exhausted, against an enemy mage in its natural environment.

He pushed his fear away as best he could and closed the distance to his enemy. He had to fight, there was no other option. He could not flee, running from a mage was typically an effort in futility, and he would be leaving good men who trusted him to die. He had no doubt that steel and muscle would avail the soldiers naught against the brand of magic the enemy used. He couldn't leave them to a fate like that, nor could he leave Wayrest to the goblin's greedy hands.

As he circled in he felt his entire left side erupt into a buzz of tingling and itching, even the numb surface of his left hand. He dove forwards, rolling through a thick clump of grass. He hit his other hand on something as he did and couldn't stop himself from yelping in pain. He pinned himself to the ground and struggled to get control over his spasms of pain before he got himself killed.

An arc of something washed out barely a foot over Endrance's body, only noticeable as it cut through the pattern of light and dark shadows of the clouds above. Even though it missed, Endrance felt its power as it withered every stalk of grass it passed through to dust. He almost blacked out as the spell passed over him. Endrance's eyes fluttered and he found himself just too tired to do anything but lay there.

He struggled to stay conscious. The spell had missed by a foot, but whatever force it utilized had sapped his vitality even though he had avoided the brunt of the spell. He shook his head trying to clear his mind. It seemed to be no use. As he lay there he struggled to move his body, move his arms… move anything.

His hand twitched, and he dimly recognized the pain that flickered in his senses. It was real though, and he focused on that one motion. He elicited another twitch from his burned hand, and the pain came back with a little more strength. Not enough to get him moving, but it woke him up enough to try to clench his fist.

Pain, pure and simple, exploded in his hand, barreled through his arm and slammed into his brain hard enough to cause him to thrash suddenly away from where he was laying. He lurched to his feet, adrenaline finally coursing through his body again. The Goblin mage had almost been on top of him, and it jumped back when its prey proved to be more vigorous than it wished.

Endrance threw out his left hand and pulled up the last reserves of strength into the only attack spell he learned to sling. "Ignatius!" he cried out desperately.

Brilliant, billowing orange flames poured from his hand in an arc nearly fifteen feet deep. It was all he could muster with his limited strength even though his rough internalization of Kaelob's flame spell had improved a little. The flames slammed into and washed around the goblin, causing the deadened and crumbling grass to combust impressively. A squealing wail rose from the flames as the goblin was roasted.

Endrance backpedaled as the fires spread back towards him. He stumbled back into the green grass and dropped to his knees as the fires quickly burned themselves out. The flame had burned too hot too quickly to spread to any of the living grass, saving him from suffering the same fate as his enemy. He took stock of his condition as a moment of quiet passed. After a moment of looking himself over he came to the conclusion that he was as close to being dead as a man could be and still be able to stand.

He heard a hacking wheezing cough from in front of him and he looked blearily into the blackened and burned remains of the field of combat. He was just too tired to feel fear as he realized the goblin wasn't dead, just a numb sensation of irritation. Its body was bent and burned by the flames, charred and smelling of roasted flesh. The thing was trying to crawl away, but its limbs were withered and twisted like spent match sticks.

Endrance gingerly pulled himself to his feet and approached, his feet crunching through ash and cooked plant matter alike. He could feel the heat through the soles of his shoes as he stopped next to the hateful thing.

The goblin wheezed and hacked, its lungs burnt too badly to utter a proper curse. Its movement slowed, and a few wheezes later it was still. Endrance looked down at it with a tired sense of detachment. He was considering checking if it was really dead when the yellow-orange gem set into his silver bracer began glowing. He looked down, lifting his arm to look at it closely. As he did so the first circle of arcane script etched in the silver illuminated in the same amber light.

A faintly visible pale golden wind arose from the slain goblin's body. It swirled up, trying to disperse, but the light of the gem seemed as a net, funneling the wind into it. It swirled around his arm as the faint light was absorbed by the bracer. As the last of it entered the gem, the second and third circles of script briefly illuminated and then died out.

Endrance stared at the bracer in a dull sense of shock. He flexed his left hand, and feeling had returned to it in that moment. As he watched, the light faded from the gem and in a moment it was normal again. Endrance felt a twinge of apprehension. The bracer had captured the remaining amount of the energy that the goblin mage had been holding in his aura. Any energy remaining disperses soon after a mage's death, but the bracer had caught the swell in energy and siphoned it into the Crystalphage.

It was a truly amazing artifact. Was his master even aware of what he gave his apprentice? He also did not know if that was all the thing could do. He looked at it again in the spell-light and knew he would have to spend hours studying the thing.

The spell-light grew brighter, and Endrance turned to see Julius trotting up to him. The soldier stopped several paces away and watched him apprehensively. He swallowed, cleared his throat, and finally spoke to the wizard.

"Sir Mage," he reported "the rest of the goblins are slain, but I only count eleven."

"The last is beyond our reach." Endrance replied, surprised to hear the words coming from his lips. "It was already on its way to report to their master when we had arrived."

Julius' eyes narrowed. "How do you know that, Sir Mage?" he asked. "Did the mage confess before it died?"

Endrance shook his head. "No, I just… I just know."

Julius eyed the bracer on the wizard's wrist and kept as much distance as was respectable. The light over his head illuminated a long groove down the side of the man's helmet. The remaining men were injured but standing.

"Did you…" Julius began, but couldn't finish his question. It was obvious that he had seen the bracer's work in action.

"I don't know." Endrance replied. "I've never seen that happen before. I am unsure what that was."

Julius shook his head. "Whatever it was, it was damn creepy, sir. Geralt's dead. We should cut free the Mathersons and destroy that drum, Sir Mage."

Endrance nodded numbly, wearily shuffling towards the captives as he spoke. "Yes. We should."

The last remaining goblin turned from the now far away burning pile that was once his mighty war drum and the bodies of his fellow goblins.

He was at the top of a nearby hill, crouched as the men only a few hundred yards tossed the last goblin corpse on top of the burning drum. He cringed as he watched his comrades burn. No one should go like that, better that they be eaten so they remain with the horde.

The wizard was comforting the last few survivors of their raid the prior day. The other captives had died during the day since their capture. The human woman fiercely held onto the one they had figured was her mate and cried over his body.

When he turned away, he froze stock still as he realized a cloaked figure was standing in front of him, as still as a statue. The creature's night vision saw through enough of the night's shadows to reveal the figure before him.

The figure was lean and tall, with slender gloved hands. It reached up and pulled back the hood, revealing beautiful aquiline features and a cascade of silken black hair. Her dark tan skin blended well with the night, and golden feline eyes stared through the goblin before her.

The messenger dropped to its knees, murmuring for her forgiveness. She ignored him a moment, standing next to him as she looked down on the men below.

"Sha'hdi…" The goblin whispered, its grasp of common a miserable mockery of the true language.

"Silence!" the woman hissed, her hair sliding across her shoulder silently as she turned her head, revealing longer pointed ears. Black steel loops and studs pierced both ears, and she had a tightly fitting single loop through her upper lip.

"Sha'hdi," the goblin tried again. "We did as you ordered. But you didn't tell us of the caravan."

"They shouldn't have gotten involved. She responded curtly. "You should have been able to sack the town with little trouble before that treacherous bastard Kaelob got involved. Somehow the whelp dragged them into it." Her golden eyes could see the young man struggling to help the four men carry or assist with the injured and dead. They would be busy for a few hours yet.

"But why?" the goblin asked. "I don't under-"

His voice cut off as the elf's hand flitted past his throat and a volume of dark blood spurted from the line traced across it. The goblin sputtered and slumped to the dirt, his eyes turning dull and his breathing stopping quickly.

"You wouldn't." She said coolly, re-sheathing the finger length narrow blade into her sleeve. She pulled the hood back over her head and vanished into the darkness once again. The night went on, a silent blanket of shadows for the dead that lay under her.

Chapter 09

Endrance woke up to being jostled roughly. He blearily looked around, wary. He realized he was in the back of one of the caravan wagons, stuffed between some sacks of grain and barrels of apples. The wagon was rolling, and he could hear people walking and chatting nearby. Whoever put him in the wagon had the presence of mind to put him on top of his bedding and pile his belongings near his head.

He sat up, and quickly realized he was naked. Someone had stripped him down of everything but the silver bracer on his arm, which had been wrapped in a simple strip of cloth. He didn't remember wrapping it, so someone must have done so when he was unconscious. He saw across his skin faintly visible lines shiny and off color, like scars that have long healed. They traced his meridian lines everywhere he looked on his body. He had never seen it before, but it was possible it was caused by over reaching his bounds.

He fumbled through his pack and labored to pull on a clean pair of pants. He was lacing them up when a woman pocked her head through the flaps on the back of the wagon's covering.

"Oh good!" she exclaimed, smiling. "You're awake!"

The woman was Geraldine, wife of one of the tradesmen on the caravan. Her curly gray hair and kind features made her fit the image of a pleasant housewife to a tee. Her clothes were clean and simple browns, the kind that excelled at hiding wrinkles and creases. She clambered over the sacks of grain and placed the back of her hand against his forehead. Her thin hand felt cool and strong, and she smiled warmly when she pulled her hand away.

"Good, good!" she observed. "You seem to be just fine now. We were worried you were going to be ill for longer."

"Ill?" he asked. "I don't remember being ill."

She pulled an apple from a nearby barrel, replacing the lid on the barrel while wiping the dripping water off on her dress with the other. She handed it over to him and shrugged.

"Julius said you fell over halfway back to camp, and they had to drag you back to camp. We got you in the light, and all we could see on you were these little black lines all over your skin like veins. You were sweating and groaning, so Julius had us look after you as he brought back the rest of the injured."

"If I was ill, why did you put me next to the food?" he asked, taking a bite out of the apple. The taste of food awoke his stomach, and he hungrily ate the apple as swiftly as he could.

"Well, Ethan had seen the marks had been on your fingers when you went to check on him before you left, and Julius said your fight that night was pretty frightening. It looked like the same thing that killed poor Geralt, but you weren't dead." She shrugged. "You had no physical injuries, so it must have been a magical illness."

He held his hands up and flexed it. The fingers had normal feeling again, and were clean. The meridians were just as faintly visible as the rest of him, though they didn't change in texture from his healthy skin.

He had fully healed from his burn out, but something seemed off. The meridian lines on his right hand seemed uneven. Compared to the mirrored lines on his left, the lines flowing from the central root in his palm through to the fingertips of his fore and middle finger were jagged and forked. He thought of the lightning and how he had kept the spell charged in his hand when he should have released it immediately. Had he somehow done damage to his meridians?

"How long?" he asked. "How many days was I out?"

Geraldine laughed. "Days?" she exclaimed. "You barely had the decency to stay down the whole night!" she pushed on his chest firmly, and he fell back onto his bedding. "Get some more rest. You earned it. I'll get some food put into you, and you can get back to sleep."

"But…" Endrance stammered.

"No buts about it!" Geraldine chided. "Julius told us how you saved his men and defeated a goblin shaman."

"But…" He tried again.

"Shh!" She shushed him again. "I'll be back in a few with some real food, so you just rest." And she disappeared out of the wagon, leaving him with his thoughts.

"Just one day?" he asked to no one in particular, baffled.

He remembered how poor he felt before he blacked out, but he had hoped he could have gone farther. It felt like for a moment his power had turned against him. He remember vaguely thinking he was going to die, yet here he was.

He closed his eyes and checked himself over again. He didn't feel bad anymore; in fact he felt great, all things considered. His muscles and shoulder was sore from the running and tumbling. His chest hurt from his heart pounding in fear pretty much the entire night. His arms and legs had a myriad of little scrapes and scratches that were already healing. There seemed to be no permanent damage caused by whatever magic that mage had used-

He knew. His head suddenly flashed with formula and theory that blinded his eyes in a sudden blossoming pain that erupted within his mind. The principle of the spells used against him burned themselves into his head, and he thrashed quietly in his bed, unable to scream or breathe from the sudden pain. The pain abruptly stopped, and he realized he was half sprawled across a bag of grain.

He quickly dug through his satchel and withdrew the spellbook Kaelob gave him. He yanked a crow quill pen from a small tube on the side and uncorked a bottle of ink. He quickly started penning the formulas that had flashed through his mind before they were gone.

It was spirit magic. He hadn't seen the effects of the spell because there wasn't anything visual about it. It had some force, but the most dangerous part was that it ignored anything without a spirit, passing through it unhindered.

He shook his head as he wrote, but the formulas remained. He could probably figure out the long form method to cast the three spells the goblin had used on him. Transcribing them out of memory on the back of a moving cart would be difficult, but he needed to do it. If he recorded them, it would save him countless months of research and hours of practice to have learned such spells the normal way.

Hours later, he looked up from his book, rubbing his eyes. It had gotten too dark to continue any writing, and he looked around. Night had fallen, and the wagons had come to a stop. He saw on the grain sack next to him a small loaf of bread and a wooden bowl of cold stew. His stomach growled at him, and he quickly ate the food and chewed on the now stale bread. He must have completely missed Geraldine's return, and by the evidence forgot about the food entirely.

His stomach sated for the moment, he took a moment to light a candle and look over his book. The first few pages were covered in arcane script and diagrams, ones he penned from memory. Small footnotes on the margins had been added as he wrote, detailing what came to mind about the spells he struggled to put to page. They would serve their purpose just fine. He was a bit confused as he read through it. It was written in arcane script, true. Most unskilled men wouldn't be able to read it at all; arcane script tended to crawl before the eyes of those without talent.

The other thing he noticed was that he had written it in cipher. The pages, even if read by a trained wizard would not be able to use the spell as is. They would have to figure out the cipher he used. He frowned, looking down at it. He read it just fine, the cipher translating in his head almost unconsciously.

He had never used a cipher before. He hadn't even made one up yet.

He sat back, closing the book. The candlelight glinted off of his bracer as he held it to the light. His brow furrowed as he studied the arcane script around the gem. The most he could make out was the innermost circle, which the spellwork was laid down to capture released essences. The second circle had similar phrasing, but used an archaic terminology he didn't completely understand. As near as he could tell the object captured was wisdom.

What worried him was that 'wisdom' in the archaic tongue could also be interpreted as 'soul'. The archaic tongue used the same word for the two meanings interchangeably in any of the texts that Kaelob had Endrance study as an apprentice.

He shook his head, and put the book away. Whatever happened had happened. He had benefited from it, but he needed to get to a library and research his gift more thoroughly before he did any more with it. The capturing of souls was considered necromancy, a taboo among the magical community. He could not afford to make a target of himself so soon in his career.

He lacked the political savvy to navigate himself through the dangerous climate of the Circle of Magi's politics. He had barely the status of a newly accredited wizard, and without any accomplishments to his name, he was afraid they would be more than willing to strip it from him. For now, it would be best for him to hide the bracer's abilities until he had a proper place to study it.

Chapter 10

It took nearly six weeks to get to Ironsoul from Wayrest. There were no further incidents, and Endrance was able to help the Caravaners in little ways during the trip. Their gratitude for saving them from the goblins had carried him far, despite numerous attempts he had made to inform them the caravan was at little risk. Several of them insisted they could never have known; they may have targeted them next.

Over that time he built a strong rapport with the hired soldiers that safeguarded the caravan. Now a man short, they used his assistance whenever he could offer it. While he had gotten pointers in swordplay or shown new exercises to strengthen his body, he felt the most exercised part of his body were his hands and feet. Every day he walked for hours, and when he was tired he perched on one of the side benches and felt the vibrations of the road through his rear and thighs.

By the time he reached Ironsoul, he was certain of three things. He would be sore for days. He needed new shoes. He needed a damn horse.

The caravan passed through the salt gates into Ironsoul proper after their travel papers were cleared by the guard. He stood just inside the gates and stared out over the city.

Ironsoul was a grand city, the capitol of the satrapies of Ironsoul. Here the high king's throne sat and here the core of his armies lay. All eight realms under High King Mastadon's rule brought their tithes and trade to this city.

Ironsoul was roughly circular, with long spoke like roads that ran in the four cardinal directions. At the ends of these roads were sixty yard towers. No guards patrols the walls, instead above each floated an azure crystal as large as a draft horse that was shaped roughly like an acorn. Although he wasn't close enough to sense their power, he had the feeling they were powerful magic sentries.

The center of the castle was an arching tiered dome over a hundred yards high and three hundred across. Complex statuary and crenellations made up its exterior, though the dome's size made even large statues seem miniscule. Banners of the kingdom fluttered in the wind from the walls, and its flags were seen flying all over the kingdom.

The second structure was not as grandiose, but at least equally impressive. In the north-east quarter of the city a tower jutted into the sky. From the southern 'salt gates' Endrance could see the tower despite the distance, and knew it easily was the tallest structure in the city, much less that he'd ever seen in his life.

The tower rose straight into the sky many hundred yards. It was a square structure, evenly spaced on all sides. The white stone blocks that formed its walls were massive, four yards wide and two tall. The stone of the tower gleamed in the day's light, and he was unable to look at it for too long or else risk getting blinded. He did not see any windows, nor did he see any banners or flags flying from it. The only feature to the shining tower was a softly shedding blue-white glow from the roof of the tower high up in the sky.

"Ah!" Ethan exclaimed, seeming to appear from nowhere. Endrance nearly fell over as he was startled out of his reverie. "That my friend, it the tower of Talos. Sure is tall, isn't it?" he asked, smiling coyly as Endrance smoothed out his clothes.

"That's its name?" the young wizard asked. He stared up at it in silence another moment before looking at Ethan again. "A building that thin should not be able to be that tall."

Ethan shrugged. "And yet, there it is. It's been here maybe thirty years or so."

"I have to wonder how long it took to build." Endrance pondered, scratching his head and staring up at the tower. "How many years and men did it take?"

"Eh," Ethan shrugged as he turned to wave the last of the wagons past. "Took about sixteen days, from what I heard." He turned back to the young mage and held his hands up apologetically. "It was before my time."

"What!" Endrance exclaimed, snapping his gaze on Ethan. "That's impossible!"

"And yet," The soldier repeated, "there it is. Fact is, no building or structure here was ever built in less than or more than sixteen days. Big, small…" Ethan shook his head as he shrugged again, frowning. "Doesn't seem to matter."

"What about the workers?" Endrance asked.

"Don't know." Ethan admitted. "You'd have to ask the steward in charge of that or a mason, I guess."

Ethan drew a small sack from his belt pouch and held it out to the young mage. "Here"

The sack held a few gold coins and a handful of silver pieces. It weighed practically nothing in his hand.

"Me and the men were talking, and we all agreed you should get Geralt's cut. You more than earned it helping us out like you did. "Ethan explained, his expression somber. "I have to go report to my superiors now, but look me up in town and we'll share a drink again, okay?"

Endrance stared down at the sack but nodded dully.

"Good. Before I go, it looked like Ked was looking for you; you should go see what he wanted." Ethan said. He gave the young mage a mock salute and a grin. "Good luck. Be seeing you again."

Endrance only nodded again as the soldier, his friend, departed. The little pouch of coins felt a whole lot heavier in his hand.

The caravan master was waiting for him at the head of the wagon train. He waved the young man over and shook his hand heartily as men and women all around him were unloading goods and loading in others. Men stood huddled around scales and officials with tally books.

Ked smiled broadly as he shook the wizard's hand. "I wanted to say thank you again for helping us on the trip here. I know we agreed upon some coin for being useful, but I don't think simple coin would be enough." He admitted, pressing a coin purse into Endrance's hand. He winked at the mage. "Tell you what, I'll let my people know who you are and they'll give you a little bit of a discount should you stop by their shops."

"I am very grateful." Endrance responded happily. "I'm glad we made it."

"So where are you headed next?" Ked asked, scratching his belly.

"Well, I have to acquire my guide, and then I'm off to the kingdom of Balator." He admitted.

"Ba...Balator!" Ked sputtered, shock registering on his face. "Why in the world would you want to go there? No mage, no matter if they were archmagus, ever willingly goes to Balator!" He tried his best to get himself under control. "Even the holy circle of magi refuses to send emissaries there!"

Endrance shrugged. "I have an invitation. A job offer, of a sort."

Ked blinked at him incredulously. "And here I thought you had run out of surprises for me."

"I do try to keep people on their toes." Endrance admitted jokingly.

Ked shook his head, clearing his thoughts. "So how are you planning on finding your guide?"

"I am not entirely sure." Endrance admitted, scratching his head as he looked at the throngs of people moving about their business. "I suppose a barbarian would stand out a bit in Ironsoul."

"True, Endrance." Ked responded. "But Ironsoul is a large place, and I think there are many miles of ground he could be coming in from."

Endrance sighed. "I knew I should have asked for more clarification from my master." He shook his head, wiping his face with a hand. "I bet he's cackling away at home."

Ked frowned at him for a moment. "What happened to your hand, son?" he asked, gesturing at the young mage's right hand.

Endrance looked down at his right hand. The markings across his skin had faded, but never completely disappeared. They were like scar tissue, nearly the same color as his skin, but didn't change color like the rest of his skin did. The jagged markings faded away at his wrist, but were noticeable enough to someone who knew him.

"Ah," he began. "I overdid myself when those goblins attacked. That's just a reminder to be more careful next time."

Ked's frown deepened. "I wish you had told me about that, sir mage."

"It's fine." Endrance reassured him. "No permanent injury, just some scars."

"No no..." Ked replied. "I wish you had told me because I need to pay you for injuries suffered while contracted to work with me." He bustled over to his cart and hauled out a strongbox from behind the driver's seat.

"Uh... what?" Endrance asked, confused. "I don't remember that being in our agreement."

Ked unlocked the box and plucked a few more coins from the box. "I know, but the circle of magi has very specific laws about the matter." He plunked the coins down into the young man's hands. "I don't want to get blacklisted because I didn't pay their mages properly."

"I'm... not familiar with those laws." Endrance admitted, looking at the gold pieces in his hands. "You probably could have gotten away without paying the extra."

"I know," Ked said with a shrug. "But I'll know, and that means that they could know, should they want to." he placed the last coin into his hands. "And that is why I am concerned."

"Where can I find the cathedral of magi?" Endrance asked. "I would like to learn more of these things my master had apparently decided to not instruct me on."

Ked shook his head, hauling the strongbox back into its place after locking it again. "I haven't the slightest idea. The cathedral of magi is somewhere in Ironsoul, but most of us without the blessing of magic haven't been able to find the place, much less enter without a wizard to escort us."

Ked turned back to the young mage. "Well, good luck on your journey, and I pray to the gods and the great magic you make it through alive. I like you well enough, son. I hope to do business with you again in the future."

Endrance pocketed the money and stepped back as the caravan master bustled past to yell at a few loaders. He found a bench to sit on and wondered how to proceed from there. He had no real clue how to find his guide, and sending a message back to his master for details was inefficient. He didn't know the first thing about the next stage of his journey.

He was unsure when the guide he was supposed to meet would show up, nor where. He had no real way of finding him, nor did he have a way of getting to Balator on his own. Whatever he ended up doing, he would have to figure this out soon.

He settled on making his way to the north half of the city. He would most likely come in from the stone gate in the north. If he stayed near the gate he could keep an eye on the traffic flowing through the area and try and spot the barbarian from there. Endrance picked himself up and made sure he had all his things with him before beginning the trek across the city. It was going to be a long day, and he hadn't even been a hundred yards into the city yet.

Feline eyes watched the young man from the alleyway across the main street from him. The dusky skinned figure remained concealed in her cloak despite being under shelter. The guards would have turned her away at the gates or even attacked upon seeing her, but she took it upon herself to gain admittance without their observations. Her kind was not readily welcome in Ironsoul. Most elves weren't.

A large-nosed, gangly young man leaned on the wall of one of the buildings that made the alley. He leered at her with interest, either trying to get a glimpse of what lied below the cloak, or just imagining what was beneath all the same. She looked to him and he snapped his eyes up to meet hers just a moment after. "So." the young man said, jerking his head at the hopeful young man burdened with travelling gear marching steadily north. "Tha's de mark?"

The Sha'hdi said nothing, but turned to look back at the young wizard who all but declared he was new to Ironsoul with every step and everywhere he looked. "I don't want him killed." she whispered.

"Whut?" the young man said, leaning forward. "I idn't ear you."

She turned her predatory gaze upon him again, and he shrank back against the wall. "Do not kill him. I just want him... inconvenienced." she looked back down the road, but the young man had disappeared into the crowd. "He still has a long ways to go before then." she whispered, the last remark unheard by her thuggish companion.

"A'ight," the man said, slinking away deeper into the alleyway. "I'ma let the boss know. You paid good money, you get good work, he says." The man turned a corner and vanished.

"Sniveling rat among men." The Sha'hdi muttered scornfully. "I'll make sure this goes how I want it, should you fail."

A guard in Ironsoul's signature breastplate armor walked past the alley right then. Either he caught a glimpse of her out of the corner of his eye, or he felt the threat of her eyes upon him, his step faltered, and he turned to look down the alley. It was empty.

Endrance eventually made it across most of the city. He had hoped to have more time to look around his first day there, but the city was far bigger than he anticipated. For someone who had grown up in a small town, seeing so many people in one place amazed him.

There were men and women of innumerable size and color moving about, doing an innumerable variety of things. Most of which he had no idea what they were doing or how. People moved on foot through the city, and carriages with horses were seen carrying passengers from one place to another. The whole mess of people, the size of the city, and the amount of noise it all made was fascinating but also overwhelming to him.

He found an inn near the north gate just before the suns set that day. He had to squeeze through a pair of people arguing about some ridiculous taxes they had to pay in order to get inside.

The innkeeper sighed and rolled his eyes as the young man approached. "I'm terribly sorry about the mess, ma'am. Those two won't move no matter what I say."

Endrance cleared his throat before speaking, and looked around the lobby before continuing. "It's sir, sir. I'm fine, I got past them anyhow."

The man squinted down at him, frowning. "You look awfully slight for a boy."

"Man." Endrance responded. "I'm fifteen."

"Uh-huh." the man responded. "Whatever you say. You need a room for the night? We have some high quality rooms left, and there's always the shelter room, you just rent the key to the trunk you lock your stuff in for the night."

"Shelter room?" Endrance asked. "What's that?"

The innkeeper laughed "You must be a first timer to Ironsoul, ain't you?"

"That I am." the young mage responded. "What of it?"

"Nothing, nothing." the innkeeper said kindly, holding up a hand as if he were warding off a harsh look. "Look boy, things work differently here in Ironsoul than most other cities. Definitely different than the satrap townships and capitols beholden to Ironsoul."

He held up a finger. "Few rules you need to observe while here. First is that there is a curfew. Be inside before midnight; don't come out for a few hours." He held up a second finger. "Next you pay your taxes." He held up a third. "Lastly, do not deface the buildings."

Endrance nodded warily. "Okay I understand the rules, but why do we have to be inside at night?"

The innkeeper leaned over the counter and looked him in the eye. "The city cleans itself up at night, boy. Anything left on the streets that ain't a fixture gets swept away, never to be seen again."

"The city itself?" he asked.

"Aye," the innkeeper nodded sagely. "Some say it's the spirit of the city, keeping itself clean. Some people say the wizards of old had bound the souls of the men who built the city to its very stones." he shook his head. "Either way the city does respond to attempts to damage it, and people wandering out after midnight aren't ever seen again."

"I see. So the shelter room?" the young man asked.

"The shelter room is free bedding for people to rest that can't afford it. Only a copper a night for a key to a trunk you can lock your things in while you sleep. It's not private, and there's some odd folk who come in, but it's enough to keep you safe. And every inn in Ironsoul has such a room."

"Ah. That's rather kind of you to have them then." Endrance commented.

"Nothing kind about it." The innkeeper replied. "One of the first High Kings ordered it when the city was founded. People used to get caught out at night all the time, even those who weren't vagrants or too drunk to know better."

"Interesting. I would love to examine that magic someday." Endrance mused.

"Just don't stick your head out the window at night, boy. Not a pretty sight." The innkeeper warned. "So you want a room or just a key?"

The mage looked behind the innkeeper. There was a wooden board with pricing carved into its polished surface. "I am not sure yet, what's the current conversion rate today?"

The innkeeper responded immediately with a tone of surety in his voice. "Eleven coppers to the Silver piece."

Endrance pulled a few coins out of his pocket. "And for gold?"

The innkeeper's eyebrows went up, but he responded just as swiftly. "Ten and a half silvers to the gold piece. Meaning one hundred fifteen copper and halfpence per gold piece."

"That sounds reasonable and your math is impeccable." Endrance began. "Do you have a room that overlooks the stone gate? I am waiting for someone to come in from there."

The innkeeper to his credit knew his place well. "I do in fact have a room. It's on the third floor and has an unobstructed view of the road leading in from the stone gates."

"Excellent!" Endrance smiled. "How much for the room for a night?"

"Well, it's a high quality room, and comes with a meal and mead." The innkeeper turned to his side and pointed at the board. "The room's eight copper a night."

Endrance flipped a coin from his hand into the air in front of the innkeeper. The man deftly caught it out of the air and opened his hand to see the shine of gold. "I would like to put in for two weeks worth then." Endrance said smartly. "I trust that if I should not need the full duration of my stay I can have the rest returned?"

The man put on his best smile. "But of course, sir. Come this way, I'll show you to the room!" he pulled the key from behind the counter and led the young man upstairs to the room. Along the way he asked a few basic questions, most about his preference of food and drink, and what times he would be out so his wife can clean the room.

The room was small for Ironsoul standards, but considerably spacious as far as Endrance had ever lived in. It was as far across as his father's home, yet there was less space inside due to elegant furniture. There lay a large four poster bed with plush crimson coverings and red curtains around it. The carpeting lain over the polished wooden floor was thick and the exact same color of red. It smelled faintly of lavender, and faint wisps of incense came from a small tray over the fireplace.

"I trust the room here is satisfactory?" The innkeeper asked.

Endrance dumped his pack and most of his gear on the bed on his way to the window. The wooden sash was polished and had a latch lock on it. The exterior shutters were open. He looked out the window before responding. The view covered the road pretty effectively, and in the distance he could see the stone gates themselves. The detail was hard to make, but he could see the traffic coming through and out of the gates. It was the closest inn to the gates, so it would have to do.

"This is fine. Thank you sir." Endrance responded. "I'd like my meal in about two hours, if possible."

"Absolutely sir." The innkeeper responded. "My wife will bring it up then." he quietly closed the door as he left.

Endrance sat on the bed. The first step of his journey was successful, and he was on his way to the next. He couldn't help but feel excited, but he also couldn't avoid worrying about everything that could go wrong. He drifted off to sleep wondering how in the world he was going to find his guide.

In the back rooms of the inn, a man in a handsome red coat and slightly crumpled matching hat sat in the innkeepers' chair. He was lean and attractive, a faint smirk on his face as he watched the innkeeper with dark brown eyes. His smooth black hair was clipped close to his head, and the hat hung at a rakish angle. The innkeeper stood across from him, wringing his hands. A gold coin danced in the newcomer's fingers, flipping over his knuckles and between deft fingertips.

The room was otherwise silent, but had a tension in the air that could be cut with a knife. The person's intrusion into his personal chambers would normally have the man shouting and possibly reaching for a weapon, but the presence of the man in red instead put him in an uneasy silence as he waited for the man's message. He wasn't even sure when the guy had pilfered the gold he got from the young man out of his pocket, but it wasn't there now.

The man in red stopped the coin between his forefinger and thumb as he looked it over. "So this young man you found paid in gold, eh?" The man in red prodded.

"Yes, he did." the innkeeper replied, worried. "He didn't look like any of the sort your kind would be concerned about."

The man in red flipped the coin back at the innkeeper, who caught it after nearly dropping it twice. "We aren't concerned about him. A client is." He stood and sidled up to the door leading out the back. "Keep us informed of his movements, nothing more. Then you can keep what he gave you." He walked out the back of the inn, whistling a merry tune and tipping his hat to a young woman who passed by. She blushed and didn't notice him lift the jeweled bracelet from her wrist as he brushed past her.

The bracelet vanished into his coat as he turned a corner and was gone from sight.

The innkeeper swallowed, and closed the door before his wife came back and wondered what he was up to. He eyed the gold coin and sighed. He had hoped that he could finally make a profit without Zadrah getting his fingers into his business again. But the infamous 'Baron of the Back Alleys' was again aware of things happening as if he were there.

The man went into the kitchens to tell his wife of the new tenant's meal, and to take a mug of ale for himself. The next two weeks were going to be a hassle.

Chapter 11

Joven rode his horse up the crest of the hill that night. The walls of Ironsoul gleamed in the moonlight, its appearance of fortitude assured safety to those who lived within. To Joven, it represented a tactical challenge. Many times the warlords of Balator had tried their mettle against the walls of Ironsoul, and as many times they had failed. Though recent treaties with Ironsoul has ceased such attacks, and removed their presence with the ivory satrap, Joven still considered the walls with the same respect one gave a lifelong rival worthy of his skill.

The moonlight caressed the bare skin of his heavily muscled arms as he gripped the reins loosely. He wore leather armor over his torso, sleeveless so he would be unhindered in a fight.

Across his chest were several straps, and upon them several sheaths and scabbards were woven into or tied upon them. Two short swords crossed his shoulder blades, their handles where he could reach them easily. On his back was slung a greatsword of black steel, its surface drinking up the moonlight and giving nothing in return.

Under his arms on his flanks were four knives at each side, where he could quickly draw them and throw, or palm them if his arms were crossed. A battle axe was strapped to his hip with a leather thong, also crafted of black steel. A dagger was securely sheathed at the sides of his hips, strapped onto the hide pants he wore. Pairs of long thin blades were sheathed in scabbards built into the leatherwork of his boots. Several throwing axes were stowed along the saddle of his horse, just in case he needed just one more weapon. He had further tricks concealed should it become truly necessary.

His blonde hair was long but held back by a steel circlet, keeping it out of his face. His visage was impressive. A man of strong cheekbones, jaw line and cleft of chin. He had shaved a few days before, and had a shadow of hair across his face. His nose was slightly crooked, like it had been broken a few times before and was never set properly. His brows were thick and the slope of his forehead gave his blue eyes a stalwart appearance, but there was an intelligent glimmer of something more behind those eyes than just the desire for violence.

He kicked in his stirrups, and his horse bolted forward. A strong beast, the horse he rode was by all considerations a massive warhorse. White hide gleamed in the night, and the black paint handprint across his face and the paint markings across its haunches made it as intimidating as the barbarian that rode it.

The cities gates were still a few hours ride away. He would have to slow down and approach carefully, lest the men on guard think he was charging on the attack. He felt no fear for such an encounter, but slugging his way through a cadre of city guards and its inevitable ending would be bad for Balator's budding relationship with Ironsoul. That and he wouldn't be able to find the Spengur if he were dead, an obvious risk when taking on a capitol city by oneself.

Joven rode on in the night, and hoped he wouldn't have too much difficulty finding the man. He had been given a description of him, and told he would be meeting him in the city, but little else. It wouldn't be hard to find someone like him in the city. His bloodline has been bodyguard to the Spengur for generations.

Each generation taught the one before it, with word of mouth and flash of steel. Taught with hard earned lessons of blood, broken bones and bruises. Each father teaches the son of sacrifice, and of devotion. Each generation is required to set aside their lives within Balator and swear new allegiance to their Spengur.

Though only one of each generation must serve, their family is required to have many sons. While Spengur can be hired with little impact on honor, there was only their bloodline to guard him. If they die out or allow the Spengur to die their tradition ends, and the Spengur would be left all the more vulnerable.

As the night rushed by Joven felt a twinge of remorse, but shoved it aside. The last Spengur was now gone, as was the ones who followed and protected him. There was nothing he could do about it. There was only one bloodline left to watch over them.

The ten men on guard at the stone gates that night had the door closed as he approached. They came to full alertness when they spotted him riding up. They rushed a few dozen feet from the gates and formed a line with their lances drawn.

Joven stopped his steed thirty yards away, and dismounted. He walked his horse up to the line of men and stopped just out of jabbing range of the lances. His face was expressionless as he took in the ten men's postures and equipment.

The men were decently trained, but had not seen real combat. Their weapons only showed the wear of being carried around and none from striking or being struck. Joven smirked; if he had been on the offensive, the men would be felled before they could mount a solid defense.

A rattle drew his attention upwards. Four more men with longbows perched upon the outer wall, their bladed arrowheads visible in the moon's light. Well, they weren't entirely incompetent, he reconsidered.

Joven's smirk expanded into a smile. He raised his arms from his sides, showing he held only his horses' reins.

"Men." Joven stated, his voice firm, but he could not keep the amusement out of his voice. "I bring you no harm, yet. I seek entrance into the city."

The closest guard stammered in response. "Well... well you can't."

Joven's smile faded. "Why not?"

"City's closed." the man responded with a little more backbone. "Come back in the morning."

Joven scowled at the guardsman. "What's the problem?"

"Nothing." the man almost shouted back. "Just come back in the morning. We open the gates at suns-rise."

Joven stared at the man, the frown upon his face as hard as if carved in stone. The guardsman gulped.

In a whirl, Joven turned and led his horse to the side, off the road. He stuck a small stick into the dirt along the side of the road, and loosely looped his reins over the stick. His horse began grazing nearby, but never let the reigns draw tight. He sat down on a grassy patch and crossed his legs, placing his hands on his knees. He would wait, and he knew his presence would bother the guards but not be a nuisance enough to attack.

He had one other trick up his sleeve he planned on using. While the guards had to remain alert and attentive, warily watching the barbarian at the gate, he would be able to rest. Joven knew how to sleep while sitting up.

Endrance woke up the next day later than he was expecting to. The combination of a month's long walk, the loss of time and the warm meal he had consumed when the innkeeper's wife had delivered it had ensured he remained unconscious. The bed being of superior quality to anything he'd ever slept in very likely had a lot to do with it.

The first hours of day he spent sitting on the windowsill, watching the gate. Nobody stood out that passed through, and he was starting to get worried by the passing of the day. Perhaps waiting and watching wouldn't be enough. He should also put himself out into the city where his guide could find him while he looked for his guide.

He thought about what he could do to pass the time, and he realized that since the task was passed through the proper channels, he should be able to find the information at the tower he saw coming in. Someone there might be able to direct him to the right person, or at least tell him who or where to look.

So his next goal would be to finding help at the tower. Then he could work on finding the guide.

In a nearby tavern, Joven asked the fourth person that hour about the man he was seeking. No one had recalled having seen him yet, and so Joven settled down to a drink. His horse was stabled at a nearby inn, and he had traded in enough furs he collected along his trip to Ironsoul to earn the silver these people wanted so badly. He could trade those for what he needed until he found his charge.

Something tapped his shoulder, and Joven glanced at the source of his irritation. A large man in ratty clothing with a large gut and holding a repurposed chair leg stood behind him. Four other smaller men stood behind him, each with an improvised weapon of some sort.

Joven's right hand slid off his tankard and towards his belt. He stopped when he felt the strip of red cloth that was tied over the axe and the loop it was hooked on. All of the visible weapons he had were tied off with a strip of red cloth, to show he didn't intend on using them during his time inside the walls. They eventually ran out of cloth strips, and told him he got the idea.

He had sworn not to use his weapons on citizens of Ironsoul while he was looking for the Spengur. So he turned to the overweight man and smiled. "Ah!" he exclaimed. "Hello! My name's Joven!" he waved to the bartender, who was trying to be inconspicuously as far away from him as possible. "Please, have a drink!"

The man scowled at him. "Look here, barbarian. Jus' cause you signed those treaties don't mean we don't remember the people your kind killed." he tightened his grip on the club. "We're gonna remind you you aint welcome here."

Joven reached up and casually caught the chair leg as the man swung it down on him. He looked over to the barkeep.

"Uh," the barbarian began, pushing back and letting go of the leg, causing the assailant to stumble back into his fellows. "Sorry if something gets broke, 'kay?" he asked. The barkeep sighed and nodded.

Endrance walked down the street, looking for someone who would be able to help guide him to the Cathedral. He passed by a tavern, and considered going in to ask the owner. He had heard from Ethan that bartenders had a wealth of information.

The door to the tavern cracked as he approached it, the wood splintering. A man on the other side screamed in pain. He heard another man yell, and the window beside the door exploded outwards. A greasy, overweight man clutching the shattered remains of a chair leg rolled across the ground to stop at his feet, unconscious.

Endrance decided to look elsewhere. That place was busy.

Joven followed the last of the hooligans out of the tavern, shaking his fist and yelling at them. He chased the remaining ones away from him, and they smartly decided to take their boss and drag him off. The passersby in the streets had barely paused in their daily routine to observe, and were already going back to business.

Just another thing Joven disliked about the people of Ironsoul. No social niceties. Any real man would have gotten up after a brawl like that and have more respect for him instead of scrambling away like a beaten dog. They maybe would even buy him a drink, or a complement on his punch. Either way, more friends had been made in Balator with means that ended with missing teeth than handshakes and fake smiles.

Joven was just turning to go back to his drink when he thought he saw a glimpse of light blonde hair on an almost womanly figure down the road. He blinked his eyes a few times to help adjust to the light and leaned out into the road. The clothes style and body size fit the description of his charge. The hair was almost exactly what the letter described. He saw the figure turn his head to smile at another traveler, and he knew for sure that he was his charge. The subject had incredibly bright emerald colored eyes.

"Fate is kind." He said to himself and tossed a silver piece at the barkeep that caught it with a sigh as he surveyed the damage the barbarian had caused.

He started out into the street when he met a wall of men. Five of the city guard stood in front of him, their faces grim. "Sir, please step back into the bar. We will have to sort this out." The lead guardsman said coolly, his hand on the scabbard at his waist. "Or are you going to continue this rampage?" The other four men watched him warily.

Joven sighed. He held his hands out to his side and slowly backed into the tavern, keeping his eyes on his charge for as long as he could. "Perhaps I spoke to soon." He muttered.

The young man continued on his way, unknowing that his guide was within sight of him. Joven's mouth twitched as the door to the tavern swung closed, cutting off his vision. He turned to the five guardsmen and had to make himself smile. If he finished this quickly, he might be able to catch up to the young man.

"Now, what is the problem?" Joven asked, attempting to sound pleasant. The barkeep flinched. The five men looked around the room as their eyes adjusted to the lighting. The head guardsman sniffed and nudged a fragment of table with a boot.

"Let's start with this." He said. "And then we'll talk about the assaults."

Joven knew that it wasn't going to get finished quickly.

Zadrah watched the kid go about his business. He walked among the other people bustling to and fro, scurrying about their lives. The kid had an air about him; one that screamed to Zadrah's experienced senses that he would be a fairly easy mark. His build, demeanor, and his eyes wide with awe at the city about him made the thief label him a kid more than any factor of age.

Though he seemed a country bumpkin, something about him bothered the thief. He couldn't quite place it, but his instincts warned him to leave the kid alone for now. He wasn't wearing any city colors or iconography that would warn the thief that his mark was a city official or mage, but nonetheless he had this nagging feeling that something was amiss with him. Perhaps he would have to delegate some of the job to lackeys after all.

Zadrah leaned back against the wall of a clothier's shop and just watched the mark for a time. He studied the kid intently, though to the casual observer, he looked to be doing nothing of the sort. He was just a man sweet talking a beautiful young lady in the semi-privacy of a dark alcove. The woman he was playing with was flattered at the wonderful bracelet he gifted her. He was able to sift through most of the bland conversation while he worked; only responding when it was needed to keep her talking with him for the moment.

Eventually the kid wandered out of sight, heading towards the gleaming tower to the east. He disengaged from the conversation with the lass using sweet promises of a wonderful night's passion, and glided after the kid. Along the way he would change his disguise, one of many tricks he used to follow targets. By the time night had fallen, they would have everything they needed to roll the kid for all he was worth, and then some.

The Sha'hdi paid in good coin. In old coin, enough so that Zadrah himself felt compelled to handle the job personally. Even though the kid was just a whelp barely out from under his father's shadow. He wasn't sure how much esteem the client felt for the mark, but they were surely overpaying him to interfere. He didn't mind that so much. He was already planning to see just how much profit he could eke out of the situation, regardless of the matter. After all, to him women couldn't get his heart racing nearly as well as profit did.

Chapter 12

The tower was far more magnificent when Endrance stood within its gates and under its shadow. Easily large enough to house his entire village on one floor, the tower was of nearly unbelievable proportions before considering its height. If turned on its side, he would spend the better part of an hour treading its length just from one end to the other. It couldn't possibly have been constructed in any normal fashion. It couldn't even stay standing as tall as it was and yet it does.

The polished alabaster stone walls cast a shadow over Ironsoul like a sundial of the gods. He could see the walls, corners, and settings for the door had elaborate script inlaid in gold along geometric patterns. They lent a scintillating effect to the already warm glow of the polished stone. Banners of the wizard who owned the tower hung from the walls surrounding the tower's courtyard. Bright white cotton cloth stitched with a gold eye upon it. The iris of the eye was a golden sunburst.

Endrance remembered the sigil from his studies of historical figures. It was the symbol of house sunseer, a family lineage of powerful wizards. His books even suggested that the Sunseer lineage predated the kingdom itself. He knew that the current head of the sunseer household was the Archmagus, Talos. Though he didn't know much about him, Kaelob told him that since the death of Archmagus Valeria, Talos had proven an adept leader.

Once within the gates into the publicly available courtyard, he saw no security measures. No guards, no warding sigils, he didn't even sense any active spells as he walked the flagstones leading up to the doors.

- - -

Of all the potential guests he had seen so far today, the young man standing in the courtyard was the first to catch his eye. Talos rose from the low slung couch he had been scrying from and sought to get a closer look. Something about the boy caught his eye. His scrying spells had revealed a modicum of magical power, but the part that really interested him was the blatantly obvious spellwork on his aura. He reconsidered. It wouldn't be blatant to anyone who didn't have the same condition himself.

- - -

Endrance hadn't even heard the man approach. He had been too distracted by the door that wasn't a door. Before him was a dome of gold, ten feet across. It's convex surface smooth and reflective. He had just been about to reach out and touch it when he realized there was someone in the reflection near him. Startled, he looked to his right. Leaning against the wall next to the dome was a man so peculiar Endrance shouldn't have missed seeing him.

Only a few inches taller but exceptionally well muscled, the man wore only a pair of snug leather pants, boots, and buckled belt. He wore around his neck a leather cord holding a triangular tooth, and on each hand was a gold ring set with rare stones. His skin was tanned and his head completely bald, including his brow. The man's eyes were a bright and almost luminous orange, a similarity shared in Endrance's green.

What was most peculiar about the man was that every visible inch of the man's skin was covered in tattoos. Black lines tracing his meridians were twisted into dozens of spell forms and arcane patterns. Even the smooth pate of his head, his eyelids, ears, and lips were not spared from the ink.

Endrance stared. The man in response passively watched the young mage as if his reaction were business as usual. At a minutes passing, he cleared his throat, and Endrance snapped out of his distraction.

"You know," the man said, sounding deliberately bored. "If you keep staring I'm going to start charging you."

Endrance pushed an errant lock of silvered hair behind his ear. "I'm... sorry." He managed to say nervously.

Before he could lower his hand from his head, the man darted up to him and caught his wrist. He had moved so swiftly that he had no time to react. When his hand touched him, Endrance's senses flared white-hot. The man had exponentially larger reserves of power than the young mage, but it was so well contained and under such strong control that he wouldn't have been able to sense his power normally. It felt to him like a band of molten power had clamped down on his wrist.

The man hardly reacted to the moment, if at all. He merely pulled Endrance's hand out before the two of them. He examined the jagged lightning marks on the boy's fore and middle fingers, appraising it with a firm but gentle grip that felt like iron to the young mage.

"Well, that's astounding." He said at last. He released Endrance's wrist, who rubbed it while flexing his fingers. "Your foundation is impeccable, but you've built nothing upon it. Are you intending on squandering such an effective technique?"

Endrance frowned as he looked at his fingers. "What?"

The tattooed man sighed. "Your scribing."

Endrance looked at the bizarre man, the confusion on his face telling him what he needed to know.

"You don't know what I'm talking about, are you?" he asked, flustered.

"Uh... No, sir." Endrance responded. "I'm sorry."

The man sighed, wiping the palm of his hand across his bald head just like a man would sweep his hair back from his eyes.

"I find that hard to believe." He started. "I'm sure you would remember the extensive and may I add intensely painful experience of getting scribed."

Endrance waggled the two fingers. "Oh, well these hurt when it happened, but I've had these marks since I was a babe."

The tattooed man's eyes brightened. "Ah, well that is a cruel but effective way of doing it." He paused thoughtfully. "And efficient too. Use far less ink."

"What are you talking about?" Endrance asked, his frustration rising.

"Do you even have any training?" The man pressed, seeming concerned. "Who is your master?"

"Yes of course I was trained!" Endrance exclaimed. "Master Kaelob has recognized me as a wizard himself just this season!"

The man blinked at the young man, stunned. "I'm sorry... but did you say Kaelob trained you?" He asked. "You are aware he's retired right?"

Endrance nearly shouted "Yes! He retired in the village I was born in!" He didn't know why, but his emotions were flaring up. Perhaps he was feeling defensive trying to justify his existence to someone with far more power than he had.

"Fine. I'll believe it for now. Kaelob never studied many sigils beyond the basics, so I'm not surprised he didn't think much of them." He looked Endrance over head to toe. "Well, they're pretty well hidden."

"Who… who are you?" Endrance finally asked.

The man shrugged. "I've earned many titles in my time, but a fellow wizard can just call me Talos."

"T-Talos!" Endrance stammered. "I'm sorry!" He exclaimed, clasping his hands together. "I didn't think-"

"What?" he responded "That I wouldn't answer the door when a fellow magic user comes along? We're not so common that I have to turn even new wizards away." He shrugged. "Besides, your aura was just asking me to come take a closer look."

Endrance smiled in relief. "Thank you for coming down and meeting with me."

"Of course, young one." Talos said kindly. "Now, wouldn't you rather continue this conversation inside?"

"Of course!" Endrance said happily.

Talos waited, watching him.

"…What?" the young wizard finally asked.

Talos gestured to the door. "Well, open it. I assure you it's unlocked." Even a newly appointed wizard could open a door."

Endrance turned back to the golden dome jutting from the wall. He reached out and touched it, pondering its nature.

Talos watched the boy work the relatively simple puzzle. He only pushed lightly on it. He examined its surface and the gold detailed frame the dome was set in. The kid had a light hearted attitude that might waver against opposition, but here his intellect brought his focus into one of the sharpest Talos had seen in a long time. Several times he watched him tuck an errant lock of hair behind his ear, a move that reminded him of someone he used to look up to. In fact, something about his eyes…

"Aha!" Endrance exclaimed, reaching out with both hands and pulling the domed surface to the side. Like a ball rotating on its point it rotated silently, until a passage rotated into view and locked in place.

"Very good!" Talos said, patting him on the shoulder as he entered. "You've opened a door."

Endrance hurried to follow the Archmagus inside.

Chapter 13

Joven stared at the magistrate, unable to keep his irritation off his face. Not only did the city watch waste his time with questions, they held him there until this magistrate showed up. Easily two feet shorter than him, and almost half across, Joven could hardly believe that this man was in a position of authority. He had an overbite so severe that he looked like a bulb was growing out of his shoulders rather than a head sitting on a neck. To top it all off, the man repeated every question he asked more than once.

He was trying his best to be patient, but if the man asked any more of the same questions Joven wasn't sure he would remain calm. This would be a problem if he had to search for his charge while being pursued by city watch for strangling this man. He was tempted though.

"So let me be absolutely sure here." The magistrate said for what must have been the third time. Joven took a deep breath and tried very hard not to scowl.

"I don't understand what is the problem." Joven interrupted. "I buy drink. Man taunts me. I ignore man. Man swings at me. I bust his head." He shrugged. "Simple."

The magistrate huffed, squaring his almost nonexistent jaw. "The problem is that I question the validity of such a claim. You had to have struck first."

Now Joven scowled. "No, if I had hit the man first I would have said so. Are you questioning my honor?" he responded, his voice seething with growing anger. It was getting harder to keep his hands off the man's scrawny neck. "I waited until the other man swung at me first." He took another calming breath that didn't do much to soothe his mood. "I was being diplomatic."

"Diplomatic is a pretty large word for a barbarian like you to be using." The magistrate quipped. "Do you even know what it means?"

Joven replied through gritted teeth. "Yes." He grated. "You let the other guy swing first." He responded. "Now, can I go?"

"There's still reason to doubt that claim." The magistrate countered. "There is no way that you could best three men-"

"Five men." Joven and the barkeep corrected at once for the third time.

"Five men when they attacked first and you didn't suffer a scratch." The magistrate finished.

Joven leaned in, putting his face more or less on the level with the irritating official. "Do you know at what age we 'barbarians' start learning how to fight?" he growled.

The magistrate then became acutely aware of the copious amount of fine scars interspersed across his face and hands. "...No?" he answered quietly.

"Well, our people start officially fighting when we're five. They don't let us use weapons yet, because we would kill each other before we knew how to use them properly. So for five years we learn to fight with our bodies. Only when we have grown strong and wise to battle do they teach us how to use weapons." He held up a finger that had more nearly invisible scars on it than the magistrate had over his whole body. "But even then we don't get to have our own weapons until make our first kill."

The magistrate took an involuntary step back. "I..." he tried to start.

"Only then can you be considered a man. I've been fighting 'men' my size since before I was your size. So when I say I bested five of your 'men', I mean it." He finished gravely.

The magistrate couldn't reply, instead he only stared at the barbarian, transfixed by fear or possibly his breath. Joven realized that he may have over done himself, so he smiled broadly as he straightened out.

"Besides!" he exclaimed. "They were all drunk. It was hardly a fair fight."

The magistrate let out a breath he had been holding in. "Yes... I suppose I can see what you mean. Your kind does seem to live up to their legends."

"You have legends about us?" Joven asked. He shook his head. "Nevermind. Can I go now?"

The magistrate surveyed the scene, his gaze reluctantly drifting back to the barbarian. "I see that all of this has been sorted out. You may go."

Finally. Joven put a silver piece on the bar and walked out into the street without any further words. By the movement of the suns Joven knew that the magistrate had wasted almost an hour of his time. The young man was long gone.

He sighed, heading off in the direction that he had seen him go before. He knew how to track prey, but this might be different. Of course, at least the other prey on this game trail could give him directions. It shouldn't take too long.

Hours later, Joven found himself standing at the base of the largest tower in the city. It was large, but Joven thought it only made itself a more appealing target during a siege. Catapults could knock it down from almost any direction. He would have to wonder why it hadn't been done before later. The witnesses he questioned directed him here, but upon arrival he found no sign of his charge, much less a method to enter the tower and search it. There was a dome of gold where the door should be. Perhaps it was locked.

Joven growled in frustration, but set about searching for someone nearby that could tell him how to get in.

As he exited the courtyard, he caught a bit of movement out of the corner of his eye. He turned and saw the heel of a boot and the tails of a coat disappear around a corner. "Aha!" Joven shouted, barreling down the lane and turning into the alleyway.

The three men he charged onto looked up in surprise. They were struggling with a small burlap sack between the three of them as they trotted down the alley, and were caught off guard when he rounded the corner.

The men looked reasonably clean, but had a disheveled look about them, and their clothes were tattered and worn pieces of the everyday clothes Joven had seen many men wearing all over the city. Their faces were sweaty and smudged with grime.

"Now what?" One of the men squeaked out, his face bunched up in a way that reminded Joven of a rat. "Oh gods, he wasn't lying! Run!" he shouted, and the three bolted down the alley away from him. Joven didn't understand what they meant, but he knew a thief when he caught one in the act. He charged after them.

The three were agile and quick on their feet, and had much less mass than the barbarian. They were starting to outdistance him. He grunted as he rushed out into the main street, looking for the men. Joven caught sight of the rat-man, who ducked into an alley across the thoroughfare. He saw the bag gripped frightfully in his hands. That was enough for the Barbarian to choose his target.

Joven ran through the crowd of people, pushing and shoving as he barreled through them. One of the other men he had chased appeared in front of him in the crowd, lunging at him with a long dagger. Joven lunged forward as well, reaching out with his hand and catching the man in the neck as he didn't even slow his pace. The dagger glanced off the hardened leather of his breastplate harmlessly. The impact of Joven's hand against the thug's throat kicked his feet out from under him and sent the dagger skittering across the street, his grip going nerveless before he could halt his thrust. Joven kept running, carrying the man in front of him with one arm.

As he entered the alley he saw rat-face waiting. He looked surprised that their ambush had failed and turned to flee again. Joven roared in effort as the muscles in his arm bulged. He wound up and threw his captive at the fleeing thief. The man sailed ungracefully for a dozen feet, bounced off the stones, and tangled up the running man's legs, sending him spilling to the floor. Whatever the object in the sack was, it clattered to the stone like metal.

The first man groaned and remained blissfully unconscious. Rat-face had only cracked his pronounced face against the stone and smashed his nose, perhaps broke a tooth. Blood poured from his broken nose as he tried to pull himself up, his breath ragged and gurgling with blood. From behind him, he heard someone scream wordlessly, having seen him hurl a man down an alley like one would a straw scarecrow.

Joven walked up to the two, ignoring the calls crying for the watch spouting from the people in the street behind him. He reached down and picked up the rat faced man as well as his stolen prize, hauling him up as he continued walking down the alley. The thief that had smartly hidden instead of trying to take the barbarian on slunk out of the shadows to haul his unconscious comrade off before the watch could come collect.

Now several twists and turns of the alleys away from the initial scene, Joven held the man against a wall with one hand. His feet dangled as he weakly kicked, trying to keep breath in his lungs.

"Now," Joven began. "What did you mean by 'he wasn't lying'."

Joven didn't relax his grip for a second, letting him squirm. Finally he could draw a full breath. The rat faced man gasped a few quick breaths before blurting out. "Ah dunno whut yer talking bout!"

Joven hooked the sack onto the pommel of one of his daggers. He took his now empty hand and slowly balled it into a fist in front of Rat-face. "What?" he said. "I didn't hear you. Let me knock some of that blood out of your nose. Might make more sense then."

Rat-face's eyes widened in fright. "A'ight, a'ight!" he called out, his speech slurred from both poor education and poor air circulation. "We been giv'n a job. 'sall! We wus s'posed ta mess wit dis kid, but afta we sacked him we saw he wus a mage. He wus spoutin sometin' about a barbarian who wus s'posed to meet him, but we thought he wus bluffing."

The man tried to shake his head, both his hands wrapped around Joven's wrist to keep him from strangling to death before the barbarian let him go. "We dunno dat he wus a mage b'fore. Den we 'ad dis idea. We keep 'im fer ransom den sell 'is stuff."

Joven shuddered, his already mounting frustration and irritation blossoming into rage. "Where is he!" he bellowed, smashing his fist into the brick next to Rat-face. Dust and shattered mortar burst out, causing the thief to flinch. The brick itself was not broken, but it had shifted an inch deeper into the wall.

"A'ight!" he squealed. "Da otha men took 'im to da storin' place. Dat's where Zadrah woulda put 'im."

Joven turned away, dashing the sniveling man to the ground. He opened the sack and looked through its contents. "This is it?" Joven asked. "This is what made you want to risk kidnapping him?"

The rat faced thief spit out a mouthful of blood. "It's really shiny, y'know?" he muttered. "It gotta be worth something."

"Which way." Joven said evenly. It wasn't a question.

"South-west of here." The thief responded, broken. "It's da biggest buildin' ah reckon's in da district."

Joven turned and stalked off, avoiding the sound of the booted feet searching the alleys. Rat face shook his head and blew clotted blood out of his nose, crawling on his hands and knees. He was too dizzy to stand yet. If he hurried, he could take a back way to the building and warn them before the barbarian ruined the deal.

He had scrambled only a few feet when he came up to a pair of shapely black leather boots. He saw dull steel skull buckles before he felt something cold and sharp whip around his neck. He tried to grab it and give him room to breathe, but his fingers were sliced so easily by the metal garrote.

"No no no..." A familiar dusky voice whispered. "That was hardly professional, now was it?"

Rat face scrabbled with bleeding fingers, but couldn't do anything to prolong his life. "I said inconvenienced, not dead. And we both know what your guild does with hostages." She whispered. "But I suppose the barbarian coming to the rescue does well enough to suit my purpose."

The Sha'hdi flicked her wrist, and the razor wired garrote snaked across his neck as it retracted. Blood blossomed across the alley stones. The wires instantly spun silently back into the thin hoop bracelet around her wrist. The wire cap fell into its place with a barely audible 'click'.

Scant moments later, the city watch discovered the still warm body of Rat-face. The word got out there was a killer loose in the city.

Chapter 14

Endrance supposed that getting kidnapped by thieves was at least mildly embarrassing. It was especially embarrassing for a wizard capable of taking out a band of goblins. If he could fight a creature of darkness and evil in its home ground, he should be able to fight off some thieves, right?

He had been too distracted by his conversation with the Archmagus. It was such a momentous occasion, being able to speak with the most powerful man in the country next to the high king. He hadn't been paying any attention to what was going on around him. Not only did they club him from behind hard enough that he was still seeing stars, they gagged him and stripped him down to his pants and shoes.

They had taken his bracer and his spell book; He didn't know where they were. He strongly hated losing that bracer, it was a valuable gift from his master. Well, the book was too, but the bracer was more like an inherited object passed down from master to apprentice, and he let it get stolen. Endrance tried his best to focus, but they had apparently some experience dealing with mages.

He was tied horizontally to a pole like someone would spit a pig for roasting. His eyes were blindfolded, and they had a rather filthy tasting gag in his mouth. To top it all off, someone had taken string and tied his middle fingers together. It was for all intents and purposes impossible to cast any spells this way. He couldn't say any words of power, form any mudras, or even aim a spell on a target. Kaelob had trained him so that he could still operate with any one of those conditions hampered, but not all three.

And his head still hurt from being clubbed hard. He at first tried to talk his way out, but he was pretty sure all they heard was babble. Endrance flinched as the back of his head twinged, but could hardly move. He felt something warm trickling through his hair, but it took him a minute to realize he was bleeding.

Time passed, and Endrance's head cleared eventually. Though he had been unable to keep track of time when he was first assaulted, he could start doing so now. He knew he needed to take stock of the situation before he could decide on his next course of action. He strained against his ropes, trying to get free. They were tight, but not so tight as to cause constant pain. He noted that, but he didn't know what he was tied to or what he was suspended over. It could be a few feet to the floor, or a bed of spikes twenty feet down.

He took a deep breath and tried to calm himself. The faint smell of oil was present over an almost overpowering scent of damp wood. Smoke, the kind that someone with a pipe would make, wafted through the air around him. He couldn't isolate any other smells. Still, it gave him some idea of where he was.

He could only pick up sounds of movement from somewhere above him, as well as the sounds of a muffled argument from somewhere nearby. It sounded heated, and he hoped that something would go in his favor soon.

A door crashed open nearby and he twitched in his bounds, startled. The argument stopped, and Endrance could hear two sets of shoes walk over stone towards him.

"Ah, I think his head's a bit clearer now, wouldn't you say?" A man's voice said clearly. Unlike the ruffians who had clubbed him, this man sounded well educated enough to use a clear dialect. His voice was smooth, but had a shift in tone near the end of his statement that gave the young wizard the impression that he was amused.

"Yeah." A rougher voice replied. This was the man who had overseen his capture. A burly man with dark skin and dark hair, dressed in tattered clothes and a chain link shirt under his vest. He had a long knife, last Endrance had seen, and the man had it on hand constantly.

"You see, dear boy." The first voice started. "We here in my business had a… misunderstanding, you see?" the voice further explained. "We were just supposed to rob you blind, and toss you out to the cold streets, but it seems that one of my subordinates had an idea."

One set of shoes walked back and forth near Endrance's side. This set was much lighter, and apparently very spry; the one walking would make little hop-step motions as he paced. "This is usually frowned upon, since we here are almost exclusively… how would you put it? Ah, opportunists of a material variety. We don't normally trade in flesh and bone."

"But now that you're here, we really don't have much choice, now do we?" the voice asked. Endrance couldn't respond even if he wanted. "So now we have all the unpleasantness of not only inconveniencing you, but also us." The man sighed, stopping a good few feet from his comrade. "What do you think we should do?" He asked finally.

"Sell him." The second man replied. "Some people in the elf lands pay the wizard's weight in gold for captives."

"Ah, but this one is so small," The first responded instantly "he would hardly make us a profit. "Besides, how are you going to smuggle a wizard over two thousand miles into their territory? That itself is a risk to both us and the cargo."

The second grumbled but didn't say anything else. The first man was quiet for a few seconds. When he spoke again, he was right next to Endrance's head, which made him jerk in surprise. He had covered a dozen feet silently.

"What about you, little mage?" he asked, his voice still amused. "We should ask the captive about his opinion, yes? Someone so young as this yet skilled enough to become a wizard must have some insight to the situation."

Endrance felt something cold and sharp press against his neck, crossing from one side to the other. The edge felt wavy under his throat.

"Now, I'm going to take your gag out. This knife is very, very sharp, so try any magic on us and you'll be bleeding out before you can finish." The first man said.

Endrance felt strong hands untie the gag, and he gasped for a clear breath as soon as his mouth was clear. He felt the sting of the knife blade, and a faint trickle of blood seeped from under its edge. It was indeed very sharp.

"Thanks." Endrance began. "I am of a personal opinion that you have your guys drag me back to where you found me and let me go. I mean I haven't seen any of you but ugly over there and I was unconscious for the trip here, so I don't know who any of you are much less where I am. It would save both of us a lot of trouble."

The first man laughed heartily, his hand still rock steady at the knife. The second man took a step towards Endrance, but he couldn't tell if the man had done anything else.

"Well well," the first said approvingly. "You still have a sense of humor, even in all this trouble?"

"I am not sure about humor sir." Endrance responded. "He is ugly."

"That he is… that he is." The first man said after a moment. He may have been waving the other man back; Endrance had no ability to tell other than a rustle of cloth. "Unfortunately we have a policy here in my band of brothers, we really aren't in the business of catch and release, you know?"

Endrance was running out of things he could think to leverage his way out of here. "Well, was it policy to change the plan to kidnap me instead?" He asked.

"Good point. A well made one." The first man replied. "But what's done is done, and we have to focus on the now."

Endrance licked his lips. Maybe now he could explain what he was trying to say before. "Well there is one last thing."

"Oh?" the first man said. "Do tell."

"I am here in Ironsoul on business. I'm supposed to be meeting a barbarian sometime today." Endrance began. "I was on my way to meet him when you guys waylaid me."

"A barbarian you say?" the man said, his amusement evident in his voice. "Why that's a pretty strange fabrication. I've heard some pretty amazing lies in my time but-"

"It's not lie!" Endrance exclaimed forcefully, hoping he hadn't just filleted his throat in the process. He didn't suddenly bleed out so he continued. "I'm supposed to be replacing the current *Spengur* of Balator, and he's supposed to escort me there. He's probably really angry that I haven't shown up, and if he finds you guys…" Endrance trailed off, at a loss for words.

"Ah, this is the same bullshit story he tried giving when we found 'em." The second man said angrily. "It's nothing but a child's fantasy."

"Well that would definitely be something to be concerned about." The first replied, either ignoring the man or taking his word into account. "But that would require him to first know you were kidnapped, and secondly find where we're holding you."

Endrance sighed. "Well then I've got nothing."

"Fair enough. Do you want to try to plead for your life or something?" the first man asked.

"No." Endrance replied. "I'm sure that won't really help here, and I should conserve my strength."

The man sounded impressed. "Smart move. You might be able to trick one of your buyers into giving you enough freedom to blast them to pieces that way. You're a good strategist, and so young."

"And that's okay with you?" Endrance asked.

"Oh yes." The man replied. "I don't really care what happens to the client after the job is done, so it's no skin off my nose. Besides… I kind of like you. Maybe if things had been different we could have been friends even."

"You do sound like a decent enough sort." Endrance responded. "My name's Endrance."

The man was quiet for a moment, but the knife came away from his neck. "Zadrah." Was all the man said before stuffing the gag back in his mouth and tying it.

"Now you just stay right here while I see if there are any local buyers in the market for someone like you." He said before walking audibly out of the room and closing the door.

Endrance was left alone in the room with the man who had assaulted him to begin with. He heard the man chuckling as he approached, his footsteps heavy and intentional. The man reeked of sweat, steel, and alcohol.

"Well well well... Ugly, you say?" the man grumbled. "Let's see who's ugly after I carve up that pretty girl's face of yours."

Despite the terror, despite the impending mutilation, Endrance could not help but roll his eyes. Again? Maybe people would stop thinking he was a girl after this thug sliced up his face. Then again, if he got out of this he would rather just cut his hair or something less permanently damaging.

The distinctive sound of a blade being drawn from its scabbard echoed through the air.

Chapter 15

The exterior of the warehouse that the thieves were holding Endrance was one of many built almost exactly the same. It was about two and a half stories tall, with rough, pitted gray stone walls with a dozen feet of open space separating its walls from the road. Like the rest of Ironsoul, the place was disturbingly clean of litter or debris. Joven had thought that the criminal controlled areas of the city would be… dirtier. At least the people around the warehouse fit his impression. Grungy, disheveled thugs socialized in small groups around the warehouse, some of them throwing dice and betting coins. They had a way of paying attention to anyone who came too close to the building, so the barbarian remained a discrete distance away and around a corner.

Joven's powerful muscles tensed as he considered his options. The warehouse building was well guarded by the same sort of men that he'd dealt with earlier. He counted maybe twelve men outside the building who were trying to appear inconspicuously minding their own business. He was certain there would be more inside. Unlike many of the men he'd fought before, these were likely inclined to use agile fighting tactics and swarm him if he just waded into them. While he wasn't particularly against such a challenge, he didn't know how many men he would have to deal with inside.

A small bit of luck came to him. As he observed their movements a man came out of the warehouse. He wore a red coat and altogether looked to be much more refined than the men around him. Joven at first thought him a client perhaps, but when the men all gave him covert nods of respect as he walked off whistling, he knew the guy must have been a superior. At least he wouldn't have to worry about that one yet.

He also had several of his weapons tied off with ribbon. While that itself couldn't even hinder him actually drawing any of his weapons, it did represent a promise he had made. He quickly checked himself over for weapons he didn't have tied off. He came up with two boot knives, a sap, a pair of spiked iron knuckles, and the finger thin blades hidden in the leather plates of his bracers. All light weaponry.

Joven replaced all the weapons except the spiked knuckles, and put those on with a sigh. They were only a pair of bars with thin steel crossbars separating sections he could fit his fingers through, with inch long sharpened spikes along one bar. It was a challenge true, but still it could be worse: It could have been boring. He would rather take on twelve men with his fists than have been genuinely bored this whole trip. At least the new *Spengur* was already making things interesting. If this was going to be any indication of fate, he was going to enjoy the next few years working for him.

The first few men who had looked as if they were sharing a pipe of pungent smelling smoke immediately noticed the barbarian walking towards them. The first stepped forward to try to steer him off while the other two flanked him on either side. They had their hands on the hilts of their knives, and the first actually drew a long blade and brandished it as he came to a stop in front of Joven.

"You better get the hell out of here, barbarian!" The man sneered, showing more than one rotten tooth in the process. The reek of alcohol and pipe weed was strong but not enough to make Joven slow.

Joven pulled a fist back and let fly a powerful blow without responding. The inch long metal spikes on the iron bar across his knuckles tore into the man's face and punched into bone beyond as the force of his blow swatted him to the floor faster than if the man had fallen. Blood and shattered, rotten teeth sprayed into the air before the target's two comrades as they watched the sudden brutality in shock.

"Can't." Joven replied as the unconscious or dead body bounced upon the stones. "You got something of mine."

The men started pulling on their knives, trying to bring them to bear on him. It was too late. He continued walking swiftly forward, throwing his arms around their necks as he clotheslined the two of them. Caught in the pinch of his powerful forearms and biceps, Joven grunted with effort as he rolled his shoulders and sharply lifted his forearms up. The move levered their heads forward at a sharp angle, and a faint crunch told Joven to let them go.

He continued on past as the two sank to the ground, as limp as wet rags. The other groups hadn't even heard the assault happen; the three didn't have the time or capacity to shout in alarm. He rounded on the five rolling the bones, knowing that the four at the far side of the warehouse would take time to get to him.

As he was within a few strides of them, one of the men stooped to pick up the dice and noticed the three bodies on the floor behind Joven. He barely had a chance to cry out before the barbarian was among them. Joven's fists lashed out powerfully, his face a steely visage of brutal efficiency. Two men who had their backs to him were down in an instant, the backs of their heads staved in. The first one to draw a blade was the one who had seen him coming, and Joven caught his blade wielding arm in one fist as the man swung at him in panic. He levered the man between him and one opponent by his captured arm, and backhanded the other as he charged in, the spikes leaving bloody furrows across his face.

That man's screams alerted the four across the warehouse lot more effectively than the initial shout had. Joven could hear their shouting and the sounds of weapons being drawn. He grinned as the battle started warming up. This was the entertainment he had been hoping for!

He twisted his grip on the first man's arm, flipping him onto his back without letting go. He yanked sharply as he stepped over him; a dull pop indicated he had successfully wrenched the man's arm out of its socket. He wouldn't be a threat soon enough to be trouble. The third man jumped at him, bringing the curved dagger down at Joven with a two-handed grip.

Joven thrust a powerfully muscled leg out, catching the man in the chest area with his boot. He heard bones crack as the man reversed direction mid-air and crashed to the ground several feet away. The barbarian whirled, swinging with his fist with all his might as the second had recovered enough from the injury to his face to try to attack. The blow caught him in the meat of his neck, and he went down in a gurgling spurt of blood.

The four remaining charged in to him. Apparently they had been concealing better weaponry than their comrades, as two of them had sickles and the other two short swords. Joven lunged forward into their midst, letting his actions without apparent concern for his own well being confuse them.

He kicked out and got one of the swordsmen in the knee with a strong side kick, splintering bone and dropping the white-faced man to his knees. He twisted with a blow struck by the other swordsman, and the otherwise dangerous strike gouged a long scratch in the hardened leather, but did no more. The two sickle wielders swung in tandem, trying to cut him off at the knees. Joven skipped back, easily avoiding the sloppy swings. He nearly burst out laughing as the two recoiled from their swings, nearly hitting each other as their failed attacks overextended into each other's space.

The first swordsman lunged forward to skewer Joven, and the big man stepped far enough to the side to let the sword slip past him. As he did so he jabbed the man in the leading shoulder twice with swift rabbit punches, letting the spikes on his knuckles do most of the damage. The man cried out in pain and his sword arm lowered despite his attempts to keep his blade up. The third quick blow to his face blinded him and he dropped, not dead, but likely miserable for a very, very long time.

The other one swung his weapon hard enough and with enough accuracy that Joven had to juke out of the way. As the man recovered from his swing Joven caught both his forearm and shoulder. A quick pull snapped the man's elbow and he howled in pain briefly before Joven hit him in the side of the head hard. As the body dropped to the floor Joven plucked the short sword out of its nerveless fingers.

He leapt forwards without looking behind him, rolling roughly across the stone as the two attacked him in tandem again, this time from differing angles. As the swings cut through the air he had previously occupied, he hurled the short sword at the one on his left. The man dropped to the ground and avoided all but a shallow slice across his back.

Joven popped to his feet and charged the only man left standing. The man's sickle sliced through the air at the barbarian's neck. The barbarian lashed out with a fist, knocking the hand holding the blade out the way. The thug's face had a split second to register surprise before it was permanently interrupted by a powerful blow.

The other man was pulling himself up as his ally fell to the ground. He looked up to see Joven standing over him, his breath coming hard from his continued efforts. The man trembled and tried to scramble away, but the barbarian merely kicked him over and stomped hard. It only took one.

A few seconds later, he had gone back over the battlefield and finished off anyone he had previously left alive. He didn't need anyone coming in behind him. He knew he had to hurry; the watch would not likely miss this place in their search for him. He strode up to the doors to the warehouse and took a breath.

The thrill of battle still flowed through him as he said a faint prayer to Kroma before winding up and kicking the doors in.

The doors crashed open, flinders of wood spiraling out from the impact of Joven's heavy boot. The barbarian rushed in immediately on the tail of the door's destruction, ready for anything that came at him. His boots stomped heavily on the stone brick flooring and a powerful battle cry echoed off the stones as he entered the first chamber.

From the back Joven heard a door slam open and the sounds of many sets of footsteps rushing towards him. He grinned as he gave the two sickles he had just recently picked up a flick and a twist of his wrists. Now the warm up was over, and he had to be as lethal as quickly as possible if there were any more than the amount he had fought outside.

Only four men poured into the receiving room, each wearing actual leather armor and holding swords. While they seemed more practiced than the crowd of amateurs that had been their perimeter guard, they were not so experienced that they didn't hesitate when they saw the blood spattered barbarian rushing into them. Joven's sickles took the first one's head off before the four could blink.

The other three brought their weapons up and engaged him as their comrade slumped to the floor, blood spilling copiously over the stones. Joven's sickles couldn't swing his blades as fast as the three could in tandem, but his weapons struck with enough power to batter their guard down.

It was immediately obvious that the three had been used to working in groups. They ducked and weaved with each other, trusting the man next to them to defend them from counter as he himself lunged in to attack. It could have spelled disaster for Joven if he hadn't gotten the first before they were ready.

The three seemed to be a match for Joven, a fact that had both sides surprised. Joven was surprised that it only took three men to match him, at the same time as the three were surprised that they were being matched by a single warrior. The stalemate lasted seconds, but it felt like minutes as their blades clashed and muscles strained to gain the advantage.

And in a second it changed. One of the three stepped to the side to flank him and his foot slipped in the spreading pool of blood on the stone. His balance was lost and in the moment he shifted to right himself, Joven was able to catch him across the neck and shoulder with a sickle. The man, though still living joined his dead ally in spilling yet more blood across the stone.

The fight got all the more desperate for the two left facing Joven. Their footing was getting worse by the second, yet the barbarian seemed as sure footed as ever. Only seconds more passed before another slipped up, and the fight was over. As the second man lunged to guard against the strike to his brother that he was sure was coming, Joven instead struck at the one standing. The one who fell got a good look at the underside of Joven's heavy treaded boot as it came down on his face.

Joven took stock of his condition. He had received a few nicks across his arms, but nothing but minor cuts. His leather breastplate had a number of new gouges in it. He was sweating and his breath came hard, but he wasn't exhausted yet.

A loud sound much like the crack of thunder blasted into the room and brilliant white light strobes through the door that the four guardians had come from. In but an instant the light was gone and the thunder but a ringing in his ears.

What was that? Joven moved in a rush but without running. He knew how to move on slick surfaces from living in a frozen, icy wasteland all his life, and trying to run would only end in injury.

The next room was empty, but the door beyond it was also open. He quickly checked for more foes as he kept moving. The next room was the main storage room of the warehouse, but it looked mostly empty and dusty. The smell of charred flesh rose on wafts of smoke as Joven saw his charge for the second time that day.

A smoldering body lay sprawled against the wall across from what looked to the barbarian as a spit. Tied to a pole suspended by two posts was Endrance, trussed up in ropes and blindfolded. His arms were tied to his side at the elbow, but his hands were free and his right hand was covered in blackened soot. On the ground beneath him were a discarded gag and a pile of thin ropes that looked like they had been burned through in several places.

The bound wizard tensed as he heard the big man enter. Joven watched him crane his head towards the door. "Hello?" The young wizard called out. The wizard's voice was light, almost melodic. Maybe his description was wrong, and they did send him to watch a woman after all. She was far slighter than most women in Balator, so at least it wouldn't be hard to find her in a crowd.

"You're Endrance?" Joven asked. "I've been looking for you."

The young wizard paused, thinking. It was not a voice he had heard before. "Yes." Came the reply. "Who are you?"

"My name is Joven. I was supposed to meet you somewhere else." The barbarian replied, nudging the body on the floor. The body had streaks of black and charred flesh across his chest and abdomen in a line. Joven studied the wall behind the corpse and saw the same blackened line streak up the wall at an angle. By looking at the line, he could see that the man at his feet had been standing right next to the wizard. Well, she may be slight, but she was still dangerous.

"So are you going to ask me any more questions, or can I get you down?" Joven asked, irritated.

"Just one more thing." Endrance said. "Did I get him?"

The Sha'hdi watched from up in the rafters as the barbarian let the young man down and hauled him to his feet. There had been a few more men waiting to ambush the man as he was helping the wizard, but she had 'persuaded' them to leave them alone. She also left Zadrah a pouch of gold and a note of thanks pinned to the back of one of his lackeys. The baron himself was not anywhere to be found, and she couldn't afford to wait around and thank him personally.

She moved silently on the wooden beams, tracking the two's progress until they left the building. She slipped silently out; tracking their progress back to the inn Endrance had taken. She herself would have to find shelter soon. Even she would not relish the pain of being outside when Ironsoul awoke.

As the Sha'hdi slipped out through a window, a figure stepped out of a nearby doorway and sighed. Zadrah held up the bloody dagger and the bag containing the rest of the gold he had been promised. He looked back up at the window and smirked.

"Pleasure doing business with you, ma'am." He said to no one in particular. The job had been far more costly than he had initially estimated. That boy was quite capable as well. Zadrah looked at the singed ropes that had been used to tie the mage's hands. He could very well have killed him without speaking, and he was pretty sure that the only reason he hadn't was that Zadrah hadn't tried to harm him and had been somewhat respectful.

The one man who had survived seeing the barbarian in the alleys near the tower had told him they had gotten the kid coming out of the tower. The assassin hadn't said he was capable of power like he demonstrated here when he had arrived. If he had gotten that powerful after just an hour under the eye of the Archmagus, Endrance either had a ridiculous amount of potential, or the Archmagus was just that good. Either way, it was best not to meddle in the affairs of wizards.

All in all though, Zadrah no longer had to split the share with the dead. Far more profit for him. Now he just had to find some more prospective recruits…

Chapter 16

"I sure hope they don't make them any bigger than you in Balator, or I'm going to be in some real trouble." Endrance said after the third long silence since he had been rescued by the barbarian. Joven looked at him out of the corner of his eye as he watched the streets below. They had made it back into Endrance's room without being accosted by either the guards or any more of the band of thieves. It was already dark and though the innkeeper was unhappy about letting him take a barbarian up to his room Endrance had managed to persuade him to let him stay at least the night since it was getting late.

Joven shrugged. "Nope." The barbarian rumbled. "My elder brother has about half a foot over me."

Endrance shook his head. "I find that hard to believe. You are the biggest and perhaps the most dangerous man I've ever met." He muttered, checking through his pack. They had managed to recover almost all of his belongings, including his coin purse. Endrance could not express how relieved he was to have the bracer back in his possession, and had put it back on almost immediately.

"Says the… man who can throw lightning from his hands." Joven replied. He was still trying to understand how the mage was actually a guy. What happened to his muscles?

"Fair, but I wouldn't have been able to fight my way out of there with lightning." Endrance replied. "I would have tapped out every dredge of my aura using that spell a few more times and then the rest of them would have gotten me. You seemed hardly winded and you killed what, fourteen men?"

"Sixteen."

"Sixteen men. I got one." Endrance finished. He supposed he should feel bad; after all, he had just killed a man. A human man. Sure he was trying to carve his face up. Sure, he was trying to sell him to slavers. Sure, it was only because it was a wildly flung spell… Endrance shook his head. Maybe he had enough reasons to be detached from it, but he didn't for a moment consider it a good thing that he had to kill him. Killing monsters was easier, they were monsters. He hoped he would never have to get used to killing people.

"What's an 'aura'?" Joven asked, breaking Endrance's chain of thoughts. He saw only a few people left out on the streets and even they were clearing out of the area quickly. Doors and windows were being closed and shuttered. The city was buttoning itself up very suddenly, which made Joven suspicious.

"Uh…" Endrance began. How to explain magic to a barbarian who grew up in a culture hating magic? "Think of it like a well that I keep my power in like you would water. If I pull too much 'water' out then it can run dry, and that would mean I'm defenseless until it can fill up again."

"So… You get tired?" Joven said, like he was emphasizing the simplicity of his statement.

"Yeah, I guess that's the best way to say it." Endrance responded. He still over thought it; Of course it wasn't exactly like that, he wouldn't get physically exhausted but it was a close enough analogy for the barbarian.

"You should exercise more then." Joven said in a knowing manner. "You would have better endurance."

"It's not as fast of a process as with physical muscles, Joven." Endrance replied, struggling to hold in the frustration in his voice. "I can 'exercise' the volume of my aura but it takes time to grow stronger and last longer."

Joven turned away and looked at the mage. "You should do some physical exercise while you're at it. You're smaller than some of our whelps." He grinned at the young man to show he was joking. Endrance scowled, but couldn't hold it for long and ended up grinning right back at his bodyguard. The man was big, true, but he was also very charming.

Endrance sighed. "I…" he began, but saw something flicker by the window and it got him to stop. "What is that?" he asked as a dull tone echoed throughout the streets outside. "Oh!" Endrance exclaimed in panic. He rushed past the barbarian and slammed the shutters closed, latching them.

"I didn't know it was that late already!" Endrance gasped, shaking his head. He was sure he had seen something… ethereal drift past his window.

"What?" Joven asked. He reached out to open the shutters for a look, and Endrance grabbed his wrist.

"Don't." Endrance said as calmly as he could.

"Why not?" Joven asked. "It's not like seeing something is going to kill me."

Endrance shook his head. "This is magic we're speaking of. Of course it can kill you by looking at it."

Joven scrutinized the young man's face before pulling his wrist out of the wizard's grip. He had been perfectly serious, and the young man's grasp was surprisingly strong. Perhaps he wasn't as inexperienced or weak as he had initially thought. Still, he found it hard not to try to look outside the window again.

Endrance sat back down when he felt he had conveyed the importance of the message. "Look I'm tired from being kidnapped and the tests that I did for the Archmagus, so I'm going to bed. If you want I'm sure the chairs are comfortable." Endrance said wearily.

"Tests?" Joven asked.

Oops. "Nothing important, just wizard things." Endrance muttered. Still, what he had learned from the Archmagus had both been invigorating and disturbing at the same time. He tried not to dwell on it too much as he blew out the lamp and drifted off the sleep.

Joven though still curious, said nothing more as he settled into a chair to wait. He could get all the sleep he needed before suns-rise, and then they could be on their way. The journey wasn't short and his people needed their Spengur more now than perhaps they ever did. The last Spengur did not leave on such amicable terms though, so his job would be perhaps tougher than any guardian in prior generations of his family.

He sat quietly in the chair, glad that it was sturdy enough to hold him. His larger weapons, the axe and greatsword leaned against the wall next to him. The other weapons remained on his person, though many were still tied down in promises. He would try to keep those promises, but now his charge was under his watch he would do anything he needed to in order to keep him safe.

The next morning Endrance awoke to see Joven was already awake and back at the window, scanning the street for something, threats perhaps. Endrance had no idea how a bodyguard did their work, and decided to leave the guarding to Joven. If what he said was right, his family had been watching over Spengurs for generations, and should know quite a bit about protecting mages.

He wanted to get cleaned up, but the bodyguard didn't look to be about to leave the room anytime soon. It took Endrance a few minutes of watching him stand at the window to build up the courage to ask him.

"Excuse me? Joven?" Endrance began, holding his pack of clothes and the large pitcher of water the Innkeep had left them that morning.

The barbarian hardly glanced his way. "Yes?" he grumbled, his attention snapping to some sudden movement in the street below. It was just a pickpocket who got caught.

"Do you think you could… step outside for a moment, so I can… you know, bathe?" Endrance finally asked.

Joven grunted. "If you want to bathe, then bathe. I'm not going to leave you defenseless." He replied, a twitch of confusion crossing his face. *Now he wants to bathe in private like a woman. What else is he going to get uncomfortable about?*

"I've… I've never had to do that with other people… watching?" Endrance supplied.

Joven sighed, turning and giving the young mage an irritated look. "Well, you're going to have to get used to it. I'm your bodyguard, which means I have to protect you, especially when you're exposed." Joven waved a hand dismissively as he turned back to the window. "Besides, it's not like I'm going to be looking at you while you bathe."

Endrance could feel his cheeks heating up. "I… I guess you're right." He said with a sigh. His job was going to take him new places and teach him new things. This was certainly a new thing to learn, yet not anything he expected. Endrance pulled off his shirt and watched Joven warily for a minute before stripping off the rest of his clothes and pouring the water from the pitcher into a basin.

He reached for a cloth to dunk into the water, and realized he still wore the bracer on his arm. It glimmered as the refracted light from the window and water basin danced across its silver surface. He had been so relieved to have it back on his arm he had not even realized it had been skin temperature despite being off his arm for hours. The arcane script encircling the Crystalphage set in its face seemed to squirm for a moment in the sunlight, but when he blinked they were still.

This object was only one of a set of two, both were objects that Kaelob's master had given him, and from him, to Endrance. Even with only one of them, this was perhaps the most valuable object in his possession next to the spell book Kaelob had crafted him. That, while enchanted and nearly indestructible was more valuable if only in knowledge.

He carefully released the subtle catches in the bracer's seam, popping it off his forearm and setting it down next to the basin. Taking the cloth in hand, he started wiping the grime and dirt off his body. He didn't know when he would be able to even take such a luxury as this again, since from what he had read of maps, Balator was many months foot journey away.

"What are those?" Joven's voice broke the silence, surprising Endrance from his inner reverie. "Scars?"

Endrance saw that Joven had closed up the window shutters. Now he was sitting in his chair again, looking almost directly at him. Endrance felt his face redden immediately.

"Joven!" he exclaimed. "You said you weren't going to watch me!" Endrance tried to cover himself up with his discarded shirt.

"What?" the barbarian replied. "I decided the best avenue to attack you is the door." He said, pointing to the door a few feet to Endrance's side. "You just happen to be in the same direction. So are they scars?"

Endrance looked down at his arms. The trace lines of his meridians were slightly visible but they weren't so easily spotted from across the room. "What scars?" he finally asked.

Joven looked puzzled. "The two on your back?" he asked. "It looks like someone tried cutting your shoulder blades out."

Endrance felt around his back, and felt there were in fact two long slashes of hot skin symmetrically across his spine from each other, nearly eight inches long. He knew he didn't have those before, but he didn't know how he had them now. "I... I didn't have these before." He muttered, glancing at Joven with worry across his face.

Joven sighed. "You can't seriously tell me you just magically got two long scars like that without knowing. Because I would bet you would have remembered physically getting scars like that." He said, picking the large mirror off the dresser and handing it to the young mage.

Endrance had to put down the shirt to hold the mirror, as it was heavy and unwieldy. How'd he casually pick this up with just one hand?

Positioning it over his shoulder, he could see the scars out of the corner of his eye through the reflection. His meridian lines in those areas were an angry reddish color, and they seemed converge on the two slashes in his back. After looking at it as long as he could awkwardly, he put the mirror down and closed his eyes, focusing his mind.

In his thoughts, he felt out his aura. It was the first thing any apprentice had to learn to do in order to learn any higher arts; it was in fact the first of the twelve sigils of mastery. His mind touched his aura, which served as the well of his power. As he rested, he gathered his power until his aura was 'full' of energy he could draw on at will. It was more than capable of growing in capacity, but that was something that came with time and practice. Part of it was a mental barrier as well as spiritual. There were other ways to fill his aura with power, but they were dangerously complex, or bordering on taboo like the first effect his bracer had shown him.

He felt his aura respond to his mind, and its power curled up around him, eager to do his will. Unbeknown to the wizard, Joven's eyes widened as faint wisps of gold-hued light brightened into view, their light coruscating around Endrance like a swirl of flickering wind. The light faded slowly like a candle on its last moments. Endrance opened his eyes, and frowned at Joven when he saw the expression on his face.

"...What?" Endrance asked. Grabbing a clean pair of pants and thrusting a leg into it.

Joven blinked his eyes clear. "You... sparkled."

Endrance glared at Joven. "What?" he repeated, this time with his own irritation.

"You…" Joven said, scratching his head. "I guess, you were… on fire, but it was a golden color." He explained poorly.

Endrance sagged with relief. "Oh. For a moment there I thought you meant something else." He said. "No, that was my aura. Certain meditations can make it visible to the naked eye when we use them."

"It doesn't do that anytime you cast magic, does it?" Joven asked.

"No. Well, certain spells may require in their long form ritual that a wizard touch upon their aura-" Endrance started explaining.

"Hold on." Joven said, holding up a hand. "You lost me there."

Endrance studied Joven for a moment as he pulled on his shirt. "Lost you where?" he asked.

"The 'certain spells' part." Joven admitted.

Endrance sighed. "The short answer is, other than some exceptions, no."

"Oh. Why didn't you say that then?" Joven quipped, standing. "You done… bathing?" he asked. "I'd like us to get going."

Endrance clicked the bracer back on his left arm. "Sure. We can get going, but I think it would be better if I got a horse. The trip is going to be a long one if I don't."

Joven shrugged. "Sounds like a good idea. My horse wouldn't carry you."

That didn't surprise Endrance. "All right, I think I have enough coin to purchase a cheap horse, if there are any around. Do you think you can help me pick a proper one out?"

Joven grinned, grabbing up his weapons and his small amount of packs. "I'm glad you asked."

Chapter 17

Joven was quiet at first, riding alongside him as the horses set a brisk pace along the beaten earth road. After a few hours and the city walls had fallen out of sight, he turned partially towards him in his saddle and said, "So how is the horse?"

Endrance looked over to him and shrugged. "I don't know. I hardly have ever ridden one, excepting a few times on a neighbor's workhorse during harvest season."

Joven chuckled. "You're going to be sore tonight then." He commented. A few more moments passed in silence. Endrance was only absent mindedly keeping pace with his horse, the paint horse they had purchased for the last of his money was a decent enough follower to not stray off the road. The young wizard seemed lost in thought, a habit that Joven noticed he entertained regularly.

"Something on your mind?" he asked at last.

Endrance blinked and looked at him again. "Oh." He said faintly. "Yes. I've… I've been thinking of my home. I'm hoping they are all right."

"Your home?" Joven asked. "So you didn't grow up in Ironsoul?"

"Well, I grew up in a village in the kingdoms, but not in the capitol city proper." Endrance explained. "The place was called Wayrest. It's a farming village a few weeks south of Ironsoul. I lived there with my father and it is also where my master Kaelob has retired."

"Yes. Kaelob." Joven muttered. "So, what of your mother?"

Endrance shrugged one shoulder. "She died giving birth to me. That's what I've been told. I don't know anything about her though, we had lived somewhere else when I was born and only moved to Wayrest when she died."

Joven was silent a moment. He didn't know what to say to the young man yet. In that situation in his culture, the child might be considered weak like their mother, unless he was to be of impressive size. But he had learned that people view strength differently here. "Are you going to miss it? Your family and your life here, that is?" Joven asked as he scratched his nose with a hand. "I mean they say you village people live real simple lives and stuff. Things are much rougher where I come from."

Endrance nodded and without turning said, "Yes, in a way I will miss my father dearly. He worked so hard to raise me, and I love him very much. But on the other side I need this change for me to grow, for me to learn more." He chuckled, "I had read every book in Kaelob's library; except for the tomes of spells he prevented me from accessing." Endrance shrugged. "Just as well, some things you have to learn on your own right?"

The two of them rode in silence for quite some time, and as they journeyed the suns crossed the sky. By the time the suns had come three-quarters its journey across the horizon, Joven looked about and pulled the horses to a stop. He grinned at Endrance as he helped the young wizard slide off his horse..

"Well, we better get started setting up camp, especially since I'm pretty sure you don't know anything about camping or living off the wild," he said, guiding both his and Endrance's horses to a nearby copse of trees.

Once the two horses were tethered to a tree, the two of them quickly found a site to camp at.

Endrance was surprised to see the spot Joven picked had already been cleared of debris, and there was even the remains of a fire having been in the center. The burnt cinders were scattered about, but there was a large scorched indentation in the center of the site. Looking about, Endrance could see that there was also several even and flattened out spots where one could lay out their bedroll and not have large lumps underneath them.

Joven dropped his pack off near the fire pit and looked around. "This place looks just fine," he said, nodding his head. "I camped here two nights ago as I was on my way to you." He frowned as he studied the ground for a moment. "But it seems something was here last night. Stay here," he said. He drew his greatsword and slid into the trees almost silently.

Endrance looked back around the camp again, remembering the tricks Ethan had taught him on the road before. He took a closer look in the long light of the setting suns and finally noticed something that had been immediately evident to Joven. A trio of long grooves marred the packed dirt surface of one of the spots people could set their tents up on.

It was quiet for several minutes while Endrance looked around the camp. He couldn't sense anything hostile, nor could he see anything lurking in the dusk-enhanced shadows of the woods. He could see much better in the dark than most men and probably as good as the elves, but whatever it was that concerned Joven was not lurking near here.

It occurred to Endrance that he couldn't see the barbarian either, and he began to get worried when suddenly a large shape loomed up in his peripheral vision. The dim light of the fading suns barely illuminated Joven's face as he stalked back into the camp, wiping his sword with a dirty cloth. Endrance sighed and walked up to the barbarian as he sheathed the greatsword.

"What was that?" Endrance asked.

He grunted, shrugging, "It was nothing important. It was just an unwelcome visitor. I convinced it to leave."

Joven turned to Endrance, his expression severe. "Okay. We need to set up camp. I'll teach you, but you need to pay attention because we're running out of light. First thing you need to get is firewood. Go into the woods here and collect about two armfuls of dried wood," He mimicked snapping a twig with his hands. "The drier the wood, the better it will be. I'll set up camp and prepare the meal once you get back." He shooed Endrance into the woods, "Hurry up! The suns are dropping swiftly!"

Endrance ran into the woods, casting his eyes about for loose sticks and branches. Quickly he gathered up as much as he could fit in his arms, stopping when he could no longer pick up anything without dropping some wood. He ran back and dumped the wood by the fire pit and looked at Joven. The big barbarian was placing several stones in a ring around the fire pit, building up a small wall around the pit. He had already rolled out the bedrolls and had a small pot sitting nearby. Endrance turned and headed back into the woods, and began searching for more wood to burn. He had grabbed most of the fallen dry wood that he could see, but he was certain he could get more by heading deeper into the woods.

The night was imminent, and in the closeness of the trees, it was as dark as it ever got to Endrance. He felt nervous out in the dark by himself. What if the thing Joven scared off came back? He carefully moved through the woods, picking up sturdy branches and sticks as he went. He had just picked up his last possible branch of wood when he came across something horrible.

In a small clearing of the woods were the makings of a horrible battle. The trees were slashed by something sharp and large, there was blood sprayed against the trunks of the trees and across the grass. Endrance could hardly tell the blood was there by sight, but he could smell it, and it sickened him. He saw a form slumped in the middle of the clearing, its spined form easily as big as a horse. He turned and quickly ran as fast as he dared back through the darkened trees. He emerged from the woods a few dozen paces from their camp, and he quickly deposited the wood near the fire that was slowly growing in the pit.

He sat down near his bed roll as Joven added some of the wood he had brought into the fire. He then put some things into the pot and set it in the fire by a hooked iron stick. He sat back and looked over at Endrance. "I'm making some stew from some supplies that I brought, but I don't have enough to last past tonight. We will have to hunt something tomorrow night."

Endrance nodded, looking into the flames. He was still disturbed from running into the bloody mess in the woods, but he said nothing. He lay down on his bedroll and stared up at the darkening night sky. Slowly the last sliver of the suns disappeared beyond the horizon, and the stars were visible, twinkling gently as the night spun on.

"So," Joven began, having picked up a stick and whittled at it with a small knife, "Tell me about what you do. It's good for my renown to be escorting the Spengur, and I want to know more about the man I'm going to be guarding for the rest of his time with us."

"Have you guarded a Spengur before?"

"No, I haven't. The last one was watched by a different family."

Endrance turned his head so he could get a sideways glance at Joven. "Then aren't they supposed to be watching me? I was told that your people guarded the Spengur in every generation."

Joven shrugged. "The last Spengur was… he died. When a bodyguard fails his duty, his family line is cut from those who are able to watch over the Spengur. Now only the house of Rothel is left."

"Rothel?" Endrance asked, his interest peaked. "That's your family name? Joven of Rothel?"

Joven grunted, watching the pot of stew intently. "There used to be twelve families who would take turns watching over the Spengur as they came and went, but now the onus lies solely on me and my brothers."

Endrance remembered something he had read in Kaelob's book, and drew it from his pack. He flipped through it and saw the chapter Kaelob had written about the barbarian families. At his time there were four families left. How many years had passed since then?

"I see. Well, that means your family was the best then, right?" Endrance asked. "Your family never failed in its duties."

"True." Joven said, adding a dry stick to the fire. "Though with your current record for getting into danger I'll be lucky if you survive until we get to Balator."

Endrance glanced down at his book, paging through to the notes on Kaelob's reception. "So what exactly is going to happen once I'm there?" he asked, trying to find the information.   His bodyguard shrugged his shoulders, grinning. "We have a feast celebrating your arrival, and then we make sacrifices to you so you help us faithfully." He said matter-of-factly. "Then you go to your new home, and in the morning begin your duties as Spengur."

Endrance looked up from his pages. "Sacrifice?"

"Yep."

Endrance continued to stare at the big man, who only smiled into the firelight. "What kind of sacrifice?"

Joven shrugged. "You know, the usual things people sacrifice. Money, animals, people." He seemed to be honest, but without any sense of malice.

Endrance shook his head and frantically began paging through his book to find Kaelob's notes. "Whoa wait a second!" he exclaimed, nearly tearing pages as he searched. "I don't want any human sacrifices! Why would you kill people for me?"

Joven looked at Endrance, confused. "Who said we were going to kill them?" he visibly went over the conversation in his head, keeping track with his hands. He eventually nodded, confirmed that he was right. "We were giving things of ours to you, without expecting them back or demanding payment." He looked back at his charge. "Doesn't that mean sacrifice?"

Endrance found a page that started explaining the feast and its sacrifices. From what he could see, the barbarian people gave up a wealth of things in hope they could get allegiance from the person they wanted to be the Spengur. They would give them a home, food, treasures, animals, and even servants. Particularly it mentioned that some of the Ergkinoa being the biggest sacrifice, as they were the ones who passed on tribal lore, knowledge, and history by word of mouth, since the barbarian people only rarely knew how to read.

"Oh. I see." Endrance said, closing the book. "I misunsderstood what you meant. I think my master had said something about that as well, I'm sorry."

Joven shrugged. "Sure. Stew's ready."

They ate in silence, and Endrance thought more about what was going to come. It was quiet while they ate, and Joven seemed to be thinking. "You know," the barbarian started, "It would be advantageous if I taught you some weapon skills either way."

Endrance sighed. "Look, I don't want to hurt anybody. I don't need to know how to use a sword." He denied, trying his best to exert himself.

Joven shrugged. "You may not want to hurt others, but that's not to say someone out there wants to hurt you. You've lived a very sheltered life up until now. I have more scars from people that I didn't want to fight than you have years in your life." The barbarian gestured at the area around him with his spoon. "The world is dangerous, and you may not be able to use your magic all the time." He finished. When they were done eating and Joven took care of the wooden bowls, the barbarian taught the young mage how to set up and break down a camp so that it would be safe to use another time and to prevent accidents from happening. By the time he was done, it was late in the night.

Endrance put his things away and laid out on his bedroll to sleep. What Joven had told him at dinner weighed heavy on his mind. "You may be right, but I still can't envision myself using a weapon. Not yet." He said, rolling his back to the man and trying to get some sleep.

He was just drifting off when he thought he heard his bodyguard whisper "I hope you never have to…"

The next day Endrance was most certainly sore, but they could not rest for very long. They travelled along the roads heading north all day at a decent clip, pausing only to rest and water the horses. They ate their lunch in the saddle, hard bread that was dry and crumbling, but dense enough to be filling. The ride was rough enough and the ache in his muscles were more than enough to prevent him from doing much else but focusing on riding the whole day. Maybe in time he would be able to ride for days without worry, but at the current time he was too green to do anything more than try to stay in the saddle.

They were still a long ways to Balator, but they agreed to make a stop in the city of Fini along the way for more supplies and to get a rest. It was still several days away so they slightly increased the pace of their horses. They made good time, and they covered several miles before they stopped along yet another wood to camp. This time they made camp well out of the woods, and Joven took Endrance along to show him how to hunt.

"Now the first thing you want to keep in mind is that if they catch on to you, they will either run away or attack you." He said, drawing one of his axes quietly. "You have to be prepared no matter what happens." He stalked along surprisingly quietly for his size. Endrance snuck along next to him, his light weight and frame making sneaking easy for him. Eventually Joven lead them to a small grove where a deer was cautiously nibbling at some leaves. Endrance nudged Joven and whispered "How are you going to sneak up on it with your axe?"

"Who said I was going to sneak up on it? Just watch me." Joven whispered as he moved carefully until he was a ways away from Endrance but still just outside the grove. He was still several dozen yards from the deer, but it seemed to have not seen or smelled them yet.

Endrance watched as Joven stood up to his full height, pulling the axe up and holding it over his shoulder, the axe head was aimed right at the deer. Endrance watched as the deer suddenly looked up, some form of animal awareness warning it of its impending doom. Before the deer could spring away however, Joven had already propelled the axe along his arm, flying through the grove in a whirl of wood and steel to impact into the doe's neck and brutally slamming it into the tree behind it. The axe haft quivered as the tree shuddered with the impact. Several leaves drifted down from its branches as the deer had a few seconds to look surprised and then die.

Joven shouted to his success, and ran into the grove to retrieve his prize. Endrance stood stock still; his jaw dropped wide open and one hand vaguely pointing to the unfortunate deer.

Endrance was overwhelmed with mixed feelings as Joven brusquely yanked his axe out of the deer's neck. He was completely amazed that throwing his axe worked, utterly surprised how fast it all happened, and most of all felt a dull sense of horror over something as beautiful and graceful as a deer dying so suddenly. Endrance could swear that the poor creature had looked him right in the eyes just before Joven's axe took the life from it. Endrance shook his head, shuddering and trying to shake off the shock.

Joven seemed not to notice, as he touched the haft of the bloody axe to his forehead before he carefully began by slitting the deer's throat and beginning the gruesome process of draining and skinning the deer. It was a relatively small doe, so it wasn't too long of a process, but when he was done there was still too much meat for them to take with them safely. Joven left some out for the predators, and hauled the majority of it with them back, making Endrance carry the hide.

Joven stretched out the hide and mounted it near the fire to dry then he quickly lashed together a rack to smoke the meat on. He swiftly and with obvious practiced ease had the deer set up and smoking in a short amount of time. After he had done this he took some of the meats and made a meal for the two of them. They ate, and with Joven occasionally waking up to tend the meats the two of them slept the night.

The venison lasted a long time, over the course of several days they ate well while they traveled. Soon they were close to Fini, and could see the city in the distance. Built on the confluence of two great rivers, Fini was practically an island to itself. The city was rich with the profits of trade and industry, and in fact many nobles and their families made their homes in Fini.   The white stone architecture of the city was collected from a nearby quarry strictly used for city development. Statues and art adorned the noble districts of Fini, and even the docks and the shops were of extraordinary quality. Gold pieces were the smallest currency of the city, and some of the services cost platinum or even gems and other wealth.

They were a scant two days away from Fini when Joven insisted that they get together some more furs and food so they could trade it for supplies. Joven turned to Endrance as they were setting up camp and said "It's your time to do the hunting boy." Joven shooed Endrance from the camp. "Now go! Catch us something!"

Endrance stalked off into the forest. He was unsure of what to do as he had never taken anything's life when it wasn't in self defense or to defend another, much less had any experience hunting. He looked back at watching Joven hunt the deer and remembered the way Joven moved and looked about. He decided then that he'd try to catch something. He wouldn't come back until he had gotten some food.

As soon as Endrance had moved a dozen yards from camp, Joven quickly slipped a pair of his throwing axes from his belt and stalked off after him. He wanted the young man to learn, but he couldn't risk the man's life just so he could learn a lesson. He would watch him from a safe distance and maybe he could catch a glimpse of the wizard's magic. He had been curious ever since the night he rescued him. How exactly did a willowy young man throw lightning from his hands? Either way, he would have to keep a close eye on the man.

Endrance slunk through the forest, his spell in mind and his hands free. He managed to make very little sound as he moved through the woods, travelling a ways until he came to a large stream that was an offshoot of the rivers of Fini. Along the stream bank were two deer, an adult buck with two pronged antlers and a small fawn that Endrance couldn't identify as male or female. The two of them hadn't noticed him yet, and Endrance positioned himself so he had a clear shot at them.

He however found himself faced with a quandary. If he killed the buck then the fawn would likely die from a predator or starve to death. If he killed the fawn then the buck could potentially have another after some time, but would still lose his young. Endrance paused for over a minute as he watched the deer drink from the water, and almost lost his resolve when he watched the shaking-legged fawn drink from the clear spring.

Endrance shook his head gently, and remembered his resolve to hunt this day. He figured that if he struck down the fawn then it would scare off the buck and he could bring it back to Joven. But didn't Joven say that they might also attack? If he attacked the buck first, he didn't think the fawn would go very far.

Joven watched from a side angle as he watched the young man think his way through the situation. At this point Joven was uncertain that the wizard realized that the buck and fawn would be too much for them to cook and tan over one night. He probably didn't, as the man had not moved to leave or find other prey. He was so focused on the young man's quandary he didn't notice the other one who came to observe.

Endrance decided to try to bring down them both. The problem was he didn't have a weapon, and using a spell could alert his prey. He could try slinging a spell, but the only ones he could think of that would take down a deer would also damage the hide and meat. Any spell that he could cast conventionally would give the deer plenty of time to hear him and scatter.

He closed his eyes for a moment, considering his options. Of the spells he could formulate in his head, the only one that seemed effective was a relatively minor one. It would take an object and levitate it with invisible force. His master was familiar enough with the spell he could cast it with but a thought and muttered word, but Endrance would have to focus enough to use it. Even then, he would have to change a critical element of the spell to make it useful.

As the young wizard rolled back in his mind all the teachings Kaelob had instilled with him about creative use of spellwork, Joven finally caught a glimpse of what else was watching with great intent.

At first it only appeared as an overly thick patch of shrub across from the deer. Joven almost dismissed it when he caught it move against the faint breeze passing through the trees. A faint outline of a feline form, easily five feet long from head to rump, its tail extending another five feet behind it, longer than a typical big cat. Joven couldn't see any fine details for a moment, until he realized that its fur was blending in with the greenery behind it. The only things that didn't change were the vertical black stripes of its coat.

Joven readied his axes and was about to charge into the glade when the big cat struck. From a crouch it pounced, covering ten yards in an instance and colliding with the buck with a roar. Even as it soared through the air the colors bled out of the big cat's back, turning a pale red color with black stripe like slashes in it. The buck had hardly any time to twist in surprise before the cat's large fangs had it by the neck.

Endrance opened his eyes in surprise, just having figured out what he would do when the roar shocked him out of his thoughts. Confused, he didn't at first know what he was looking at. The buck was lying in the grass, its neck broken and bleeding from a large bite, while a red and black striped cat easily as massive as Joven batted the fawn to the ground with a sickening crunch.

Endrance froze, partially in fear and partially because he didn't know what it would do next. Maybe it would leave with its prey, and he could search elsewhere. Or better yet, return to Joven and let him know what happened.

The great cat looked directly at him, and Endrance winced. Joven was too far away to get between the cat and his charge before it would get to him, so he wound up his arm and prepared to throw his axe with all his might. The young wizard knew as he stared into this creatures eyes that this was one of the moments where it was kill or be killed. Its eyes pierced into his, and he could sense the ferocity of the predator in front of him. It wouldn't rest until either he or it was dead.

All three parties burst into action at the same time. The cat roared and charged across the open grass towards the trees in a graceful lope that was frighteningly quick for its size. Joven gauged the speed of the attacker and let fly his axe. Endrance thrust his hand down into the dirt at his feet and pulled up a peach pit sized rock.

The great cat must have noticed the axe in flight and shifted its course, the axe handle slipping over its head by a scant inch. Endrance held up the rock as if he were offering it to the beast and fixated the altered version of the spell in his mind. The cat leapt into the air, mouth open and claws splayed in the darkening sky.

"Vexo!" Endrance cried out, closing his eyes in fear as the spell went into effect. He felt a strong drain on his reserves, and he realized too late that in his fear he had thrown too much energy into the spell. The rock departed his palm with a loud crack as splinters of rock scattered everywhere, puncturing his palm several times. The rock itself was flung away from him with such great force that it shattered into smaller chunks as it shot cleanly into the great cat's mouth. None of them came out the other side, but the cats roar died in mid air and the beast clipped the young man as it came down hard on top of him.

Joven nearly screamed in rage and fear for his charge. Bounding towards the young man, he saw the cat lay there unmoving and the top half of Endrance's body sticking out from under its furry coat. The wizard was struggling, trying to push the beast off of him but it was far too massive for him to move.

Endrance hadn't seen or heard Joven's approach yet; the cat's roar and charge had both dulled his hearing and amplified his nerves. He was pushing at the crux between its neck and shoulder when the cat's eye rotated to look at him directly. Endrance froze, terrified that he had only hurt the thing.

A moment passed that was so tense Joven couldn't see a way to interfere without possibly doing more harm than good. The great cat stared Endrance in the eyes; its own slit-pupil orb seemed to glow with animal ferocity while the mage's were wide in both fear and wonder. He saw something pass in its vision, something the young man thought to be satisfaction, and in that moment the light faded from its eyes.

Endrance let out his breath in a rush, and closed his eyes as he tried to recollect himself. Joven called out his name, and the young man finally became aware he was approaching.

"Joven!" he exclaimed. "Oh thank the gods!"

"Look what you got yourself into this time!" Joven exclaimed mockingly, trying to hide how honestly scared he was for the young man. It was almost the end of a very short career right there.

Endrance looked down his body at the cat that pinned him down. "Yeah, I think I caught something that would be profitable, though." He reasoned.

Endrance thrust out his left arm to Joven as it was the closest. His sleeve fell back from the bracer on his arm, and the yellow-orange Crystalphage set in the silver flared with its own light before Joven could grab his hand. The barbarian leapt back as a wind rushed about the young man and the cat.

Like before, the first circle of arcane script lit up in golden light, and from the flesh of the dead great cat faintly visible golden wind erupted from the beast and swirled around the bracer. Only when it had all funneled into the gem did the lights and winds fade. Endrance stared at the artifact on his arm with a detached sense of curiosity and dread.

Endrance tried to reach out with his other hand, and winced as the stone splinters in his palm jabbed his nerves. He carefully pulled them out one at a time and dropped them aside.

"I have some cloth that can be used as a bandage in my pouches." Endrance said, holding out his bloodied hand. "But they're under this thing."

Joven watched him warily for a moment, struggling between his sworn vow and his fear of the wizard's magic.

"It's done. Please help me out from under this." The young man pleaded. His legs were growing numb.

The barbarian grimaced, but walked around and grabbed his right hand, and with a firm pull managed to extricate the slender young man from under the massive cat. "What was that?" Joven asked.

"They are called blood tigers." Endrance said, sounding distracted as he quickly removed a dinner plate sized patch of cloth and began wrapping it around his bleeding hand. "Magical creatures, they can use magic to appear like their surroundings."

Joven blinked at him and then shook his head. "Not that!" he said, poking the young mage's upper arm. "That."

Endrance looked down at the bracer. "Oh. Well, it seems that blood tigers have an appreciable amount of magical energy stored in their auras, and my bracer was able to capture it before it dispersed."

Joven shook his head, trying to understand. "So wait the… blood tiger was a wizard too?"

Endrance crinkled his nose at the thought of it. "No. Not like that. It itself is a creature of magic, and therefore has magic in it. It is inherent to them."

"I think I understand." Joven admitted after pondering it over. He surveyed the area, noting where his axe was.

"How did you get here so quickly?" Endrance asked innocently, poking at the tiger's head. A trickle of blood leaked out from between its teeth, but otherwise it looked perfectly healthy.

"You think I would let you wander off into the forests around here without supervision?" Joven said. "I didn't think you would mind if I kept an eye out for you."

"So did you just... miss the tiger, then?" Endrance asked.

Joven scowled at him. "You're the one who said they're magical, how was I supposed to spot it?"

"Fair enough." Endrance responded, patting the dead beast on its head. "Well, I think we got some hides and meats for when we get to Fini." He concluded.

Joven leaned on a tree trunk and looked at the two deer some ways away. "Yes we do, but did you take the time to think that we can't carry all of this back, much less be able to skin and cure the hides in one night? Or cook all that meat?"

Endrance's face went blank. "What?"

"It takes a lot of time to cook such a large animal," Joven said in irritation, waving at the buck near the stream. "And we can't eat that cat, can we? The fur would be good, but we're going to lose a day at the least curing all this meat and hide."

Endrance thought it over a moment. "Wouldn't just leaving them here be a waste?" he asked, puzzled.

Joven used both arms to flip the tiger onto its back. He grunted with the effort, his muscles bulging as he heaved. "Yes." He responded, producing one of his many long knives. "Which is why we are going to stay until the job is done. We do not waste." He made the first cut along the collarbone, and then pointed at the young wizard with the knife, a bead of ruby blood dancing on its tip. "Let that be the first lesson you learn of our ways."

Endrance nodded, his eyes focused on the droplet of blood. "I understand."

"Good." Joven said, and returning to the task of skinning the blood tiger. "I will do my best to teach you to not offend my people before you can take care of yourself, but just in case try not to do anything until the Ergkinoa can teach you properly."

"I will try." Endrance asked.

"Why didn't you do that lightning thing, like you said you did with the thug that kidnapped you?" Joven asked, speaking over the gruesome noises he made skinning the great cat.

Endrance shrugged, though he knew Joven wouldn't see it. "I couldn't clear the spell I had been preparing out of my head in time. Unlike most of my other spells, I had been making it on the spot from another spell I had already learned and memorized. Since I had been so focused on the information in the spell, it would take far longer to clear my head of that spell and mentally recall another spell without chancing me accidently mixing some of the components from both, and that can have catastrophic repercussions.

"I had to use the spell I had at hand, and hope I had correctly repurposed the spell enough to prevent it from misfiring. Otherwise it would have been on me before I could do anything else." The young wizard concluded.

"So…" Joven stated flatly, glancing at him over his shoulder. "You didn't have time to grab a different weapon and used the one in your hand?"

Endrance glared at his bodyguard. How did he have the ability to simplify such complicated processes and then make them sound so… silly?

"You really aren't as stupid as you make yourself out to be." Endrance observed.

"Yeah," Joven said abjectly. "It seems that we uneducated barbarians can be just as smart as you people can be." He paused a moment, then resumed his work. "Well, maybe not you or Kaelob."

"What?!" Endrance sputtered. "I wasn't talking about your people. I was talking about you."

"The difference?" Joven asked.

"I base my opinions off what I've observed. While you appear to be ignorant to the general population, and make a show of avoiding any writing stating your inability to read, I have noticed you reading over my shoulder, when I have out the guide book Kaelob wrote." Endrance concluded.

The barbarian halted before he made the final cut. "Oh." He said quietly. "You noticed that?"

"Yeah." Endrance replied. "I'm not entirely unobservant. I was taught a few tricks by a professional soldier named Ethan."

"Then this Ethan has earned some of my respect." Joven said, making the final cut and peeling the hide from the tiger. Endrance's eyes widened as he caught a glimpse, and then turned away before he lost control of his stomach.

"What should I do now?" Endrance asked.

"Watch." Joven said, with some force. "And learn."

Chapter 18

He saw the tiger attack him over and over again in his dreams, but each time it seemed all the more disturbing. The dream was vague, with ephemeral whorls of terror and red and black stripes, which ended with its fangs sinking into the young wizard's neck. Endrance awoke screaming, but was horrified to see that Joven was really a blood tiger in disguise and he was the one about to get skinned.

Endrance awoke again, this time to the real world, a wordless cry on his lips. He could see the stars above, and must have been asleep several hours. Joven glanced over at Endrance, having completed his task of skinning and cleaning the animals long ago. The hides were stretched on their racks after only a few hours soaking and the meats were beginning their long smoke. He was cooking something on an iron plate, and it smelled delicious.

"I was just going to wake you up." He began, scraping the hunk of meat off the iron plate into a wooden bowl and sliding it towards Endrance. "Eat up, you earned it." Joven turned back to his own meal as Endrance picked up the plate. A venison steak sat in his bowl, well cooked as well as a few vegetables and half a loaf of travel bread. Endrance's mouth watered and he realized then how hungry he was. He took a bite from the bread and was going to dig into the steak when he became aware he had no utensils. "Joven, I would love to eat this steak but I seem to have no knife to cut it with." He stated.

Joven chuckled and rolled a small bundle over to him. "Use these." He said. "I made them for you. They should fit your hands perfectly."

Endrance unrolled the long and thin bundle to see that Joven had crafted for him a pair of knives, each with a fresh sharp steel blade set into a handle crafted from the buck's antlers. The handle was the main part of the antler and the off shooting prong was positioned so that it was the finger guard. The blades themselves were single edged and slightly curved back near the tip, making them excellent at slicing and stabbing work. The blades themselves were not ones Endrance had seen Joven using. They were Ironsoul steel, and high quality.

"They're beautiful," Endrance said.

"They're also good trophies. You can show those to anyone in Balator and they will know to give you some respect."

Endrance looked up at Joven in surprise. "But... I didn't kill the buck."

"No you didn't. You killed something far stronger." He responded. "We have had a few blood tiger attacks before. That would have torn through a few men before it could be taken down, yet you finished it in one shot of a rock."

"I couldn't have hit it that hard." Endrance said demurely. "After all the rock didn't go out the other side."

Joven huffed in laughter. "You didn't see what I saw once I got the hide off." He began merrily. "First thing is that cat's hide is a lot tougher than prepared leather. Second, tigers have been known to fight on even if they lose a limb. They're tenacious."

"I know." Endrance said, remembering the absorption his bracer had left him with. For an instant he felt the beast's instincts swell up against his mind. He closed his eyes and forced the thoughts down until he had control again. Like with the goblin shaman, it looked like the active personality behind the information he gained from the tiger would fade in time, but for now it was very real. He would have to be careful lest a particularly powerful one take him over.

"And once I got the hide off, I discovered that your little rock broke into several pieces and bounced down its spine and around its rib cage, pretty much turning everything inside there into mush." Joven concluded. "Some monsters are not so tough on the inside, and their very armor keeps something from punching its way out."

"So it was more effective because it wasn't strong enough to go right through it?" Endrance asked.

"Her. And yes." Joven replied.

"Her?"

"Yes. A female, recently mated as well." Joven's face was serious.

"Let me guess…" Endrance said knowingly. "That's bad."

"Very." Joven said, checking over the assorted smoking racks.

Endrance sighed, and as he considered the option the information suddenly appeared in his mind, confirming his suspicions. "She was mated." He concluded.

"I don't know." Joven said, "If she was I say we could be in some serious trouble. Reports I've read say they're incredibly vindictive. One such pairing we encountered was like that. One day one of our men managed to kill the male, and the female went mad. Didn't even care about the other men around him; they weren't even there. She died, but only after she had torn the one who killed her mate into pieces."

Endrance gulped, and then looked down at the steak before him. It looked far more like a last meal than it was a reward for a good hunt. He carefully picked up the daggers he had been gifted and started cutting into the meat. If he was to die, he would rather it be on a full stomach, and perhaps in his sleep.

"Like I said," Joven repeated, noticing the worry on his charge's face. Perhaps he had gone too far explaining the creature. "I don't think she was mated, or he wouldn't have been far behind. I also did what I could to confuse its scent, drained both deer on the same spot as the tiger so I don't think it could pick up the few drops you left behind."

Endrance sighed. "That's not going to help." He said morosely. "They're called blood tigers for a reason." He took a bite of steak and chewed it thoughtfully. "The other magical ability they have is to track by drawn blood. They're better than even the best of a king's bloodhounds. They're better because their magic allows them to do so. They can stalk prey across a country off of one drop of blood so long as it was there. They don't even follow a trail, it's like their nose becomes a compass that leads them to the source of the blood they smell."

Joven huffed, tearing a hunk off his steak with his teeth. "If you knew so much about the blood tigers, why did you let me talk on about them?"

"I don't" Endrance said. "I only know what their name is and what information came with her aura. Namely the natural magic power she could use. Scent and camouflage, that's all." He crumbled some of his bread into the steak's juices to soften the bread up.

"You learned that when you did the wind eating thing that you did back there?" Joven asked.

Endrance rolled his eyes. "Yes."

"Does that mean you know how to camouflage yourself like they do and track by blood like they can?" the barbarian asked innocently.

"I-" Endrance stopped, thinking about it. Information stolen from the dying cat flooded his mind again, the feral force behind it weaker than before. The knowledge of how remained, albeit in an instinctual manner than an intellectual one. However he lacked the proper physical parts needed to make it work. "I could, if I had a blood tiger's skin and their nose." He concluded in pleasant surprise. "That's pretty amazing, but impractical."

Joven grinned as he poked one of the racks with a stick. "I know what winter coat you're getting." He said jovially.

"…Thank you, Joven. You are a true friend." Endrance admitted. If he could figure it out, even tanned the hide might still be able to blend into the surroundings.

"Well, You are the Spengur, not to mention a kid off on your own for the first time taking on a job that you have no way of being properly prepared for, in a kingdom where everyone values strength of body and prowess over the mind, not to mention that you have the build of a foppish debutante and would be looked at poorly by even the peasant-folk of the kingdom…" Joven ticked off facts on his fingers as he stared out into the night air.

Endrance stared at Joven as he went on a while. "You…" He began. "You are not nearly as stupid as you pretend to be."

Joven winked. "Just don't tell anyone okay? I have a reputation to keep up here."

Endrance looked down at the two knives in his hands, and at the meat stacked on his plate. "It is really okay to do this? Kill an animal, and then eat it?"

Joven grunted as he chewed on a large chunk of steak. "That's the law of nature, Endrance. Eat or be eaten."

Endrance nodded, using the knives to cut up his steak so he could eat. He chewed on his steak for a few minutes in silence then asked.

"Foppish… debutante?"

More days passed as they prepared the hides. The meats were sufficiently dried by the end of the second day to consist as travel rations, a meat jerky that could be thrown into stew water to soften up if needed. The hides took more care and watch, or else some predator would steal into the camp and ruin their work.

During this time Joven taught him what he could about surviving the wilderness, and kept a constant vigil in case the mate of the hide he was preparing came looking for revenge. Endrance in his own way did so as well, and by the third day he had finally penned a new spell using borrowed structure from spells he had studied before. Cobbling together a spell like that was never efficient until it could be refined and it definitely would be considered vulgar; however it saved on much time and resources designing all the elements of the spell from scratch.

The new spell he tested out when it was his turn to watch that night. After Joven had settled down at his usual spot and went immediately to sleep, Endrance stood in the center of the camp. He faced the forest around him, the camp fire's heat bearing directly on his back only a pace away.

He consulted his spellbook one final time, and locked the components of the spell in his mind. This would take some time to set up, but if it worked then he would start memorizing it so he could sling it at a moment's notice. He raised his hands and went through the proper hand and body gestures one more time, making sure he had it right. Lastly he recited the proper words of power, carefully enunciating each one in the proper sequence.

All the components assembled, he committed to the casting. He wove the three together, using the knowledge he had, fed it power with his aura using elaborate mudras, and chanted the words of power to give that power shape. It was a difficult process to cast a spell for the first time. Once he became more familiar with the workings of it, it would be easier. If the spell worked at all how he thought it should.

As he finished the final word of the spell, his body was twisted around and his hand flung out at the campfire. "Flaratorus." He said, his voice low but forceful.

The campfire, which at this point had been running low, blossomed into full strength, and its flames unleashed a wave of air-rippling heat that spread out in a ring and disappeared. Cool night air slowly seeped back into the camp, and the fire died back down to its natural strength. Now anything that entered into a certain radius that had some magical energy would find their aura made brightly visible to anyone. The same time, the fire in the center would flare up and crackle loudly if that happened, drawing attention to intruders.

Endrance had no way to test it yet, so he had to remain alert and vigilant. It should work regardless of their stealth abilities, unless they were magically shielding themselves from specific spells like this. He theorized that since blood tigers weren't capable of spellcasting, defeating such a defense would be impossible for them.

Of course there were flaws in the spell; it would only last so long as the fire remained. In order to prevent it from swiftly draining whatever power he had stored, he had designed it to use the campfire as a source of power. It meant he had to put more fuel in the fire as it burned half again as fast as natural, but it was better than trying to sustain such a spell without sublimating a natural source of energy. He would have been drained of power and exhausted within an hour or two. Though that would be a good practice method to strengthen his aura-

A crack of a branch in the woods nearby drew Endrance's attention to the tree line. He scanned the forest and could see several sets of eyes reflecting the firelight back at him, but all remained a safe distance away. He spotted one set of eyes that were far bigger than the others. As his eyes adjusted to looking away from the fire, he could make out the eyes of the other blood tiger.

It was possible that the male great cat was smaller than its mate, but Endrance couldn't tell through the dark and the tiger's natural blending ability. He could only make out the eyes hovering in the trees, on a branch that looked too small to support the full weight of one of these predators.

Endrance stared back at the cat, his emerald eyes shining in the dark much like the cat's amber ones glared back at him. Their gazes met, and for a moment the last vestiges of the animal instinct he captured struggled to rise to the surface. As the tiger in the woods bared his fangs at him, Endrance could feel his own lips curling into a snarl of his own.

Without taking his eyes off the predator he pulled the two knives from his belt, and held them ready, the blades down. "I see you…" Endrance whispered. He raised his hands over his head, holding the blades into the night sky so the tiger could see their deadly glint in the fire light. The blades, curved as they were and pointed towards the ground, looked almost as a set of fangs themselves.

The two of them held their positions, neither one of them moving in the night. Endrance knew only that to back down would be to invite death, and the only thing he could do is be prepared for the inevitable fight, or get it to abandon its hunt. So for the moment he didn't move and in his head he prepared to throw lightning if he really needed to.

Tense moments passed, and the sounds of the night seemed to drown out in the silence of their battle of wills. Occasionally the fire would pop as an ember burst or the wind would blow detritus between the two, but neither blinked as their eyes were locked. The other animals in the vicinity, having either sensed or seen this clash of wills in effect vacated swiftly. It seemed even the other denizens of the forest wanted nothing of the business between a wizard and a supernatural hunting beast.

A trickle of sweat trundled down his temple, over his cheek, and down the smooth curve of his jaw line. It balanced there on the point of his chin, precariously indecisive of its departure. Seeming eons passed until it finally dropped from his chin and began its agonizingly long yet instantaneous decent to the ground below.

The great cat blinked as Endrance remained resolved, sweat dripping from his face. Its fur shifted back to pale red tinged white, and its fangs disappeared as it closed its mouth. It seemed in an instant to lose interest in the young man, and dropped from the branch, sauntering away slowly. The cat was in fact much larger than its mate by several dozen pounds.

Endrance remained in his posture for until the cat was out of sight, and even then remained for another minute. He let out a breath and sank to the ground in a rush, the blades thunking into the dirt by his knees, their handles sticking up into the air.

"I… I am not cut out for that." Endrance muttered, wiping the sweat off his face. Relief washed over him and he shook his head, trying to clear the tension from his thoughts. "I can't believe that really worked."

None of the other animals came back towards the camp during his watch. He woke Joven when it was his turn to get some sleep and made sure to tell him about the spell on the campfire. He crawled into his sleeping bag and almost immediately fell asleep.

When he awoke in the morning, a dead bird the size of his torso laid placed on the ground in front of him. It looked to have been taken down by a large cat, and hadn't set off Endrance's spell, if the spell even worked. Joven hadn't seen it before and he was alert the whole night. Endrance stared at the thing for several minutes, and wondered if the bird was a warning or a peace offering.

Chapter 19

The hides were soon done, and the two carefully packed up everything and continued on their journey. Neither one of them wanted to camp in these forests again. They travelled as fast as they could, and were within a few hours ride by the time the suns had started setting.

"Endrance." Joven shouted, his horse in the lead as they raced down the road towards Fini.

"I know!" Endrance yelled in return. "Let's just keep going until we get to Fini!"

They raced along in the gathering darkness, their horses lathered in sweat and breathing heavily from the effort. They slowed their mounts when they got to the first of the great bridges leading to Fini proper. Endrance's paint horse seemed grateful for the relief, but the young wizard couldn't help but notice Joven's steed seemed ready for more. The barbarian had to keep tight check on the reins.

The great bridge was made of large gray stones, sturdy and solid. Set well above the banks of the river, it arced gracefully towards the city walls on the other side of the river. The bridge was wide enough that two wagons could pass each other and not brush the low walls on the sides. The bridge was long enough to cross the entire of the river, and was a single smooth curve across the top. The underside was made of several arches of increasing size across the river. Its massive arches were large enough in the center that a sailing vessel could run full sail underneath the bridge and not risk crashing into the stones.

As they crossed the bridge, they saw that the city was active even during the night. Large fires were burning in stone basins along the bridge, and there were travelers approaching the gates on the far side of the bridge as they crossed. Endrance leaned over in the saddle and watched the dark waters of the river flow under him, the stars of the night sky rippling across the surface like a writhing mirror in the dark.

On either side of the gates at the end of the bridge were guard houses, and four guards stood nearby each. The guards wore suits of chain mail, with steel skullcaps and tabards bearing the insignia of Fini across their breasts. They had a small steel target shield strapped to their backs and at their waists steel longswords were slung. They were stopping other travelers as they entered the city, asking questions before they let them pass.

They let the travelers pass, and then it was Joven and Endrance's turn to stop before the guards. They stopped the two of them as they approached, and the guards eyed Joven warily as they walked up to him.

"State your names and purposes." The first guard demanded, twitching a bushy mustache that protruded from his lip. "And are ye holding any contraband?" he eyed the two with an experienced gaze.

Joven slapped his hand against his chest, ever playing the dumb barbarian. "Me Joven. He…" Joven's gaze followed his hand as he pointed at his ward. "He… End… Ender…" Joven scrunched his brow as he seemed to struggle to concentrate. Endrance took his queue. "My name is Endrance." He replied, nodding his head to the head guardsman.

He seemed unimpressed. "What's your purpose here in Fini?" he demanded gruffly.

Endrance smiled. "I am the Wizard Endrance of Wayrest." He stated, nodding his head at the man. "I come to the city to restock supplies before continuing my journey north. Would you let me pass please?"

The guard snorted as he considered them, his mustache bristling. He had seen his share of poor people hoping to make it big in Fini, but this was the first time he'd seen someone with the guts to attempt impersonating a wizard. If the kid was telling the truth, he was either far younger than any mage he'd ever seen or was of elven descent. "Great, another elf blood…" He grumbled, waving the two in. "Very well, welcome to Fini…" He turned away as the two walked their horses past the gate.

Endrance and Joven entered relatively unhindered beyond that point into the main of the city. Along the sides of the roads a great many buildings were packed end to end next to each other, so much so that much of the time there was literally perhaps a hand span's space between two buildings, if there was a gap at all. Every building was made from the same white stone, and almost every building on the main street bore a pennant with the kingdom seal upon it.

The streets were relatively busy, lit by torchlight, and the two were tired from their extended ride but needed to go about trading for supplies before they could find an inn. They searched around as they rode into the city, and eventually found a stable that satisfied Joven's standards. They housed the horses and took up a room at an inn across the street. The place was expensive, a gold piece for the night, but the room was large, had two beds, and had a bath they could use. There was even mention of a warm meal in the morning.

As they settled down, Joven took the time to strip off his armor and perform regular maintenance on his gear. Endrance sat on his bed and tried his best to keep his nose in his book, but after a few minutes of the barbarian taking care of his gear left him staring. The man had changed into a sleeveless shirt and clean pants, and left his dirty boots by the foot of the bed.

The young mage watched as Joven set a package the size of a loaf of bread to one side on the bed, and then began laying out his weapons. The greatsword was first, followed by his battle axe, his short swords, an array of knives, a pair of sickles, long daggers, punching spikes, throwing hatchets, a sap, and one odd looking club with three spikes on one side and iron rings around its haft. His eyes were wide with awe. How did the man manage to carry all that, much less hide half of it?

"That seems like overkill." Endrance said flatly.

"You don't have just one spell to kill your enemies with, do you?" Joven asked in reply.

"No."

"Why not?"

"Certain creatures may have resistances to particular types of magic, or they may be adept at countering certain spells. Having a variety of offensive magic can help you survive a fight if that happens."

"Well, that's why I do it."

"You've had enemies that are immune to steel?"

Joven chuckled as he undid the string on the package to the side. It opened up to reveal several corked jars and several tools that invariably had to do with cleaning and maintaining weapons.

"No, nothing I've ever met was immune to steel itself. But I have met some creatures that just got angry when you bashed it on the head, or had scales that could turn even the best of blades from it. I have so many different weapons to handle because there are so many different kinds of things I may have to kill them with." Joven took a cloth and one of the jars and carefully went over his greatsword before opening it and applying the oils that were in the jar.

"Endrance." Joven called his name, and when the mage looked up stared him in the eye. "If you want to learn more about this, then take out your knives and watch what I do. I will teach."

Endrance watched, and learned. It was the first lesson in something physical, and he had to learn to be careful handling the knives that Joven had given him: they were very sharp.

While they were working on cleaning the assorted arsenal, Endrance noticed that Joven had a dark mark on his neck that disappeared down his collar. He pointed to the man's muscular neck and called attention to it.

"What's that?" Endrance asked.

Joven touched the side of his neck and grunted. "Ah." He said. "Tattoo."

"A tattoo? Of what?" Endrance pried. He was trying to learn more about the man whom he was going to be trusting with his life. Learning about things like that might give him some insight into him and perhaps the people whom he was going to be working for.

"Oh. It's just my totem." Joven responded. "My uncle was good with ink and a needle, and I was pretty confident of my abilities." He grinned. "I didn't make a sound when he did it."

"Your… totem?" Endrance asked. "I've never heard of that before." Yet another time he pulled out the guidebook that Kaelob wrote and paged through it.

"In Balator, if you have enough honor, your family can ask the Spengur to divine their newborn child's birth totem, something that is set in the stars. It is a great honor for the king to allow the family to ask the Spengur for such a task. One's totem animal can tell you a great deal of their future, and only those who know their totem animal may go on a vision quest." Joven explained. Endrance found nothing about totems or their significance in the book.

"So how would you find the totem of a person after their birth?" The mage asked.

Joven shrugged. "One of the prior Spengur had made a drink that you could take that would grant you a vision. Many who had taken it had claimed that their totem animal visited them in their dream." The man shrugged, his muscles straining at the simple cloth of his shirt. "I do not know for sure if this works for those who have not been told their totem before, but whenever I take it I see it."

Endrance nodded. "What is your totem?" he asked.

"Bear." Joven said simply. "As it should be."

"Yes." Endrance said in agreement. "I couldn't think of anything more fitting for you."

Joven shrugged, having cleaned and maintained over half his gear. "Why do you ask so many questions about totems?" the barbarian asked. "Did you not know your own totem?"

"Sadly, no." Endrance replied. "We in wayrest didn't believe in totems and Kaelob never told me about that stuff." He shook his head. "Never even talked about that at all, now that I think about it."

Joven grunted. "I think there is still some of the paste that we mix in my pack somewhere. Let me check that for you." The barbarian put the sickle into Endrance's hands and went to his pack. Endrance noticed a plethora of tiny nicks and notches on the blade of the sickle. It looked like it was going to need some time at a whetstone before oiling. While the barbarian rummaged through his pack, the young man picked a thin whetstone from the tools pack and followed the directions Joven had given him. He tested a few brisk strokes down the edge, not along it, and seemed satisfied with the motion. He didn't even notice Joven look up from his pack and check to make sure he was doing it properly.

Joven returned when he had finished what he could with the sickle. As he handed it back, Joven dropped a small leather pouch into his hands. It seemed heavy for its size, and shifted as if a thick liquid was inside.

"You'll need some ale, or something to mix it in." Joven stated. "Go get some, and I'll keep watch while you go on your vision."

"Why ale?" the young mage asked.

"Alcohol makes the process happen faster." Joven said. "And taste better. Take it from me, you don't want to know what it tastes like mixed in water."

Endrance went down and found the innkeep as he was closing up the front. After some bartering and another of his precious few gold coins remaining he returned with a bottle of white wine. Joven quirked an eyebrow at the wine, but shrugged.

Endrance undid the cap on the pouch and squeezed the paste out into a wooden tankard from the cupboard in the room. It was a thick, brownish paste with black flecks and green strands in it, and it fell into the cup in clumps. The smell wasn't too terribly pleasant, an acrid and bitter odor that curled itself up in his nose and made his eyes water. He finished squeezing out the paste and poured in the wine until the tankard was half full, stirring the mixture with a wooden spoon. The wine did much to reduce the odor, but the drink was now a disguisting sludge color.

"Are you sure this is the right stuff?" Endrance asked. "It looks foul."

Joven leaned over and looked down into the cup and grimaced. "Yeah." He said gruffly. "Looks about right. Drink up."

Endrance held the tankard in one hand and tried to figure out how to stomach the concoction. If it tasted a fraction as bad as it smelled he was going to be gagging the whole time. He pinched his nose, held the cup to his lips, took a deep breath, and drank the contents quickly. It tasted horrible, and he almost spit it back up, but once it touched his lips it seemed to just slide down his throat into his stomach as if it had a mind of its own.

He stumbled to his bed and crawled up on it. He sat upon the covers and waited for the drink to kick in. He felt the drink sitting warmly in his belly, felt it coiled inside him. It seemed to start spreading through his body as the warmth wound its way through his legs, his arms, and then curled itself around his mind. The world seemed at once to become more intense, colors leaping out at him like they were being projected from their sources. Joven worked on sharpening the other sickle. The steady rhythmic sound of the whetstone on steel was soothing, and he felt like he could drift away in its beautiful noise forever. He started to taste the feel of the soft sheets beneath his palms, and it was sweet to him. He almost fell over despite the fact he was sitting, and had to prop himself up with an arm.

The air strummed at the beat of his heart, and… things flickered at the edges of his vision. He could feel the very meridian lines scribed on his skin pulsing not with his heart but with the flow of the world around him. He stared at his hand, watching the darkened lines of the two fingers on his right hand quaver and jump on his skin, as if they were trying to escape. The reddened scar like confluences on his back vibrated angrily as he breathed. He was starting to feel very uncomfortable.

He struggled up onto his knees, the shifting chaos of sensations around him making even moving difficult. His back ached sharply once, then again and again in an ever increasing frequency. He tried to speak, but only gibberish came out. Joven barely glanced up at him before returning to his work, no stranger to watching someone under the effects of the foul drink.

The ceiling started rattling, and Endrance stared up dumbfounded as the planks of the roof trembled on their rafters. White light shone from between the cracks and seams of the boards, and brightened before the boards resounded with a crack, and started peeling up into the light. As his eyes adjusted to the brightness, he saw only an endlessly distant sky above him, a brilliant blue expanse for which he could see winged figures flitting about the clouds in the distance.

A shadow fell over him, and Endrance looked up to see what had shut the suns away from him. Above him glided down a tremendous scarlet bird, with its wingspan so large it could block out both suns as it drifted down to land on the bed in front of him. Its feathers were brilliant scarlet, and towards the tips seemed to bleed into a fiery orange for which licks of flame danced every time the beat of her wings stretched them to full extension. As it landed its wings stretched out, blocking the suns but limned in their own fiery light.

It was easily large enough it could have scooped him up in its claws and carried Endrance away to a house sized nest if it wished. Endrance couldn't help but kneel in awe of such a powerful and majestic creature. The bird seemed to take in Endrance deeply with one brilliant burning ruby eye. Endrance could see himself reflected within the eye. But the reflection seemed strange to Endrance. The other him he saw had burning arcane runes spinning in a circular orbit behind him formed of burning, glowing lines of power. As he watched, more lines burned into place, forming a pair of circles, one on the inside of the runes and the other outside, bracketing them in a circular band.

The bird cried aloud, its shriek a chorus of hundreds of eagles that pierced Endrance's mind to the very core and filled his nose with the smell of burning cloth. Flames washed out from the bird in a brilliant coruscating display. Overwhelmed, he fell forward on his face and collapsed, unconscious.

He awoke, and the smell of burnt cloth still lingered in his nose. He sneezed and carefully pushed himself to his hands and knees. His body ached horribly. It felt like his bones had gone dancing without him and were just now settling back in from a long night out. His head was filled with a ringing sound and his heart pounded hard in his chest. The skin of his back burned like it had been lashed with a whip repeatedly.

He shook his head, and his vision cleared enough to see he was still on the bed, but it looked different. He stared at it for what felt like hours until he realized that it looked like the pattern of the cloth was scorched. He looked up, and blinked again in confusion.

Silently, the room around him was in complete disarray. While none of the furniture was broken, almost everything was knocked over or tilted on edge. The bedposts were blackened, and smoke rose in wisps around him. As he turned his head to the right he saw both the innkeeper and Joven standing by the door. It looked like the innkeeper was staring in shock while Joven barred the door with a mighty arm and mouthed something to him.

The ringing started clearing, and Endrance rubbed at his ears. No, his bodyguard wasn't mouthing words at him, he was actually shouting at him.

"Endrance! What happened? Are you well?" Joven exclaimed, his voice sounding strangely distorted.

Endrance tried to push himself up to just his knees, but dizziness overwhelmed him and he fell back on his hands again. He shook his head again, and crawled to the edge of the bed, falling on his face again on the floor. He stood carefully this time, gripping the scorched posts for support. He felt very much off balance.

"That… felt very, very real." Endrance concluded. He kept his eyes locked on Joven, as the rest of the room had a way of spinning around when he wasn't paying attention to it. Stupid room; it needed to hold still like the rest of reality.

"Endrance, what did you do?" Joven asked. This time his voice sounded almost normal, maybe only an octave higher. Endrance tried shrugging and fire shot up and down his back. He cried out, and fell to his knees.

Joven abandoned the door, and rushed to help him. "What happened to your back?" Joven asked, gripping the sides of his arms. "What did you do?"

"What?" Endrance asked. "I didn't do anything… I just did what you told me to. Was I casting spells?"

"No. You were sitting on the bed there and suddenly you glowed with those lights like that other time." Joven said. "Then suddenly it seemed to get even brighter and burst out from you like a flash fire. From it came some kind of push that knocked everything down, even me. And when I stood back up, you had that on your back."

"I had what?" Endrance asked, he craned his head to the side and looked over his shoulder. In the reflection of a nearby knocked over mirror he saw what the source of his pain was. The spell inscribed lines of his back had formed a miniature version of the circle he had seen in his vision. The lines etched in his flesh burned with energy it was draining from his aura.

Even for the scant moment he watched, the circle continued writing itself on his flesh, marking more and more elaborate arcane symbology into his back. As the pain increased in volume for every mark the spell scribing inflicted upon him, Endrance did the only thing he could think to do then: he fainted.

An hour later, he was conscious and aware enough to talk again.

"Does it hurt?" Joven asked. He had apparently smoothed things over with the innkeeper and righted most of the toppled furniture while Endrance was unconscious.

The young man sat on the edge of his bed. He had awoken an hour later, and by that point the circle had finished working itself into his skin. The lines no longer glowed with power, but were a dull orange-ish color that was slowly turning black each time he checked it. The meridians on his back had been forcefully changed and realigned, something that would have been mind numbingly painful no matter who the subject was.

Now the circle was dormant. His body still hurt; the aftereffects of the drink, falling on his face twice, and the muscle strain he inflicted on himself contorting in pain had left him exceedingly sore. He stared at the reflection in the mirror for moments, but did not comprehend what he was seeing. Only after a few minutes of staring at it did he realize that he was just too tired to concentrate on mentally discerning a reflected image of the arcane language.

"It doesn't hurt anymore." Endrance admitted. "Now I just hurt all over." Maybe he could get Joven to help him get a better look at the circle.

Joven grunted. At some point he had managed to convince the innkeeper to leave and that there was less damage to the room than initially thought. The barbarian had put everything back that he could, and dumped the few broken pieces of pottery and one mirror in a corner.

"I am almost afraid to ask." Joven began, "But what in the hells happened to you?"

Endrance attempted a shrug with minimal success. "I… I think I somehow inscribed a spell onto my back. While I was under the effect of that drink you made me take."

"Made?" Joven grumbled. "You wanted to have it."

"No, you're right." Endrance admitted. "But I had this vision of this amazing, huge bird with wings of fire and ruby eyes. Then when I snapped out of it the room was trashed and I was scribed."

Joven's eyes squinted suspiciously. "It was a firebird? A Fjallar?"

"Ja-what?" Endrance asked.

"Fjallar." Joven said carefully. "It's a fiery bird in our histories, the story behind has been passed down since the first days. Its presence was a symbol of great change. Some say the end of the world."

"Is… Is there a totem that the… Fjallar is represented in?" Endrance asked. "Because I didn't see much else during the vision."

Joven shook his head. "I do not know. You would have to talk to the Ergkinoa about it; they are the masters of our history and culture. I thought you would have ended up a field mouse or forest fox."

Endrance frowned at his bodyguard. "Field mouse?"

Joven grinned. "Yes." He held his hands together to indicate something tiny. "Very rare totem."

"I can imagine why." Endrance muttered.

"So what is this scribe thing you said you did to yourself against your will?" Joven asked. Somehow again he had managed to make what happened sound ridiculous to him.

"I'm not entirely sure." Endrance said after a long suffering sigh. "I can't get a clean enough look at it."

"Do you want me to hold a mirror for you?" Joven asked.

"No. It's something complicated enough as it is, trying to translate a reflection of it would be even more difficult." Endrance admitted. "How is your ability to write?"

Joven grunted. "I can't even see the symbols clearly. They're squirmy."

Endrance nodded. "Oh, right, I forgot about that. Maybe we can get an impression?"

Joven scrutinized the young man's back. "Well, looks like there was some bleeding. I think I can take a cloth and…"

The barbarian tore a square of the white inner sheets of the young wizard's bed, and laid the square across the mage's back. After carefully smoothing it across his skin, he peeled it off gingerly. The cloth stuck to his back over the areas Endrance had been scribed, evoking a hiss of pain as the cloth pulled up.

The barbarian laid the cloth across the top of one of the tables, letting the blood do what little soaking in it had left to do. Endrance grimaced when he stood, but was able to walk over to the table and sit down in front of it. When the cloth had soaked up the little traces of blood, Endrance flipped the sheet over so he could read it from the other side, so it would be like looking right at his back.

He was better able to make sense of the spell scribed circle now. From what he had been taught by Talos, having runes inscribed was a very rare thing; very few spells required them. Though his understanding of runes was only the basics, he could make out a few runes that copied over well enough to make sense of.

The circle had other arcane lines worked through it, and he wondered how drastically this had shifted his meridians. They had to have been stretched out, or expanded upon in order to make these lines and markings. The young mage tried discerning the purpose of the circle, but could only come to one conclusion.

"Well, it's not a spell." Endrance admitted after a long few minutes of scrutiny. "At least not a spell that is activated when I power it like the lightning spell scribed on me."

"Then what is it?" Joven asked.

"It's an ongoing effect scribing." Endrance stated. "Archmagus Talos had several of them but he said they were more costly, difficult, and painful to inscribe properly. Now I understand just how much more painful and costly it was."

"Costly?" Joven asked. "What did it cost?"

"As far as this is concerned, it cost space." Endrance replied. "I only have so much space on my body for spellscribing to work on. This circle covers all but the upper area of my shoulders and the lower part of my back. Talos inferred during his conversation with me that an ongoing effect scribed takes many times more space than a spell of the same power."

"Why?" Joven asked.

"It's complicated." Endrance said, not sure how he would explain it to the barbarian. "A spell is only active for when I empower it. An ongoing effect is always going to be active. It takes more lines and therefore space to make sure it remains active."

"Yeah. That sounds complicated." Joven admitted with shrug. "Is it going to kill you?"

Endrance was quiet a moment. "I don't... think so. It just hurt like I was getting skinned alive."

"Ah!" Joven exclaimed. "I knew a man who had almost had that happen to him. They managed to stitch the skin back on his arm."

"Really?" Endrance asked.

"Yes." Joven said with a chuckle. "His eyes were so big. I've never thought a man that strong would scream exactly like a little girl."

Endrance shook his head. "I don't know how to respond to that."

Joven shrugged. "Anyways. Get some sleep if you can. We need to get to work tomorrow getting our supplies together. We won't be able to afford another night here. Not after having to pay to replace the stuff you broke."

Endrance shrugged sheepishly, the pain having faded to an annoying itchy burn. "Sorry."

Joven smiled at him. "No. It was very impressive." He said in a congratulatory tone. "I don't think you could have broken half of that stuff otherwise."

"Right." Endrance said. "I'm going to try to sleep."

Joven merely nodded, and sank onto his bed and stared up at the ceiling. Endrance tore the remains of his shirt off and threw himself on the bed, laying on his stomach. The pillows smelled faintly of burnt cloth, and the top sheet had a large square torn out of it, but even so he was able to fall asleep in minutes.

Chapter 20

Endrance rode his horse hard, even though the layer of snow across the terrain and heavy snowfall made it incredibly dangerous to do so. He had lost track of Joven several long minutes ago, back when the howling had started catching up. The barbarian had urged that they take a fast pace once they left Fini proper and were passing through the snowy territory before they left the kingdom's borders.

For a while an occasional wolf's howl had been heard far and distant, wavering over the snowy woodlands that they trotted through. However half an hour prior they were startled by a howl that was close enough to shake loose some flakes from the pines that rose up around them. Joven then pushed the two of them forwards at a much faster pace, but the lone wolf's cry was joined by several others. It was only when their pursuers burst into view that they were able to see that it was a pack of wolfmen, not wolves, that hunted them.

Endrance raced his horse as fast as he would dare to through the pines as he tried to keep going in the direction that Joven had pointed out to him. The increasing snowfall and the uniformity of the snowy lands made it almost impossible to determine exactly what direction he was traveling in. They had not even seen the suns over the last several days since they had left Fini and traveled north of the river confluence the city sat on. They must have gotten off of the roads in the snow and the constant storms made it almost impossible to find any signal fires.

Even now, though his bodyguard had fallen behind, Endrance could hear the sounds of pursuit. Several animal grunts and growls trailed behind him as his mount dashed through the snow. Occasionally he heard the faint echo of hoof beats behind him, and Joven's battle cry would reach his ears, followed by the sharp yelp of an injured animal. His bodyguard was doing his duty, but some of the wolfmen had circumvented him and continued pursuing Endrance.

The young wizard leaned forwards into his saddle, and pulled the glove off his right hand with his teeth as he tightly gripped the reigns with his other gloved hand. The pale red tinged fur of the tiger's hide was a decent insulator from the heat, and if it was as tough as Joven said it might protect him from more than just the snow. He switched hands and pocketed the glove with as close to a snarl as the young man had the ability to imitate. At least he had developed a spell to alleviate the cold if he needed to.

The sounds of pursuit increased, and the occasional snap of a branch or rustling bush got closer, and Endrance realized that these wolfmen had the advantage of terrain and knew better these lands than Endrance ever could. At this rate capture or death would be inevitable. He had to get away from them somehow. Even a few dozen yards advantage could save his skin.

The wizard risked a glance over his shoulder, and was terrified to see three furry shapes rushing through the snow on four limbs, nimble in addition to their obvious power and muscular forms. From what Endrance saw, the wolf men wore armor and weapons like a human or elf or dwarf did, but their equipment seemed strange and more primal, made of roughly shaped metals and crudely cut leather. Their bodies were massive, bigger than the average human with shaggy gray and white fur that covered their skin. They had completely wolfish heads, and shaggy wolf tails that waved in the wind as they hunted him. Their eyes however had an intelligent quality to them, though they were filled with blood lust as they pursued their prey.

Endrance dashed his horse to the right, and then to the left, trying to shake the wolves as he sought desperately to escape their hunt. They were relentless however, and easily foiled Endrance's attempts at escape. His horse was breathing hard; the poor thing would be tiring soon. If the horse tripped or slowed too much he might as well give up now.

The young wizard knew that if he didn't do anything he would be brought down by these creatures. Though he was terrified for his life, he realized that he needed to act to save himself. Calling upon the reserves of magical energy within him, Endrance twisted in his saddle abruptly and cried out wordlessly as he pointed with two fingers at the leading wolfman that was pursuing him.

In his mind, he just channeled power through his fingers, and the spell scribed meridians on his body shaped the power into the correct form to make the lightning spell work. His bare hand crackled with power and lightning welled deep from his chest, down his arm, and to the tip of his fingers, where it leapt through the air at his foe. Which was why he'd removed the glove; He'd found out during his stay at Zadrah's hideout that the lightning would burn through any cloth or rope around his fingers, and he didn't want to ruin the only pair of winter gloves he had.

There was a sharp *crack* as lightning split the air. The dim wintery day was brightened tenfold as the snowy terrain reflected the light like mirrors and steam erupted in a line as the lightning vaporized any snow falling within a foot of its power. There was a spray of blood as the wolfman recoiled, his left shoulder nearly destroyed and rendering the arm useless as the lightning crackled through his body. Bloody droplets spattered the thickening snow and the sides of an elder pine tree as the injured wolfman thrashed painfully, tossing blood-flecked clumps of white into the air.

Endrance started to cast a second volley when he suddenly realized he had let go of the reigns and was not steering the horse. He snapped his attention to what was in front of him right as a large pine branch loomed in from the obscuring snow, crashing into him and cleanly unseating him from the horse. The young wizard saw stars for a moment and then white as he slammed into the snow covered earth.

The impact onto his back set the still healing lines in his skin burning again. Dazed and in pain, Endrance could not help but lay on the snow with the world spinning in his head. He saw a shadow dart past, a silhouette that was most likely a wolfman chasing down his horse. The disorientation started to clear when the other wolfman's form loomed over him. In a panic he scrabbled at the snow trying to push himself away from his canine assailant.

The wolfman carried a crudely crafted steel axe in his furry hands, and it stood upright on hind paws. The armor was crafted of bands of steel bolted onto leather straps which creaked in the silence of the snow filled night. Snow crusted the edges of the roughly hammered and nicked steel bands. Its fangs bared, the wolfman lifted his axe high over its head with one hand.

"Outsiders!" It growled through the sound of the windblown snow. Its voice was brutal, human sounding but gravelly and strange. "Begone!" it brought the axe down with dangerous swiftness. Endrance yelled in fear and desperately rolled to his right in an attempt to avoid the blow. The axe crashed into the ground with a resounding thud, kicking dirt and snow into the back of Endrance's head as he rolled to his feet.

The young wizard scrambled through the snow, the cold biting into his uncovered right hand. He had to get far enough away to hit him with his lightning, or else he was as good as dead. The wolfman snarled again, taking one step forward. Endrance kept the wolfman in his perception, stumbling back as it moved slowly but purposefully towards him. The faintly falling snow wafted around and through the warrior's ruffs of fur as he passed the trees and sparse shrubs. It was almost a serene scene, the young wizard noticed.

The wolf's step was sure and steady despite the invisible tangle of forest floor underneath the concealing comfort of several inches of snow. The way he carried the axe in his furred hand, the shrug of his shoulders as he both limbered up his arm for the swing as well as shift his armor to prevent it from impeding the lethal stroke. He was leaner than the mage originally had thought; thick fur covered ropey muscles instead of sheer bulk. Though the creature's snout and face was that of a large wolf, it had a very human expression. Unexpectedly, Endrance could see that this savage warrior looked regretful.

"Please!" Endrance shouted. "Wait!" He held out his hands pleadingly. "We don't have to kill each other! We can still make peace!"

The wolfman's left ear twitched, and his pace slowed a small amount. "Too late." The wolfman growled at him, his voice lighter than expected but still as gravely. Endrance was able to pick up what made this one's voice strange, it had a lilting quality to it that reminded him of a dog's whine. Perhaps speaking in human tongues hurt their throats.

"You have seen our Bastraum, and you have slain our kin." The wolfman concluded. "This time, there will be no peace!"

"Bastraum?" Endrance asked, but was only answered by the Wolfman's renewed charge.

As the wolfman's stride ate up the short distance the wizard had gained, he raised his axe over his head again with a howl. Endrance flung his hand out and called upon the reserves of power in his aura. The sudden discharge of electrical power sent the settling snow scattering from his shoulders as lightning was unchained yet again.

The wolfman lunged to his left, ducking under the crackling beam of power that thundered through the night sky. Endrance stumbled back as he tried to both adjust his aim and to believe that it was possible to dodge a lightning bolt. His heel caught on a root, and he fell backwards onto his rear as a sharp pain shot up his leg. The blunder saved his head, as the wolfman's swipe arced through the air where his neck had previously occupied.

In a blind panic Endrance threw more of his energy into his scribed spell. The still aglow spell form entwining the first two fingers on his right hand blazed into brilliance again. This time his fingers itched painfully and Endrance winced at the sudden change, but the lightning came forth with as much force and brilliance as before.

This time the spell was far too close to dodge even with his animal reflexes. The blast hit the wolfman square in the chest, filling the air around him with the smell of scorched fur. The lightning carried his foe several dozen feet away and into a tree trunk, his howl of anger cut short. Clumps of snow fell from the boughs of the tree, scattering around the still smoking form slumped at the bottom.

Endrance took a breath, then another. His head hurt from the fall off his horse, his hand hurt yet again from overusing the lightning spell, and he suspected he had twisted his ankle when he had fallen. He tried to rise, and after a moment of using a tree trunk as a brace he was able to gain his feet again. He stumbled towards the wolfman he had slain. He had come to rest against the very tree that had knocked him from the horse and had guaranteed a life or death struggle. He needed to try to follow his horses' tracks before the snow covered them up. As he approached, the stench of burnt meat and fur grew stronger.

He would like to think that it was morbid curiosity that led him to take a close look at what he had done. As he surveyed the damage his spell had caused, he realized for the first time that he had never yet actually seen the results of his magic. Sure, he had used the spell before, even killed before out of necessity, but he never had actually seen the effects it had in any detail. He knew it was effective, but every time before it had been dark, or he had to look out for others, or he was blindfolded... This time he had to see it, if he wanted to be able to follow the trail and find his horse.

The body was quite recognizable, though much of the fur across his front had been scorched black or burned away entirely. There was a neatly burned hole the size of the young mage's fist in the chest of his armor, and through which he could see a charred mess of burnt gristle and bone. The iron bands of his armor had heated white hot for an instant during the blast, and were now glowing a dull red as they cooled and cracked in the cold winter air. The body twitched, and the whole thing was just too much for him to handle.

Endrance dropped to his knees near the corpse and vomited up the simple meal he had consumed that morning. With the expulsion of his stomach contents there followed a wave of guilt that threatened to completely incapacitate him. This was a horrible thing he had done, and it was something done without a moment's reservation. He had snuffed out a living, breathing thing that could talk and might even have been able to reason with him, if he had just given him a chance.

The spell wasn't even the worst of what he could do. His master had taught him all manner of theoretical ways of using even simple magics to great effect. He realized just how easy it would be to kill someone. Even simpler for him, as all he needed to do was point and strike things down from afar with his scribed lightning spell. What if he stopped caring about things like right and wrong? What if he lost control?

He wouldn't. Endrance shook his head, wiping at his face with a handful of fresh snow. The cold felt good on the still tingling fingers of his hand, and he pulled himself back to his feet.

He could become a monster, a horrible magic using killing machine, but he chose not to be. He decided that this power he had been born with and trained to use properly was for him to use as he saw fit, and he saw fit to do good things with it. He could do great things with it. He would not let himself stoop to becoming cold hearted or abusing his power because he would be letting down all that he had the potential to be.

He didn't believe that he was meant to do wrong things. He couldn't conceive of it, but the ease in which he had utterly destroyed the lives of the enemies who had attacked him was a grim reminder that he could annihilate the innocent just as easily. He took a shuddering breath in the cold, but he could not look away from the reality of what he had done. He wouldn't be able to rationalize the power he had anymore; it was something he was going to have to come to live with, and overcome.

He turned to the body of the dead wolfman, and bowed his head towards the corpse.

"Thank you," Endrance said aloud. "You fought with your heart and I regret that we had to meet like we did. I learned something very important today because of you, but I would rather we both lived. I can never repay you for opening my eyes." He touched the two fingers of his right hand to his forehead, the same way that he had seen Joven do with his weapon any time he killed something that he hunted. The barbarian explained that it was a gesture of thanks, both to the weapon that it was true, and to that which had been slain by it. A faint smudge of ash remained on his forehead when he lowered his hand.

The wizard scanned the forest around, searching the snow for the trail of tracks to lead him to his horse. It was then when out of the swirling snow and weak winds that the third wolfman's form became evident to him. The beast man had been standing still as a statue in the snow, watching him for an unknown length of time.

The wolfman was larger than the last and had armor that was of cleaner, better quality craftsmanship. His body was as muscular as the other had only appeared, seeming much better fed and more experienced than the one who laid dead nearby. It had a straight sword made for chopping with a square edge, but it was still strapped across his back. The reigns to Endrance's horse was in one hand, and behind the wolfman was the shadow of the paint horse, standing skittishly but without panic.

The wolfman remained in his spot, but tilted his head as he considered the wizard before him. The wolf's eyes were surprisingly human and crisp blue like the sky on a bright spring day, and he regarded Endrance before him with an expression that was either curiosity or mild surprise. His ears were tilted in different directions, away from the general direction of the blowing snow, but there was no doubt he could hear the wizard speak from where he stood.

"You." The wolfman stated, his voice nothing like the one Endrance had fought before. It was smooth, rich, and utterly indistinguishable from a human's. "You thank your enemy for teaching you, even when he refused you peace? You feel guilt, even though he attempted your life? You would cry over the bodies of your enemies?"

Endrance watched the wolfman warily, but nodded. "He taught me a very important lesson about the power over another's life, and how it isn't something to be abused. I could have ended up seeking only to cause destruction like the kind he had sought for me, but I choose to be better than the worst I could possibly be."

The wolfman tilted his head further, but his attention was focused on his dead comrade, not the young wizard before him. "Yra'ag." The wolfman said aloud after a moment.

"Yra'ag?" Endrance asked.

"That was his face-name. Never forget the one who taught you what it was like to kill." The wolfman lifted his right hand for the mage to see. A claw mark like scar made a geometric pattern in the fur of his hand, indistinct in the snow but still enough to be obvious. "Those who have learned the lesson in our pack carve the name in our hand, so that we may never forget."

The wolfman hooked the reigns onto a branch nearby him. "Our pack was not meant to fight with your kind. You came within a few strides of our Bastraum-our home, as your language says. Our youth were too… Ga'th. Too hot headed. Those who have not given their lives to your warrior will be punished, and we will continue on our way."

The wolfman turned from him, walking quite humanly away. Right at the edge of sight he turned his head to take Endrance in with one eye. "I wonder if our pack and yours can really have this 'peace' you have asked for." And in an instant he was gone, a swirl of snow in the dim forest light.

Endrance shivered, approaching his horse. The horse seemed grateful for his company, and a quick inspection revealed no damage had been done. He mounted again quickly, and as he lifted the reigns his right hand twinged again painfully. He held his hand out before him, and inspected the injury to his fingers. The lines of his meridians were a reddish color. It looked as if it would be a while before they darkened back to the black lines that indicated the energy was fully dissipated.

He sighed and dug his glove from his pocket, putting it back on his hand before turning his horse back to look for Joven. It wouldn't be too hard, after the wolfmen called off their attack, the only things in the forest would be him and his bodyguard. Though the encounter with the wolfmen was unusual to say the least, they were still within the territory of the Ivory Satrap. They should be safe for a ways longer.

. . .

The Sha'hdi hated this area. So much snow and so much white meant she had to don white leathers, something that was not usually tailored in Salthimere due to their more tropical climate. Even in the temperate zones an assassin could wear black on any given day and expect to not stand out like spilled ink on linen.

Even so, she was finding chances to interfere with the young man more and more difficult. Not only was he getting better at defending himself and keeping himself out of trouble, the bodyguard had been getting more alert as time passed. Already she suspected that the barbarian had caught on to fact that she had been following them. Even though her talents and skills were far greater than any human could hope to achieve, she was not without hunger, or need for warmth.

She would have moved against the young man directly, but that was not what was needed yet. She would be free to directly assail him if… once he made it to Balator. She hadn't even needed to do more than kill off a few enemies that might have gotten the advantage over the two travelers. In this last encounter with the migrating pack of wolfmen, she only had to kill one of the pups that had attacked. She slipped up behind him as he closed on the horse the mage had lost and slit its scrawny throat before it could so much as howl.

She couldn't help but grin at her own skill. Wolfmen were almost impossible to sneak past conventionally. Even their pups had nightvision comparable to the elves, hearing sharper than any other race alive, and a sense of smell as strong as a hunting dog. Only those of her order had been able to reliably deal with wolfmen targets, a skill that fetched a great price when they were needed.

She was certain that the elder wolf had seen her as she disappeared back into the snow, as he came upon the horse at almost the same time that the pup had. It mattered not, the wolfman had policed the animal and was taking it back with him instead of killing it like the young one had been about to do. She trailed him a while before she was certain of his motives. Once he left the presence of the mage, he wasn't important enough for her to be concerned about.

She watched from an upper branch in a snow laden tree as the young man reunited with the barbarian and continued their journey north. The young man was progressing nicely. A little ahead of schedule, but magic was such an organic thing; it moved at its own pace.

Chapter 21

"What do you mean we have to go with you?" Endrance asked.

The soldier of the patrol that had caught up with them cleared his throat, his breath puffing through the thick wrap of cloth around his face. Only his eyes were visible from over the wrap and under the helm's brim. He seemed hostile, but not aggressive.

The soldiers who had come upon them as they made camp were easily identified as Ironsoul troops by their uniforms and kingdom emblems across their shields. They wore winter gear instead of the regular armor the soldiers farther south wore. Their armor was a heavy long coat made of an internal layer of fur and an external layer of leather. In between the layers were light steel plates that were inferior from the normal breastplates, but better than just leathers. They wore heavy fur gloves and boots, and their helms had a fur inner layer before the steel domes. Thick cloth was wrapped around the lower parts of their faces where their helmets failed to cover, and only their eyes were truly visible among them.

"I told you to come with us now!" the soldier repeated, agitation evident in his voice. "You have to come back with us to the fort for examination!"

"But... Why?" Endrance asked as he turned with the soldier and the seven other men at arms that had approached them as the two were setting up camp that night. Now the camp was half set and these men were demanding they start moving now.

"I don't have to explain it to you!" The soldier was practically shouting. The sword at his hip cleared its scabbard. "Come with us now or I'll just assume you're resisting."

The young mage kept his eyes on the tip of the sword as it wavered in the firelight before him. Endrance didn't even need to look in Joven's direction to know he had his hands on his weapons. The man probably had also plotted out in what order he would have to kill who so they could escape. Knowing him, he probably would succeed as well.

Endrance held up his gloved hands with the palms out to show he was being accommodating. The back of the right hand glove was now marred by amateur stitching, spelling out 'Yuraahg'. Endrance had no idea the proper spelling of the name and had to sound it out phonetically. Even if it was improperly spelled, its very presence was a grim reminder to him of what it meant to take a life.

If they had to defend themselves, the two would fight against these men. But Endrance hoped not to as they were men of Ironsoul, and merely doing their duty as best as they were ordered. Maybe there was still a chance to talk it through with them.

"Excuse me, soldier." Endrance stated as clearly as he could. "I am the Wizard Endrance, en route to the borders of Ironsoul, and I have done nothing deserving of arrest. But if there is reason to do so anyways then say it, and we will accompany you back to your fort."

At the mention of being a wizard, several men of the patrol blanched and exchanged looks. The one who had been doing all the talking only narrowed his eyes and took a step forward aggressively.

"A likely story." The man growled. "Now sub-"

Endrance had been preparing himself for this since he began his own request. He could already tell the caliber of the man before him, and figured him for the type of watchman who used his power and status to bully others who had to submit to the law. As the man showed that he wasn't going to be civil, Endrance already had all the power he needed gathered for the spell he was going to cast.

He thrust his left hand towards the snow around the man's feet with his fingers outstretched and he released the spell energy into the spell he was slinging. "*Deserpo!*" he shouted, interrupting the man, and the effects were immediately and drastically noticed.

While slinging the spell reduced its power by a fair margin, he had compensated with more than enough extra power to make up for it. The snow at the man's feet seemed to explode into an exponential amount of volume, forming a pillar of snow with the now frightened soldier within. In less than a second the snow compressed around the man, leaving him incased in a column of ice that kept him completely immobilized. The light of the fire Joven had made barely half an hour ago flickered through the column's crystalline structure, and glanced off the plate of the soldier's helmet within, creating interesting fractal light patterns.

By virtue of the spell he had spent countless weeks designing, it was meant entirely to be an immobilization method when he was in cold terrain. The words of power were arranged in such a way, and memorized the same, that one trapped within the ice was still capable of breathing so long as a fair bit of the ice was exposed to air as well. Otherwise he would have just sealed the man in his icy tomb; countering the spell would take longer than most men had air.

The rest of the patrol backed away fearfully, but had not broken ranks. If the mage had pressed his attack on the rest, they would have surely fled. As is, they held their weapons and shields at ready, and had fanned out, encircling the two that remained in their spots. Endrance turned to stare purposefully at the next closest man.

"Now, where were we?" Endrance said cheerfully. "I believe I was just stating that I'm a wizard with all that title entails, and would like to know why you want to detain me."

The man gulped, but put his weapon away. "Sir Mage." The man stated nervously, using the general honorary title for mages. "We apologize for offending you. We are only acting on our orders to bring in anyone suspicious within an hour's ride of the fort."

Endrance smiled, and held his hands out at his sides. "I was suspicious?"

"Well, you are travelling with a barbarian." The soldier stated. "Uh… Sir Mage."

Joven scoffed but said nothing.

"Even a wizard like me finds that a bodyguard can be extraordinarily helpful when I am travelling abroad." Endrance explained, choosing to not waste time trying to explain the whole of his story. "What is the matter?"

The soldier waved the other men down, and they sheathed their swords. After regrouping, the men sat down near the fire so they could explain in relative warmth. Every few moments one of the men would glance at the pillar of ice standing just outside the warmth of the firelight.

Endrance and Joven sat opposite, but Joven had enough foresight to start repacking their gear while the men talked to Endrance.

Endrance looked over at the man encased in the frosty column and asked aloud. "Do you think he's learned his lesson?"

The man who had spoken to him before stared at him wide eyed. "You mean he's alive?" he asked incredulously.

"Yes. I designed the spell to allow him to breathe, but I would wager he's getting mighty cold in there. I suppose he could freeze to death if he stays there much longer than the few minutes he's been trapped." Endrance replied casually. "I could let him out; if you think he's figured out I am who I say I am."

The men around nodded immediately. "Yes sir mage!" the new lead soldier replied. "Please forgive him!"

Endrance waved his hand in no specific direction. "Alright, please wait here."

The young wizard climbed to his feet, and plodded back to the encased soldier. He could feel the remaining energy in the ice he had conjured. Left on its own, the spell would be able to maintain itself until the summer suns came and the rest of the granted energy was expended keeping the ice formed in the heat. He placed one gloved hand on the ice structure and closed his eyes, feeling out the structure of the spell he had cast with his senses tuned by years of training.

The ice crystal was of his own construction, so he was very swiftly able to disassemble the spell to its breaking point. After a minute of concentration, he pulled his hand from the crystal, flinging it behind him as if he were tossing something behind his back. The spell energy rapidly vacated the crystal, flowing into his hand in a barely visible rush of gold tinted wind leeched from the ice and into his palm, sweeping up his arm and disappearing into his chest. Instantly the ice formed around the soldier reverted into a cloud of snow with a faint *poof* sound.

The soldier collapsed to his knees as a mass of snowflakes drifted down around him, dropping his sword and shield as he coughed and shuddered. Shivering, he looked around, confused and freezing. His eyes finally focused on the outstretched hand of the very mage who had frozen him, and his gaze followed his arm up to the young man's face, which smiled at him as he stared at the wizard with incredulity.

"Now," Endrance began. "Shall we try this again more civilly?"

He nodded. After a moment he realized that Endrance was offering him a hand up. He took it, and with some effort the young mage had him on his feet again.

"What is your name, soldier?" Endrance asked gently.

"H-h-hill, s-s-s-sir-r-r…" The soldier repeated through chattering teeth.

"Alright. Soldier hill, come sit by my nice and warm fire and we can discuss what the big rush was. Seeing as you're in no condition to travel quite yet I think we will have time to talk. Does that sound alright?"

The soldier nodded, his skin pale from the cold. Endrance helped him over to the fire, where he sat so close to the flames he risked falling in or setting his clothes aflame. Joven picked up the discarded sword and after examining it a moment, tossed it to the ground near the man who had obviously forgotten he had let go of it.

After sitting back down across from Hill and giving the man a few minutes to warm up, Endrance took a deep breath and lifted a hand to prod the man to continue. "You were saying something about the two of us having to go back to your fort with you?" he said.

The second man spoke up while Hill was still warming up. "There was a murder deep within our fort, and our commander told us to chase down anyone who might have been involved."

"All right, who was murdered?" Endrance asked.

The man sighed. "He was the regional tribunal."

Endrance raised an eyebrow. "Someone like that would not have been unprotected while within your fort. What was he killed by?"

"His throat was slit, sir mage. We found a bloody knife stuck into the desk just nearby the tribunal's body." The soldier shrugged. "Our commander has detained everyone in the fort and sent us out to check for others who may have been fleeing. We didn't really expect to find anyone, but there you two were, easily found by that campfire." He finished, gesturing towards the fire.

"Ah. I see." Endrance said. "If you would like us to come with you, I can understand you need to follow orders. But we have been moving in your direction, not away from it."

"Still, our commander would still want you to come with us. Being a wizard, he might even use your help."

"If you all insist, we will detour with you. But I have a duty to perform, and cannot tarry for very long."

"All I ask is that you come with us back to the fort. You can convince the commander to let you leave once you are there."

Endrance nodded, pushing himself to his feet and looking back over the camp. Joven had been hard at work during their conversation, and the camp was almost entirely repacked. All that remained was the campfire. Looking around, Endrance brushed snow off his trousers and looked down at Hill.

"When you're ready, we'll get going." He said.

Four hours later the eight soldiers and two travelers found themselves within the gates of the border fort. The structure was built of stone on the top of a large hill in the middle of an open field. It was built with three great square towers that rose above the walls, where many slits carved into the stone allowed soldiers to see farther than anywhere else within miles. The rest of the fort was squat and rectangular, rising only two floors but likely having at least one dungeon or underground storeroom.

Buried in the winter snows, the tower was nearly invisible in the blustery cloudy nights, where the visibility was incredibly low, even with the altitude advantage. Endrance was exhausted, cold, and sore from walking the horses through the storm and stumbling in the dark through snow blanketed obstacles. About an hour and a half in he realized he could make his journey easier by walking in the steps of the leading soldiers, but even then he still stumbled and was sure he had sprained an ankle but was too numb to feel it.

He had his warming spell, but it would only tire him faster and he had been uncertain how far they had to travel. They would have been able to ride up to the fort within fifteen minutes or so during the day and without snow, but with the conditions being as they were their journey had been excruciatingly slow.

Once inside the gates, Endrance finally cast the warmth spell he had devised before. Taking a deep breath and holding it so it warmed up a fair bit, he released the spell and shielded himself from the cold and snow. The snowflakes disappeared into flecks of water as they touched upon his aura and evaporated into tiny puffs of steam. He would warm up swiftly even if the commander were to have them thrown into a cold cell.

The soldiers within were dressed similarly to the patrol that had found them, and though only a few seemed to be awake or out at present, the fort was easily large enough to house a garrison of sixty men and then a dozen or so supporting servants.

The commander of the soldiers stationed at the fort was waiting for them when they arrived. Though he comported himself with the demeanor of a man who was unsettled by nothing, he was not so steely that he completely concealed his surprise when his men brought them in as an escort instead of as captives. As the group approached, a few soldiers who had been waiting nearby brought out tin cups with hot broth in them to hand to the men.

The commander approached the one who had led the squad that had retrieved the two travelers. Pulling the man aside, they had a quick and quiet conversation before the commander dismissed the soldier back to the group and walked over to the young mage and his bodyguard.

The man was tall, though not as tall as Joven. He wore a thick winter longcoat much like the other soldiers of the fort, but it had conservatively placed metal plates across the chest and shoulders on top of whatever was inside. The plate additions stood out from the rest of the men, but his helmet was the same issue as theirs, as was the sword and shield he wore on his person. As the man approached to talk he pulled the scarf from his face, so that he could speak more clearly.

The man from behind the scarf was an older man, with a thick, shortly cropped beard and mustache of black hair. He had a scar that started on his left cheek and went straight down across the edge of his jaw, leaving a pale cut through the hair on his face. Weathered and beaten, the older man was still in remarkable shape and his brown eyes had lost none of their sharpness. He looked the two of them over in an instant, taking in the entirety of their tired, cold forms as well as their horses, and came to the conclusions he was looking for.

"Sir mage." The commander stated stiffly. "I apologize if my men had handled you improperly. We do not seek to quarrel with a wizard of the circle."

Endrance inclined his head to the man, attempting a tired smile. "We had a small disagreement about courtesy, but the matter was rectified rather quickly. Think nothing of it."

The man grunted and nodded. "Very well. Please, accompany me to my quarters, and we can discuss the issue that is at hand here. Your man is free to follow, and …Private Hill will be tending to your horses with all the care we would give our own." The man glanced at Hill, who winced but immediately went to take the horses away. "If this is acceptable to you, we will see about scrounging up some food and drink for someone of your stature."

"Acceptable." Endrance agreed. The commander turned and led them into the central building from which the three towers rose. "I have a question." Endrance asked as they approached the large reinforced doors to the fort. "Why would Hill be in charge of those men if he was just a private?"

The commander kept his stride as he responded. "He wasn't."

"In charge?"

"A private."

The interior of the fort was very sparse, clean and nearly empty. The halls were simple stone, devoid of furniture or decorative wall hangings. The doors were sturdy, metal frames set in stone, with steel reinforced wooden doors set flush with the walls. The hard soled boot steps of the soldiers droned out the softer steps of Endrance's shoes and the rough textured boots that Joven wore as they followed the commander. The majority of the place was dark, and only the lanterns that hung from the ceiling at the intersections provided any light in the winter's night.

He led them deep into the fort, past several halls that were darkened even to Endrance's better than average night vision. The trip led to a door near the rear of the building, to a room that was far more warmly lit and furnished than the cold impersonal halls they walked before. The commander held the door open for the two, and closed the door as he entered.

The commander's room was not richly furnished, but it was well done. Thick rugs covered the stone floor, and a fire burned in a triangular stone basin in the corner of the room, built three feet up from the floor so one could sit next to the fire or adjust the wood without needing to stoop. A few feet of floor around the fire was bare of rugs, showing the same quality of stone that the rest of the building was crafted of.

Thick tapestries hung from the walls, many of which were of simple repeating patterns, pleasant, but not anything inspiring or thought-provoking. There was a bed in the corner next to the fire, a simple sturdy wooden piece with thick blankets and simple bedding. At the foot was a single trunk, where he would keep his few personal belongings. Little more than a dresser and mirror was against the wall between the bed and the fire.

In the corner opposite of the fire was a heavy desk of simply cut wood. Upon it were many pages of parchment, quills, vials of ink, books, a map of the local area, and a compass. Here was likely where he planned the movements of his men. Here was also where he wrote reports that were sent back to Ironsoul by courier or other means.

At the corner where the front of the desk met the wall was a pair of stools stacked on each other. As Joven and Endrance stood in the center of the room, the commander pulled out the stools and set them down in front of the desk, walking around it, he settled into a sturdy straight backed chair.

He pulled off his helmet and set it on top of the map, rubbing his temples as the two took their seats. His hair was short cut but a dense professional soldier style, black with streaks of silver that made him appear all the more respectable. He looked wearily at the two as he leaned back and took them in. Endrance and Joven sat quietly as they waited. While Endrance felt the urge to say something, he didn't know what to say.

"You can call me commander Gural." The man said after a short moment. Out of the distracting sounds of the winter night and the other men, Endrance could hear that Gural's voice was strong, commanding, and surprisingly soft. He also couldn't hear the usual fluctuation of tone that most people had when they were as tired as this man looked. That meant that he must have had some form of voice training like Endrance himself had. Interesting to be sure but not unheard of; military leaders can benefit from having fine voice control nearly as much as a mage could.

"Well met, Commander Gural." Endrance said, giving him a tired smile. "My name is Wizard Endrance. This is my bodyguard, Joven." He introduced them, gesturing to Joven as he mentioned him. The barbarian smiled a toothy grin, sitting at a false ease on the stool, his arms crossed.

Gural nodded as he acknowledged them, and placed his hands on the desk as he leaned forwards a bit. "I trust you have been told what has happened here, and why I ordered my men to bring you here."

"That is true." Endrance said. "We were making our way towards the border, and had just been settling down for the night when your men approached us."

"I understand that this is most inconvenient, markedly so for a wizard belonging to the circle." Commander Gural admitted. "But we have an emergency of some importance here and we needed to try and catch anyone in the area who might have been fleeing the scene." The commander leaned on his elbows and clasped his hands. "Would you be willing to tell me what it is you're doing trying to leave Ironsoul?" he asked. He had spoken softly, but it carried a quality that said his request would not be denied.

Endrance leaned back in his stool, and nearly fell over as he had forgotten these seats had no back and were narrowly built in the first place. Joven held a hand out without looking and caught him before he spilled embarrassingly. Red faced, the young mage murmured a thanks to his bodyguard and looked back to Gural.

"We are on our way into the untamed lands, to the barbarian capitol of Balator. There I will become their next Spengur." Endrance explained succinctly. "Joven here is to ensure I arrive there safely."

Gural took the information without changing his expression or breaking his analytical stare. After a few seconds of silence, Endrance was starting to feel uncomfortable with the man just staring at him. So he mustered up the small dredges of energy he had left and gave the man a genuine smile.

Gural sighed and sat back in his chair, wiping at his face with a gloved hand. "All right, I believe you." He said. "But before I could let you go I would be in poor conscience to forsake asking a wizard's professional help in this matter."

"Oh?" Endrance asked. "What kind of help could I be?"

"You wizards are all far better educated than ten of my men combined." Commander Gural replied. "You might be able to help us make sense of the murder, help us know who could have done it."

Endrance shrugged. "I would be happy to help when asked, but I am exhausted; I've been on the road all day and then should have been asleep hours ago. I can take a perfunctory look now and put my mind to it after I get some sleep."

The commander looked at him and blinked.

Endrance sighed. "I'll take a quick look tonight, but I need sleep or I'll make mistakes. That could be worse than if I didn't help at all."

"Ah." The commander said. "That will work for now. We've already moved the body so you can take a look at him tomorrow."

The young wizard thought for a moment of the blasted wolfman he had left behind earlier that day. He shuddered, but swallowed and nodded. "Sure. I can do that tomorrow."

The rooms that Endrance and Joven had been given were directly next to the room where the murder had happened. The room was barely big enough that there was room for a single cot, a trunk for gear, a small table and chair, and a similar fire pit like the one commander Gural had in his chambers, though this one was smaller and wasn't already burning when they were ushered in. Joven took the room closest to the victim's, and Endrance plopped into bed in the room next to that one.

He had looked over the room the tribunal had been killed in, but he had been so tired and worn out by that point that everything had become a long fuzzy blur. He had taken notes of things that stood out to him, but even as he stripped off his shoes he could not recall what it was he had written down. He sat on the bed and shucked his clothes, tossing them on the chair so the melted snow water could evaporate as he slept.

He checked the fire pit to make sure it had fuel in it, and lit it with a simple spell that most apprentices learn early on to ignite candles and lanterns for their master. As the heat from the fire spread warmth through the room, Endrance finally released the warming spell. The relief was immediate for him; it felt like a spiritual weight had been lifted from his shoulders.

He rubbed his back as best he could, touching the lines shaped into his skin by his meridians. He could almost imagine he could feel them under his fingertips, though he knew on some level that they didn't change the quality of his skin in the slightest. Even after the amount of time he had since its appearance, the purpose of the circle on his back continued to elude him. From what Archmagus Talos had told him, it was impossible to scribe an effect or spell you didn't know upon your body, and how perfectly you know the spell affected the spells efficiency and potency.

If that was true, what did he mark onto his back and how would it even work if he didn't know it?

Kaelob's education was very heavy in the basics and exploring what could be done with just those basics, but he only went into a few branches of advanced magic during Endrance's apprenticeship with him. He couldn't begrudge the man; Kaelob had always said that he wasn't trying to influence Endrance's education towards one branch or the other.

"I'm only building the foundation for your own tower of learning." Kaelob had told him. "That way, it's sturdy enough that you can build anything you want upon it and it would budge not an inch!" His explanation had a lot more gesturing and flailing about, but his statement was the sum of his reasoning.

As Endrance lay back on the mattress and started to doze off, he idly wondered if this circle came from the basics he had been taught, and he had just not recognized it yet.

He awoke without explanation a short time later, his breath coming hard and a trickle of sweat running down his face. He felt a moment of confusion. Were the goblins back? It almost felt like he had felt a beat of the goblin drum. He shook his head, and took control of his breathing. It wasn't nearly as hard to gain control of his panic, and he realized he didn't feel the familiar sensation of magic in the air.

He scanned the room, trying to find the source of his awakening. Nothing stood out to him. As he searched, the adrenaline spike of panic faded, and the exhaustion from the prior day seeped back into his mind as he found nothing out of sorts. He did find his gaze drawn to the depth of shadow in the corner across from the fire pit. A nagging sense of fear crept into his spine, a thin string of instinctual self preservation that tickled at his mind, barely felt through the fog of his nascent slumber.

"Hah." He mouthed, blowing air through his teeth. "Look at me, jumping at shadows like a child again." He closed his eyes as he lay back upon the mattress. "I can't let something like a little darkness scare me." He drifted back off to sleep a few short moments later.

Only then did the Sha'hdi relax. Cautiously, she melted out of the pool of shadows in the corner of the room, her predatory eyes fixed upon the young man who had nearly pierced her hiding place. She crept up to the side of the bed, as silent as a whisper of a single snowflake in a winter sky.

The kid had been sleeping fitfully when she gained entry to the room, but seemed unaware of her presence at first. She had stood there for several minutes as still as a statue as she watched the young man's near angelic features. Though not nearly as beautiful as an elven child would be, he had a quality of his face that reminded her of someone whom she used to know. The faint trace of elven blood in his appearance was noticeable, but hardly accounted for much, many male elves had dalliances with human women that they fancied for a few years and then discarded.

She had then considered her orders, and wondered if such a strange assignment was worth the price that was set. She was Sha'hdi, an assassin of the highest degree and of the closest intimacy; it wasn't in her nature or training to toy with her prey for even a fraction as long as she had with this one. A faint smile curled the corner of her lips.

After all, she had thought as she touched the grip of one of her lancet thin black steel knives, *it would be so easy to just execute him now, and his bodyguard would never-*

She had pulled the blade a scant half inch from the sheath when the young man had suddenly groaned and his eyes fluttered. She had slunk back into the shadows of the room, and with a simple thought had bent the shadows to conceal her. As she did so he had awoken with such speed and panic, it gave her the impression that such a simple application of natural magic had been like dropping an armload of steel pans.

Once concealed, she observed him until he fell asleep again. Now as she stood beside the bed once more she recognized one reason that she had been paid so exorbitantly to subtly harass the young man. He had potential, even she could see that.

The sha'hdi slunk silently to the door, listened for any foot traffic in the hall beyond, and then excused herself from the room. Perhaps some other day she would get to enjoy the pleasure of ending this mage. If he proved interesting enough, she might consider doing it at a discount.

Chapter 22

Endrance didn't sleep nearly as long as he wished he could. Still, a bed in a warm room was better than the nights out in the cold. His throat was definitely grateful, as he wasn't inhaling cold air all night long. He wouldn't have to perform quite so many vocal exercises before he would feel comfortable casting a spell. Last thing he needed to have happen was for his voice to crack or give out during a complicated spell casting.

He immediately regretted moving. His body ached from almost every conceivable spot, sore or bruised from impacts or even aching from pulled muscles. The day before had been very long in the saddle, and combining it with being hit off a horse with a tree branch at full gallop as well as a life or death struggle with a wolfman made it one of the worst days that Endrance could remember. He wearily rubbed his thin limbs as he tried to work out some of the soreness, and blinked his eyes multiple times as he gazed around.

The room had dimmed and the ventilation leaked cold air again, as the fire pit had almost entirely died down. Endrance wasn't sure what time of day it was, but now he was awake again he was too sore and aching to go back to sleep so soon. At least his mind had rested well enough.

Adding some extra wood to the fire pit, he heated a tin cup of water and steeped it with a pinch of his favorite herbal mixture. He sat quietly for the few moments the hot embers and newly lit wood did its work. Only after the aroma of the bittersweet herbs and oils wafted up from his cup did he see to cleaning himself up and getting dressed. His body protested the whole way, but he eventually got fully dressed in his spare set of clothing. He pulled the blood tiger hide winter coat on over his clean shirt and breeches.

This time he examined his hands before he went out. The day before he had overused his spell scribed lightning by not allowing the meridians time to clear. That had caused painful burnout that normally only happened when a mage used more power than they were capable of handling safely. The result was that his fingers were bright red around the zig zag lines in his fingers, as if he had burned himself with a small flame. They would likely sting for a day before they healed; longer if he had to use them again.

Outside, he found Joven standing waiting for him. He was dressed and armed and ready to go to war if it should happen to break out at this little fort in the middle of the snowy plains. He gave Endrance one of his signature grins, and patted him on the shoulder.

"Slept well?" Joven asked. "It's been a while since you've had a bed to sleep on."

"Yes." Endrance replied, wincing at the pat which reminded his sore body to speak up again. "I slept well enough, I suppose. How long was I asleep?"

"Over five hours!" Joven exclaimed. "Isn't that good?"

"Of course…" Endrance muttered. "I would have preferred a few more though."

"Bah!" Joven exclaimed. "You've been sleeping five hours a night for weeks now, you should be just fine."

"Most of those days," Endrance responded, his voice nearly a growl. "We don't fight for our lives and then stay up several hours later than usual."

Joven shrugged. "It has still been better than military service would have been. And we still have to finish here and then make up for lost time."

Endrance sighed, hanging his head with a frown. "Right. I'm still sore as hell though."

Joven shrugged. "You're new to fighting. Going to be a while until you get used to it."

Endrance scowled at him, his ache adding a little bite to his words. "First, I'd rather not have to fight like that anymore, and second-"

Commander Gural cleared his throat, alerting the two to his presence. Endrance snapped his mouth shut. He didn't need the commander to see them bickering over this or he might lose some credibility, which would be bad this early on in his career.

"Commander." Endrance began, nodding his head to him. "Good morning."

"Good morning, sir mage." Gural responded, raising an eyebrow. "Did you make any observations last night I should be aware of?"

Endrance shook his head. "Not yet. I've had a look around and kept some notes, but I'll need time to analyze it, maybe see if there's anything magical I can glean from the room."

The commander sighed but shrugged. "As I expected would happen. I've had my scouts out searching for anyone who might have escaped since the murder, and they have come back with bad news, but not related to this."

"That means one of two things." Endrance admitted. "Whoever murdered the tribunal either had a magical means to escape across the snow covered fields around the fort or…"

"The murderer is still here in the fort." Gural admitted. "And my other news might be worse."

"What's that?" Endrance asked. He was already getting the idea that the day may be as strenuous as the last was.

"One of our scouts found wolfmen tracks and a few of their corpses south of us." Gural reported. "There are a sizeable number of them inside our borders."

Endrance and Joven exchanged a glance. Gural watched them, his eyes narrowing. "But something tells me you already knew about that." He concluded.

"Of course we know about them." Joven responded. "Who do you think killed them?"

Endrance glared at Joven, but didn't say anything. Gural's face twisted into a snarl. "This is something you should have told me immediately!" He swept his hand out in the direction of the few of his men who had been standing alertly nearby. "Wolfmen inside our borders is a serious threat to Ironsoul! Even as a wizard you should know it is your duty to protect the people of our land!" His voice had risen to a shout, echoing down the stone halls.

Endrance winced, unused to people actually yelling at him. Joven took a step closer to him protectively. Endrance shook his head, waving his hand dismissively. "They were hardly a threat." Endrance stated evenly with a scowl.

"That's not for you to decide; after all you're not responsible for the northern borders of the Ivory Satrap, are you?" Gural shouted. "That's my decision whether or not it is a threat!"

Joven stepped in front of Endrance, his own temper rising. "Hey!" He shouted his face a snarl of anger. "We took care of the wolfmen! There's nothing left for you to worry about!"

"That just makes it worse!" Gural responded, his hands clenched into fists.

Joven blinked. "What?" he demanded. A silent moment passed, and Joven's temper cooled in his confusion. The anger in Gural's face vanished instantly, a ruse that seemed to have evoked the responses he was looking for. The corner of the commander's mouth ticked downwards, and he snapped his fingers.

"Among the dead wolfmen we found one of them that had been killed in exactly the same way as the Tribunal was." Gural stated, his volume lowering. "Now I have to take you both into custody, as you are the only ones who could have done this."

The men who had been standing behind the commander walked forward, hefting a pair of heavy crossbows and training them on Endrance. Joven lurched, his newly ignited rage being restrained by the fact that he couldn't get between Endrance and both shooters in time. Gural took a single step back and spoke in an even, level voice.

"Now, please accompany these men into our dungeon, so that there aren't any further incidents. If you aren't the murderers, then cooperate. If you open your mouth, mage, my men will fire upon you. If you do not do everything they say, they will fire upon you. Work with me, and we will try to get you out of here as soon as we catch the culprit." Gural made way for the four men who came to relieve Joven of his weapons, and the two who had their crossbows trained on the young mage kept the barbarian from retaliating even though he practically boiled in rage at this sudden turn of events.

Endrance watched this sudden change in a daze. Was this really happening? Was this just a dream? It sure didn't look like one to him. He kept his mouth closed and his hands pressed to his sides. One of the soldiers leaned down in front of the mage, putting his face on level with his. He held up a gag made of a latched bit of metal, wood, and rope. "This is for you to wear sir mage. If you would slowly open your mouth…" he said as he held the gag up to Endrance's face. The rope went into his mouth, the bands of steel on either side of his face kept it sitting around his head, and the iron latch in the back was locked so that it would be impossible to pull the thing off without biting through the half inch thick rope.

It took them only a few minutes to take them to the underground dungeons. There they had been locked into separate cells. Both were stripped to their boots and breeches, and Endrance still wore the gag. Though it was repulsive and he gagged every time he thought about it too much, he was able to breathe and he could still attempt regular speech. The gag was more than effective enough at muddling the precision of his lips and tongue when forming words of power, but he still could sound out basic tones without much hindrance.

The dungeon was dark, damp, and smelled of stale hay and stagnant water. A single fire burned in a fireplace on the far wall from the doors in, and the heat hardly spread across the stones into the four cells occupying the room. In between the cells was an assortment of torture and interrogation devices. A table with built in manacles was the centerpiece of the set, with barrels containing water to one side, and a smaller table with instruments spread across it on the other. The cells were walls of bars, spanning between the floor and ceiling on three sides, with the very solid stone blocks forming the back wall. One other cell in the room was occupied; a man lay on a wooden plank that formed the cell's bedding with his back to them, asleep.

Blood stains across the floor around the table had spread several feet in every direction, but looked long dry. Instead of any one travesty spilling enough blood to stain this chamber, the marred floor was a product of several decades of 'guests' being kept and questioned in the fort. It was one more depressingly nauseating reminder of where they were.

Joven couldn't pace the small cell, easily able to grasp the bars on opposite sides as he stood in the center. Instead he sat on the wooden plank of a cot and seemed to be lost in thought. The barbarian considered everything in the room that he could see, so that if it came down to it he could escape from there and break out his charge. He had been willing to entertain his charge's insistence on following Ironsoul's law, but now it was directly interfering with his duty to his own kingdom. He hadn't even seen this fort or it's people when he first crossed the borders into Ironsoul.

Endrance did pace the cell, nerves wracked and nearly hyperventilating through the gag. At first he thought this would be over soon, but now he wasn't sure if the commander intended on letting them out at all. As he paced he thought at first he could smell the blood staining the floor, his imagination given strength by the unknown.

An hour later, he was certain he could smell the blood on the floor. He didn't realize it, but his breathing had slowed, his pace stilled, and his eyes were wide open. Having fixated on the smell, the need to vomit had faded. Instead, his stomach rumbled and he realized how hungry he was. He had nothing to eat but his herbal tea, and while it did help stave off hunger, he hadn't anything to eat since the day before. He took another deep breath through his nose, and the smell of blood welled in his nostrils. It was almost as strong in his mind as if he had a bloody nose or lip, and for some reason it only made him hungrier.

Joven looked up when his ears picked up a low growl coming from somewhere in the room. It sounded like a cat of some sort was stalking prey, but when Joven looked up there was only the three people in the room. The man hadn't awoken, but Joven saw Endrance staring at the torture table in the center with wide open eyes. The young mage had a strange expression on his face. Joven had expected him to be afraid, but instead saw… yearning?

"Hey." The barbarian spoke up. The young mage didn't seem to hear him. By this point Joven could tell the low toned growling was coming from Endrance's throat. "Hey!" Joven said sharply, slapping his hand on the bars. Endrance twitched and looked at him with startled eyes. The barbarian was certain he had imagined that the young man's pupils had been slit right before the mage blinked at him and were normal, though they still did seem almost illuminant in the darkness of the chamber.

The young mage seemed disoriented, so Joven continued to speak at him. "Hey, Endrance… snap out of it. We're going to get out of here without a problem, just you see. Don't panic, we'll be out of here in no time, even if I have to break us out."

Endrance nodded, sank down to the ground and sat. The smell of blood had faded, and as he focused his thoughts inward he felt a familiar impression in his mind. The instinctual presence of the blood tiger had resurfaced, it's self assure confidence stepping in when his own instincts didn't know what to do. He shook his head, pushing it back down and retaking control. He had thought the presence had faded as time had passed, leaving only the information behind. Apparently either he was wrong or the strength of personality behind the subject affected the rate it faded, or if it faded at all.

He couldn't know for sure so soon; he had only seen the bracer absorb energy from two subjects, the goblin shaman and the blood tiger. He hadn't absorbed the energy from the wolfman, perhaps he had fallen too far away when he died. The same must be said for the thug that nearly carved his face up. At least he was able to figure out there was a maximum range of absorption.

Now if he only knew if the absorption affect was beneficial or detrimental. It didn't matter at the moment; they had taken the bracer off him when he had been arrested. Still, the knowledge he gleaned from them might be useful if he could just apply it to this situation…

The iron clad door leading into the chamber clacked as the bolt on the door slid open. A man in an insulated armor coat walked hesitantly in, followed by commander Gural. The door was closed behind them by a man guarding the door from the outside. The commander walked past the two cells Endrance and Joven were in, and stopped in front of the other occupied cell.

Rapping his hand against the bars of the cell, Gural tried rousing the subject. "Elf!" he exclaimed. "Wake up already."

The figure stirred, and rolled onto his back before sitting up. Endrance was uncertain why they hadn't noticed, but the other captive in the chambers was an elven man. As the nervous man stirred and fed the fire with wood, they were better able to see him.

The elf was willowy and tall, not quite as tall as Joven but couldn't weigh more than half of the barbarian, maybe less. Dressed in a well tailored tunic and breeches of violets and gold trim, the clothes were of exceptionally high quality, even after their rough treatment in the dungeons. He wore soft leather boots and gloves, the kind with a folded cuff at the wrists and ankles. They too were scuffed and dirtied, with a few nicks in them at the bends in the leather.

Only the clothes seemed to show any stress from the ordeal. The man himself seemed not only unperturbed by the experience but refreshed by it. He was of incredibly fair skin, and had smooth, angular features and his violet eyes were almost preternaturally clear like pools of glass from which he viewed the world. His face was serene, and his hair was shoulder length, and seemed to be perfectly straight and slinky despite hours spent laying on the boards that passed as cots in the dungeon, the hairs shifting over each other as he moved, straightening out on their own.

Endrance thought he had problems with people thinking him either beautiful, a woman, or both. If this elf was any example of the species, it was no wonder that humans wrote poetry of their beauty and grace. It at least made his heritage more understandable; who couldn't fall in love with someone if their kind was on average as good looking as this man?

Perhaps it was the lingering traces of the blood tiger in his thoughts, but something else about this elf told him to be cautious around him. Maybe it was the way that he moved as he stood, or how the elf carried his self when he approached the door to his cell, but something about how he moved reminded him of a great cat. Like all his speed and power was coiled up underneath a guise of grace and gentleness.

The elf stopped just on the other side of the bars from Gural. The corner of his mouth ticked up in a smirk as he addressed the base commander.

"I take it that you are finally through with this madness and are ready to release me?" the elf asked, his voice smooth and almost mocking.

If Gural was provoked, he didn't show it. The commander jerked his thumb at Joven before replying. "Got a pair of cellmates for you, play nice. One of you three might be the murderer."

"Oh most indubitably." The elf commented in mock sincerity. "I'm sure that you will get to the bottom of this so that the rest of us travelers can be about our business without any further hindrance."

"Quiet your mouth, elf." Gural snapped. "I still am not convinced that you are legitimately allowed to wander the kingdom unwatched or without escort."

"I provided you with the proper papers, didn't I?" The elf asked.

"Those can be faked." Gural dismissed. He eyed the man a moment, and then changed the subject suddenly. "Since you've been around the area before we picked you up, had you encountered any hostile creatures?"

"Picked me up… I suppose you could call it that." The elf jabbed. "But other than a few wild wolves and the occasional rabbit of extraordinary bravery, I'm afraid my journey was most uneventful."

"Wolves… or wolfmen?" Gural asked.

The elf didn't even blink, instead just quirking one eyebrow in response. "I get the feeling that you are trying to implicate me into something. Unfortunately I've never seen neither hide nor hair of a wolfman for years, not since my last journey through the north."

Gural sighed. "We're going to have to ask you to remain here for a little longer, until we can find the killer, until then, feel free to introduce yourself to these two." He turned to the far wall and gestured to Endrance's cell. "He's not supposed to talk, so don't bother."

The commander looked at the mage and his bodyguard and shook his head. "Do either of you have anything to confess?"

"Yeah!" Joven exclaimed, gripping the bars of his door. Endrance winced. "I have a duty to perform, and you're getting in my way of doing it."

"That's too bad." Gural responded.

Joven looked the man in the eye, his face a scowl that would scare the most hardened of killers out of their skin. The next few words came out as a growl, his voice at its most threatening. Endrance from his position noticed the elf take an involuntary step away from the bars separating their cells, though his expression seemed neutral.

"Let us out now or I promise you this will end very, very badly for you." The barbarian intoned. The commander's stern expression flickered with worry as the bars under the barbarian's hands creaked in his grip.

The other man in the room had made himself as unobtrusive as possible. Gural didn't balk, but it did take a moment for him to collect himself to respond.

"I can and will not!" he exclaimed. "Not only do I have a duty to my kings and country, but now you're threatening a commander in the army-"

"No threat." Joven interrupted. "Fate. It *will* happen."

Commander Gural drew himself up, and turned to the other soldier in the room. "No food for this one. Not yet." He ordered. "Perhaps an empty stomach will help his disposition."

The commander departed, leaving the three in their cells, and the remaining soldier nervously left a chunk of bread and a wooden cup of water within reach of Endrance and the elf's cells before silently excusing himself. Silence reigned in the room for a few seconds before the elf crouched and picked up his food through the bars.

"Always a charming individual, that man." He said, taking a bite of bread with perfectly straight white teeth. He sipped his water and swallowed the dry bread with effort. "And his hospitality is second to none."

Endrance picked up his food and stared at the dry hunk of bread and the cup of water and wondered how in the world he was supposed to eat it with his mouth gagged as it was. A moment passed and then he finally shrugged, giving up. He looked over to Joven's cell and saw the barbarian was watching him. He held out the bread to the man, and rolled his eyes. Joven watched him quietly for a few seconds, but nodded.

The young mage tossed the bread at the barbarian's cell, which Joven easily caught. Endrance tilted his head back and drank the water as best as he could with the gag. Some of it caught in his throat and he dropped to his knees coughing and sputtering through the rope. He again gagged, barely able to keep from vomiting.

"Hmm… that seems to be a rather cruel punishment to put a lady through." The elf commented.

Joven banged his fist on the bars of the cell between the two. "He's no lady! Aelfar!" he exclaimed. "He's a man, and a wizard."

"More like a boy, really." The elf replied, sitting back on his cot and eyeing the mage quietly. "But a wizard, hmm? How did they capture you intact? I've seen wizards that could bring fortresses like this down with a few minutes of effort."

Joven sighed. "We were guests here."

"I would like to point out that you still are guests here."

"Regular guests."

"Ah."

"But somehow they think we killed the tribunal when we were not even near the fort."

"Well, you have a wizard."

"What?"

"You have a wizard. He could easily teleport into the tribunal's chambers, cut his throat, and teleport back without too much difficulty."

"They… they can do that?"

"Of course they can. And they cannot discount his ability for his apparent age; the more powerful the wizard is, the longer they live. This 'boy' here could have been that apparent age for decades."

"What?"

"You aren't the most precocious of people, are you?"

"Not really. I find that hitting things solves most of my problems."

"What about the problems it doesn't solve?"

"I hit it harder, aelfar."

"Ah."

Endrance wished he could contribute, since much of the conversation was almost painful to hear without the ability to add to it. He let out an exasperated sigh and banged his head against the bars. It wasn't like he was completely helpless; he could still throw lightning if he needed to, and none of the soldiers in the fort could avoid the blast in their metal armor.

That wouldn't help him get the cell door open, nor would it help with fighting his way through the rest of the fort if they came at him in a concentrated effort. Nor would he be able to do anything about a decent archer with a well-aimed crossbow quarrel. He hoped he would have time to prepare better next time he gets captured by an army. He banged his head against the bars again. Wait, next time? He was too quickly getting acclimated to this adventuring lifestyle.

"You there. Boy." The elf caught the young mage's attention. Endrance lifted his head from the bars. "Mmmph?" he mumbled.

"So did you do it?" The prisoner asked.

Endrance shook his head, sighing.

"It wouldn't be your style, anyways." The elf replied. "Any mage powerful enough to teleport through barriers into an enclosed room wouldn't even need to cut a man's throat like that. They would have a dozen varieties of magic that would kill them just as completely."

Endrance looked at the elven man and let out a sigh of relief. Finally, there was someone who understood. The young mage shrugged and fidgeted with the rope. It was too tight in his mouth, he wouldn't be able to pull it away from his lips enough to allow him to cast a spell, but he could pull it far enough to relieve the pressure on the corners of his mouth.

"My name is Valzoa, heir to the Alastrel line. I do apologize for the quality of your lodgings." The elf said sardonically. "I would have cleaned up but it appears that our host has some issues with the rules of hospitality."

Endrance shrugged. The rope was abrading his mouth; he would be bleeding from this by the time the suns had reached their zenith. He hated the lack of control he had, as well as the ability to defend his position in the accusations against him.

"Alastrel line?" Joven asked. "Aelfar have bloodlines like we do?"

"Of course." Valzoa responded. "Though usually our bloodlines are very long lived. Mine happens to be one of the more affluent ones in all of Salthimere."

"Half a what?"

"Affluent. You could say I have more money than you could fit in this fortress, and that's just my portion of the gold."

"So your line makes money?"

"Collects it, really. What about your line?"

Joven puffed up his chest. "I am of the line of Rothel, bodyguards of the Spengur of Balator."

"Rothel?" Valzoa asked. "I'm familiar with the name, and the profession." He turned to consider the young mage in the cell across from him. "So this is the one who is supposed to be the next Spengur?"

"Yes."

"And if he is detained here or killed?"

"Then my family line will no longer be allowed to guard the Spengur, leaving the replacement with nothing but their Draugnoa for protection. My line is the last, and if I fail the line will die out with me." Joven stated grimly.

"You have an honorable task before you." Valzoa observed. "And as a noble of the elves, I hold that in high esteem. I can tell you've been honest with me, and I think you've just been caught up in some unfortunate circumstances. I wish I could help you get on your way somehow, but for the moment it seems that neither of us is likely to go anywhere."

The door out of the room unlocked and slowly opened, drifting fully open on its hinges. No one entered, and the three of them craned their heads trying to see what was going on. Nothing happened; no man entered, nor did anything else change. Nobody spoke into the room, and the only sound was the crackling of the flames in the fire pit.

Valzoa raised a delicately trimmed eyebrow. "Perhaps I spoke too soon?"

Joven had the best view of the door and the hall preceding it. Peering as best he could, the barbarian didn't see the two men who had been standing watch before. The hall was empty.

"I don't see anything." Joven reported.

The elf looked about the room, seeming to be searching for something. "We should get out of here."

"What?" Joven asked. "Wouldn't that just get us in more trouble?"

"What do you smell?" Valzoa asked, his eyes shifting smoothly from shadow to shadow.

Joven sniffed the air. Endrance was wary but curious enough to focus his sense of smell.

"I smell nothing." Joven responded angrily.

Valzoa glanced at the young mage and reached around to the locking mechanism of his cell. "Your young friend there seems to smell something significant.

Joven turned and checked on his charge, and saw Endrance was clinging to the bars, his eyes wide. The young man smelled something that made the fragments of instinct inside him go wild. In the wafts of air passing through the open door he distinctly smelled the smell of fresh blood.

Chapter 23

Valzoa fidgeted with the keyhole of his cell door, and after a few short moments the lock disengaged with a loud clack. The elf stood straight and gave the door a slight push. The door swung open with a loud creak, swinging wide open. He cautiously strode into the open room and looked around as he crossed to the mage's cage.

"Let me see if I can get this door open." He said, reaching for the door. Endrance stuck his hand through the bars and stopped him, covering over the lock with a palm.

"What?" Valzoa asked, looking up at him. Endrance turned around and rested the back of his head between the bars. The elf could see the lock of his gag shoved up to the cell bars. "Oh." He muttered. Valzoa grabbed a long thin needle from the torture instruments askew on the table and went to work. Joven tested the bars of the cell quietly. They weren't made of the best quality steel, and the years of being in an underground damp location had only helped reduce their durability.

Valzoa finagled the latch open, and the gag fell away to clatter to the floor. Endrance licked his lips and worked his sore jaw. "Thanks." He said, turning back to his rescuer. Valzoa peered at him impassively for a moment before nodding. Endrance felt that the man had been taking a close look at his ears and eyes. He must have seen the telltale signs of elven heritage.

"Any time. Do you need assistance getting out of your cell?"

"No. I will take care of that."

"Very well. I will attend to your barbarian friend." The elf conceded.

Joven grunted with effort as he applied his full effort to the bars of the door frame and the bars of the cell. He pushed against the door with one hand while pulling the bars of the wall it was anchored on with the other hand, his face turning red with effort as he mightily set to breaking out of his cell. The metal of the door's bolt was weaker than the bars, and when confronted with that much shearing force, groaned, and then gave way. The door jerked open, and then drifted slightly off center as Joven pushed past it, the door askew in its frame.

"Oh." Valzoa admitted with amusement. "It seems that my assistance is no longer necessary."

"Vexo." Endrance murmured; the palm of his hand against the back of the locking mechanism for his cell. The whole while Joven was working his way out of his cell Endrance was collecting his thoughts and judging the power he would need for the spell. The power he settled on flowed from his chest, out his mouth and down his arm to his palm.

Steel cracked in a sudden burst, and Valzoa leapt back gracefully as the cell door not only broke open but flung to its fully open position. The hinges creaked and gave out, dropping the door to the floor as Endrance surveyed the spell's effect. As the bars stopped rattling he stepped calmly out of his cell, a pleased smile on his face.

"That was satisfying." He admitted with a grin.

Valzoa watched the young man with a larger amount of respect than he had before. "That was a very finely controlled show of power there, boy."

Endrance glanced at Valzoa before waving Joven over. "My name is Endrance," he began. "And I am no boy; I am a man and a recognized wizard."

"That you must be." Valzoa acknowledged, bowing his head slightly in respect, an amused smirk gracing his expression. "Though I believe that we must take this conversation and put it aside for now, I fear that there may be something else we should be concerned for."

"I smelled blood." Endrance offered. "Fresh blood."

"Your sense of smell is better than I expected of someone with so little elven heritage remaining." Valzoa remarked.

"It's not that," Endrance replied. "About a week or so ago I... I absorbed the wisdom of a blood tiger. Ever since then I've been acutely aware of fresh blood when it has been spilled around me."

"You've drank from the ruby chalice already?" Valzoa asked, a perfectly trimmed eyebrow arose in question.

Endrance shook his head. "Is that what they call it?" he asked.

"Indeed."

"Then yes. I guess." Endrance admitted. "I'm still not sure how much I'm supposed to grasp, but it's only echoes and fragments."

"It would be." Valzoa agreed, guiding him over to Joven. "It's something that takes time to be able to control. Now can we focus on getting out of here alive?"

Joven stood at the doorway, his face pale. Outside, the two men who were supposed to be on watch were dead; one had been strangled, the other had been run through the eye by a narrow blade. Both had been quick, there hadn't been much blood spilled in the process. The strangled man's neck was wrung out like a single strong thread had been wrapped around and tightened. The key to the dungeon was still in the key hole of the door. There was no other sign of people in the hall.

"This is bad." Joven stated. "I didn't hear anything going on out there. They could have been killed right after the commander left, or moments before the door opened."

"I, too, didn't hear anything either." Valzoa admitted.

"Who could have done this?" Endrance asked.

"While I do not think it will do you much good, you two should arm yourselves." Valzoa suggested. "I have seen this kind of work before by reputation. There is only one professional that can do this much work so perfectly, and I am loath to accept it."

"What is it?" Endrance asked. Joven recovered one of the fallen men's longswords.

Valzoa took a breath and held it for almost two minutes before he replied. "This is the work of the Sha'hdi. The moon elves."

"The moon elves?" Joven asked before Endrance could say almost exactly the same thing.

Valzoa took the other longsword, and gave it an experimental flick of his wrist. The blade responded perfectly in his grasp. "How much do you know of the land of the elves?" Valzoa asked.

"Nothing." Joven responded.

"Only what Ironsoul has in the viridian satrap's libraries." Endrance stated. "So nothing I can verify."

"Shame." Valzoa stated. "The land of the elves, Salthimere, is a dichotomy in both politics and topography. The northern lands, the ones that lie closest to Ironsoul are the lands of the northwinds. There the Suo'hdi, the sun elves. We are the elves your kind has seen the most of. We're much nicer to you folk than our cousins would be."

"But Ironsoul is almost constantly at war with you all." Endrance stated.

"Precisely." Valzoa exclaimed. "While we're more focused on higher ideals and artistic endeavors, the Sha'hdi is much more cutthroat and cruel. They are the night to our day, our winter to our summer… Our balance. To them, their idea of artistic expression is how skillfully they can cause misery to others."

"That's… Pretty damn horrible." Endrance admitted.

Valzoa shrugged. "It is what it is. They do not kill or cause pain without reason, and they are quite capable of great deeds of good, but their society is too esoteric to explain in the short time I'm willing to remain in one place."

"Fair enough." Joven said. "How do we get to our stuff?"

"Good idea." Endrance stated. "I really need to get to my spell book. And my bracer. And those daggers."

"They put my things in the next room. We should be cautious. If we are still alive at this point, it is only because she wants us to stay that way for now." Valzoa directed them.

"She?" Endrance asked.

Valzoa stalked down the hall cautiously. "The poison blades are the best of their civil servants. They're all female."

"Civil servants?"

"Assassins."

That told Endrance all he needed to know about them for now. The three of them crept cautiously down the hall to the next door. The door was closed but not locked. Joven carefully pulled the latch on the door, and swung it open, the longsword in his hand ready to chop down the first thing to come at him. The room beyond was dark, but the lantern light from the hall illuminated the dim room enough that Joven could see that no men waited on the other side.

"There is no one here." He stated.

Endrance looked around the hall before entering the room. Inside he could see that there were only a few chests, a table and a pair of weapon racks. Almost the entirety of both racks of weapons contained Joven's equipment, the black steel blade of his greatsword glittered faintly in the light from the hall.

Valzoa went directly to the weapon racks and withdrew the only weapon that was not the barbarians. He held up a beautifully crafted rapier in its scabbard. A pearl handle designed to perfectly fit his hand, and fine gold and silver basket guard in the design of two beauteous sylphs entwined with each other as wind and leaves danced around them. The scabbard was a pure white wood with silver and gold detail following the same theme. A thumbnail-sized diamond was held between the sylphs, and many smaller gemstones were set along the scabbard. A sapphire the size of a robin's egg was set in the pommel.

He drew the first few inches of the blade from the scabbard, and the blade slid clear silently. The thin blade of metal was milky white, and gleamed brightly in the dark. Endrance could feel the trickle of magic coming off the unsheathed edge for the moment before Valzoa closed it and reattached the scabbard to his hip.

"That is a very valuable weapon." Endrance commented.

"Indeed." Valzoa admitted. "It is called 'The Dancing Lovers' in our language. One of five enchanted blades, each of a different element."

"Five?" Endrance asked. Joven had almost finished adding the weapons back to his person and strapping back on his armor that had been dumped in one of the chests. The barbarian handed the bracer and his pack to the mage, and Endrance checked through everything while the elf explained.

"The five elements? Wind, Water, Earth, Flame, and Life?" Valzoa asked. "They should have been part of your education as a mage."

Endrance clasped the bracer back on his arm, the familiar warmth of its presence comforting. "We are taught that there are only the first four."

Valzoa's mouth ticked into a momentary frown. "And yet again I am reminded in the flaws in your people's teachings. Life is an elemental force, as strong as the others, and sometimes stronger."

Endrance made sure he had the rest of his things before turning back. "I'll have to read up on that some other time, but at the moment we need to get out of here alive."

"Agreed." Valzoa seconded. Joven rolled his eyes and moved out into the hall, tossing the longsword back with the dead men and drawing his more familiar battle axe instead.

"We need to stick close and move quickly." Joven stated. "Stay right behind me and keep your eyes out for this assassin."

"You know the way out?" Endrance asked.

"Counted the steps." Joven stated. "I should be able to get us back up to the ground floor."

Valzoa stood in the back seemingly at ease, but his hand never left the handle of his rapier. The three moved down the hall, and Joven invariably led them to the steps up. The trip was quick, and they did not find another person nearby, nor any sign of them having been in the immediate vicinity.

They ascended the stairs cautiously in the dark. No one stepped out to challenge them; no blades came out of the dark to strike at them. They emerged in the better lit main halls, and found nothing out of sort, except that the hall was empty.

"Do you think they killed everyone?" Endrance asked.

"They?" Valzoa countered. "If it is a Poison Blade, then one would be all that is needed."

"That can't be possible; this place had easily forty men!" Endrance exclaimed.

"Forty men who didn't know she was coming." Valzoa stated calmly, his eyes peering into the shadows. "It might as well have been a single person. The thought they had the assassin resting in their dungeon, and let their guard down. What I'm trying to figure out is why she had slain the two outside our door but left us alone and alive."

"A good question." Joven interrupted. "Let's think about it later!" He waved them on angrily. "The lot of you would rather think this thing over instead of do something to save your lives." He muttered as he stalked ahead towards the doors to the courtyard. Endrance looked at Valzoa and shrugged. The man had a point.

They crossed several closed doors, but heard no activity. Several of the lanterns that hung at the intersections had been extinguished or were missing entirely. They found no signs of activity until the three made it out into the courtyard.

Snow drifted through the air, but there was no real snowfall to speak of. Scattered through the courtyard were at least a dozen unmoving forms on the snow. Joven and Valzoa took up defensive positions as Endrance brushed the snow off of one of the fallen men. He cleared the snow from the face of the soldier, and immediately saw the puff of fog coming from his mouth.

"They're alive!" he exclaimed, examining the body. "Unconscious, I think. Asleep."

"Good." Joven reported. "Let's see if our horses fared better."

"This is where we're going to part ways, my friends." Valzoa responded. "Go and get your horses and get out of here. I will take my leave through other methods."

"But how will you escape if you can't move quickly?" Endrance shouted looking back as he and the barbarian ran towards the stables.

"I hold the Dancing Lovers; their element of winds is more than just a sharp edge or quickened blade." Valzoa declared, drawing his blade. Even several yards away, Endrance could feel the aura of magic on the fully unsheathed rapier. He turned from the elf and followed Joven into the stables.

Valzoa closed his eyes and concentrated as he heard the two mount their steeds and guide them out of the fort's gates. He listened as the sounds of their horses faded off beyond the reach of even his enhanced hearing. He took a deep breath, and turned to a dark recess in the fort walls.

"I know you are there, Sha'hdi, you might as well give up the charade." He said aloud. His weapon held lightly yet ready in his gloved hand.

The shadows seemed to peel away from the assassin as she confidently strode out of the dark and into the open air. Casually she walked over the unconscious men with predatory grace and a lithe gait. Valzoa raised an eyebrow, but otherwise gave no indication of surprise. The Sha'hdi spread her empty hands at her sides and smiled broadly.

"You caught me, lord Alastrel." She said, sounding flirtatious. "Now what will you do with me?"

"Hmm… you seem to be aware of my identity, but alas, I do not know the pleasure of what beauty it is that's trying to end me." He returned coyly.

"You can call me Jalyin, of house of blades." She purred, walking in a loose circle around him, her hands gliding across her white leather armor seductively. "And I have no interest in your life, lord. In fact, I find you being alive to be much more pleasing to me."

"So it was not I you were after." He said.

"No, unfortunately." She responded with a wink. "A shame; you would have been a challenge to bring down."

"So is it the boy or the man you were after?" he asked.

Jalyin chided him, waggling a finger. "Now now, that wouldn't do to break my solemn oath to the Poison Blades, even for such a handsome stranger as you."

"So you think I'm handsome, huh?" he quipped. "Well since you are a Poison Blade…"

"Yes." She responded.

"And I am technically a lord of Salthimere." He continued.

"Do go on." She prodded.

"Then I would offer to pay off this bounty you have." He concluded. "You see, I had come to like that young man, and would hate to see him fall so soon in his career."

Jalyin exaggerated a frown, still stalking around him. "I'm so sorry, my lord." She began. "But you should know that once we have taken a job, we finish it."

"Unless you are slain or your employer is no more." Valzoa responded.

"I don't think even the inheritor of the largest banking clan in all of Salthimere has the reach to even touch my employer." The Sha'hdi observed, taking a step backwards as she spoke. "And I do not believe that trying to slay me now would be any more fruitful."

Valzoa studied her in silence for several seconds. The two locked gazes upon the other, and for moments that felt like hours, they studied the other's eyes. Valzoa broke the stare at last, shifting his weight and shrugging.

"That would be true, Jalyin." He concluded, flicking the tip of his rapier as he kept his arm limber. "It would be a shame to render such beauty asunder. And perhaps there is a solution that can at least help assuage my desire to assist them."

"Oh really?" she said. "So you think I'm beautiful, huh?" she returned. "And what solution would you offer then?"

"I cannot pay you to cancel your contract," Valzoa admitted. "But that doesn't mean I couldn't pay you to… delay a few days. Give them a sporting chance."

She smirked. "Ah, that would not be against my contract, since the details of my task are at my discretion."

"And that way I get to live, you get to live, and at least for a while longer, they get to live." He concluded. "Does that sound agreeable?"

"Agreeable enough." She accepted.

Valzoa used his free hand and disconnected a thick, bulging money pouch from his belt and tossed it to her. The assassin caught it with one hand. Her eyes never left him as her nimble hands swiftly opened the bag and felt their way through the pouch. She withdrew a few of the coins and held them out where she could see. The coins were two inch diameter electrum coins, with the engraving of House Alastrel's Treasury upon the faces. A small six sided ruby was set in the center of each coin.

"This is quite the amount." She acknowledged. "Are you sure the child is worth it?"

"Every day I purchase here is another day he has to become stronger." He stated. "And perhaps if he lives long enough, he would be able to save himself from you."

She gauged the weight of the bag, and the value of the coins. "Each of these is worth a few hundred pieces of gold."

"And there are twenty five of them in the purse." He said.

She tucked the coins back in the bag and attached it to her belt. "You have a deal. This is enough to distract me for some time, but not forever. I am paid more than this for the job."

"How long have I bought him?" he asked.

She considered. "I would ordinarily say three weeks, but since you've been such a fine elf to chat with, I'll make it a month, human days."

Valzoa nodded. "Then I will take my leave. Though beware; if I find that you broke my agreement-"

"Do not worry about such things!" she interrupted. "I am a Poison Blade. We never violate a business agreement once we have been paid."

"I have the ears of several in the king's court." Valzoa said, his voice more cheerful than threatening. "I would hate to have to report… poor job performance."

"One month." She whispered, already regretting making the small concession she did. "As you have paid for."

"Very well." Valzoa agreed. "I am off."

With that he whipped the tip of his rapier around him like one would trace a circle around them. He brought the blade up as he did so, and the snow swirled around him faster and faster as winds picked up in speed. He thrust the point of the rapier into the sky, and the winds lifted him up into the sky like a shot from a catapult, his violet and gold figure dwindling quickly into the distance.

Jalyin watched him take off with unconcealed surprise. The male had more than a few surprises up his sleeve after all. If he had mastered such a magic, she couldn't help but wonder what else he was capable of. Perhaps he could have beaten her in a straight fight after all. But why didn't he press the matter? She frowned briefly before disappearing into the snow.

Maybe he had been seriously flirting with her. It was an odd thing to consider; she only did so because her looks and actions could be distracting, and therefore gave her an advantage. Was it possible that he saw through the act, or was he just dense enough to think she was honestly flirting with him?

Either he was exceedingly savvy for a noble, or he was just a good actor. No matter what though, he had purchased the boy some time away from her attention. A month without her directing trouble towards them; after all he didn't need to know that she wasn't paid to kill them yet. She took one last look at the courtyard as some of the men started to stir. They would soon find that their prisoners had 'escaped', and would relay that information back to Ironsoul proper.

Now the boy wouldn't even be able to run home, should he try to escape from the things her master had planned for him. Everything was working out smoothly, and she made a large amount of money on the side. It sounded like the beginning of an uneventful month for the wizard.

Chapter 24

Endrance and Joven eventually found their way again, and continued to ride along their path. They had to keep moving and despite the cold and the poor weather; opportunities to camp like they did before were no longer possible. It was just too risky with just the two of them.

Endrance and Joven moved for as long as they could, and only set up a camp once the suns were both gone over the horizon. They found a small area that offered reasonable enough coverage, several trees grew closely against a small snowy hill only a dozen feet tall. They built their campfire on the other side of the trees from the hill, using its size to cut the wind that blew at their backs while they had been riding.

Endrance sat against the trunk of a tree, watching the lazy drift of snowflakes as Joven dragged several branches cut from nearby evergreen trees together to make a basic shelter. They had tents, but they needed to be able to abandon the camp quickly in case more wolfmen came upon them. Joven tossed the branches he was dragging up to the campfire and scowled.

"I don't know how well protected we are going to be tonight." He started, observing the night sky. The clouds were scattered and snow was drifting lightly from on high. "If the assassin is as good as that elf was saying, she'd be able to find us without trouble." He concluded. He started assembling a lean-to so Endrance could get some rest.
"You know it would probably be safer if we split up after tonight. Tomorrow I'll make a big distraction, draw anyone's attention away from you, then make my way to Balator on my own." The big man commented offhandedly as he finished tying together several spread out branches, making a shelter of green pine needles that if anything cut down the chilly air and caught the snow. "I am better able to take care of just myself in these dangerous situations, and if it would get you out of danger that would be even better."

Endrance shook his head, tossing a faint glitter of melting snowdrops into the air. "No, Joven." He denied. "I don't know how to survive in the wild like this, in foreign territory, by myself." He huddled in his winter clothes, trying to stay warm. "Besides, I wouldn't know what to say or do once I actually got to Balator. That part is also your job. No, it would be safer if we moved together on this."

Joven shook his head, drawing his axe and producing a sharpening stone. "Suit yourself, little one." He looked up at the night sky. "Then I will need to wake you early in the night, and have you look out for assassins while I sleep. I will be no good to you exhausted."

Endrance accepted. "Fine. I can do that." He crawled under the lean-to, and lay on his bedding. Pulling the blanket over him and wrapping it around himself as best he could, he tried his best to sleep. He lay there a while, able to see glimpses of the campfire and his bodyguard through the boughs of the improvised shelter. The precise, methodical sound of stone sliding against steel as Joven sharpened his axe was almost hypnotic. The snow blanketed everything, and the other thing Endrance realized as he drifted off to sleep was exactly how quiet things were. He imagined as darkness slipped across his vision that he and Joven were the only people in the entire world.

He didn't dream that night, but instead kept almost waking up. The night was so cold, so quiet, that the littlest noise or change in environment seemed alarmingly distinct. His sleep was one of being only barely warm enough to drift off, but too cold to become comfortable. He fitfully slept for several hours when he was awoken roughly by a strong hand.

Endrance startled awake, ready to dash for safety when he realized that his bodyguard was trying his best to gently wake him. He looked up at Joven and at the night sky, and blinked away the drowsiness. It was still very dark out, and the campfire had fallen low. Joven looked tired, dark bags beneath his eyes. He also couldn't conceal the faint tremble through his body as he shivered slightly. Even with all the furs he had donned when it started snowing, the cold would creep through all his body heat.

Endrance pulled himself out from under the blanket and shelter, and pulled out his book. Opening it, he turned his head to Joven. "Get some sleep, I'll watch out for now."

Joven nodded assent, and crawled under the shelter. "Oh good," he said. "It's still warm in here."

The young mage flipped through the pages and sat quietly near the dying fire. While he could see fairly well into the woods with the limited moonlight provided by the slightly cloudy night, the fire was also warm and he needed that much in order to stay alert. He held the book in his left hand, using a finger from the same hand to keep the page. With his teeth he pulled the glove off his right hand, tugging at one finger at a time until it was loose enough to take off.

The young man dropped the glove in his lap and flexed his fingers in the cold winter air rapidly, trying to move warmth back into their bones. Once he felt confident he could twist them in the correct patterns, he quietly mouthed a few words of power, his right hand changing position and closing and opening fingers in the precise order required. He finished his brief chant and pointed with his right hand at the dying campfire. He couldn't even feel the draw on his reserves of magical energy as it flowed from the spell formed in his body through his hand, and jumped to the campfire.

The burning coals and embers immediately burst up into a full crackling campfire. Their flames flickered with blue and white as the flames were not fueled by wood but with magic. The area around him lightened, and he felt the heat of the fire increase satisfactorily. Glancing around, he found there were in fact a few pieces of wood set nearby the fire. It was likely Joven had set them aside for him to use.

He tossed a few pieces of wood into the fire, so that when it ran out of magical energy to burn it would still have fuel to keep burning. He would have to either find more wood for the fire later in the night, or just fuel it with the spell again. He smiled, realizing that the little wizard's trick he used was the first real use of his magic during his journey that was purely helpful. He slipped the glove back on his hand and resumed keeping watch on the camp.

He could probably cast the spell in his gloves, but their thick and bulky nature would make certain hand gestures difficult. Movement was incredibly important for wizards, as it took a flexible body as well as mind in order to cast difficult spells. Most combat spells were simple enough that in war mages could go into battle wearing some decent protection without it interfering with their combat spells. Anything more elegant than a fireball or blast of lightning however, and the mage would have to at least shuck his gloves. Most wizards preferred to go unarmored in any case, as armor was constricting and uncomfortable and there were spells that were far more protective than a piece of metal. Endrance laughed to himself as he thought about it. He supposed wizards were a spoiled bunch, indeed.

He stared into the dark of the trees around him, and wondered how many forests like the ones he and Joven had been traveling through were there in the world. This forest was different from the one he grew up near, with evergreen trees instead of deciduous, and the space between individual trunks was much further apart. Every animal seen here had a winter coat, grays and whites. Most were either very large, like the creature Joven called a moose, or very small, like snow rabbits.

His stomach growled then, and he realized that neither he nor Joven had a chance to eat during their escape from the dungeons earlier that day. He put his book down next to his pack as he dug through it, retrieving a small pouch that contained smoked and dried venison. Finding the meat too cold to eat, he skewered it on a stick and left it near the fire for a few minutes while he looked around some more.

The trees around him were quiet, and now that he thought about it he realized he didn't see any of the signs of wildlife around him that Joven told him to look out for. The area was genuinely empty. He felt a sense of creeping unease pass through him as he turned around to survey the entirety of the camp. He saw and heard nothing. The horses remained crowded near the campfire, their reins loosely tied to a stick set in the ground.

He plucked the now heated venison from the stick and chewed on it as he continued to try to find the source of his suspicions. He came back to the hill, and thought he could climb up on top and get a better look around. Finishing off the chunk of meat with a hard swallow, he packed up his book and carefully crept around the trees next to the hill. He took his first step on the hill when he then realized what his subconscious mind was telling him was wrong.

The first thing he noticed now that he was in mid step up the hillside was that his boot slid on the hill's surface before finding purchase. Stepping back and kneeling down, he carefully wiped the several inch thick layer of snow from its surface. He was expecting grass, ice, or even rock beneath the layers of fallen snow, but not white, thickly pebbled hide. Looking up slowly, he realized the hill was in fact very slowly, very subtly, shifting up and down. It was sleeping.

Fear shot up Endrance's spine. Terrified, he carefully, slowly backed away from the sleeping mound. He got several feet away from it when he finally broke and scrambled back around the trees to the campfire and the shelter. He squatted down near the fire and thought fiercely, uncertain what needed to be done. *A hydra!* Endrance thought. *How in the god's names did we miss that we set up camp next to a sleeping hydra!*

He didn't know if they hibernated, or just dozed for a few hours at a time. What he did know was that if the thing woke up any time soon, they would not be long gone enough for his satisfaction. He crept his way over to the shelter, and patted Joven's booted foot as gently as he hoped to. "Joven!" he whispered, "Joven wake up!"

To the barbarian's credit he woke up instantly alert. "What is it?" he responded, and Endrance could hear the sound of a knife being drawn from within the shelter. "The assassin?"

The young man glanced back through the trees. The hill still hadn't moved.

"Worse." He whispered back. "A hydra."

Joven jerked from where he was laying, almost spilling the shelter over as he wormed his way out from under it. "Where?" he half whispered, looking around in panic. "How did one sneak up on us?" he asked quietly.

Endrance jerked his head towards the snowy hill nearby. "We snuck up on it." He responded, looking very worried. "Do they hibernate or just sleep?"

Joven made an uncertain face. "I don't know! I only see them when they're trying to kill us!" he whispered angrily. "We should get out of here. C'mon."

They carefully grabbed up their gear and tossed it on their horses. The horses hadn't had a lot of rest, but they had no real choice.

Endrance was kicking snow into the fire when his boot caught a branch that had been buried in the snow. It broke with a loud piercing *Crack* that resounded through the night air, and chunks of burning wood scattered across the campsite. He winced, and the two of them slowly turned to look at the pile of snow nearby.

The hill was still at first, but their hopes fell as the snow shifted. The hill rose higher, and sheets of the snow slid off it as the Hydra rose to its full height. Joven and Endrance stared up at the beast as its eighteen foot tall shoulders towered over them, and three draconic heads rose from the snow on long, muscular necks. The three heads looked around angrily, and one almost immediately spotted them. The other two turned to orient on them immediately and fins on the sides of their heads fanned out as they screeched at the two humans in unison.

Joven and Endrance looked at each other, shared a grimace, jumped on their horses and bolted. Snow kicked up from their mounts' hooves as the horses needed no encouragement to flee for their lives from this foe.

The hydra screeched again, its cry echoing out across the snowy woods. Endrance could see the sound shaking snow off the boughs of the trees ahead of them as it lurched into pursuit. The thing was eighteen feet tall at the shoulder, easily forty-eight feet long from tail to the farthest head. It propelled itself along at them on four heavily muscled and long clawed limbs. Its white pebbled hide made it almost seem to blend into the snowy land around it as it charged after them.

Endrance couldn't help but wonder if this was a good example of his life to come. He kept his eyes on the forest in front of him as this time getting knocked off his horse would be surely fatal. He could hear it behind him, and even hear the thing's breathing as it chased them down. The two riders parted around a small cluster of trees, and Endrance's hopes fell even further when the hydra crashed through them rather than slow to go around.

Joven looked over at his charge and shouted through the din of hooves and encroaching monster. "Endrance!" he shouted, "Break off! I'll lead it away!" he swerved his horse to the left, shouting at the hydra as he waved his axe. Endrance watched his bodyguard leave in a panic. He couldn't leave his friend to die like that. He also waved his arms and yelled as the hydra started to veer off after the barbarian.

The maneuver actually did work out slightly in their favor. Two heads remained focused on Joven, while the third turned towards Endrance. Not able to split two ways, the three fought for control of their legs, slowing the monster a small amount as it stumbled.

Desperate he tore off his glove, and after a split second to aim at the great beast's bulk, let fly a blast of lightning. The spell worked as it was intended to, charring the hydra's hide, and all three heads whipped around to snarl at the young mage.

"Endrance! No!" Joven shouted from the other side of the beast. He wheeled his horse around as the hydra came to a stop, reorienting to go after the pest that burned it. He slammed his axe into its holster, drew his greatsword, and charged at the beast. Endrance launched another lightning bolt at it, scoring it across the neck of its rightmost head.

One of the heads saw Joven's charge, and the leftmost one snapped at him as it flicked its tail at him. Joven saw the head dart in, and swung at it as it came in, gashing its maw and deflecting its bite, but the tail hit its mark slapping against the barbarian's chest. The hardened leather armor cracked and he was unseated and flung from his horse in an instant. The barbarian crashed through a snow covered bush and skidded to a stop a dozen feet from where he was before.

Endrance could not see what was happening on the other side, but he could tell Joven was actually trying to fight the thing. The hydra was hesitantly trying to follow after him, as it was dealing with attacks from both sides now. Endrance rode his horse far enough away from the beast to keep out of reach and he released a third blast. Three blackened patches burned against the hydras hide, but would be mosquito bites compared to the thing's size.

He was being careful, timing his shots to allow his scribed spell to 'cool off' after each blast. The cold winter air seemed to help greatly, but even if that wasn't a problem he was taxing his reserves of power. He would have to figure out a way to kill the thing quickly.

Joven pulled him self up from where he landed, still keeping a grip on his greatsword. He reset his grip on the weapon and charged in to attack the thing. He had to keep it from killing his charge; that was his sworn duty. He rushed in, his sword swinging at the head he knew would be coming in to bite him. He felt blade bite into flesh and bone, and cold blood sprayed across his face and armor. He had managed to lop the lower jaw of the left head clean off, and it was screeching and flailing around in pain. Joven saw the tail sweep in this time, and leapt up into the air. The bony protrusions on the end of the tail just barely missed his boots, and he brought his sword down on it as it passed back under him.

Endrance saw the thing's tail sweep over to the other side of the hydra and come back suddenly missing a few feet off the end. He smiled; that meant Joven was still alive. The center head had been trying to decide which morsel to eat and now turned to the right head, screeching and nipping at it. Together the total number of heads turned towards the barbarian on the other side.

It seemed to Endrance that even if he used fire there was no way he would be able to burn it enough to keep it from killing his friend. He had to figure out a better solution. In fact, the only spells he knew that dealt with fire at all were his...

Endrance tore the glove off his left hand as well. He figured he could try it. He weaved his hand gestures like he did before with only his left hand, intoning the words of power in gasps as his breath came harshly. He finished the spell, pumping a significantly larger portion of his magical energy into the spell than before. Instead of releasing it right away, he held tentatively onto the energy of the spell as he thrust out his right hand and held his left over it like he was trying to shield his face from it. He released the spell as he channeled one last blast of lightning.

The world went white as thunder pierced the night. Light, piercing and brilliant, shot through the air and hit with tremendous force against the hydra's hide. Endrance couldn't see anything, nor could he hear anymore. All he felt was the sensation of nearly every drop of energy he had left draining out of his aura, through his body, and out his hands. The fingers of both hands burned for only a second before going numb, and he was afraid he could have burned out the meridians in his fingers, or worse yet outright destroyed his hands.

Joven was cast in sudden shadow as thunder and lightning pierced the night behind the hydra. The blast of lightning punched into the monster's body, causing it to fall onto its side as the heads convulsed. Ashes and black charred blood rained down around the hydra as it thrashed in agony before it finally fell still.

"Joven!" the barbarian heard Endrance's voice shout from the other side of the beast. "Let's get out of here!"

The barbarian ran to his horse, which had faithfully remained nearby but still as far away from the fight as it dared. Jumping on, he kicked its sides, and they shot off into the woods. He found Endrance blindly riding his horse away from the dead hydra in the same direction as he. They met up again as they left the beast behind, who would be in no condition to give chase if it did in fact survive such a powerful stroke of lightning.

He whistled at Endrance as they rode silently into the night, trying to get as much distance as they could. "I have to say," he commented as they rode on. "That was pretty impressive! It takes at least ten of us to hunt down a hydra of that size." He gingerly felt along the cracks in his armor. Nothing felt broken fortunately. He looked his charge over, and found he was only holding the reigns loosely with his left hand and his right arm hung limply. His pupils had shrunken to pinpricks

"What happened to you?" he shouted as their horses bounded through the woods. The young man was plainly coping with a lot of pain as he rode along, biting his lip as he struggled to return his bodyguard's look. "Did the hydra get you?" he asked, ready to slow the horses down and help him.

The young mage shook his head, wincing. "Burnout!" he blurted, "Happens when you don't cast spells the way they're supposed to be cast."

The young man raised his right arm with obvious pain, and Joven winced as he saw the young man's right hand was scorched, blackened along the fingertips and burned raw all the way to his wrist. An injury like that would be crippling if he needed to cast any further spells. His fingers were awkwardly held, as if he wasn't aware of their presence.

"Gods, boy!" the bodyguard exclaimed, and Endrance dropped his hand again. Letting it hang in the cold snowy air felt much better than trying to move it, and he was not about to try and test his body's ability to recover from burnout quickly. It might take him years to recover, if he recovered at all. While it did work, in retrospect amplifying the lightning spell seemed like a dumb idea. Couldn't he have just put more power into the spell through the spell scribed?

He shook his head and let Joven lead them, feeling too drained to do anything else but hold onto the reins. Whenever he over charged the lightning spell that was scribed on him he burned his fingers anyways. At least he had tried to find a workaround. He winced again as his back twanged in pain as well. He must have pulled something on top of nearly destroying his hand.

They rested for a couple of hours, neither of them actually sleeping. They continued their journey when the suns rose, and they made their way through trackless forest utterly exhausted. The gods had mercy on them as the entire day and night after the attack from the hydra was uneventful. They rested as best they could, and continued to travel as fast as their supplies and the terrain would let them.

A full two weeks later they finally broke out of the northern forest, coming out onto a great snowy plain. On the horizon a mountain range was visible, and in it the capitol mountain of Balator. The biggest of the range, it was easily half again as tall as any of the other mountains. This far out from the kingdom, they were only able to find a farming community, and after wearily dropping silver pieces for a room that would have rented for copper, the two finally were able to rest knowing they had made it into the barbarian lands. It was of far more relief to Joven than it was to Endrance.

Endrance sat in a wooden chair at the farming community they had found. It had been only a day since they rode into the place, ragged and tired from the constant moving and fighting. He told Joven he needed a full day to rest, and the bodyguard was too tired to disagree. The farmers had been more than gracious enough to help them, and gave them a room at their house to sleep in and offered them a place at their table for their evening meal. Joven's family was apparently well known in the barbarian lands, and they gave him these things out of respect for his family's work.

He carefully flexed his right hand as he looked it over. The burns looked much better after two weeks of healing, but he had no idea how much the cold had affected his recovery. His hand had gradually returned to a pinkish color, with red blotches that spread across it and it no longer hurt to move his arm. The fingers still twinged in pain when he flexed them, and the swelling still hadn't gone away entirely, but he could feel things with them again.

What bothered him was that the scribing on his finger had gotten more complicated. The zig-zag lines and spellwork that had been the completed lightning spell now had additions to their work, making it slightly more complicated than before. The marks now came completely to the tips of his two fingers, and converged into little black dots at the points. The completed lines ran all the way down that half of the palm and back of his hand to his wrist, where it faded away.

The young wizard took to heart the lesson he learned that cold night. Spells can be made more powerful when overcharged with energy, but burnout could cause serious damage. When he put too much energy into the spell, he was overloading the conduit the spell flowed through -- his hand. His body was not capable of safely channeling a spell fueled with that many times more energy than should be done. If he had tried any more energy than that he would likely have lost his hand.

In all it showed him that he was overly relying on the one spell he had scribed on his body. He reached over his shoulder and gingerly touched his back; The only spell he knew how to use. From the small amounts he was able to figure out from his meditations, the spell on his back required enormous amounts of power. He was afraid to try it out without knowing more. Given the situation of how he got it and the damage he did to the room he was in, it was entirely possible he could break something or someone testing it out.

Endrance pulled out the hydra hide book that Kaelob had written. He felt a part of his mind go back to that night with the hydra now, and he pushed the thought from his mind. He opened the cover of the book, and began studying his master's notes on the barbarians he would be working for.

Most of the barbarian lands were snowy plains and mountains. The barbarians gathered in tribal towns, each group of them trading and fighting with the others around them. Many tribes lived in cities or townships scattered throughout the barbarian lands. Their biggest city was called Balator, and there the largest and most powerful barbarian tribe resided. Ruled by a strong king, and with armies of warrior men and women, Balator was the established capitol of the Barbarian people. The people of Balator were the essence of what most civilized people thought of when someone used the term 'barbarian'.

Balator was currently ruled by a powerful king, a giant of a man named Kalenden. He had taken power when his father died two decades prior, while Joven was just a child. The strongest tribe in the barbarian lands by right gains control of Balator, and over the last three generations it had been held by Kalenden's lineage.

Endrance had not seen much of the barbarian culture personally, but from what he saw in Joven he was having some of his perceptions altered. His bodyguard was strong and definitely a huge man, but he also had the intelligence and a sense of justice that was stronger than some of the 'civilized' people Endrance had met. He saw things as they were, and made decisions about things he observed concisely and he accepted the consequences of his choices without hesitation.

Altogether, he hoped the bulk of the people he would be meeting would be like that. He could see by watching the farming community they were staying at that they were normal people like those who lived further south. This northern part of the continent was large, but wreathed in winter for all but three months of the year and was considered scarcely inhabitable by 'civilized' society. Even Ironsoul, the kingdom closest to the barbarian lands, kept only an outpost-fortress there and that was it.

From Kaelob's notes, the people were incredibly superstitious and many of the common folk followed many strange rites and observed many strange taboos. Endrance noted one of Kaelob's cases where he found a man working a field with a large mouthed bass tied to the top of his head via twine. The young mage was going to have to learn to be more open minded about what people thought made a difference in magic. He was just glad that Balator actually had healers with real experience healing, instead of some kind of superstitious medical practice. He would not want to have a trout on his head on top of a cold.

Endrance was interrupted by a knock on the door. He closed the book and cleared his throat. "Come in." he said, shifting in his lighter clothes. His winter gear was getting scrubbed clean, after having worn it for weeks on end it had been in bad shape. Even the hide of supernatural creatures could get filthy if you wore it for long enough.

An old woman edged into the room. She was the mother of the family that lived in this house, and her wizened and wrinkled form was proof that she had worked a great many years of her life at the farm. She looked at him and bobbed her head. "I drew a bath for you, poor dear. You still look chilled to the bone." She said, ushering the young man up and out the room. "Come, the water is nice and hot!" She all but shoved him out the room. He tossed his book on the chair, and let her push him out mostly because he found he really enjoyed the idea of a hot bath. As she was moving him, her hand touched the back of his shirt, and he felt the meridians on his back tingled and itched at the same time. Endrance walked jerkily as the contact both tickled and felt incredibly strange to him.

The woman must have felt something, because she let out a short hoot and addressed him again. "Oh dear," the old woman said, "Who did that to you?" she asked.

Endrance shrugged, wriggling his shoulders, trying to get her to stop touching the circle on his back. "I kind of did it to myself... could you please stop poking it?" he said, glancing at her. "It tickles a lot."

The old woman laughed as she turned him back around. "Youngsters these days, so eager to earn their battle scars." She shook her head as she continued on. "There's no honor in self inflicted wounds, dear."

She pulled open a door to a room in the center of the farmer's house. The center of which had a stone bath which was about eight feet across inside. The bathing room had a fire in a fireplace nearby, and the wooden planks around the bath had splashes of water across them. A large wooden bucket was nearby, set aside and empty. There was a shelf on the wall holding a few sparse cleaning soaps.

The old lady let Endrance in and then said. "Go ahead and get soaked, dear. Your boyfriend will be here in a few minutes." She smiled kindly at him and started backing out of the room. Endrance turned to her as she was shutting the door.

"Excuse me, but I'm not a girl!" he exclaimed, worried.

"Whatever you say, dear." The old woman continued smiling as she closed the bathroom door, leaving the young mage alone.

"Great." Endrance muttered as he pulled his shirt off and folded it up. He set it on an empty shelf nearby. "The old woman thinks I'm a girl." He kicked off his shoes, setting them on the shelf as well. "Fantastic."

He stripped down, and stepped into the bath. The water rose as he sank in, the edges of which lapped at the wooden planks around the bath. Quickly his agitation faded as he felt the cold melting away from him. He had been out in the cold weather for so long that he had been chilled to the core, and even though he had slept in the warm room last night he still hadn't warmed up all the way through. He let out a sigh of relief as he could feel himself starting to relax.

He had closed his eyes for a few moments, and heard the door open behind him. He looked up to see Joven walk into the room. The barbarian glanced down at the young man in the bath. He quirked an eyebrow at Endrance, "How's the water?" he asked. The big man was wearing light winter furs, which he was already in the process of stripping out of.

Endrance looked at the big man, then the bathtub. "Uhh..." he stammered, "The water is hot, but I don't know how I feel about sharing the bath." He looked away from the barbarian as pants were shed. "The old lady already thinks I'm a girl." He finished.

"Oh?" Joven said, climbing into the bath. The water welled out over the floorboards. As he settled in he floated a bar of soap over to the young mage. "That will likely happen a couple more times before we get to the capitol."

Endrance carefully glanced at the barbarian out of the corner of his eye. The angle of the water and the poor light from the fireplace obscured him seeing anything immediately offensive, though he felt incredibly uncomfortable in the situation. "I... don't know how to feel about taking a bath with you, Joven." He said, grabbing the soap and gingerly washing his injured hand. "I've bathed alone since I was a little kid."

Joven shrugged, rubbing his shoulders and neck with a bar of soap. "Too wasteful out here. Drawing and heating water takes time and work, better used if it gets more than one person clean you know." He scrubbed his underarms, and nonchalantly interjected "I had to bathe with my three brothers all the time when I was young, then with the men I trained with in Balator as I grew older."

Endrance began carefully cleaning himself. He was sitting half tuned away from his bodyguard in the water, and was trying to scrub his shoulders when he realized just how much they ached. "Ouch!" he exclaimed rubbing at his own shoulders. "I really need to get a good look at the spell on my back." He admitted.

Endrance had finished bathing and was stepping out of the tub when the old woman entered the bathing room. She stopped and stared at Endrance's naked tattooed form as he froze when she entered. She stared at the markings on his back in silence, and his embarrassment drove him to cover up.

"Uhh..." Endrance said, reaching out and grabbing a towel off the peg it hung on with an awkward smile. "I guess I'm done with the bath." He concluded lamely as he quickly covered his decency with the towel. He looked up and remembered his tattoos. He laughed nervously. "I'll... just be going back to my room. Ok?" he said, grabbing his clothes and boots and squeezed past the stunned old woman. After he left, she turned to look at the barbarian who remained comfortably in the bath. He looked up at her and shrugged. "Kids these days." He said with a smile. "Always so decent, you know?"

Endrance quickly dried off and dressed in his room, and sat in the chair again while he tried to think of a way that the situation didn't feel horribly awkward for him. That night when they sat down with the family for dinner, he could feel them staring at him the whole time they ate. While he silently ate his meal, he thought about what had happened. The woman had been shocked not just by the way his body was marked, but he had seen recognition in her eyes as he had passed her leaving the bath.

While the barbarians didn't condone their people practicing magic, that didn't mean they weren't ever born with the latent ability to become mages. She was likely someone who would have been a possible apprentice when she was young. This could work for him.

As dinner was finishing up, he turned to the old lady. "Ma'am," He started. "I need to talk to you in private after dinner."

"Oh no, dear." The old woman objected. "I have much to do cleaning after the meal."

Endrance looked at Joven pleadingly. Joven looked the woman in the eyes and frowned only slightly.

"But my daughters can take care of that tonight." The old lady corrected. "If a son of Rothel insists that I talk with you."

Endrance talked to her for a while, and eventually got her to agree to help him. In one of the rooms Endrance sat facing the back of the chair, his shirt off. The woman sat at a table behind him, several sheets of parchment set across the surface. She had one of his quills and a bottle of black ink. He dozed half asleep and comfortably full and warm for the first time in weeks as she fastidiously copied every line and mark of the circle on his back over four pages of parchment.

He had chosen her to help because she was the only one in the household who had the ability to write and draw, as well as her latent ability meant that the arcane script wasn't as likely to shift or squirm under her eyes. While she didn't have the education to understand it, her natural connection to magic would help her grasp the image of the language of power enough to copy it down.

After she was done and the ink had dried, he carefully examined the script. It was intact, and quite legible. For being an old lady she had remarkably steady hands. He thanked her and offered her another silver piece, which she only reluctantly took before scurrying away to her family.

The next day Endrance mounted up with bleary eyes and sluggish movements. He had been up studying the symbology later than he intended, and was unhappy to have to get moving so soon. He was able to systematically identify some of the properties of the spell, but he was not finished yet. All he had garnered was that it took a steady supply of energy from his aura to do… something.

Together they rode in a odd silence, having now spent enough time around each other to not feel awkward not saying anything but the occasional word to each other. Endrance had started to look to Joven not just as a bodyguard, but as a true friend to him. Over their journey they had spent some time before sleeping talking with each other about whatever it was that came to mind at the time, and Endrance really started to feel that he had made a connection with his bodyguard.

Several more days passed, and many of them were much more comfortable than their trip through the border territories. They occasionally got to sleep at a village or outpost along the way, and Endrance got to see more of the barbarian people and their culture. He was surprised that it was in fact true that many men were nearly as large as Joven. Even some of the elderly barbarians who had lost quite a bit of mass to age were larger and of bigger build than Endrance knew he himself ever could be.

He noticed however whenever he entered an outpost that he never saw any women among their rank and file. Endrance, after having waited until they were quite a ways away from any possible eavesdroppers asked "Joven, you said that even the women are trained to fight. How come there aren't any women in the troops?"

Joven shrugged and patted Endrance on the back, nearly knocking him off his horse. "Well Endrance, the womenfolk are trained to fight by their fathers and brothers, but only men join the military. Women do enough duty to our people by producing strong sons and fighting to defend their homes when we're attacked." He winked at the wizard. "We do have a company of all female volunteers though, and they are a sight to behold." He grinned. "Beautiful warrior women, clad in armor and bearing the swords of their fathers or lost loved ones. If that isn't the ideal woman, I don't want to know what is."

Endrance realized then that even though Joven had basically said that women were really only good for raising children and keeping a home, that the women living in Balator were given more rights than most ever had in other cities. Their people considered it enough of a service to their people that they bear their children and keep their homes, while other societies would think that those tasks were the only things they were good at. It made sense then if a woman had the might of arms to prove that she could fight then she should be allowed to. At least here they could pursue those things without drawing discrimination, and if Joven's distant far off look was indication, gathering some admiration as well.

"But what if the women really want to serve in the regular military?" he asked. "Can they?"

Joven nodded. "It's uncommon, but it happens. You may see one or two occasionally in Balator itself. However you should be careful not to aggravate the ones with red hair. They are cursed women and must be avoided."

Endrance knew that the people of Balator were incredibly superstitious, but that seemed extreme even for them. He had read about many places that shunned others who had certain traits that they found either unappealing or were signs of being evil or cursed.

"So," Endrance began "Because someone has red hair they are cursed? That seems very hardhearted of your people."

Joven blinked in surprise, looking as if he was confused about what Endrance had just said. "What, you haven't seen a redhead before?" Joven asked. "They are indeed cursed."

"I have seen people with red hair before… and they were completely normal." Endrance countered, gesturing with a hand at a farmer in a nearby field as an example. One of the older men had a head of copper colored hair. "Like that man there. Is he cursed, just because he had red hair?" he asked. The man, realizing that people were talking about him kept glancing over his shoulder at them as the distance between him and the two lengthened.

Joven glanced over his shoulder at the farmer, winked as he caught the older man's eye, who quickly turned his attention back to the field in front of him. Turning back, Joven scoffed as he jerked his thumb back over his shoulder. "That man? That's not red hair. Sure it's kind of red, but I mean color of a man's-fresh-blood red hair." He said, "You run into a woman with hair that red, you very well will be in need of a god's help should you anger her."

Endrance was still puzzled. "Do they have a temper then? Is that it?"

The barbarian looked at him sternly as he spoke, "Those folk, with hair as red as a dying man's blood, be cursed with a terrible rage." His face was unusually serious. "They're cursed by the Furie, a spirit of anger and rage. When they lose their temper, they become like wild animals, with the strength of demons." He explained. "I thought everyone knew that."

The young mage knowing that Joven was being quite serious, decided not to press the matter anymore than he had already. He had seen during their skirmish with the wolfmen what Joven's rage was like, and it was terrible enough that he would never want a barbarian's anger directed at him. However the idea that a malevolent spirit enhanced certain people's rage so that it became a force that even monsters feared gave shivers down his spine.

They continued on through barbarian territory, and though the trek got colder and colder they had increasingly sparse encounters with anything threatening. When they started running low on supplies Joven showed him how to make snare traps as well as hunt smaller game. To Endrance's relief Joven did not in fact hunt rabbits with his great sword, instead using a sling with stones.

The entire while they traveled they needn't worry about their direction; the mountain of Balator was visible in the distance. It took them another couple of weeks traveling to get close. They were able to find relatively safe territory to rest at, excepting for one blizzard that kept them holed up in a shelter for two nights. They had traveled wandering paths through the mountains, careful to stick to the road even though the snow made finding their way through the rocky terrain dangerous.

They came through the last mountain pass to see the mountain of Balator was finally within reach. They arrived at the gates of Balator at mid afternoon, and were able to see the greatness of the city that lay before them. The lowermost bowl of the city was in fact only half a bowl. A half-circle carved out of the mountainside, the first bowl had the largest diameter. Ten miles across, the first bowl was entirely farmlands. There they grew cold weather vegetables and kept cattle and other farm animals. Pigs were seen commonly wandering around the farmlands, and fences kept them away from the crops. The mountain streams were frozen, so though they had access to pure freshwater all year round they did not traffic in fish except during the summer thaws.

The second bowl beyond the gate was accessed by a large sloping road that traveled up the mountainside in loosely sweeping curves, giving switchbacks and plenty of places for defenders to fall back to. The bowl was predominately additional farmland, but also contained most all of the housing for the farmers of the first two bowls. This area was the first part of Balator to boast natural security as the mountain walls were carved to form actual barriers.

The designer of the city had made the transitions up from one bowl to the next to utilize choke points in the way the bowls were carved out of the mountain. Once past the gate, the rest of the bowls had bottleneck paths into the bowl above it. Since the bulk of the city's flat ground was carved out of stone, the materials carved up had been used in the construction of the city's buildings. It was not uncommon to see houses carved out of the sides of the very bowl they lived in.

The bowls decreased in diameter significantly each level up it went. While the first bowl was ten miles across, the second was a mere six. The third was five, fourth was three, and the fifth and sixth bowls were approximately two miles across. The seventh bowl was only a mile, and the eight bowl a half mile. The eighth bowl of Balator had only the castle built within it however, as well as the surrounding grounds. The seventh bowl held the many temples and churches of the religions the barbarians followed alongside a few other important buildings. The sixth held the military, with their training ground and barracks, camps, quartermaster, command buildings, and other structures. The fifth bowl down to the second was entirely housing and markets.

The walls around Balator were extremely thick gray stone quarried from the very mountain they lived on. Endrance could not see how far they spanned but he was certain they encircled the entirety of the city. The individual blocks were nearly eight feet by eight feet, and mortared expertly together. If the soldiers of Balator's people were as tough and as fearsome as Joven's example led him to believe, Endrance figured the only people crazy enough to assault the barbarian kingdom would be other barbarians.

Endrance and Joven rode unhindered through the first bowl of Balator, and Endrance could feel a growing sense of excitement as well as unease inside himself. He was nearing his objective, but was also feeling anxious as well. The city meant an end of their journeys, and though it was an end to their danger it also meant an end to the time it was only him and Joven travelling together.

This was it, he realized. It was the end of the life he knew. From here on he would be staying in this foreign place far from anyone he ever knew, living with people who may very well hate him. He would be far from help, and no one to turn to if he was overwhelmed or frightened. He took a deep breath as he steadied his thoughts. This was what he agreed to do, it was his first task. These people even if they disliked him, would be depending on him. While his life was going to never be the same again, it wasn't necessarily a bad thing.

They approached the gates of Balator, to find them open. A great many traders from other tribes clustered around Balator's gates, each talking and dealing with others around them. Some of the guardsmen actually posted on the wall watched the tribesmen with the practiced boredom of someone who had been on this post for many years. Nothing new to see there, excepting for the lone barbarian, with the tiny man in tow.

There was a pair of barbarians in heavy furs and chain armor standing in the front of the gates. They each carried a three bladed ranseur as well as each had a sword buckled to their belts. They were each nearly as large as Joven, and they definitely had similar musculature. They regarded Endrance with but a cursory glance in passing, crossing their weapons before the opened gate. Joven and Endrance came to a halt as they spoke.

"Stop," one began. "Joven?" The man recognized Endrance's bodyguard and seemed pleased at his comrade's return. "You returned from your journey. Has everything gone well?" the guard asked in the common tongue, his voice thick and burly. The other guard merely nodded his head, appearing as stone faced as any statue of a barbarian.

Joven flashed his broad smile and waved over to Endrance with a strong hand, causing him to lean back as Joven's fingertips would have otherwise slapped him in the face. Endrance could tell that Joven was making a show of it, and so he figured that he would do his best to stay out of it until he learned more about the way barbarians spoke to each other.

"Yes!" Joven exclaimed, leaning over and patting Endrance on the back as he talked. A faint "Oof!" slipped from Endrance's lips as Joven continued. "I was tasked to bring the new Spengur, and so I have!"

The two barbarians looked at Endrance with a look of surprise on their faces. The young wizard could see the barbarians weighing Joven's words against what they saw before them. And it seemed that Endrance had fallen short as they both nearly doubled over laughing.

"Her?" The second guardsman stammered out as he laughed. "You sure you didn't get hit on the head and confuse this…waif with the Spengur?" he slapped his knee as he laughed loudly. The first guardsman took a moment and feigned looking over the young wizard while scratching his chin. "Is it a he or a she?" He asked curiously. "I would almost wager it was a little girl, but she would be far too scrawny and meek to be one of *our* children!"

Endrance had never been so embarrassed about his looks before. Sure, he'd had people make fun of his build before. Sure, he'd even been confused for a woman on many occasions, but a little girl? Never before had he ever wished he had taken up some form of exercise. He should probably cut his hair or something. If only he could grow facial hair…

Regardless of what Endrance thought, he could feel heat rising in his face as a blush of embarrassment rushed in. This was not the first time that a barbarian here confused him for being a girl. This only seemed to encourage the two barbarians who laughed even more.

Joven thrust out his jaw, and Endrance could see the muscles of his neck rippling as he took a breath to speak. His voice came out low, but commanding and powerful. The bodyguard had had enough.

"Now listen here you… two," Joven began, the tone of his voice killing the laughter mid throat as the two guards were made to remember just who they were laughing at. "I have traveled according to the wishes of the king and our tradition's instructions. This is the Spengur." His voice emphasized the 'is' of his statement. "You will do your best to respect the Spengur, or else a punishment worse than death may be visited upon you." He growled, kicking his heels and prodding his horse forwards. Endrance followed as they passed between the chastised sentries and into the kingdom proper. "I've seen this 'girl' you mocked so callously slay a hydra with summoned thunder and lightning. I would be wary if I were you." He finished, his voice bore complete sincerity as he left the two behind.

Endrance smiled privately as they passed the great gates, knowing that even in a kingdom full of such barbarians, Joven would prove an able and more than adequate guardian.

They rode into the second bowl in peace, and Endrance got to see the things his master's book detailed to him. He had the book out, and was paging through it as he read about things he was coming up to. A large water reservoir in honor of the first king of Balator, a brewery that only produced a mead that barbarians were renowned for, and other little details that Endrance was surprised to see matched the notes in his book. The fact that these places remained despite hundreds of years of tribal life was a testament to barbarian steadfastness.

They reached the sloping road to the third bowl, and though there was only a modest checkpoint, Endrance could see the bowl entrances were made so they could tactically block them off, preventing easy access to the bowl above it. Essentially an attacker would need to besiege the city seven times in order to capture the castle at the top.

At the checkpoint, Joven pulled a young man on watch over, leaning in his saddle and whispering something in his ear. The man's expression went from one of interest to one of surprise and anxiety. As soon as Joven straightened out in the saddle the young man was off, running up the road towards the far side of the bowl. Joven looked at his charge and winked.

"Sending a runner to let the king know you're here." He flashed a toothy grin. "Gives him time to get ready to receive us, you know?"

As he rode along at a gentle pace led by Joven's horse, he watched the people of the city he would be working out of, the country he would be working for. He thought that though their ways may be foreign and simple to him, he knew that he would not let his master down. He had much he had to learn, and he would devour that knowledge and excel just like he used to.

Chapter 25

The young mage was received at the entrance to the sixth bowl by a large cadre of men. The barbarians were dressed in fine steel breastplates detailed in black iron filigree. They wore steel longswords at their belts and steel shields on their arms which bore the seal of a wolf emblazoned in black iron across the surface. Their gear was of top quality, and they carried themselves with the discipline any military would be proud to display. Ten of them were spread out across the road, their weapons sheathed but their demeanor severe. Their posture was not aggressive, and Joven raised his hand in greeting.

"Hail, brothers!" Joven called, dismounting from his horse. The men clamped their free hands to their breasts, and nodded their heads to him.

One of the soldiers, who bore a trio of long scars across his face, stepped forwards. "Joven, we were instructed by the king to take you two to meet him." He said, his voice sounding like it too had been slashed by a wild animal. He glanced at the young mage and scoffed. "Sorry," he said, "One and a half."

Joven laughed and patted Endrance on the shoulder, nearly bouncing him off the horse he stood by. "Don't let this one's size fool you. His magic is mighty."

The cluster of soldiers collectively spat upon the ground. "All the more reason to not like him." The leader said. "That magic's deceptive."

Joven frowned. "And never will you meet a more pure hearted user of it. Let's be on our way, I'm sure there's much for the new Spengur to see before the feast tonight."

The leader nodded "And we need time to prepare the sacrifices." He waved a hand, and the other armored men fell into a loose circle around them. "Come," the scarred man said, "Let us show you the true heart of our kingdom."

The group of soldiers led Endrance and Joven through the sixth bowl. Endrance was amazed to see the size of the military that the barbarians trained and kept working there. Everywhere he looked, he saw men and women exercising, sparring with each other, being instructed in all manner of combat arts, and even forging their own weapons and armor.

"How big is the military here in Balator?" Endrance asked. "There seems to be half the people in the city here."

The leader laughed, exchanging a look with some of his comrades. "That's cause the other half is off duty!" he exclaimed; a frightful smile across his face. "Everyone in Balator serves in the military. At least for six years." He shrugged. "Many stay for longer."

Endrance had never seen so much martial prowess in his life. There were soldiers practicing with weapons he didn't know the names of, men and women suiting up to go on patrols or perhaps even to battle, and commanders shouting out orders that echoed across the entire bowl.

They were nearing the exit when he saw something that was even more unusual. One building was separated from the others, and had its own training ring just outside of it. That on its own was not unusual, but the ring holding several young women in white fur armors was. As he watched, the women on the outside of the ring encircled two of their number as they squared off in the center.

"Who are they?" he asked, pointing at the women.

Joven nudged him with an elbow. "They're the Ergkinoa." He commented as he watched the match begin as well. "Looks like they're having a match."

The two women wore white fox fur armor, soft hide boots, and a scabbard for a dagger tied to their left arm where they could draw it quickly if needed. That was all they wore, even in the numbing mountain cold. They squared off on a circle of packed dirt and sand, and the others watched with somber expressions. One of the women carried a heavy blade, a slightly curved chopping blade with a flattened point on the end. The other twirled a pair of short swords as she prepared to fight.

"What's happening?" the young mage asked.

"The lead soldier shrugged. "They're determining who get's sacrificed to you tonight, that's all."

"That's all?" Endrance asked. "Why are they fighting then?"

The leader let out a sigh. "Because we have to sacrifice our most capable Ergkinoa, so they can protect you in case someone tries to assassinate you." He seemed agitated. "We used to have enough bodyguards, but now that we are down to the house of Rothel we have to chose our finest warriors among the Ergkinoa.

Endrance was quiet for a moment as the two women leapt into action. He expected the girl with the heavy blade to be slow but was surprised at the speed she brought her weapon to bear. The heavy blade arced through the air and with casual ease batted one of the other woman's short swords away. She darted in with her other blade while her other arm was still recoiling but the woman using the heavy blade had spun out of harm's way, bringing her blade full circle to attack her opponent again. She twisted her wrist at the last second, swatting her opponent in the face with the flat of the blade. Endrance flinched as he heard the slap of skin against metal and the other woman flipped backwards to land in the sand, her face spraying blood.

The Ergkinoa jumped to straddle the fallen one and pressed the edge of her sword against her target's neck. Endrance was sure she would cut her throat right then and there but the woman on her back shouted something and the keeper stayed her blade. Standing, she shouldered her blade and walked away without looking back.

"Ah, that one's Bridget." One of the soldiers said. "Looks like you got a good one. She's a brutal warrior." The man's smile was broad and he elbowed the man next to him. "I'd take her on any day of the week, if you know what I mean."

Endrance didn't know what he meant, but the leader responded by swatting the outspoken man on the back of his head. "Quiet you!" he barked. "You know they wouldn't do that with you!" He scowled at the man until he turned away. "Besides, a girl like that you'd have to best in a fight 'fore she'd lay with you." He muttered.

Endrance looked up at Joven, who shrugged. "Either way sounds like a good time to me." He commented to his charge, and ushered the young man on as the group started moving through the passage to the seventh bowl. "Ergkinoa aren't as well trained as me, and they have almost no experience outside Balator, but they need to be able to fight too."

"But I thought you were supposed to be my bodyguard." Endrance stated, sounding more like a question.

Joven nodded. "True, but there are places they can go that I cannot." He looked down at the young mage. "Didn't your book tell you anything about that?"

Endrance shook his head. "Just that they are given up to me."

Joven grinned. "Well, that's going to be fun." He said. He seemed amused by something, but as usual Endrance could get nothing from the barbarian's toothy grin.

The road up to the seventh bowl revealed a neat and orderly arrangement of stone buildings, several of which had arching rooftops and symbols of different religions upon them in many manners of colors and methods. The primary religions almost dominated the western side of the bowl, with grand buildings and many people who come and went through them daily. The less popular religions had barely small huts and Endrance could even see a few had meager shrines that seemed stuffed into out of the way places.

The altitude was high up enough that a blanket of snow covered everything, and gave the place a much more serene appearance than would be expected of a kingdom of barbarians. At many places down the main road were stone and steel structures where a large fire burned, providing light and heat along the roadside. The snow had been trampled and melted in many places down the main road, and he could see much of the refuse the people here made was burned at the fires.

"There is one place here you will want to keep note of." The lead soldier gruffly instructed the young mage. "That is the longhouse you will be living in." he pointed to the eastern side of the bowl, which had a small, unused road that led through otherwise unoccupied land to a building in the far off distance. "Why you have a wooden house where everyone knows stone is better is beyond me." He grunted as he pointed to the open terrain between the main road and the longhouse, "Nobody in their right mind built anything within several hundred feet of the longhouse."

"Why is that?" Endrance asked.

"You use magic." He said, like that was all the explanation he needed. "Why would we want to live near you?"

"Yeah." Endrance remarked, looking at the marked distance that the barbarian people had gone through to avoid people with magical talent. "Makes me feel very welcome, it does."

The lead soldier shrugged.

The group climbed the much steeper incline to the eighth and final bowl of the city. The castle loomed up over their heads as they approached. Endrance could see through the snow that the castle appeared at first as a standing structure, but was mostly carved out of the mountain its back was to. Roughly pentagonal, three of the walls were nestled into the mountainside, while the remaining two came together in the front, their crux meeting at the front gates. There several more soldiers in steel and black iron armor waited for them.

The personal escort broke off at the gate, leaving only Endrance and Joven at the gate. There waiting for them was a man who must have stood seven feet tall. His massive frame dwarfed the young mage and even made Joven seem average. The man had pale skin like his bodyguard, with pale blonde hair that hung to his jaw. He had intelligent blue eyes that reminded Endrance of Joven, whose face had lightened up when he saw the man before him. The man wore armor of hardened leather with steel breastplate, pauldrons, hip guards, vambraces and shin guards. Black iron filigree gave his armor the appearance of being a man of great importance, and his weapons of steel and black iron added lethal weight to his presence. A two-handed greatsword hung at his back, and a longsword hung at his hip.

"Balen!" Joven called, raising his hand and clasping the man's, his face that of joy. "I'm so glad to see you after such a long journey!"

The man smiled, and Endrance could see a similar toothy grin in this man. "As am I, Joven!" he released the grip and clamped his hand across his chest, and Joven did the same. "I hear you travelled farther south than any of us are willing to. How was it?" his voice was deeper and more forceful than Joven's.

"Was pretty warm down there," Joven began; a smile across his face. "And the prey there was weak. I hardly had a challenge until we got back up north!" he shrugged.

"You must be Joven's brother." Endrance said. He held out his hand, knowing he would have to put a strong foot forwards.

Joven looked at the young man's hand and almost grimaced at what he knew was coming. Balen looked down at the wisp of a person in front of him and smiled as he reached down and grasped the young mage's hand. "And you must be the new Spengur." He said, his massive mitt engulfing the mage's hand.

Endrance knew what was going to happen, and instead of shying away or expressing pain got as good of a grip as he could and squeezed hard in turn. The sound of a bone popping was audible, but neither one indicated it was theirs.

"You can call me Endrance. A pleasure to meet you, Balen." The young mage greeted his friend's brother, using every drop of willpower to keep from straining his voice in pain.

The handshake lasted but a moment longer than would have been normal, and the two disengaged their hands. Balen shook his hand out visibly, and Endrance did the same. "That's quite a grip you have for being so small." Balen remarked, smiling as he watched the young man rub his hand trying to get blood back into his extremity.

"And you have the strength expected of someone so mighty." Endrance replied.

Balen turned to his brother and commented. "I like this guy." He jerked his head towards the inner courtyard. "Come, I am to take you to see the king."

The interior of the castle proper was much more attractive. The black stone of the mountain was polished to a mirror shine inside, and many beautiful tapestries hung from the walls. Suits of armor and display weapons adorned the walls, and a thick carpet rolled down the halls. Torches were set in black iron brackets, and the firelight was more than sufficient to light the rooms.

An easily defensible foyer led into a main hall, which bore to the left and right, with a large double door in the center which led to the throne room. The throne room was expansive, with room for dozens of men to stand about without ever bumping elbows with their neighbor. The room was flanked on each side with eight stone pillars, smooth cylinders with detailed etchings of the deeds of the barbarian kings across their surface from top to bottom. Though there were only eight pillars, six of them had been filled with etchings. The remaining two, the ones closest to the throne, were almost entirely blank. The one to the right hand side of the throne had a third of its height covered, almost all of it with the exploits of the current king on it.

The king's etchings were tightly packed and started with him becoming king at the death of his father king Gurn, who had died suddenly one day while out hunting with his guards. Everyone had died in the wolfman ambush that day, including Joven's father, Daelen. Ever since then Joven's family suffered the hit to their prestige, but was still a powerful house within the kingdom. His older brothers served the new king faithfully and loyally.

The rest of the king's exploits included the slaughter of the wolfman tribe that ambushed his father, the subduing of a snow hydra in single combat, and many others which were incredibly violent and overly aggressive acts. Even his wife, a reputably heartless woman, was his conquest as he had taken her from another barbarian chieftain. It was said that she didn't flinch as she was forced to carry her own father's head all the way back to Balator under the king's escort.

Sitting upon the throne at the back of the room, one hundred yards from the foyer and the entrance to the castle was one of the largest barbarian men Endrance had ever seen. Quite easily seven feet tall, the king's black hair hung down past his shoulders loosely but clean and well combed. His face was brutish and strong, but his black eyes were sharp and bore an almost serpentine intelligence about them. The king's body was of incredible stature, with bulging muscles and strong corded limbs. His hands were broad and his knuckles bore many scars from fighting barehanded hundreds of times. He looked upon his young wizard much like a general would look upon a formation of his warriors; critically, with a detachment that came from watching their men die on the field. He sipped at a chalice of black iron with a golden rim and eyed the trio approaching across the room.

The ruler's sign of being high status was not any kind of ornate crown but rather equipment of great quality. The king was wearing a breastplate, pauldrons, and vambraces of Balator's best known material, black steel. The process of turning black iron into black steel was a difficult one, but produced somewhat heavier, but much sturdier steel. The king's sword, a black steel bastard sword, was propped up against the arm of the throne. It was a wicked weapon, its double edged blade had many hooked barbs across the edge, making it tear through flesh easily. Its dark surface gleamed dully as it reflected the light of the dozens of torches throughout the room. He wore a crown that was more than a simple golden ornament;

the black steel circlet had golden trim and gems, but was built to be worn into battle and protect his head from attacks.

The king remained seated, a look of disinterest across his face as the three stopped several dozen feet from the king. Balen and Joven kneeled, and Endrance quickly emulated their movements. They hung their heads down, and so did he. The floor was polished enough that he could see the reflection of the room around him in it.

The king stood, and waved a hand. A servant rushed up with a platter and the king set his chalice upon it. As the servant scurried off the king spoke for the first time.

"Rise." He commanded. His voice was strong but surprisingly not grating or rough like many of the other barbarians that Endrance had encountered.

Endrance felt a shiver shoot up his spine, and as he stood he realized he was trembling. Adrenaline had started flowing through him, though he was not in a life or death situation. He felt fear and more surprisingly anger rise slightly in him as he waited to hear the king's next words. It was an unusual feeling, like he had been riled up or was ready to fight, but he could not for the life of him figure out why he felt that way.

The king seemed to not notice this change, and stood, coming down the steps. He moved with practiced ease in his heavy armor, and Endrance was unsure if the man even felt its presence anymore. The king paced in front of the young man, looking him up and down critically.

Endrance felt his anxiety rising, and he felt something deep within his chest ache sharply. Maybe he was overreacting to the presence of the king, or his appearance had been enough to cause his anxiety to boil over into panic. He struggled to keep his emotions in check and waited to hear from the king.

"You must be the one we sent out to retrieve." The king stated flatly. "When I heard that you were the recommendation of the Wizard Kaelob, I knew that if anyone would be able to do this, you would." He smiled and though to some it would be a charming smile, Endrance thought it reminded him more of a serpent baring it's fangs to strike.

"Yes, sir." Endrance replied.

"Come now, call me King Kalenden. I'm sure we can work together to handle the coming times smoothly." He said his voice assuring. "I look forward to seeing you get established and working to better my endeavors."

"Yes King Kalenden." Endrance said respectfully. "I will serve you and your people as best as I am able to."

"Don't downplay your abilities, mage." The king responded. "If you were trained by the Wizard Kaelob, then you should be more than ready for this position." He turned away from the three and walked back up to his throne. "I have already ordered the feast to be ready by tonight. Please take this time to rest and recover from your journey. Return here at nightfall." The king sat back onto his throne, smiling as he could see their travel-worn possessions. "Balen, I need to discuss something with you afterwards. Joven, Spengur. You may leave."

Joven and Endrance bowed, turned and left the throne room quickly. As they were walking through the foyer to the inner courtyard Joven asked Endrance a question.

"So what happened back there?" he asked, concern showing on his face. "I could see you trembling the whole time we were in there."

"I don't know," Endrance said, rubbing his shoulder as they walked. The feeling of anxiety and anger faded as they walked into the cold afternoon air. "I guess I'm just nervous or something."

"You can feel magic, can't you?" Joven asked. "That's what you were explaining to me before, right?"

"Yeah."

"Well, if I remember, the royal armor is enchanted." Joven supplied.

"That... That could be it." Endrance accepted. "If it's powerful enough it would definitely make me feel uncomfortable."

"Well, we can go visit my family. My mother would love to see me after being gone for so long." Joven offered. "She can make anyone feel welcome."

"Sounds good." Endrance said, feeling how tired he really was. Why was he so strung out? It felt like he had just survived a near death experience.

"Great!" the barbarian exclaimed. "She'd love to see you. Her father was bodyguard to the second to last Spengur, and she's always been curious to see another one."

The two of them went down the bowls to the fifth, where Joven's family home was. His mother turned out to be a very nice woman, and though she lived alone most days now, she was more than happy for the company. They visited for a few hours, and she made Endrance promise to come down the mountain for stew someday. All too soon time had passed and the two found themselves back at the castle, the suns having just barely faded on the horizon.

The castle had been lit by several braziers and incense floated heavily through the air. The hundred meter hall had three long lines of tables down its length, and each was stacked with foods of all kinds. Hundreds of men and women of Balator milled around awaiting his arrival. Instead of happiness or glee, their faces turned somber and dark when he entered.

Men in armor escorted him to the far end of the room, where the king and his family sat at their own table, which spanned across one end of the three rows. At their table was placed a roasted hog of massive size, as well as plates bearing all kinds of cooked foods, baked breads, and sweet delicacies. Goblets sloshed heavy with wine, and servants moved amid the crowds, taking the lull in activity to refill a few guest's drinks.

The king turned to the assembled collection, his goblet held in one hand and his other held up for all to see. He spoke in a loud voice that carried from one end of the hall to the other, something he had much practice performing in his years of kingship.

"People of Balator!" Kalenden exclaimed. Again, Endrance's anxiety spiked, but he closed his eyes and clamped down on the feeling as the king continued. "For some time we have been without our Spengur! Without the one who would protect us from the evils of magic!"

The people slapped their hands on the tables in unison several times. The king smiled. "But that is no longer!" He shouted, gesturing a hand towards Endrance as he opened his eyes once more. Everyone was staring at him, their faces grim. "This one will stay with us and protect us from evil by using that very magic against it!"

Again, the barbarians slapped their hands on the table, and Endrance could see the only one really smiling during the process was Joven. From his place, the king shouted aloud over the sound. "Bring on the sacrifices, so that we may gain his service!"

Several of the people at the tables stood and approached. A total of eight stood in a row before the king's table. The first stepped forward and spoke loudly.

"To the Spengur, we give to him two passels of hogs with sows, so that he may always have food!" He declared. Everyone burst out in cheers and encouragements, thanking him for making such a great sacrifice, and congratulating him on his selflessness. Endrance would have felt uncomfortable enough just hearing the man give him so much, but it was all he could do not to bolt for the door as the rest of the group made the man out to be some kind of martyr before him.

"Thank you." The king said, and the man returned to his table.

The next stepped forward, a woman. "To the Spengur, we give him a year's measure of grain, a year's measure of vegetables, and a plot of our best soil, so that he may grow his own foods." She proclaimed somberly.

Again, people cheered, the king thanked her, and Endrance felt worse. This followed for the remaining six people, who had given up clothing, equipment, even a chest of gold pieces. The whole time the people of Balator cheered them as heroes, which only made him feel like he was the villain, extorting such a bounty from their people. He thought it was over when the king dismissed the last of the eight.

Instead, King Kalenden walked around the table, holding his hands out and his palms splayed, seeming to bask in their attention as the sound of the barbarians thumping the table droned louder and more insistent. He took a deep breath and cried out, his voice piercing through the noise.

"Do you think your king is not ready to give as much as his people?" he shouted aloud. The people resounded in the negative, cheering him on. He turned to Endrance, and the wizard stood nervously, gripping the end of the table. The king pulled from his pocket a silver necklace chain, bare of any ornaments or decoration. The people pounded louder and cheered harder.

"Come forward, Endrance of Wayrest." Kalenden called to him.

Endrance gulped and walked around to stand before the king. The man towered over him, and the muscles of his forearms rippled as he handed the ends of the necklace to him. Endrance became acutely aware that the man's bicep was thicker than his neck.

The king stepped back and spread his hands again, leaving Endrance holding an end of the necklace in each hand. "And now, I give to the Spengur the gift of our history! Bring forth the Ergkinoa!"

The pounding on the tables stopped in an instant. The silence rang through the chamber as the entrance doors opened.

"Say goodbye to these brave women, and know that their sacrifice will ensure that the Spengur is always prepared to battle the evil of magic!" The king exclaimed into the silence.

No man or woman spoke, nor did they move, nor did they gesture to the three women who entered the great hall. They collectively hung their heads in mourning as they passed. The Ergkinoa had changed out of their fur armors, and wore simple white dresses and a single silver ring on their left hand. They wore no other ornaments, or shoes, or jewelry of any kind. The cloth of their dresses was sheer enough that Endrance could see the lines of their bodies silhouetted by the light of the braziers passing through the cloth.

He shook his head and blinked his eyes clear. Why weren't they wearing more clothing? The women seemed unaffected by the cold stone floors, and the three of them kneeled as one before him.

The first one was a woman in her twenties, almost six feet tall and leanly built. Her hair was platinum blonde, and she had icy blue eyes. Her body was muscular but still feminine. The dress clung to her body around her slender breasts and buttocks, and her face was pleasant to look at, with angular cheekbones and full lips. In all, she had a mature beauty that would take the breath from any man she so desired.

The second was the woman he had seen earlier in the day. This woman was at least six feet tall, her body muscular and lean. She seemed to be about twenty. Her dress was tight across her body, but it accentuated her strength and power rather than any femininity. Her face was strong, more tanned than the other two, and her brown hair was short and framed her fierce brown eyes. She did not seem pleased to be in the room with him at all.

The third woman was barely out of being a girl, likely closest to Endrance's age. Her black hair was curly down to her shoulders, and her black eyes deep and soulful. Her face was more rounded than her sister keepers. Her body was neither statuesque or muscular, but rather toned and slender. Her dress clung to her body tightly, and though shortest of the three, her body sported the greatest curve of breast and hip. Every time Endrance looked her in the eyes she looked away.

The women quietly remained kneeling in a half circle in front of Endrance. Someone else would have enjoyed watching them kneeling before them, but the young mage felt nothing but embarrassment for them. He looked to the king, wide eyed and unsure of what to do.

"Are they to your satisfaction?" The king asked.

"Umm." Endrance stammered, looking back at the three. "Y-yes?"

The first woman stood, and from her hand plucked her ring. She reached out and gently grasped his left hand and took the end of the necklace from him. She slid the ring onto the chain. She looked him in the eyes, and he saw sympathy before she spoke, her voice hardly loud enough to carry father than the king.

"And in so doing I die to my king, giving my life so that the kingdom be served." She intoned a phrase that seemed rehearsed, though her voice was pleasant to the ear. She placed the end of the necklace back in his hand, and walked around him to stand behind and to the left of him. The ring hung in the light, and the young mage could see something engraved upon the surface.

The second woman, Bridget, stood before him. She scowled at him openly as she yanked the end of the chain from his hand and plunked the ring onto it. "And in so doing I die to my king, giving my life so that the kingdom be served." She growled, and went to stand next to the first. He was pretty sure it was the growl, but her voice wasn't as pleasant.

The third woman approached, tears in her eyes as she kept looking up at him then quickly throwing her gaze down. She grabbed at his hand without looking, and Endrance held the pinched chain between his fingers and grasped her hand to guide her. She twitched, and a shudder went through her. At the same time, Endrance felt a jolt through his hand, as if he had been struck by a very weak form of his own lightning. His heart started pumping, but not out of the desire to flee, but the desire to be there for her.

He blinked the sensation out of his eyes, and helped her slide the ring onto the end of the chain. He took the end back and let go of her hand. The pounding of his heart finally started to slow.

"And... in so doing I-I die to my king, giving my-my life so that the kingdom be ser-served." She stammered out, ducking her head and walking to stand in her place. Endrance watched her move aside, perplexed. She was still taller than him, and likely stronger than him, but she seemed so very scared. So one hated him, one was afraid of him, and one felt sorry for him. Great.

The king stepped forward. "It is finished!" he cried aloud. "Your three daughters no longer belong to Balator, but to the Spengur! As they have died, they give up even their titles. For here on, they are Draugnoa!"

Everyone was seated, and Endrance finally got to sit down and take stock of the situation. Joven sat to his left, and the three to his right. No one else sat within ten feet of his end of the king's table. He leaned over to Joven and whispered to him between mouthfuls of admittedly good food.

"Wait." Endrance whispered. "I thought they were Ergkinoa."

"They were." Joven explained. "The owl women are what they were called while they lived. But since they have 'died' to our country but still remain behind, our people have taken to calling them Draugnoa." After watching the three women a few seconds he continued. "They're the ghost women now. Dead but can still be seen and heard."

"That seems pretty extreme." The mage observed. "And belonging to me?" he said. "Are they slaves?"

Joven grinned, a strip of roast hog stuck between his teeth. "No no..." Joven responded. "More like your wives."

Endrance turned to look at the three, who were eating their food more delicately than Joven. They paused mid bite, watching him as he stared at them, like he was about to say something to them. He waved them on, and they resumed eating. He turned back to Joven.

"Wait, wives?" he asked.

Chapter 26

The building that housed the Spengur was a longhouse, with one floor but several rooms on either side of the moderate center hall. Double doors were in the front center of the house, with only a window on the long ends. The building was two dozen feet wide, and six dozen feet long. The walls were formed of wood, with decorated moldings in the corners and along the floors. The ceiling had two main beams that crossed from end to end of the house, and several other beams crossed those. Their intersections had support pillars which formed the corners of the rooms within. The ceiling above was one large open space, which all rooms looked up into. Many comfortable furs were laid over the worn wooden floors. Four braziers stood in the main room, one in each corner where their contents burned quietly, providing both warmth and light to the comfortable room. A faint waft of incense trickled through the room, pleasant but also too faint to distinguish. In the back and center of the room was a low backed wooden chair with a single cushion in the seat for comfort. Tapestries were hung from the walls, well away from the burning braziers. They depicted many different things, from starry night skies to dragons battling with barbarian warriors.

The double doors flung open, and Endrance stormed into the room. His entire demeanor showed both confusion and extreme distress. His shoulders hunched, his face contorted, and his pace quickened he paced back and forth in front of the chair in the back of the room, his hands lifted as if he was holding something in his hands that obviously wasn't there. He raised his hands in frustration and with a heavy sigh dropped down into the chair, the air seeming to deflate out of him.

The women quietly stood in a half circle in front of Endrance's seat. They waited silently as Endrance peered at them from behind his disheveled hair, his face like that of a man faced with his demise. He sighed again, rubbing his face. "Tell me again what just happened?" Endrance requested his voice soft but confused.

The eldest of the three nodded as she stepped forwards. "My name is Anna." She began. "What don't you understand? The feast is complete, your sacrifices are being brought in the morning, and you are now officially the Spengur."

He waved his hand. "Yes yes, I get that part." He muttered. "All that I understand, but what happened after that has me confused."

The woman looked puzzled, frowning slightly as she thought back. "What was confusing about what happened next?"

Endrance raised a hand pointedly and replied, "The part where Joven said that you three were my wives?"

Anna nodded affirmatively. The brown haired woman scowled, and the young one blushed. Anna spoke again, her voice comforting and explanatory "It is tradition in Balator. The Ergkinoa are sacrificed to the Spengur so they may serve only him from the day that he is chosen, to the day that they die. The Draugnoa are no longer people of Balator but property of their Spengur. This way they will have no conflicting loyalties."

She stepped forwards and knelt before him. "Please, accept us and use us as you will, great Spengur."

Endrance was shocked. He was barely past fifteen, and the first day of his first job he was… married? Not only was he married, but to *three* women?

"But…" Endrance stammered. "I don't even know any of you. How can I be married to someone I don't even know, much less love?"

Anna nodded. "We know what you mean, dear husband. But there will be time for you to come to know us, and for us to come to know you." She smiled at him soothingly. "We will serve you from here on out until our time to die, or you send us away, no matter if you love us or not. It is our duty."

Endrance shook his head. "But, I don't want to force you into a marriage you don't want!"

The brunette spoke up, "Bridget." She identified herself before continuing. "It's not like we have a choice, Endrance. We are all born of the owl totem. Our sign is rare, and the owl has by tradition only been allowed to marry the Spengur. If we were not to marry you we could not marry at all for as long as we lived in our lands." Her voice was throaty, unlike Anna's smooth and velvety voice. "I'm no happier about this than you apparently are."

"I'm not against it!" the raven-haired keeper interjected. She blushed when he looked at her again. "I'm Selene, by the way." She muttered as he looked at her.

Endrance sighed, standing up and approaching Anna. He placed a hand on her shoulder and spoke in an assuring voice "Please get up. You need not lower yourself before me as if I was your master." He smiled at them as she stood again. "I do not 'own' you, nor do I dislike you!" he began walking back and forth before them as he spoke. "I was just caught off guard by the situation. My master believed I was both intelligent enough and mature enough to handle this task and I shall not prove him false. I will need your help to succeed, and I would be a fool to deny your assistance. You know more about Balator than I likely ever will.

"Now I may not know you yet, but we will have plenty of time indeed to get past that obstacle. I am sure that you will all serve to the best of your ability, and I am confident that we can all get along. You are all beautiful women, and I would likely have fallen in love with someone like one of you easily if things had not already been arranged. Now I don't know how I feel about being… bonded so quickly, but I will manage."

Endrance considered now the course of events in his life. Now in his early fifteens, he had a position in a generally feared if not respected kingdom, he had a bodyguard that was also one of his best friends, and was now bonded to three of the most beautiful women he had ever seen. Even through the optimism of his good fortune he knew that something like this could not have happened by circumstance, and he was certain that he would find out quickly what lurked beneath the surface of this otherwise perfect career.

Endrance had been told numerous times that the world outside of his village was greatly different from what he grew up knowing. It was violent, strange in some places, and many parts of it were evil. He knew to be suspicious of something that seemed too good. He knew that this situation was almost the literal interpretation of the phrase 'too good to be true'. His father taught him how through honest, hard work one makes it to the places they dreamed of being. *So what does that place me at then*, Endrance thought, *if I came up from a life of relative peace and luxury into a position many wizards had to fight tooth and nail to get into with practically no effort on my part?*

Endrance shook his head, clearing himself of errant doubts. "So," He began, pulling his hair away from his face, "What happens next? Are you supposed to teach me about my duties or something?" His expression dropped to worry when he saw them exchange a glance and nod at the same time. "What?" he asked worriedly "Did I forget something?"

"We need to agree on our… sleeping arrangements." Anna stated. Selene blushed and looked down, while Bridget rolled her eyes and looked like she had eaten something sour.

Endrance blinked at them, perplexed. "Well, I'm sure there's some bedrooms around here somewhere." He said, walking to the door to the right of the entrance. Opening it, he saw a large bedroom with a massive bed covered in many thick furs. "Oh," he exclaimed. "Here. This one's big enough we all could fit on it. Easy."

Bridget snorted, shaking her head and walking away. "Forget it." She blurted out angrily. "I sure as hells am not going to sleep with him." She walked to the opposite end of the hall, taking the door into the rooms beyond. Endrance scratched his head. "Well I guess you wouldn't feel comfortable sleeping in the same room as me yet…" his voice trailed off as the door slammed shut.

Selene remained still, uncertain if she should follow Anna or Bridget. She raised a hand nervously. "Anna?" she said uncomfortably. "I don't think I feel ready to do it yet either." She said, looking timid. Anna shrugged.

Endrance felt a sudden rush of panic as he realized they were inferring another part of marriage. The physical part. He gulped and shook his head. "Wait!" he exclaimed. "That's out of the picture!" he shouted. "I don't know any of you nearly that well! That is not going to happen tonight!"

Selene looked relieved but also embarrassed. She half smiled apologetically, "Sorry." She muttered. "I… I just can't do even that much." She went off after Bridget.

Endrance turned to Anna and sighed. "Oh dear." He said, running his hands through his hair. "Well, I'm sure there's another room on that side you can use."

"No, I think I'll sleep in this room." Anna said coyly. She walked towards the big bedroom. "It's a comfortable looking bed, and there's more than enough room for the both of us."

Endrance let out a long suffering sigh and plodded in after her. As he closed the door he heard her say "You can sleep here too, but beware I don't prefer to wear anything to bed."

The next morning came with him awakening sprawled across one side of the bed, with Anna lying at his side. He had given up any pretense of modesty after a while and just lay there naked. She idly traced her hand across his back, something that both felt relaxing and made him mentally uncomfortable. "Your back… Where did you get those?" she asked, propping herself up on an arm and looking his markings over.

Endrance sighed, "It looks pretty scary huh?" he said. He tried to keep his eyes from wandering off of her face as they talked.

She nodded. "And painful. It looks like someone just went to work with a tattooing needle on your back in one run."

He wasn't certain what to say. He figured he would carefully approach telling her the truth. "It was done in one night. Well, they're kind of self inflicted, I guess you would say."

She raised her brows, curious. "If you did this to yourself, I would have to say you are either insane or incredibly talented."

Endrance rolled onto his back, taking the subject of their conversation out of sight. "Well, a little of both really; it wasn't something I had control over. I kind of inherited something more than most normal men do."

"I see. I'll have to find out what you mean by that sometime." She responded.

"I'm sure you all won't be able to miss it." He said. "Can we talk about something else now?"

Anna leaned in and kissed his cheek. "I have to go help with the day's preparations." She said, stretching in front of him. "Go ahead and come out at your leisure."

The young mage was simultaneously glad and disappointed when she dressed and left the room. He hadn't slept very well, being so vulnerable sleeping next to someone for the first time, and had rested fitfully. He closed his eyes now and let out a sigh of relief. He drifted back off to sleep without realizing it.

Rays of warm sunlight poured from the only open window in the bedroom, illuminating Endrance's face as he slept. The bedroom was built in the same style as the main hall, though somewhat smaller. A large multi-hued rug covered the center of the floor and the large rectangular bed sat near the back. Near the door to the main hall was another door leading to a storage room roughly half the size of the bedroom. Across the room near the open window was a long table pressed up against the wall, with mainly alchemical tools displayed across them. Near the bed were two large armoires, one on either side of the bed. There were articles of clothing within them, most of which belonged to one woman or another. Everything gleamed with the shine of having been recently dusted and polished, and though many of the tools displayed throughout the room hadn't been used in over a generation, they were in top shape and ready to be used soon. A third door was near to the back of the room, very easily missed.

Endrance stirred, and suddenly remembering the night prior snapped awake with a start. Seeing no one around, he quietly slid out of the furs on the bed. Realizing he was naked, he quickly searched about for his clothes. Finding many articles of clothing, but none his, he turned to the armoires. Inspection of one's contents proved futile as it was immediately evident it held only women's clothing. The other however had an assortment of articles of male clothing, many of which were sized to fit him. Finding a few that seemed to go together, he swiftly and quietly dressed. He then carefully made his way to the door he vaguely remembered entering through the night before. He paused, his hand on the door latch as he looked back at the rumpled bed.

Endrance pulled the latch free and stepped into the main hall beyond it. Selene was moving about the hall, cleaning and dusting as she hummed some song he had never heard before. She was wearing warm clothes with a many pocketed leather apron across her waist. He could hear the other two throughout the longhouse, going about various chores and cleaning. Walking past the girl to the door leading to the rest of the longhouse he caught the glance of Selene, who gave him a shy smile and a blush. Immediately an image entered his mind, a memory of her face from the night before, shy and scared. Endrance blushed nodded at her as he sped past, giving her his space.

He entered the next chamber of the longhouse, and found several doors along the sides of the hall, four in total, and two on either side. The rooms to the back of the longhouse were a kitchen and library, and the other two were guest chambers. Anna was at the end of the hall, arranging some mountain flowers in an earthen vase. She set the vase down on the window ledge as Endrance approached and she turned to greet him. "Good morning, dear husband!" she greeted him cheerfully.

He nodded at her, smiling pleasantly as he approached. "Morning, Anna." He responded, coming up to stop in front of her. She looked him in the eyes and smiled as he was acutely aware of what subject came to mind as she began speaking.

"So my dear husband was last night… all that bad?" she asked, reaching out and caressing his cheek.

The young wizard sighed, smiling despite himself. She was very beautiful and had not done anything to him. In fact, if he didn't take control of his imagination it would quickly put him in a rough spot.

Anna raised an eyebrow, silently urging him to speak. "The thing is," Endrance began. "I am not sure how to… I've never done…" He shrugged, embarrassed to be bringing this up and feeling lame. "It's not that I'm not capable, I just don't think it would be possible for me to be any good…"

From behind one of the doors nearby he heard a girl laughing. Anna glanced at the door. "Back to your cleaning Bridget!" she called, and the laughter beyond the wooden portal fell silent.

Endrance gulped, trying to loosen his frozen voice. Intimacy was new to him and he found it hard to control the emotions rushing through him. He knew little of these women save for their names and their devotion to their tasks. Yet despite the little they knew of him, they were willing to give their lives over to the task of supporting him, much less giving their bodies to him? He couldn't comprehend it and his frustration boiled over, thawing his voice in an instant.

"I don't understand!" He blurted out suddenly, stepping away from her and leaning against the wall, his back to her. Glancing over his shoulder he responded. "You three know me not, yet you have been preparing your entire lives to serve me! You met me for but a day, and you agreed to give everything to me?"

He slammed the hand he was leaning on into the wall, too angry to be surprised that the blow split a crack up the wall. "How?" He demanded. "How can you do so much for someone you never knew?"

The sounds throughout the longhouse stopped as his voice rose, and doors cracked open as the wizard's bonded peeked through, silent. Anna pursed her lips as she waited for the young mage to finish venting his anger. He fell silent, his glare both angry and sad at the same time. She cleared her throat and smoothed her clothes as she began to explain.

"Dear husband." She started, "We were chosen at birth to be raised to serve the Spengur, no matter if there was one or not. The last generation grew old and were retired waiting to serve a person that never came. While I am certain we were expecting a somewhat older Spengur, we were instructed very specifically to treat you no different than any other man." Her expression bore a hint of sadness as she continued. "You were told how we were not allowed to be with any other than the Spengur, so you know that I would be faced with either a life of solitude without you, or exile if I tried to make a life outside the kingdom."

"For the sake of all three of us here, we have dreamed for the day we could meet our charge. I was at first reluctant; you looked to be too young, but Joven had insisted you were indeed a man." She shrugged, "You will come to understand in time. Our people consider one turned a man when he has killed his first enemy, proving that he is mature enough to take part in our people's struggle to survive. You had slain both bandit and wolfmen on your journey here, and are proven a man. That alone would have proven your adulthood."

"And you must understand that now we are dead to the kingdom. The people will speak to us as strangers to their homes. Our families mourn our deaths this very day, for they may no longer accept us in their homes. We three have had since Joven was dispatched to retrieve you to come to accept the end of our past life and accept that our new lives are now bound to yours. Please give us time, and we will prove our worth to you."

Endrance closed his eyes and thought about it. He did know that they were unable to marry anyone other than the Spengur, and they must feel fortunate that they have that person. Otherwise they would be stuck being unable to marry, or form any kind of romantic relationships without abandoning their old lives and peoples entirely. Though this felt to him like an arranged marriage, it was their culture and their way of life. He didn't know how or if he should question it.

The wizard sighed, dropping his hands and sighed in surrender. "I suppose you're right. You have many reasons to take to this situation like you have. I apologize for my outburst; I am the kind of person who takes the time to weigh the situation before making a decision and this came through as a rush to me; I didn't even know exactly how close you were supposed to be to me." He turned back to Anna, who had patiently waited for him to respond.

The eldest Keeper nodded, coming close to him and embracing him. "I understand, dear husband. Caution is a trait that will do you well in your position. We had all the years of our training to come to this decision, while you were thrust into it unknowingly." She released him, and looked him in the eyes. "Now, it should only be a bit longer for us to finish our daily tasks, and we will begin teaching you the basics of our culture and where you fit into it all. Feel free to take a bath, and we shall be ready by the time you are finished."

Endrance acquiesced, and walked down the hall to pass through the main room and back to the bedroom. He paused at the door and looked back at Anna, who was still standing passively by the vase and flowers. "About the bath, do I need to draw water or anything? I don't remember seeing a washbasin in the bedroom." He queried.

"Oh," Anna replied. "I can help with that. The other door in the bedroom leads outside, where through a little path there is a personal hot spring we use."

The young mage thanked her and slipped out the door. Selene had resumed her duties and acted as if his little outburst had not even happened. He walked past her, and since she didn't acknowledge him he did not either. He knew that he may have made a mistake publicly displaying his anger at the situation. They had much of their life decided for them, and when they thought they had been given to someone who would be a good husband or bond he seemed to have rejected them. He passed through the bedroom and out the back door to the secret path. He decided he would have to work to make sure they knew he wasn't rejecting them.

The path was soft earth flanked on either side by the coarse mountain rock the longhouse had been built up against. The path was incredibly secure, the rocky stone rose a dozen feet on either side; one would quite literally have to fly to get on the path any way other than going through the longhouse. He followed the path down a short distance, and it opened up into a small basin in the mountain, nearly sixty feet across. Taking up nearly forty feet of the area was a crystal clear spring, seeming only three or four feet deep at the center. Endrance could see shimmers of heat in the cold mountain air over the spring as the water gently stirred by some unseen current. Endrance saw that a wooden stand had been setup on the rock near the spring, with many perfumes and cleaning supplies had been set. Looking them over, he could tell that much of the soap was specifically for each of the Draugnoa. The rock of the spring sloped up to the edge, forming a natural ramp down into the water.

He picked out a towel from the rack and set it near the water, as well as a lump of soap. Slipping off his clothes and shoes, he let out a sigh as he settled into the relaxing waters. Leaning up against the side of the spring wall, Endrance let himself float out. It was indeed a relaxing experience, and he was able to take time to sort his thoughts out as he soaked. He realized that first of all, he would have to come to accept the barbarian's way of doing things long before he could come to be able to provide them with the assistance he had been employed for.

His silent relaxed musings were interrupted by an itching sensation running up his back. At first it was barely noticeable, but when it began to strongly irritate his skin he stood up in the water. Something about the circle on his back was reacting to the water, and he opened up his senses as broadly as he could in order to investigate.

He felt the background flow of natural power in the world, but it seemed different here than it had to him anywhere else. The ambient energy seemed to be pooling around the spring. He waded deeper, feeling the power's eddies and flows as it seemed to be collecting in the water. He scooped up some of the water, and his senses could feel the water itself wasn't the source of the energy. It was more likely it flowed through someplace powerful, and the excess energy 'rubbed off' as it passed through.

He had a moment of realization. If he could tap the power flowing through the spring, he could safely activate the spell tattooed upon his back without worrying about being completely drained. He waded through the waters, standing in the center where the water was almost chest high.

He closed his eyes, feeling the flow of power in the water interacting with his aura. He focused on drawing that power in, connecting it to his own. He hesitated a moment, scared to continue. There were many ways this could go horribly wrong, and his imagination was more than happy to provide a few scenarios to him.

He shook his head. His master Kaelob wouldn't have hesitated to experiment. After all, Endrance had studied the circle and as best he could tell while it was complicated it should be safe to activate. Archmagus Talos had not indicated that scribed spells would be harmful to the person who had them, so it should be safe enough to try out.

He held his breath, and released a trickle of power into the circle. The scribed lines glowed as power flowed through them, like water ran through channels in a river. When the full of the circle was empowered, Endrance lost control over the stream of power. More specifically, the spell started pulling harder, and he lost mental control over how much it was drawing.

The water around him started rippling, rolling away from him as the circle on his back. The water increased in temperature as the circle drained the extra power from the water instead of cooling. The temperature in the air around him also spiked. More water pushed away from him, steam rising from it as the spell quickly ran its course. Though he hadn't moved, the water was flowing away with such force he was standing only up to his ankles in a visible bowl of empty water in the middle of a violently stirring spring.

His back burned painfully, and he staggered under the sudden pressure he felt on his back. His aura became visible; a flickering gold colored fire that seemed to swell up from his back like it was a bonfire. The lines of the circle burned as it carved further detail into his back. Within the confines of the circle simultaneously etched three smaller circles, ringed in arcane script of words of power. The circles within were arranged so that there was one close to his neck, while the other two were larger and touched the sides of the smaller circle. Endrance cried out in pain as the sensation of his meridians being shifted again brought back the very disturbing sensation of his own power turning against him.

As the spell ran its course, Endrance felt a strange need coursing through his mind, riding on the torrent of power draining into the spell. He needed something, to focus on something in his mind, and give the spell shape. As the spell went unfinished so did his agony over the magic that would either end with him burning himself out or draining his well of power into nothing and dying.

It might have been the vision he had the night the circle had first been scribed, but his thoughts immediately went to the fire bird that had appeared. It had a name, but at the moment Endrance didn't care to think of that; he only envisioned what it was and what he saw. The bird was easy to remember, its presence having burned figuratively into his memory.

As he focused on the memory of the bird, he could see it in his mind as clear as if it was right before him. He could see its powerful size, its majestic presence, the span of its wings that blended into licks of flame. The creature that watched him with ruby eyes that pierced through him.

The smallest of the three inner circles shifted as the lines swirled inwards, filling it in with a complicated icon of a bird with outstretched wings. Endrance nearly dropped to his knees in pain, and he barely noticed trickles of hot blood dripping down his back. The sigil completed, and the young wizard cried out in pain one last time as the spell completed its course.

The air crackled and wavered with heat, and the golden wind whirling around him pushed the water away from him as the circle finished its function. A disk of void filled the entire large circle on his back, the edges ringed in golden fire. The sensation was a strangely relieving vacancy of sensation across his back, and Endrance almost passed out from the sudden lack of pain.

Out of the void in his back burst a small ball of flames as large as both of the wizards fists held together. It shot out into the air over the water, arced around the natural stone walls of the mountain, and came around to stop suddenly in front of the agonized young mage. The instant the ball of fire stopped moving, the void closed in on itself, leaving an angry red glowing spell circle tattooed upon the majority of his back.

Water splashed back into the empty section of the spring, though it seemed to have dropped in volume by several inches, only going up to his abdomen. Endrance looked up and stared in wonder at the small ball of gold and orange flames that hovered before him. The flames burst away from the center like a puff of smoke, and there hovered a small scarlet bird the size of his hand, whose wing feathers brightened into lightly glowing orange tips without flames. It in some ways resembled a young chicken, in that it seemed very young and small compared to the majesty of the adult creature he had seen in his vision before.

The bird and Endrance stared at each other for a few seconds before Endrance finally half shrugged his shoulders.

"Huh." He said through a wince as his body protested moving. "So that's what it did."

The bird chirped a strange staccato of sounds, like three lesser birds calling right on the end of the last. It chirped again, and flew in a circle around his head, seeming pleased with the wizard's presence.

Indeed. Endrance heard in the back of his mind. *That is one of its features.*

He craned his neck trying to keep track of the miniature bird of fire. "Did you just-" He was mid sentence when while tracking the bird he saw the three Draugnoa standing at the edge of the pool in shock. Selene covered her mouth with a hand to stifle a gasp. The bird flew around their heads, chirping happily its strange triple chirp.

Endrance thought quickly, they seemed more shocked than anything else. Even Bridget seemed amazed. He smirked, looked Anna in the eye and said "You see? You were going to find out sooner or later!"

Endrance sat in his low backed chair in the main room of the longhouse. He had dried off and dressed in a pair of pants and shoes that had been provided to him by his Draugnoa, but his back was still far too tender to put anything on it. As it was, he sat leaning one elbow on the low arm of the seat, the other arm holding out so the bird that he had somehow summoned could perch on his hand.

"So, let me get this straight." Endrance began. "You're a... what again?"

A familiar. The words appeared in his mind. *You summoned this one to be your companion, did you not?*

Endrance half grimaced. "I was trying to ascertain the exact nature of the spell scribed on my back. It so happened to somehow summon you, after I envisioned one of your kind while the spell ran its course."

And no finer creature could you have called. The familiar told him. *This one is now sure you have fantastic taste.*

Endrance blinked at the bird, which was looking at him with its head half cocked. "What is that you are doing?" He asked.

What is this one 'doing?' The familiar asked.

"The thing where you're speaking in my mind?" Endrance asked.

Since this one has become your familiar, the bird instructed him. *We have formed a mystical bond. It allows this one to communicate with you even though you somehow haven't learned to speak the language.*

"Bird language?" the bewildered mage asked.

Yes.

"How come your 'voice' in my head sounds so... basic?" the young mage asked. The entire time the bird had been communicating with him, the tone he was hearing was simple. The voice could have been male or female, young or old, but it had no variance.

That is because you have yet to form any kind of bond with this one beyond the basic one you formed when you completed the summoning. The more you know about this one, the more distinct and individual this one will become.

"Ah I see." Endrance muttered.

This one also advises using the link to communicate with this one, as your females are beginning to question your state of mind. The bird advised, bobbing its head.

Endrance blinked several times and looked beyond the bird perched on his hand. Anna, Bridget, and Selene were milling around the chair, watching him like he himself had started talking to a rock.

"You've never seen a familiar before, have you?" Endrance asked.

"No." Bridget replied.

"Neither have I. Isn't it fascinating?" he asked.

"No." Bridget retorted. "Can I kill it yet?"

"Of course not." He replied.

"Damn." She muttered, narrowing her eyes at the bird, who only tilted its head at her and chirped.

Endrance hadn't tried mentally communicating with the thing, but he figured he would have to give it a try.

Can you hear me? The young wizard thought, imagining the thoughts reaching the familiar. The bird turned and regarded him with a ruby eye.

Indeed. The bird replied. *You have figured it out.*

Okay. Endrance replied. *I need to know a few things about you and how you got here.*

Ask.

What is your name?

You may call this one Gullin.

Thank you, Gullin. Are you male or female?

I, the bird used the first person for the first time, *am male.* The same time, the bird's voice in his head started to have variance in his tone. It sounded more masculine, but also more musical, much like the voice of singer or poet. It still seemed off, but it was much more personal than before.

Thank you, Gullin. Now, how does the circle on my back work? Endrance asked. He needed to know if this was something he would be going through regularly.

It is a very complicated spell, for which I am surprised you remained conscious during the scribing. The bird observed, hopping back and forth along his hand. *It has three functions.*

Those are?

The first you are aware of, the smallest of the sub-circles is a familiar circle. It is what summoned and bound me to you. That spell function is going to remain active for as long as I am in this realm.

Do I need to 'send you back' or anything?

Not necessarily. However, in order to use either of the other two spell forms you would have to return me. Gullin replied.

Will that break our bond?

No. Now that it has been formed, I will return to you without fail every time you call. Also, if I should be injured beyond simple remedy I can recover in a few hours in my home realm.

What if someone tries to kill you? Endrance asked, glancing at Bridget. The three had decided to leave him alone now that he was just silently communing with the little bird he had summoned.

That is one malady that cannot be remedied. Gullin told him, his voice disturbingly the same tone as before. Endrance realized that while the bird had a voice, he was not hearing any emotion conveyed.

What are the other two spell forms? Endrance asked.

They haven't been formed yet. Gullin replied. *However I will be able to help you with that as we both increase your power and skill.*

So they do nothing for the moment. The wizard confirmed. *Good. We will have to look into that later. Now, how can you help me get more powerful?*

The bird took flight, bobbing through the air around him and eventually landing on his head with a chirp.

I am a fjallar. Gullin stated. *I am a being of power, and though I am young, I have much understanding in your practice of magic.*

Young, huh? Endrance prodded, looking up at the bird as he looked down at him. *How old are you then?*

Only forty thousand days. Gullin responded. *I am barely a hatchling by our race's standard. It was why you were strong enough to call me.*

Forty thousand! Endrance didn't think he could sputter mentally, but he did. *That's... over one hundred years old!*

Yes. Gullin stated. *Is that old for your kind?*

Endrance shook his head, and Gullin had to spread his wings to keep from being knocked off.

Yes. That's older than most humans live.

But you aren't fully human, so you should live longer.

I know about the elven heritage, but I'm not sure how much that will affect it. Besides, won't mastering magic improve my lifespan anyways?

Indeed.

Okay. Endrance said. *I need to get to work, please feel free to sit anywhere you like, and chime in if you have anything to say while I'm learning.*

The fjallar popped off his head and flew in a lazy circle around the room, he eventually plopped straight into one of the braziers in the back of the room, and the fire didn't seem to bother him in the slightest. The bird let out a little sigh, and fluffed his feathers and dozed off.

Endrance stood and stretched. His back had stopped hurting, and he nodded, pleased.

"All right." He said, calling the attention of his Draugnoa. "I am ready for you to teach me."

Chapter 27

Endrance studied hard the following several days the barbarian culture and history. His Draugnoa were very informative, but could only relay information through word of mouth. He found to his distress that they had been forbidden from learning how to read, instead having to tell the history of their people orally. Since they were no longer bound to Balator's ways directly, he could order them to learn to read. He would rather they decide to learn on their own though; he didn't relish having to order them to.

He took notes of the key parts of Balator's history, the cultural differences he found between most of the common people to the south and the barbarians themselves. He found that the 'barbarians' that most people referred to applied to almost anyone living up in the harsh northern territory, not just the people of Balator. Most of the common people thought of barbarians as brutal bloodthirsty warriors, but from what Endrance had witnessed that impression was false.

He was certain there were dozens, if not hundreds of warriors as big and powerful as Joven, Balen, or King Kalenden was, but they were not the majority of the people. Sure on average a northerner was taller or broader than your average commoner in a more temperate zone, but they were essentially the same. Those that lived south of the frozen north only saw the big and strong barbarians because they were the only ones who ventured south of their territories.

After his second week he started to take visits from the barbarians in general. It took two weeks not because he was unprepared but rather it took almost two weeks for someone to build up the courage to visit the Spengur for help. His first case was an old woman who had seen the prior Spengur when she was a young child, and had finally a chance to speak to him in person.

He sat in the low backed chair in the main hall of the longhouse, while Anna and Bridget stood on either side of him. Selene, being the least intimidating of the three had been delegated to letting people into the longhouse to see the Spengur. Joven stood watch outside with another soldier of Balator, a precautionary move until Endrance was better accepted by the community. His fjallar familiar was perched on his shoulder, looking intently at anything that moved. Selene still couldn't believe that he was a fjallar totem. They were one of only two totems rarer than the owl.

The old woman walked into the longhouse, her cane scraping the wooden floor and sometimes catching on the furs as she moved along. Helping her was her son, a farmer who had come out of a desire to protect his mother. The man was lean and tough, but had no real education other than farming. He scowled at Endrance as he helped his mother walk on her cane across the room to stoop in front of him.

Endrance was concerned for the woman, and waved Selene over.

She approached, listening for his instructions. Her shyness had faded slowly over the last two weeks, as she had spent much of the time around him and teaching him. It gave her a feeling of control of the situation, being able to instruct him so, and it helped her adjust to interacting with him more readily.

"Yes, Endrance?" she asked. She hadn't begun using the phrase 'dear husband' like Anna was prone to do, but Endrance wasn't really sure whether that was a customary saying or just something Anna did. As he had gotten to know them, he was sure it would be something she would do.

He leaned over in his seat to be close to her ear. He was looking at the elder woman and didn't notice Selene tremble as he got closer. "I was wondering." He whispered. "Is it wrong to offer her something to sit on? She looks to be having some problem staying standing."

Selene didn't respond right away, and Endrance thought she was thinking through the nearly forgotten and abolished customs when visiting the Spengur. She eventually nodded her head. "It... It should be fine; I will get her a stool." She whispered back, quickly pulling away from him and walking out in a brisk pace. She shuddered as she left the room into the hall beyond.

Being close to him made her conflicting feelings for him all the more jumbled. She didn't dislike the man, not in the slightest. In fact she found him surprisingly attractive for being one of the shortest and scrawniest men in the city. It was actually kind of nice that even though she was the shortest and youngest of the Draugnoa, he was actually shorter, and skinnier than her. He also paid attention to the three of them, and seemed to honestly care about how they felt, and not if they could still perform their duties.

It was some other feeling that rose whenever she was near him. She felt anxious, on edge. Her pulse quickened when he was nearby, and she felt like she was about to go into a sparring match again. She shook her head and stepped into the guest room she was sleeping in and picked up the chair and carried it out of the room.

She had not yet slept with him, not even slept in the same room. She was uncertain why, since she knew it was an eventuality. She liked his looks, he had a sweet and caring personality, and she could see when he cast spells that he was very good with his hands. Still something about how she felt around him seemed off, so she stayed in one of the guest rooms until she figured it out. Bridget had taken the other and practically made it her home. It seemed that she refused to even consider the idea of eventually moving into the main bedroom with him.

She carried the chair back into the main hall to hear Endrance and the farmer in conversation. She walked up and set the chair behind the old lady as the two conversed, and the woman was more than grateful to sit down for the while.

"Our crops are failing!" the man shouted, waving a small sack that he now held in his hand. Bits of soil and dirt fell through the weave, and Selene figured it was a sample of his crops, soil included. "Last season we had to fire one of our workers for stealing some of our tools. When I confronted him on it the man cursed my land!" he seemed as angry about the crops as he was being here. "I want you to go to my farm and remove the curse from my land!"

Endrance nodded, taking a split second to thank Selene for the chair. She blushed and stepped aside; waiting for anything else she could help in. Already she was thinking of gathering the cold weather clothes and boots for a hike down the mountain, as well as to pack some things for the trip since it would likely take the rest of the day.

He held out a hand, as if expecting something. "May I see the bag you brought me?" he asked gently. "If your land is cursed, then I may be able to see what it is from that."

The man looked at the bag in his hand, and the young mage's hand. He seemed unwilling to actually walk the distance and hand it over personally. Selene stepped forward, her hands cupped to receive the bag. "Let me take it to the Spengur." She said gently.

The farmer dumped the bag into her hands, a disgusted look on his face. "Keep it," he said, "Stuff's all wrong anyways."

Selene walked over and handed the bag to Endrance, who opened it and pulled a pinch of soil out of it. Pouring it into his palm, he sniffed it, and sprinkled some of it back into his palm. Frowning, he looked at the farmer. "Tell me," Endrance began, "How often do you irrigate your crops?"

The farmer shrugged. "Enough, I guess." He responded. "Ma always used to do it before I did, now she's too old to, so me and my men do it all ourselves."

Endrance nodded, dumping the soil in his hand into the bag again. He stood, and the farmer took an involuntary step back. "I suppose this season your crops took too long to sprout, and have been growing slower than anyone around you?"

The farmer agreed. "Yes, and much o' them's dying off too."

Endrance handed the bag to Bridget, who scowled at him but said nothing. "Very well then. I will need to take some time here to examine the soil, and I will return with a solution." Endrance smiled kindly to the old woman. "I will find out what is going wrong with your family's crops." He glanced at the Draugnoa. "Selene, if you would be so kind as to keep them company, I will be at the alchemy table. Anna, Bridget, please come with me."

The young mage entered to his bedroom, sitting on a stool next to the alchemy equipment as he waited for the two of them to arrive. Pouring some chemicals, he held out his hand to Bridget. She set the bag into his hand, and he rummaged through it, sifting his fingers through the dirt.

"So do you think it's a curse on his land?" Bridget asked.

Endrance shook his head. "Of course not!" He found a suitable sample of the soil and carefully dispersed a pinch of it into the chemicals in a vial. The clear blue liquid turned cloudy, and he muttered 'aha' as he looked through the vials of chemicals for something specific. Gullin, hopping about on the table, carefully slid a vial in front of him which he picked up and unstoppered.

Anna frowned as she tried to make sense of what he was doing. "Then what is it?" she asked.

Endrance looked up at her as he poured a drop of another chemical into the vial. The solution turned clear and colorless. To the Keepers it seemed it was now filled with water. He held up the vial and commented in a matter-of-fact tone, "It's the soil." He put the vial into a rack and looked at it as he explained.

"A few years ago I was studying under my master when one of the farmers in our area had a similar problem. He was a first generation farmer, and didn't know what he was doing wrong. Kaelob looked his farm over, and after testing the soil informed him that his irrigation methods left too much salt behind. It happens more often south of here I would wager, since much of your irrigation water is melted snow and hasn't had much time to pick it up flowing through rivers and similar salty areas." He shrugged. "It was likely building up over several years, and only now started affecting his crops."

Anna looked at her young husband, impressed. The young man wasn't yet sixteen, and had already learned so much about things he wasn't even trained in. "And you just happened to know this?" she asked, holding out a hand to help the young man from his stool.

Endrance smiled faintly. "I asked a lot of questions when I was a child."

Bridget blew air through her teeth. "You should have spent some of that time getting some exercise." She said under her breath.

Endrance hadn't missed the statement, but chose to ignore it. "Come, we need to let him know what is going on." He said, walking out of the bedroom, Keepers in tow.

The farmer looked surprised that the trio was only gone for a few minutes. He looked at his mother, and back at the Spengur. "You found the curse already?" he asked. "Can we go now and remove it?" he looked hopeful.

Endrance sat on his chair, and looked plainly at his visitor. "I have some instructions for you." He said. "If you follow these instructions your crops will pick up and may even be fully recovered by harvest time."

The farmer scowled, but listened.

"You need to increase the amount of water you give your crops. Fix the irrigation so that everything gets extra water for the rest of the season. When the season is over, you need to re-plan your furrows so that everything gets equal amounts of water."

The farmer interrupted then stepping forward and angrily jerking his thumb at his chest. "You are trying to tell me I'm doing a bad job on my crops?" he shouted.

Endrance tilted his head. "No, I am trying to say that you need to change a little thing, and you will be fine. There is no curse on your crops, it just needs an-"

He was interrupted again as the man shouted angrily. "You don't know nothing you filthy mage!" he cried, pulling a knife from his belt and charging the short distance across the hall towards the young wizard. Endrance was surprised how quickly the man turned to violence, but remained seated like he had been instructed to.

The farmer never got a chance to attack. Selene, who had been waiting passively nearby the two visitors burst into action. Her eyes wide and her expression blank, she slid into the farmer's left side, her left hand grabbing the wrist of his left arm and her right elbow sank into his side. He stumbled as she pulled his arm down and kicked his foot out from under him, flipping him over his own head to land on his back with a loud *crack*. Air rushed out of his mouth and he gasped for breath. Gullin cawed at the man, but hadn't taken flight when the fighting burst out.

The main doors of the longhouse burst open and Joven barreled in, to see the man pinned to the ground by Selene, her knee on his shoulder and her knife against his throat. Her face was still blank, and Joven had to call out her name twice. She seemed to snap out of it, and stepped away from the man she took down, looking more flushed from embarrassment than exertion.

Joven picked up the man and carried him out of the longhouse. The old woman watched her son go, and after being offered a hand up, thanked the Spengur for his assistance. She said she would monitor the fields, and make sure her son did as he asked. Endrance smiled and said farewell as she departed.

He turned to Selene when the guests were gone, and whistled. "That was amazing!" he said, looking her in the eye. "You just took the man down like he was nothing!"

She turned her eyes away, still feeling anxious. "I don't know about that, I just did what I needed to." She said.

He embraced her briefly, and he felt her stiffen in a moment of resistance. Her scent filled his nose, like fresh rain in a clean fall evening. "You did just fine!" he said. Releasing her, he stepped back and looked at Anna. "Is that all for today?" he asked.

She nodded, tilting her head to the door. "Those two were the only people to come visit for the first day. Though I'm not sure strong arming the first person out was the best idea."

The wizard sighed. "Yes, well I can't very well let them stab me freely either."

Bridget snorted derisively. Selene tittered and tried to be quiet, and Anna rolled her eyes. "Let us worry about the physical threats against you, dear husband." She assured him "You have more pressing concerns than people who are angry at the truth you lay before them."

That night out of concern for the safety of his guardians if they were likely to get injured protecting him, spent several hours searching for a spell of healing he could learn. Only during the nights did he really have the free time to spend deep within his spell books. He made progress learning many of his prior Spengur's spells, including many spells that were several hundred years old and generally forgotten by even the most studious members of the magical community.

He wielded his magic sparingly, and only used it after great consideration to how it would help his people. They would eventually come to accept him as their own, as they began seeing the positive consequences of his advisement. He quickly came to feel for them as a people, despite their paranoia of magic. It reminded him that no man is a master of all things. Just as they knew little of magic, he knew little of battle.

It was a few days later that Endrance had been called to investigate something that set his nerves on end. He received an official request from Balen, asking him to investigate a cave that had been discovered just outside the first bowl of the city. He had traveled there early in the morning, and had to pass through a rough mountain pass to get to the patrol that had discovered the source of their concern.

Endrance arrived at the path leading to the cave, where two grim faced guards in leather armor and wearing axes waited nervously for his arrival. He hiked across the rocky terrain to the guards, Joven in tow. Gullin, who travelled everywhere with the Spengur, came to rest on his shoulder whenever the young man stopped moving for more than a moment.

He had managed to convince the Draugnoa that Joven would be all the protection he would need outside of the longhouse, and his bodyguard was quite happy to be able to spend time away from the stationary task of guarding the longhouse. The two soldiers nodded at Joven and gave a slight customary bow to Endrance.

"This way," one of the soldiers spoke, leading the way down the path. "The cave is up here." The men led the way, picking their way through the rough rocky terrain. "I don't know how we missed this path before; it was very easy to spot today." The other man at arms, shaking his head replied "I can't believe everyone's missed it. Even for all these years we've patrolled around our very capitol."

The path led the way to a small cave entrance, jagged and rough, almost giving the appearance of a sharp-toothed maw. While it was tall enough to allow Endrance easy entry it was short enough to make Joven duck under its spiny entrance. The interior of the cave was dank and dark, the faint *drip drip* of melted snow water echoing through the chambers beyond. The first chamber of the cave was merely ten feet wide and fifteen long, with a ceiling varying between eight and seven feet. The stalactites clustered in the center requiring the two of them to take a circular path to the adjoining passageway on the other side of the room.

The passage was short, leading into a much more expansive chamber, as the cave led deeper into the side of the mountain the bowl wall was carved out of. The room was nearly forty feet in diameter, almost a perfect circle in fact. Reaching nearly twenty feet high at the center, the room had plenty of space for any number of tasks. There were no stalagmites in the room, which seemed odd to the wizard as he examined his surroundings.

The main source of illumination in the chamber was a circle of five large black candles on twisted black iron candlesticks, tall enough to reach eye level. The flames of the candles burnt an unnatural green color, an obvious indication of something being amiss even if the rest of the circle wasn't in the room. The candles stood in a circle in the center of the room, each six feet apart from each other. Drawn across the stone floor of the cave around and under where the candles stood was a pentagram of some kind of black substance. The outer ring of the circle ran under the candles and made a complete ring around the pentagram.

Joven remained at the entrance to the dark chamber, while Endrance paced around the circle, analyzing it. He pulled out a blank book he had taken with him for the purposes of keeping notes, and took care to sketch out a copy of the circle that lay painted on the floor. Magic wrought using mystic symbols could be very dangerous, especially if accidentally triggered by an unaware victim. Endrance was acutely aware of the slight weight of Gullin perching on his shoulder, and was reminded how much a properly prepared circle could achieve.

I would not suggest powering this circle. Gullin stated. It had been weeks, and still Endrance had been unable to discern any kind of mood from the bird.

I wasn't going to. Does this look like a demonic circle to you?
Yes.

Endrance scraped a small amount of the blackened substance for identification, though he was pretty certain that his tests would reveal it was human blood. For some reason it seemed that humans, of all the sentient races, were the most useful resource when it came to the dark arts of demon summoning.

An ancient council of wizards had tried to find the answer why. Using the best arcane tools they had at their disposal, and even summoning many higher ranking demons they attempted to divine an answer. The most logical solution they could find for all their trouble was that it had to do with the human's lifespan, or lack thereof.

A human being lived anywhere from fifty to a hundred years old, but in that amount of time they could accomplish as much if not more than a dwarf, who lived nearly six-hundred years, or even the elves, who lived sometimes over a thousand. Even the industrious gnomes, as few and far between as they were, lived typically two centuries.

The young mage personally believed that the human spirit's potential was the key element that gave their bodies the potency and appeal to the forces that would consume them.

After completing his notes and gathering the evidence he and Gullin could, Endrance pondered the nature of the circle itself. While it was a pentagram, it was possible that the circle was for any number of purposes. They could be used for protecting as well as containing; however the wizard knew that one wouldn't need that much human blood to form a protection circle. Endrance sniffed the air as he leaned towards the circle. The sharp acrid smell of sulfur was still lingering in the air around the candles. He stepped back, firm in his belief that something had been summoned and captured by the circle. He would have to compare the symbols to what Gullin knew, as well as to the older books the prior Spengur left behind.

He considered then what should be done with the room. The demon has already been summoned, and the summoner very likely had become aware of the kingdom's notice of their cave. He waved Joven over, who cautiously approached.

"Hey Joven." Endrance started, pointing to one of the candles, "Try and blow it out." Joven stared at him, "What?" Endrance asked, finding it hard to contain a laugh as the barbarian's face suddenly went from caution to fright.

The barbarian frowned at him. "You are the master of magic here… And you want ME to blow out the creepy evil candles?"

Endrance shrugged. "I thought you were supposed to be my protector?" he nudged his friend, who nearly swatted him over in response.

"Nuh-uh!" he exclaimed. "YOU blow it out."

The young mage couldn't hold it anymore and broke out laughing. Joven watched him for a second, and then laughed as well. Endrance looked the barbarian straight in the eye when the laughing stopped. "No, seriously." He said firmly, "Try to blow out the candle."

Joven scowled, but took a breath and puffed at the candle. The green flame barely even flickered. He looked puzzled at the candle and took a deeper breath, and blew at the candle with all his might. The flame jumped but once, but came nowhere close to blowing out. Gullin chirped in a way that seemed remarkably like laughter.

Endrance nodded, gently nudging one of the candlesticks with a finger. "It's as I thought. The candles are enchanted. You probably would need an enchanted weapon to even scratch them, and I'm certain that now they have been set it would be incredibly difficult to move. They've been lit for who knows how long and have barely lost an inch of their foot length, I would guess. These things are some pretty high quality items."

He waved Joven back over to him. "Let's get out of here, and get this problem taken care of."

Carefully making his way outside, he signaled the soldiers over. With great care he instructed the men to gather two of their best stonemasons, and for them to bring their best tools. The guards left to go up the bowls to retrieve them, and the wizard and his bodyguard settled down to wait. After a few hours of waiting two stonemasons were seen picking their way up the mountain path, laden with the tools of their trade. Carefully whispering into the mason's ears, he sent them into the dark cave.

Joven, who had waited patiently to hear about Endrance's solution, finally couldn't wait anymore. "Tell me, what kind of help can those mason's give to fix the problem inside? Did you not say that you would need enchantments to bring those candles down?"

The wizard smiled, waving at the entrance as he talked. "Well it's simple. We're going to carefully cut weak points into the ceiling of the cave and then collapse it on top of the circle. While it won't destroy the candles, it will prevent anyone from even entering the cave; much less use the circle which will most likely be invalidated by the thousands of pounds of falling rock."

Joven nodded, understanding at last. "So... You can't remove the circle, so you're going to destroy all the stuff around it so no one can get to it?" He smiled approvingly at Endrance's nod. "Good!" he exclaimed. "I like that plan!"

He heard the sounds of the stonemasons beginning tapping at the walls and ceiling inside the cave. He smiled at Joven. "Well, let's make sure they get the job done then go home, okay?"

Joven nodded. "Sure, I suppose. Can we stop somewhere along the way? I hate having to stand guard outside your house all the time."

Endrance looked up at his bodyguard. "Well, you could always wait inside. It's much warmer in there."

Joven shook his head. "I probably should. It's not like you get many visitors unannounced anyways."

They watched the stonemasons work for several hours, and when the cave had been collapsed to their satisfaction, returned back to the longhouse. Along the way back Endrance stopped at a shop and purchased the painting equipment he had wanted to get when he set out on his journey there.

Later that day, Endrance was reclining in his chair and listening to Selene reciting one of Balator's more obscure rituals to bless the crops of not the coming season but three seasons in the future. It was boring, and even Selene didn't seem into telling it. The door to the longhouse was opened unannounced and a soldier bearing the steel and black iron armor of the king's personal guard strode into the room. Selene fell silent and eyed the guard suspiciously as he approached.

Anna moved to intercept the man when his pace did not slow when he got close to the Spengur. She stepped directly in front of the guard, halting him. The guard stared dispassionately at the woman. "I am here to deliver the King's summons to the Spengur." he growled, his voice menacing. The woman didn't as much as flinch as she held her ground.

"You do not approach the people's Spengur so directly!" she scolded, slightly shaking her head as she chided the King's messenger. "Even the king knows not to threaten the Spengur!"

The guard snarled his hand flying to the ax over his shoulder as he attempted to make a show of force. Bridget, who had been quietly approaching from the guards left, darted in and grabbed his hand, pulling it past the weapon handle and yanking it behind his head with one motion. The other hand held her slender dagger, whose point was a scant hair over the skin of his now exposed armpit. "I love men in armor with big... axes." she purred. "They practically offer their vulnerable spots to us when they try to draw their big, unwieldy weapons."

The guard flinched, grunting in pain as she pulled down hard on his trapped arm, but did not struggle. She twisted his wrist and he yelped as he felt a bone audibly pop in his hand. "I'm sorry." he muttered. "I'm Sorry!" he howled as she tickled his underarm with the point of her dagger "I'm sorry for being improper to our most respected Spengur and his Draugnoa!"

She nodded, slowly releasing his arm as she stepped back from him. The King's Guard rubbed his shoulder as he rotated his arm around working the pain out. A bruise was already forming on his wrist as he inspected it. He exhaled as he brought his attention back to his initial task. "Wise Spengur, the King wants you to come see him immediately." he bowed. "Please be at the castle as quickly as possible." He straightened, grimaced as he moved his wrenched arm. He turned and disrespectfully left without another word.

Endrance looked at the two women who were watching the man leave. "So, is it alright to be manhandling the King's guard like that?"

Bridget waved the man off as the doors swung closed. "Psh!" She blew wind through her lips as she dismissed the man verbally. "Royal Guards are wimps!" she derided. Anna nodded. "They are almost entirely for show, really. They think they are much more powerful than they really are." She nodded, as if affirming something in her own head. "The King has no real need for a guard..." she finished, her voice trailing off.

"Why doesn't he need a guard?" Endrance asked, his curiosity triggered.

Bridget shrugged. "Why else? The King himself is one of Balator's most feared warriors! He has been fighting-"

"And winning." Selene interjected quietly.

"For nearly twenty years. He is one of the strongest men in Balator, and has foiled several attempts on his life without suffering any harm." Bridget finished. "He is the prime example of the strongest of our people." She then mused, "Now that's a man I wouldn't mind spending time with."

Endrance chose to ignore the comment for the time being, and stood from his chair. He picked up his carry satchel which held his all important spellbook as well as other writing utensils and ritual materials. He had not reached the level of practice with his spells to erase every doubt that he had not perfectly memorized their forms. This consequently was the reason several of the spells he cast before were either inefficient or took much more energy than they should have.

Endrance had hoped that he would have more time to devote to improving his magical capabilities, but his duties to the people and his continuing education of the kingdom's multitude of laws, customs, and superstitions had been keeping him busy. He didn't even have time to send off letters to his father and Kaelob, much less spend hours studying the wealth of magical knowledge in his storeroom.

He had dressed this time in a thin shirt, and had to go back into the bedroom and change clothes. He added on a thicker layer of clothing and an overcoat. The winter air was especially chill this evening, and he did not relish having to walk up the mountain.

Outside stood the customary standard of a pair of two men standing guard. He glanced at the two of them, noticing that he did not recognize them from any of the guards Joven had personally introduced him to. "You new?" he asked, and one of the guards nodded.

The young mage smirked. "Well, I suppose since Joven is off duty this afternoon, you are aware you were supposed to actually *stop* people who charge into my home, right?" another silent nod spurred him on. "Don't want to talk?" he asked. The guard shook his head, and Endrance could see that the man would not be here if he had not been ordered to. "Well, if I understand things right, you will get reassigned if you are unable to perform your duties here, correct?" The guard gulped, but nodded after a brief pause.

"Good, good." He said, nodding his head. "Just checking in case your orders changed."

The man was beading sweat across his brow trying to stare straight ahead, and flinched when Endrance suddenly turned away from him. Walking a few paces away, he turned back to the men at his front door.

"I have to go see the king now." He began. He cast the warmth spell, and the constant swirl of light snow stopped falling on him in its entirety. "I expect you to be more diligent in the future, understand?"

Endrance chuckled as he left the two with their jaws hanging, but winced when the cold mountain air managed to slice right through his meager warmth spell and into his clothes. His breath came in weak puffs. Being in cold weather and high altitude was almost too much for his weak spell to handle. Fortunately he only had to travel a short distance to the castle.

Banners hung from the windows and across the double reinforced doors of the castle. Two men stood guard at the front door while two more patrolled around the perimeter. They wore the markings of the King's Guard, and wore steel plate armor and sharp steel weapons that were all in perfect condition and bore the black iron filigree that marked them as the king's personal retinue. The men stared at the young man whom snow would not fall on, and bore with him a bird with glowing ember like feathers.

The wizard walked up to the first guard at the door and smiled. "Good evening!" he greeted, waving mildly at the armored man. "I was summoned to meet the king?" he prodded, trying to get the man to react.

The barbarian shook his head to try to clear it, and nodded affirmatively. "Yes, the king will see you, Spengur. He awaits you in the throne room." he turned from the young man and signaled for the door to be opened. The large double doors creaked open. Endrance clapped the guard on the shoulder as he passed by. He didn't see the man shudder as he left.

Endrance paced steadily into the grand hall and across the floor of polished black marble. His strides weren't slow, but they weren't hurried either. He had arrived in a good time, so he was not concerned he would be late. The king was watching from across the great hall, and so Endrance was more focused on not falling on his face than being early to the summons.

Endrance studied his king's face as he approached, trying to get an idea of the purpose of his visit. Kalenden leaned back on his throne, almost slouching as he rested his chin on one mailed fist. The king's face never betrayed what went on behind those critical eyes however, leaving the wizard guessing as he knelt before his ruler. "King Kalenden, you called for me?" Endrance spoke out, his head remaining bowed.

Again, he felt himself becoming anxious. His nerves crawled, and he felt like he was just waiting for a fight to break out. He found his hands were clenched into fists as he remained bowed. Something about this place was driving his senses crazy.

The king remained silent for several long seconds before grunting and replying. "Rise, Spengur." he commanded, and the wizard complied. "I have called you here to talk to you in private, young one." King Kalenden waved his hand at the four guards standing attention at inconspicuous places around the room, and they each took a nearby door and vacated the throne room.

King Kalenden smiled at him. "Anyways! The great eclipse is coming in a few months, and I need to make sure you know what your duties are for this event."

Endrance nodded. The king continued. "You know that the reason you were brought here was that against my desires, the people of Balator demanded that we have a Spengur." He grimaced. "I do not think you are necessary, or even useful. Let me make that perfectly clear."

Endrance nodded. "I however," Kalenden continued, "I am a generous ruler, and will provide for my people if they believe they honestly need it. They want you, because they believe that there has been a plague of trouble rising up as this eclipse approaches, and they grab for anything to help them feel safe." He pointed up at the ceiling of the throne room. "The signs say that the eclipse should be in three months."

Across the smooth stone surface was a mural of the stars out in the sky, with the moons out clearly. There were four total, each of varying sizes. The largest was the white moon, which could be seen almost anywhere in the world at night. Second was a green moon, which usually only came out during the months of summer. Third was a blue moon, which showed during winter seasons and during the summer solstice. The last moon was a subject of much debate in the magical community, as it was thought to be nothing but a black disk that traversed the sky only when great suffering was about to happen. Some wizards urged it was a remnant of some great necromancer's work during some mage war over two-thousand years ago. Others believed wholeheartedly it was just a black rock.

The mural depicted the four moons ordered from largest to smallest left to right in a semicircle arcing away from the throne. It showed over the throne both suns side by side, rendered in brilliant whites and yellows. And the night sky near the moons faded into day over the throne.

"This is the time where both our suns and all the moons will eclipse at the same time, and won't again for hundreds of years." Endrance explained. "It is a time greatly tied with prophecy. And the people, as superstitious about magic, still have their stories."

The king watched the young man silently. Endrance could tell he would have to explain further, though he was sure the king already knew. "There is a prophecy told about the joining of the moons and suns. This prophecy says that on that night a child will be born to certain conditions who will become the greatest hero of all time, uniting the whole of the good people against the darkness who would destroy it."

King Kalenden smiled broadly. "Excellent. You have learned something after all. Good. That will make explaining this all the easier."

The king leaned forwards in his throne, his hands clasped together ominously. "I have ruled here for quite some time now, by our standards. I want to make sure that no one would see fit to question my rule for until I am quite happy to give it up."

The barbarian king arose from his seat, casually picking up his sword and fingering the tip as he spoke, though Endrance found that his sire's body language said anything else but casual. "My wife, she is nearing the end of her second pregnancy, and I'm certain she will be giving birth on the eve of the eclipse." His expression was dark, almost threatening. "It would be best for *my* kingdom that you decree *my* child the prophesied one." he paced in front of his throne. Walking back and forth, having found his sword quite to his approval, he now carried it over one shoulder with his wrist counterbalancing upon the handle.

Endrance felt a moment of panic. He did not know what to do in this situation. The king was quite literally ordering him to make a false declaration about the upcoming prophecy! The young mage had very little experience with selfish men, but he was quickly getting the idea what kind of things a man would do with his power, if it meant keeping his or gaining more power.

The king eyed him impatiently. "That is what is best for my kingdom, don't you agree?" he asked, his voice almost a growl as he glowered at him. The Spengur did not miss the barbarian king's hand wrap around the grip of his sword.

The young man quickly nodded, cowed. "Yes, sire!" he blurted out. "If that is what you think is best my lord, I will do what I can." he finished, feeling weak and at the same time dirty for letting himself be intimidated into agreeing to something he would never do normally. But what could he do?

Kalenden stared Endrance in the eyes, searching for even the slightest hint of disloyalty. Finding the young man sufficiently intimidated, he suddenly smiled broadly, which made the mage think again of a serpent grinning, if one could. "Good!" he bellowed, pulling the handle of his sword down and flipping the blade back up over his shoulder and leaning it once again against the throne. "I would hate to have to prove to the people just how unnecessary I think you are." King Kalenden sat back down upon his throne. He waved his hand dismissively. "Now be gone, mage." he muttered. "I have more important things to do than to have you standing around here."

As the young mage left the throne room, the King sat quietly on his throne. He waited, and after the Spengur left the hall beyond he spoke aloud.

"Well?" the king asked, to nobody in particular. "What do you think?"

The shadows pooled around his throne flickered in the torchlight. They darkened into blackness and took on physical form as it swelled up beside the throne. The sha'hdi emerged, watching the doors to the room beyond close.

The moon elf leaned up against the throne and laid her head against the king's shoulder, breathing into his ear as she spoke.

"I think you know what he will do." She purred into his ear. "A young child like that is full of ideals and dreams of heroics."

He grunted, never even looking her in the eyes. He continued to stare down his throne room, deep in thought. "Still…" he said, shifting in his seat and causing the shadow elf to nimbly step away from him. "He's trained by the Wizard Kaelob. Knowing that man, he taught his apprentice more than just magic."

"I can see…" The shadow elf faded into the shadows behind the king's throne. "He's already improved so much. Our master will be most pleased, don't you think?"

Though she had only just disappeared, the king knew he was alone again.

Chapter 28

Endrance found rest hard to come by that night as he slept with king Kalenden's words echoing in his ears. He wanted to be true to the people of Balator, as well as to himself, but he was certain the king would probably have him executed or worse if he didn't comply. Endrance rolled over in bed, and in the dark he could clearly see Anna was resting peacefully. She was sprawled along one side of the bed, and Endrance had the middle. There was far more space on the massive thing for more, but he was in some ways happy that it was empty.

He still felt down about the other two Keepers. The whole thing was confusing for him in many ways. If he did do more than just sleep with one, what would that do to the other two? One seemed to like him as far as he could tell, but something held her back. He honestly thought she was very attractive, but he couldn't put his finger on it. Something about her appealed to him greatly, though he wasn't sure what it was. Perhaps it was her shy nature. He had been taking care working to get Selene to feel comfortable around him, but still she shied away.

The other one, Bridget, seemed to be torn between doing her job and hating him for being as she saw it, 'weak'. He smiled to himself in the dark. *If only she knew.* He knew with some of the spells he had been researching he could be stronger than her despite her constant exercise and practice with heavy weapons, but she had years of combat experience behind her that he did not. If he was going to prove himself an equal to her, it would have to be in something that they were equally capable.

Looking around the room, he had the feeling that something seemed off. The young mage quietly eased his way up out from under the sheets, and carefully vacated the bed without waking Anna. Hopping silently onto the floor, he slipped on a silk robe and silken slippers, and searched for what felt out of place.

He felt almost immediately a cold draft across his feet. Investigating, he found the door to the bath outside was open a crack. Knowing for certain that it had been closed when he went to sleep, poked his head outside. The light of the moons illuminated a new set of footprints in the sand leading to the bath. He quietly made his way to the bath, hoping to not make too much noise. He shivered as the cold high altitude mountain air drafted through his robes with little effort.

The air surrounding the spring was quite warm however and once he emerged from the path leading up to the bath he felt much better. The moons provided enough illumination that he could see clearly across the spring. The stars of the sky were so clear up on the mountain, and their reflections across the spring looked like a second sea of stars, so close he could just jump in and be afloat in the ocean of lights.

He could see a female figure in the spring, sitting with her back against the pool edge. Her back was to the path approaching, so he was certain she didn't see him approach. He was about to speak when he heard her sobbing. Staying quiet, he carefully padded up to the side of the pool. He stood only a few feet from her, but she was too distracted to notice him.

She was crying quietly, her sobs sending little ripples across the pool as she shook. She looked so vulnerable, curled up naked in the water. He could not resist the urge to help her. Slipping out of his slippers and robe, he took a step towards the pool, taking care that she could hear his approach.

Selene startled at the sound of something disturbing the ground behind her, and not having the slightly improved vision that allowed the mage to see in the poor light, she half stood half crouched in the water, alert for danger. Endrance noticed the faint glimmer of starlight across a small curved dagger she held in her hand. The loveliness of her body's curves was distracted by Endrance's curiosity of where she had been hiding the blade.

"I see I'm not the only one who enjoys a midnight bath." He said in a friendly tone.

Hearing his voice she visibly relaxed, slipping back down into the water as she set the dagger back on the stone edge of the spring. "I'm sorry Endrance." she stated flatly. "I didn't hear you approach." she sighed as she stared into the subtly shifting water of the bath. Endrance sank into the water, sighing as he felt the warm water rush across his skin. He glanced over to Selene, and saw she was trying to still sit in the bath while modestly covering herself with her arm and crossing a leg.

"I can see that you are bothered by something, dear." Endrance began. "What is it?"

She shook her head. "Nothing, Endrance." She began. "Nothing I should bother you about."

Endrance flicked some of the warm spring water at her, making her flinch and look at him in the dark with irritation. "Nonsense!" he jested. "There is not a thing you couldn't bring to me if it's a problem. Isn't that part of why we had been bonded together? So that you can help me?"

Selene nodded. "Well that doesn't go one way you know. I also get to help you out with stuff too." He finished, leaning close enough to her that their shoulder's touched.

Selene shied away, turning her back to him. He waited quietly a moment, hoping she would respond. She glanced at him from over her shoulder, and turned away again when he met her gaze.

"I can't tell you," she said, "I can't tell you because…" she shook her head and went quiet.

Endrance laid a hand on her back from where he was sitting. He felt her jerk slightly when he made skin contact, and as he scooted up to her he could feel her trembling through his hand. She trembled as he remained close to her.

"You're shaking." He stated, rubbing her back with both hands now. The water was warm enough, but the air could have been chilling her.

"I can't help it when I'm near you." She said, staying still. She was worried she would make him angry if she pulled away from him.

"Oh?" the young man asked, pausing. "Why is that?"

She shook her head again, tossing her pretty black curls and Endrance was again reminded of rain as her scent passed through his nose. "I don't know!" she exclaimed, slapping the water with her hands in frustration. "I don't know why!"

"I look at you and I see a sweet, attractive young man who really cares about me, who goes out of his way to be kind to me, and deals with me when I can't deal with others. I see the man who doesn't judge me even though I hesitate to perform my duties as your woman, and still!" she half turned to look him in the eye, her gaze both scared and angry. "And still I want to attack you whenever you're around!"

Endrance stared at her, baffled. She turned away from him and sobbed again, her trembles never abating.

He knew exactly how she felt. He had felt that way every time he was near the king. He didn't know what caused it, but thought it was just his nerves. Now he was hearing that one of his Draugnoa was experiencing the same thing, but towards him.

"Tell me something." He requested, taking his hands away from her and sliding back from her in the water. "Have you ever been to see the king?" he asked.

She nodded in the dark, the tips of her hair dancing across the spring's surface. "Yes, we saw him several times during our training." "What about in person? Like being maybe fifty feet or closer?"

She paused, thinking. "I during the ceremony when we were bonded to you. Why?"

"Did you feel the same way you do towards me when you were around him?" he asked.

She shook her head. "No, I didn't."

Endrance sighed, slouching back in the water. "Well there goes that idea." He muttered, splashing the water as he thought. "I feel exactly like you do towards the king."

She turned to look at him. "You mean I'm not the only one feeling this?"

The young man looked at her and smiled. "Nope." He stated. "I feel like taking a swing at King Kalenden whenever he's nearby me. I don't know why either."

Selene sighed, sinking in the water to her shoulders. "I'm relieved." She said, looking up at him from the water. "But you don't also… feel strongly for the king, do you?"

Endrance shook his head. "No, I'm actually kind of intimidated by him." He paused as what she said clicked in his head. "Thank you, Selene." He said. "I think I'm coming to 'feel strongly' for you too."

She frowned. "Why do I feel the way I do?" she asked.

The young mage straightened up, leaning his head towards her. "Maybe it's because you have something conflicting with your feelings."

"I do feel that I really could love you, I just feel so afraid when I feel that aggression rising."

"Maybe you just need to decide on how you are going to feel and give in to one or the other." He suggested, remaining where he was in the water. "Then the other feelings would go away."

She rose in the water and walked towards him "I do…" she whispered "Want to love you." She pulled him close and wrapped her arms around him, despite the near invisible tremble in her body. Her lips were a short span from his. "I… I…" she whispered, her face flushed in the darkness. She could feel herself heating up as she realized how close they were, how there was nothing between their naked bodies but a little spring water.

Their breath mingled, and neither of them could tell who moved in to kiss the other first. He had felt the power of lightning shoot through him before, but it couldn't even compare to the powerful jolt that went through him. He stopped caring about the world around him, just the two of them. He could feel her melt into his arms, and her passion burning through her lips.

Their kiss parted, and they were both out of breath. Selene looked him lovingly in the eyes and touched his cheek. "I think you were right after all." She said, playing with a lock of his hair with a finger before embracing him again.

"I guess I am." He said, returning her embrace.

They remained that way for a while, and Selene looked him in the eyes, the light of the stars glittering across her limpid black eyes like a new celestial body. She leaned in and kissed him again, briefly. Inclining her head, she kissed his cheek, and then his ear.

"I think…" she whispered. "I think I'm ready, Endrance." She nuzzled his neck, and he felt tingles across his skin. The smell of spring rain filled his senses as time ceased to have meaning for just this one night. Whatever happened beyond that moment under the stars, he would always have the memory to carry him on.

Much later that night, he was certain he heard Anna mutter "About time" before rolling over and going back to sleep when the two of them finally climbed into bed. He was able to sleep perfectly fine, with Selene contentedly wrapped in his arms.

The next day Endrance took few visitors as he worked hard to prepare himself for the eclipse as well as study the findings of the cave from the day before. Joven had returned on duty early that morning and Endrance had him brought in. The barbarian bodyguard mock scowled at the Spengur as he entered the library across from the guest rooms. "Why did you get two of my best men demoted yesterday?" he asked as he stepped up beside the mage as he pored over the couple of books he was studying. Gullin tapped a symbol in one of the books and Endrance nodded and jotted something onto the notes he was taking.

Endrance didn't even look up from the table as he replied "Oh those two? They let an obviously aggressive man through my doors without so much as announcing him, and they refused to do much more than stand at the door even after confronted about it." He turned the page of his tome and scratched a note on a piece of torn paper with a quill.

Joven grunted. "Remind me next time to get some more open-minded men on guard." he stated.

"Or at least a bit more dedicated to their jobs would do nicely." Endrance replied cheerfully. Joven stared at him quizzically until he noticed a spring in Selene's step as she passed by. He grinned, chuckling to himself as he watched her pass.

The wizard had been up since breakfast checking the books of the Spengur's library, comparing them to the notes he had made in the cave the day before. Though the tomes of demonology and summoning were old and very informative, they lacked many key parts that would be needed to actually use them to summon much more than an imp. What they did have however, was an extensive listing of different types of demons and what their specialties were, as well as notes as to their behaviors while on the worldly realm. Gullin was able to provide much more detail about the particulars of summoning in general, so progress was halting, but moving along.

He held up his notes from the day before. "I have been doing some checking up on the work of our mysterious summoner." he started, pointing to a set of angry looking symbols he had sketched. "You see these? They are part of a set of elder symbols. Only master summoners and demons themselves know how to use them properly."

Joven squinted at the paper, confused. "But what do they do?" he asked.

The wizard set the page down. "The symbols when done properly, grant the summoner a great advantage when gaining control of the summoned demon. It reinforces their control over their subject, while weakening its resolve."

The barbarian quirked his brow. "And if done wrong?" he prodded.

"Quite simply, done any way but the right way, and it is you who has your resolve drained, and the demon's reinforced."

Joven winced. "Ouch. How bad is that?"

"Pretty bad." Endrance answered. "The demon usually in those cases breaks free of the summoner's will and then goes on a rampage free to wreak havoc on the material world, after having horribly tortured and killed the offending summoner." He tapped his finger on a large book with a red leather binding. "This book explains it all. I think I could spend the next ten years learning about the craft of demonology and I would still have decades more to learn."

Joven scratched his chin. "Does that make wizardry easier to learn than demonology?"

Endrance shook his head. "Both are equally difficult. Some people just have a talent for one or the other. I heard stories about people who practiced both, but learning two distinctly different styles of magic is taxing, and takes much longer to learn from either. I suppose if one had the time they could fully learn what they want from one, and then work through the other, but that would take centuries of continuous hard work and risk."

Joven continued on his questions. "If it's so dangerous, why do people practice demonology? Wouldn't they rather take a safer profession?"

The wizard shrugged. "Power, what else? Demonology is a quick and dirty way to power. Even an untrained dolt who knows little of the craft can summon a demon if the conditions are right. Demons are incredibly powerful allies if you can get one on your side. Some of the more powerful ones can even grant the summoner's wishes, in return for freedom. This practice can lead to great power, but is also so dangerous and risky that usually only the insane and the black-hearted pursue it."

Joven pointed at the loose stack of parchments on the desk. "So, what else do you have?" he asked curiously.

The young mage shuffled his pages, producing one of the other sketches he made. "This set of markings indicates the type of contract the demon is being summoned for." He opened another tome and pointed to a matching set of symbols. "There." he said, scrutinizing the text below. "It looks like the demon was summoned to serve for a year and a day as a personal consort." He furrowed his brow, piecing things together. "I find that sex as it is, is amazing enough that why on earth would someone want to risk mind, body and soul to have it with a demon?" he asked, looking through his stacks of pages.

Joven shook his head and looked around the library. He wasn't going to go into that conversation with the young man. "Is that day part important?" he asked, squinting at a shelf of books.

Endrance stopped paging through his notes and looked back at the barbarian poking through his shelves. "Huh?" he commented, unsure what he was talking about.

"The year *and a day*." Joven stated. "Is that extra day on the end important or something?"

The young mage shrugged. "It seems to be the commonly accepted limit on how long a demon can remain bound. The books I've read today tell me that any longer risk them breaking free of their imposed contract and I've already explained what happens then."

"Ah." The barbarian said. He picked up a book and flipped it open. He pinched a page and turned it, but cringed when he heard the paper start tearing. He closed the book and put it back, looking from the shelf to his ward with a sheepish grin on his face. "Oops!"

Endrance sighed, shaking his head. The young mage quickly sorted through his pages as he looked for other information. Finding the page he desired, he opened yet another tome near the edge of the desk. Leaning over it, he compared symbols until he found a match several pages in.

The wizard pondered the situation, and devoted his considerable intellect to the task. He considered the succubus, the timing and the coming eclipse and other possible outcomes. Sadly, he knew fairly quickly what the most likely course was. "Joven." Endrance called to his friend and bodyguard. "Please go find out for me exactly how many children will be birthed on the eve of the eclipse?"

Joven grinned, clapping a closed fist over his breast. "Right away, Endrance." And without another word set out. He in all reality probably wouldn't be able to know for sure, but he could find out a rough number.

The young wizard thought about his options with the eclipse, and knew that he had to be there for each birth to check their babe for the markers that might indicate they are the hero. So the two things he had to figure out in the weeks ahead was to find out the specific markers for identifying the hero, and to figure out how to get to each of the births in the same night.

Several hours later the door jumped in its frame as someone knocked a little too hard on it. The women placed their hands on the daggers strapped to their left arms, waiting. Endrance chuckled as he got up to answer the door. "Must be Joven." he stated, unlatching the door and opening it.

The big barbarian on the other side grinned at the Spengur as he waved a loosely rolled scroll in his face. "Hey Endrance!" he exclaimed. "I figured out how to get you to all the births in no time at all!" He swept into the already crowded room, seeming not to notice the women now crammed into one side of the open space of the small library. He laid a scroll down on the desk and unrolled it right over the wizard's papers and books. It appeared to be a map of the eight bowls of Balator and their general building layout. "See, what I think we can do is to get all the women who may be giving birth the night of the eclipse into the churches, nearby the Spengur's longhouse here in the seventh bowl." He pointed to the cluster of large buildings in the bowl. "That way we can watch the pregnant ones, and shift the ones who actually are going to give birth during the eclipse itself to your main hall here," he pointed at the longhouse on the map. "Here we can handle the delivery of those who give birth while the moons eclipse the suns and you can check each child as they are born for the signs of the prophesied one!" The barbarian slapped his hand on the scroll, causing a puff of dust to escape from under it.

Endrance smiled at his friend. "That's a good plan, Joven." the young mage sighed as he looked back down at the page. "The only problem is that I cannot get to the only real truth of what identifies the prophesied child!" He exclaimed, shaking his head.

"Well friend," he responded, "that's what makes it fun!" he laughed as he swept back out of the room, possibly to prepare for the search.

Endrance worried about his predicament. If he didn't do what the king asked, then he would likely be killed or worse, fired from his position as Spengur. If he did what he asked, then he needn't put all of the coming up effort into it; He would just be declaring the king's son the prophesied hero anyways. He rubbed at his temples with a hand while trying to clear the dread creeping around his heart.

"May I ask you a question?" Endrance asked, his voice meek.

Anna held out her hands passively. "Whatever you wish to ask of us, dear husband." she said.

He closed his eyes and thought deeply about telling them about the King's words, but first he needed to know that he wasn't going to endanger either his life or theirs. "If I told you something, and it was a very dangerous piece of information, do you have to tell anyone about it?"

Anna shook her head. "Anything you say to us in confidence will never be told to another outside of this room." she answered calmly.

"Even if it was the king who ordered you to talk?" he added.

Anna smirked. "Remember that we are dead to Balator; Even the king cannot force us to tell that which we do not wish to discuss. They call us the Draugnoa for a reason." she replied, a noticeable level of sarcasm on her voice.

Endrance shook his head. "I'm sorry," he apologized "I should have remembered that."

Bridget spoke up, finally moving from her position on the wall. "The Ergkinoa was a part of Barbarian Culture long before King Rothel united the tribes of barbarians in this region and formed Balator. The laws of our sovereignty from the rest of the kingdom are laid in the foundation of our kingdom's laws. And since we were a 'sacrifice' to you, the only one who has control over our actions is you." She inclined her head towards Endrance. "And while I don't have to like you, I still have to serve you to the best of my ability."

"And why is that?" Endrance said sharply, sitting up in his chair. He was aggravated by the stress of the coming eclipse and just couldn't let her one-sided commentary go by this time. "Why do you hate me so much?" he scowled as he stood from his chair.

Anna and Selene exchanged glances, and promptly left the library. The door had barely clicked closed when Bridget responded.

"Because you are weak!" she hissed, shaking her fist at him. "Look at you! So scrawny and you don't even try to get in better shape!"

Endrance shook his head. "I train every weeks end with Joven."

She scoffed. "Yes, with knives!" she pulled hers out and with a casual flick stuck it into the wall near Endrance's head. "Even children can use knives!" She scowled at him fiercely. "A strong woman like me deserves to have a strong husband, but all I have is such a pathetic reed of a husband!" she shook angrily. "And they expect me to *sleep* with you?" her shoulders shuddered as she laughed to herself. "I would break you, boy!"

Endrance felt angry again, this time he knew exactly why and where it came from. "Well then come on." He said quietly, his hands balled into fists. "Let us see then, just how weak you think I am."

She laughed derisively at him, turning away. "No way!" she exclaimed, "I wouldn't waste my time beating a wimp like you into paste!"

Endrance took a step closer, his eyes flashing angrily. "Oh?" he said, his voice mocking. "I think it's because you're afraid I'd punish you for striking me." He shook his head condescendingly. "Maybe you're just being a coward."

Her eyes flashed angrily, and she whirled on him, swinging her fist in a strong right hook. It was just what Endrance had been expecting, but he made no effort to move out of the way. He *wanted* to feel her hit him. He *wanted* to sort this out with her.

Her fist collided with his cheek, and he reeled with the blow, bounced off the wall to his right, and remained on his feet. He looked at her through his now tossed hair, his eyes still shining angrily. He drew up some of his power, and careful to prevent anger from warping the effect of the spell whispered the word of power. "*Ursare.*"

The power flooded his muscles with the strength of a bear, and though he physically didn't transform, he also felt the temperament of an angry bear form in his mind. Her fist had barely left a red mark on his pale skin. "Is that all you got?" he said, tilting his head up. He raised his left hand and beckoned to her. "Come now," he said, raising his other hand in a fist. "Let's do this your way."

Anna and Selene waited out in the hallway patiently. Selene almost went into the room again when she heard the sound of someone striking another, but Anna held her back. "I think it would be best if we stay out of this." She said smartly, looking at Selene. "They have needed to sort themselves out for some time and Bridget's hard headed enough that I think this is the only way."

Selene nodded. "Yeah," she said, walking with Anna towards the bedroom. "She always did like learning the hard way. I hope she doesn't hurt Endrance." She said. "I'll go get the bandages." She offered as another crash came from the library.

Inside, Bridget punched him a second time, this time a quick jab to set herself up for a haymaker, piling all her strength into a heavy punch. The jab connected, tossing his head back, but he was able to see the haymaker coming and threw his hand up in defense. Her fist smacked into his open palm and stopped cold. She looked at their hands in shock as he closed his hand on her fist.

"My turn." He said, pulling her close to him as he wound up with his other hand. Bridget threw her other arm up to block his punch, but the blow sent her reeling back. She slammed into the side of a bookshelf, shaking books off their shelves and raining them down around her. She lurched away from the shelf, shoulder ramming him into the wall. She couldn't understand why he was still standing, but when he let her slam into him and grabbed her with both hands she knew she may have underestimated the young man.

He spun her away from him, and his foot slid on a loose piece of paper. She crashed back first into the door for the library, and the wood cracked and splintered. Bridget brought a leg up and kicked Endrance away from her as hard as she could, and the door gave way as he resisted most of the blow. He skidded back and she tumbled into the hall in a rain of flinders. Rolling to her feet she saw her husband walk into the hallway steadily, his posture angry but confident. He stepped up to her as she swung, taking the blow to his face, and swinging with his right fist.

Anna watched the fight with some degree of surprise. She wasn't sure how the mage was matching her in a straight fist fight, but he was holding his own. In fact, he was proving to be stronger and tougher than her, even though he was very unskilled. Selene rushed back into the hallway and skidded to a stop, dropping the roll of bandages onto the floor in surprise.

She was a more skilled fighter than he, but he wasn't trying to avoid her strikes and taking the opportunity to hit back. As his fist impacted with her abdomen and she crashed through the door to the guest bedroom that was hers, she realized he was taking her hits on purpose, and striking back to prove a point. She backed away from him for a moment, holding her stomach as she recovered from his last strike. He paused for a moment, almost in consideration of her, then stepped into the room and swung a wild punch.

She ducked his blow, and grappled him around the waist with her left arm. Hooking his leg with her right, she easily tossed the lightweight man over her shoulder. He sailed through the air and crashed into the simple wooden night table, smashing it completely. Bridget sidestepped a table leg as it flipped past her and threw a sweeping kick at her husband's side as he pulled himself up. Her foot impacted with his left side, forcing a 'woof' from him as she knocked the breath out of him again.

Throwing a second kick, the young man threw his left arm in the way, blocking her kick. She pulled her leg back to go for a third, and he rolled into her remaining leg, knocking her over him and into the wreckage of the table. The two pulled themselves to their feet unsteadily, panting.

She lunged forward, trying to grab him and throw him around again. He grabbed her arms as she grabbed his, and the two struggled to gain control of the clinch. His strength was in fact greater than hers, something that surprised her greatly. However she had better leverage being half a foot taller than him, and he didn't have steady footing. Twisting her waist while sweeping her foot, she picked her husband up into air and slammed him down upon the bed. The wooden frame cracked as he impacted hard, and the breath left him as bedding flew everywhere.

"Give up?" she asked, struggling to hold him down.

"No. You?" he responded after catching a breath, his lip bloody and a bruise forming on his cheek from having been struck there numerous times.

"I didn't think you where that strong." She admitted. Endrance could tell he was getting through to her, though her grip hadn't slackened. "Why do you hide your power?"

He grunted as he struggled to break free. "I really just don't like conflict." He couldn't break out of her pin no matter what way he tried. "I don't think that a person's physical strength counts…" he grunted. "I think it's your inner strength that you should be impressed with!" he exclaimed, throwing a knee up and launching her over his head into the wall. He was uncertain if he had overdone it when the wall cracked and she crashed down on top of him. The impact was more than the simple bed could take, and it shattered like so much kindling.

She was still conscious, and lay on top of him in the pile of the ruined bed without struggling. The both of them were battered and bruised. She looked him in the eyes and for the first time he didn't see disdain in them.

"Anyone can work out, train for days on end, and become physically strong." Endrance whispered as the two of them lay there unmoving. "But a strongman despairs if he fights something stronger than himself." He felt that these words were as much for him as for another, so he kept speaking. "A person, who grows strong of character, will, and spirit will find a way to survive, even when they are pressed on all sides by many foes stronger than himself." He knew that he himself would be proving this theory in the days to come.

"You know…" she said quietly. "I think I could come to like a guy like you…"

He looked up at her and made a show of examining the wrecked room around them. "It seems we broke your room." He said. "I think it would be best if you came and stayed in the main bedroom."

She nodded. "I think I would like that."

He kissed her on the forehead and then his head fell back. "Good." He responded. "I don't want to have this conversation with you again, okay?"

She laughed briefly, but winced as pain flared up again. "But I like foreplay." She joked.

He winced. "Oh, don't make me laugh; I think you broke one of my ribs."

She shifted so she was lying in the wreckage at his side. "Hey, it's what I do." She boasted jokingly. "If something wasn't broken I wasn't taking you seriously."

"Glad to see that you take me seriously." He said, breathing shallowly.

"I do now." Came her reply.

"So, do you want me to try out my healing spell?" he asked. "I'm going to use it on myself first of course."

"You used some kind of spell to give yourself that strength, didn't you?" Bridget concluded.

"Yeah, like I was going to be able to win a contest of strength with you without using my own talents. Just like I was talking about." He explained.

"I guess magic isn't so bad." She admitted. "But I want you to do that spell thing on me sometime."

"Why?" he asked. The spell had worn off after only a minute, but it had been long enough.

"Because, if it made you that strong, imagine how strong it would make me!" she said with excitement.

Endrance sighed. Anna and Selene came into the room and helped them into the main hall so he could heal their wounds. The spell worked fantastically for broken bones and bruises.

***

Days later, he had made no further progress.

"I just don't see it!" he exclaimed. "I have read all the texts here about the prophesied one, and I cannot find this last book they are referencing to!" He shoved the stack of books away from him and stood, turning to face his Keepers. "Do any of you know where this 'Journal of Lehtor' is?" He waved his hands at the whole library within the study. "I checked every book here, and couldn't find it."

The women exchanged a knowing glance, and then looked at their husband seriously. Anna stepped forwards, nodding. "We have heard of this journal, dear husband. When our order, the Ergkinoa was established, our education began with the writings from that book."

Endrance nodded, "So we go get it where you were trained then?" he inquired.

The Draugnoa shook her head. "We cannot, dear husband." she replied. "We have been educated by word of mouth alone for centuries now. We cannot read any of the books in this library, much less the Journal, which is written in a language that even prior Spengurs couldn't read."

Endrance frowned at Anna. "So then where is the book?" he asked, concerned.

Anna shrugged, but Selene added, "It was buried in the tomb of Rothel, the first king of Balator. The king decreed on his dying breath that the Journal was too dangerous to be kept in mortal hands and so it was entombed with him."

Endrance rubbed his face, exhaling. "I knew this was not going to be easy."

Endrance shrugged as he kicked his feet up on the desk, resting on a pair of books that didn't even bow under his diminutive weight. "That is we have a few weeks to actually find the tomb itself, since the king wished his burial site kept secret, and then we have to figure a way in, get the book, get back here, decipher the secret language, and get the information I need, oh and there's a high probability that the tomb is heavily trapped and there may be other dangers involved."

"We will stand by you, Endrance." Selene encouraged. His heart warmed again at hearing her voice. He didn't know that when he wasn't around she still struggled with the unnatural desire to attack him.

***

It was as hard as expected to find the hidden tomb of Lord Rothel, first king of Balator. He looked at the map he had first, trying to figure out where the tomb could possibly be hidden; until he realized that the maps he was looking at were several hundred years too recent. Digging through some of the first Spengur's things, he was able to find not only an at the time current map of the Kingdom, but also the first spellbook.

Endrance almost danced across the room when he discovered the book lying at the bottom of a trunk, buried at the back of a closet in his storage room. He also had to stop himself from gripping the delicate book too tightly, for fear of utterly shredding the fragile crumbling pages. He eventually would find a spell that would allow him to mend damaged objects, but for the next couple of days he could only stare at the closed book whenever he had the chance and wonder what kind of ancient magics the wizard kept within the dusty, fragile pages.

The older map was copied down dutifully by Anna, and they used the new copy to mark historically significant places on it that King Rothel was involved in. Most of these sites were no longer accessible, or were moved due to increased expansion of the kingdom, since in the early years Balator only had four bowls completed and the other four would be finished over the course of many decades after Rothel's death. Eliminating sites that were built in the four most recent bowls carved out of the mountain, they compared sites in the first four to buildings and other formations that corresponded from past to present without periods of having been torn down or dug up.

They were able to find five potential sites, though the Draugnoa were uncertain which would be the correct one. Endrance marked the locations on the map copy they had made, and started to work on figuring out if there was a pattern in the map markers.

He gathered the Draugnoa in the bedroom so they could talk in relative private. After thinking it through he decided to call Joven in as well. The barbarian came as soon as he had posted a replacement guard for the front door and the wizard had him lock the doors on the way in. Joven leaned against the closed door leading to the main hall, while the women sat on the edge of the bed. He sat upon the chair next to his worktable, and faced them all with his head in his hands at first.

The young mage looked up, placing his hands on his lap as he spoke. "I need to know from you that you will not share what I am about to say with anyone. I know you are to keep secrets, but this is of the greatest importance." he took turns to look each of them in the eye as he continued on. "If this kind of information gets out you may be placed in danger or worse." he finished.

The women nodded in agreement, and Joven shrugged. "Stop being so dramatic, Endrance. Out with it!" he exclaimed.

Endrance nodded. "I will put it simply. King Kalenden wants me to fake the results of my findings when the eclipse happens."

The Draugnoa exchanged glances, concerned. Joven's eyes widened with shock. "Wait," he exclaimed. "You're saying the king, our king, wants you to... lie about who is the prophesied child?"

Endrance nodded. "He insisted very strongly that it would be the best for our kingdom that his son be named the hero of prophecy."

Selene shot to her feet, her face angry. "You can't do that!" she exclaimed angrily. "He can't just tell you to lie to our people like that! It's against the laws... and it's just not right!" her fists were balled at her sides, her lips pursed though she still managed to look pretty in doing so. Anna nodded at her statements while Bridget patted her on the back.

Endrance nodded, beckoning Selene over to him. Sitting her down on the ground in front of him, he stroked her hair as he looked out over her head at the others in the room. "Selene is right. No matter how much the king would threaten me, I cannot perpetrate such a deception." he looked down into her eyes and smiled warmly, and her expression softened.

Joven pushed himself away from the door and spoke up. "Wait a minute!" he exclaimed. "He's the king of Balator! Why would he do something like that?"

The young mage sighed. "Joven, I have no reason to lie to you. You have been and always will be my most trusted protector. I do not tell you these things lightly. The king has decided that he would rather risk destroying a two-thousand year old prophecy in order to further his popularity and increase his personal power. A king who fathered the great hero would be respected across the entire barbarian community, much less the world."

Joven shook his head. "No!" he said. "My brother is general of the king's armies! He meets with him regularly! He would have said something if the king was doing something underhanded!" he rebutted. He stomped angrily as he spoke, the metal buckles on his armor clinking as they tapped the hardened leather.

The young mage stood, holding his hands out at his sides passively as he slipped past Selene. "Joven," he started, walking towards his bodyguard. "I am not saying the king is evil, I am merely saying what he has tried to get out of me."

Joven looked distressed as he accepted the wizard's words. "So," he said finally, "what do we do now?" he asked.

Anna stood. "We will support the Spengur, even if the king himself were to try to retaliate." she stated, a cold fact no one would refute.

Endrance shrugged. "I am going to declare the correct child for what he is. If the king is lucky, his threats and manipulations may have been unnecessary. If not, then I'm sure to have a very angry ruler banging on my door day after the eclipse."

Selene spoke up. "Endrance, you are in a better position than you realize." she said.

The young mage looked over to her. She ran her hands across her dress as she spoke. "You are the only man of magic in the kingdom, and even the king must defer to you in matters of magic. If you publicly declare the true child of prophecy, then the king cannot say otherwise."

Endrance nodded. "True, but that doesn't make him any less likely to try to kill me."

"But it does my husband. The king cannot strike at you for performing your duties as the Spengur. Your ruling is final. He could try to get rid of you with more covert means, but that is the reason we are here."

Joven grunted and crossed his arms. "Any of us here will fight to the death to protect you, no matter the source." he frowned. "Even if the king were to order me to do otherwise." the phrase left a bad taste in his mouth.

The young mage smiled, reassured. "Thank you all," he said gratefully. "Thank you so very much for your loyalty. Don't worry; I assure you I will ensure the prophecy comes to pass!"

The sha'hdi listened from her hiding place nearby. As was her kind's abilities, she crouched completely undetected in the shadow of the worktable the Draugnoa and that barbarian lout were facing. The idiots could even walk right next to her and not know she was there until she reached out and killed them. She smirked, knowing they might not realize it even then.

It seemed the mage had decided to go against the king's orders after all. She smiled. So the brat had a backbone after all. This was turning out much better than expected.

Chapter 29

Using the information he put together from the maps, Endrance and Joven were able to plan their visit to those sites over the next couple of days, preparing for each individually. The two of them looked at the body of water within the kingdom's walls first. The body was too small to be a lake, but too large to be a pond. The water was the reservoir for the expansive farmland of the first and largest bowl of the kingdom. Farmers had packed the dirt around the water and even laid stone around the edges, though they did not line the bottom of the reservoir.

Joven and Endrance stood at the edge of the water the next day and looked at the calm surface while they puzzled the next step. The suns and a few scant clouds lazily drifted across its surface and it looked much like a large mirror had been lain out amidst several fields of grain and vegetables. The shadow of Gullin swooping by, flying high in the sky drifted across the water lazily. Joven kicked a pebble with the tip of his boot and watched it drop into the water, sending concentric ripples across the surface of the water. Endrance looked up at the barbarian as the big man turned to him with a question on his lips.

"So... why are we here again?" Joven asked, scratching his head.

Endrance shrugged. "This site is supposed to be historically significant. So I'm going to look for the chance the Tomb of Rothel lies beneath." he explained.

Joven nodded. "Ah I see..." his nod stopped. "So, now that we've been here, it's about time we started heading back, right?" he asked, looking around and seeing nothing of interest. "What was so important here anyways?" he finished, stifling a yawn.

The wizard closed his eyes a second, thinking back to the explanation his Keepers had provided him. "This is the site where king and the first 'Spengur' met, as well as where they parted ways for the last time. The king and his Spengur were both very close friends, and it was after he left that king Rothel created the laws about the Spengur and their general sovereignty."

"Ah!" Joven exclaimed. "So the first Spengur left because of some moral objections?"

"Indeed. The Spengur then was a very powerful wizard, but something the king asked him to do did not sit well with him, and he refused. When the king tried to force the wizard to do so they argued here, and instead of complying the wizard cast a powerful spell, shouting he would never return so long as Balator was run by Rothel's lineage. His spell blew a large crater out of the first bowl, and in the explosion the wizard disappeared, never to be seen again."

Joven pointed at the center of the reservoir. "But we can see there is nothing here." he expressed. "So what are we looking for?"

Endrance gestured at the water. "A clue, perhaps even the tomb itself."

Joven snorted. "Well obviously nothing is here."

The young mage scoffed, shaking his head. "There is always something there; it's just beneath the surface."

"Of the water?"

"Maybe the water, or perhaps the earth beneath it. It hadn't been converted into a reservoir until a year after Rothel's death."

"So he might be buried here?"

"Like I said, possibly." Endrance sighed, sitting down at the edge. "It would be nice if it was here though."

"Why's that?"

"I don't relish the idea of spending another several days researching and gaining nothing. Besides, I have reason to believe that there is something here, but if it's not here I don't know where else to look along the line."

"What line?"

"I detected a subtle change in the flow of energy as it was carried…" Endrance started, trailing off as he glanced at Joven. "There was a trail left by magic that coincides with a few historical sites." He simplified.

Joven nodded. "See. You can learn after all."

Endrance stood, dusting the small amount of dirt off his backside as he looked over the water. "Well," he said "time for me to get to work."

The wizard dug into the satchel he kept slung over his shoulder and pulled out his spellbook. Flipping through the pages, he found the spell he was looking for. He held the book by the spine in his left hand while he tracked the words and symbols he was reading with a fingertip from the other. He read through the pages twice, and repeated the phrases multiple times as he did so. His fingers twitched as he thought through the motions needed to weave the energy, and in his mind calculated the amount needed for the spell.

Surprisingly little, it seemed for such a powerful magic, and the motions were less stylized and more functional than many of the newer spells. He closed the book a minute later, certain he had the formula right. Putting the book away, he began casting the spell. Hands and fingers wove intricate lines of faintly glowing bluish energy that pulsed to the intonations of his voice. He gathered up the spell as he completed it, reaching out with his right hand over the center of the water and spreading his fingers in a fan as he exclaimed the last word of the spell. The energy dispersed from his hand, and invisibly swept out across the water.

Immediately the effect of the spell was evident. From the point where his palm obscured his vision, the water immediately froze solid; from bottom to surface, and swiftly the ice spread across the water until the entire reservoir was one piece of ice. Even the faint ripples in the water caused by the mountain breeze froze, leaving the surface almost perfectly smooth and clearly reflective. A small ripple in the water had frozen in motion, leaving concentric rings of waves in ice.

Joven's jaw practically fell off its hinges and Endrance whistled. "Wow!" the wizard exclaimed. "That was completely more effective than I had thought it would be!" he walked out onto the ice and looked about himself excitedly. "I mean I had hoped but… Wow!" he finished, kneeling onto the ice and running his gloved hand over the surface as smooth as blown glass. It was frozen so completely that it wasn't even slick with partial melt, just cold and smooth like marble.

Very impressive! Gullin told him, the bird chirping cheerfully as he swooped down and landing on the ice out in the middle of the reservoir. *You didn't even need my help.*

Joven recovered slightly, taking a hand and closing his mouth manually as he tromped out onto the ice carefully, his metal shod boots gouging little nicks in the ice as he walked. He stopped in front of the young mage and stared at him.

"Umm..." Joven began. "That was... amazing!" he exclaimed, still somewhat dazed.

Endrance stood, excited. "I know!" he shouted "Wasn't that great!" he exclaimed, his deer-hide boots slipping slightly on the ice and he wobbled, his enthusiasm nearly toppling him over. Joven reached out and caught the young man, letting go once he had stabilized. "I think that spell is incredibly effective!" he continued, skating across the ice slowly as he took it all in. "I mean, the spell didn't even call for a body of water but look!" he slapped his thigh, whooping. "I think it made it all the more effective!" Gullin took to the air and flit about the area, seeming to be even more joyful as Endrance's mood brightened.

Joven looked at him confused. "I don't understand, Endrance. How can a spell that freezes water not need water to do so?" he asked.

Endrance started skating around the ice more steadily now and picked up speed as he circled around the barbarian gleefully. A farmer had come up to retrieve some water for his crops and stood his mouth agape as he watched the Spengur ice skating over his water supply. Endrance, not noticing the man nearby, began to explain. "Well, the spell itself was a spell I copied from one of the oldest spell books an earlier Spengur left behind!" he exclaimed merrily. "And it was actually a spell that creates a wall of ice out of the water in the air around where the wall is made! I had cast the spell hoping to make a walkway out over the water so we could look down at the center and see if we could look for the tomb-" Endrance skidded to a stop in front of the barbarian. "But the spell absorbed all the water of the reservoir and froze the whole thing! Isn't that great?" he puffed from his exertions. Gullin dropped onto the young man's head, and sat on its feet, using his hair as an impromptu nest.

It is too cold though. The familiar remarked. *I prefer the element of fire.*

Joven scratched his head. "Yeah, I guess so," he began "But is it going to stay like this forever?" he asked.

The wizard shook his head, waving a hand and causing the familiar to chirp angrily as it took flight again. "No," Endrance responded. "It will melt naturally once the magical energies I put into the spell wears off. The magic itself just gathers the water together and freezes it. It's not 'magic' ice or something, though it should stay frozen until it runs out of energy."

Joven looked Endrance in the eye. "We live in a mountain that is almost always just around freezing, Endrance. If it had to thaw that much water on its own it could take months."

Endrance scowled. "You're no fun!" he joked playfully. "Fine! Fine! I was going to melt the ice after we checked anyways!"

The two of them made their way to the center of the frozen reservoir. Looking straight down, they were able to see a stone disk set in the bottom of the ice. It had the symbol of king Rothel on it, the wolf that Endrance had seen before on the king's men. Three circles of ancient script encircled the symbol. Joven squinted through the ice and Endrance took out a piece of parchment and a stick of charcoal, carefully he laid the parchment against the ice and quickly sketched a copy of the disk at the bottom of the reservoir.

"Is that it?" Joven asked.

The young mage shrugged, sketching the pattern of markings across the stone below. He had to be careful, the frozen ice made discerning fine details difficult, and he had to double check his work. "It could be. Or it could be a memorial marker or something."

He stood up, and rolled the slightly damp and very cold parchment up, slipping it into his bag. He tugged on Joven's arm as he went to leave. Several other farmers were now gathered at the edge of the ice and were glaring at the two of them as they had worked. Joven nodded grimly. "I think we should give the farmers their water back." Joven muttered as he and Endrance made their way back to the shore.

The wizard smiled at the farmers, who stepped away from him fearfully. Joven glared at the few who held farming implements that could be used as weapons. The young mage then turned his back on the men, raised his hands, and closed his eyes, reaching out with his senses towards the ice.

Endrance could feel the strands of magic from his spell lingering in the water. Magic that was still active always had a connection to the caster, until either the spell or the caster expired. If it was in the nature of the spell, it could continue on after the mage's death, but usually effects brought out by the caster only lasted while their will existed to keep the magic coherent. Certain spells could have power invested in them and left alone, running until their power was exhausted.

Endrance reached out with his will, feeling along the line that connected him to the spell. Through it he could learn many things about the spell that he would not have known from reading the book. The most important thing was that the ice would remain in the current atmosphere for around two months before the energy invested in freezing the ice had run out, allowing it to thaw as normal. The high altitude of the mountain kingdom and the continuously cold climate would make sure that it needed very little of its energy to stay frozen.

He extended a hand towards the water, grasping the thread of his spell with his will and body. He focused and then willed the spell broken, using an equal amount of energy to counteract the spell's energy. He realized later that he perhaps could have canceled the spell in a less dramatic fashion, but at the time he had already committed. The ice suddenly seemed to vaporize as a great volume of mist erupted from the surface of the ice. As the mist cleared the farmers could see the water below rippling gently, thawed. Normally the water would still have been frozen, but the act of countering the energies of a spell caused it to thaw. Since Endrance used the same amount of energy canceling the spell as was used to create it, the spell was effectively negated and the water restored to its normal state. *Maybe a little bit warmer*, Endrance thought. *I forgot that the spell had already expended some of its energy, so I may have put just a bit too much into the counter spell.*

Yes you did. Gullin remarked. *It took more power to freeze the water than maintain it. And since it would naturally thaw you wouldn't need to use exactly the same amount.*

Endrance and Joven left without saying a word, and the farmers whispered amongst each other superstitiously as they departed. One of them stuck a finger in the water and nearly fell over when he found out the water was actually warm. As the wizard and his bodyguard left, Endrance caught a glimpse of some of the older men stripping off their shirts as they waded into the reservoir.

***

The translating stage of his work proved to be more difficult, as he had to keep going back to the books and re-translating certain symbols as he found many of his current translations made no sense in any grouping. The script around the circular stone was uniformly spaced and had no punctuation, so he was uncertain where to begin or end the translation. He brushed his hair away from his face, frustrated as he went back to the books for the fourth time that hour. The Draugnoa eventually drifted off, having their chores and duties to perform as he worked on a one-person task. His familiar dozed perched on the hot metal roof of the oil lantern he was using for light.

He never noticed the newly replaced door sliding open, nor did he hear the faint creak of the hinge as it closed again. Endrance sighed noisily as he scribbled on yet another piece of parchment as he struggled through the ancient words. He did however, notice the flicker of one of his candles as a faint draft of wind caused it to dance on its wick. He glanced behind him, hoping to see Selene, but saw no one neither standing behind him nor sitting in one of the few other pieces of furniture around his library. Shrugging, Endrance turned back to his parchments. "It's gotten late, I really should check to see what time it is," he muttered, turning the parchment over. He spotted the symbol he needed and replied to himself "...after I get this phrase finished."

A dark figure slowly and deliberately descended from the ceiling, releasing its grip on the rafters above once its feet had silently touched down onto the earthen floor. The intruder watched her young prey go about his business unawares. She waited for one, two, three heartbeats, relishing the fact that she could move on to the next stage of her contract. She slipped a thin wire from a blackened metal loop about her wrist, and with great care she padded up to the chair Endrance sat in, spreading the length of wire between her hands, using black metal caps on her thumbs to safely handle the weapon.

Outside, Joven approached the longhouse. He had the evening off, but wanted to see if he could get Endrance to join him for some drinks at his favorite watering hole. The barbarian had spent months travelling with the young man, but never had the chance to see if he could hold his liquor. It would be an amusing prospect and the drinks might put a few hairs on his chest. Gods knew he needed them.

His grin faded swiftly as he noticed no men on duty outside the longhouse. He was sure the men were still supposed to be on guard, the people had still expressed unease about the Spengur's presence, and Balen had insisted the guards stay until the eclipse had passed. There was no one there. More men shirking on their duties Joven would have to discipline personally.

He growled angrily, approaching the doors. Immediately he noticed spatters of blood on the ground, sending him into full alertness. He slammed into the double doors leading into the central room of the longhouse, blowing them both open. They hadn't even been locked. The fires in the corner braziers were out, casting the room in a dimness that made it hard to see clearly in.

A faint purple mist layered the ground throughout the main room, and two white dressed forms slumped across the floor. Joven slapped a hand over his mouth, holding his breath as he thundered across the floor and banked left through the open door to the hall leading to the Spengur's library. He had to leap over yet another form he hoped was only unconscious as he barreled at the door at the end of the hall.

Endrance had barely looked up at the crashing sound coming from outside. He was busy with his work and he dismissed it as unimportant. Gullin however, had awoken and saw the sha'hdi lurking right behind the mage.

Endrance! Behind you!

She lunged forwards and her lethal wire found its mark.

Joven burst through the door as Endrance jumped in his seat, his fingers scrabbling at his neck in panic. Joven removed his hand from his mouth as he shouted in rage just as the woman gave her wire a sharp yank. Endrance's eyes widened in pain as crimson welled out from a line across his throat, and his body jerked involuntarily. Scarlet sprayed the books before him as his lifeblood escaped him, and wordlessly he collapsed forwards, his head falling onto bloody parchments. Gullin went into a panic, fluttering about and cawing angrily.

The woman smirked at the barbarian at the door as she simultaneously stepped back from the garroted mage and snapped her hand, causing the razor wire to retract back into the ring on her wrist with a *snick*. Joven charged, raising his ax. The assassin laughed mockingly as she gracefully skipped back out of the barbarian's swing. She danced about him as he swung again, just barely missing her and demolishing a bookshelf instead.

"Silly human!" she laughed as she moved around him, avoiding his blows with practiced ease. "You can't hit the sha'hdi so easily!" she laughed again as she faded just out of the ax's surely fatal blow. "You came a hundred years too early to take me on!"

Endrance was in darkness, he could feel his life blood flowing out of him. If only he could speak well enough to cast the healing spell he had devised.

Gullin! He ordered, trying to get the bird to snap out of his panic. *Listen to me!*

The bird responded but kept fluttering around. *What do want me to do?*

Can you help me cast the healing spell from before? He asked, finding it harder to concentrate, even though only a second or two had passed.

Form it in your mind, and I will do the rest. The familiar instructed, landing on his head and leaning over the crimson pool of his blood. *Hurry.*

The assassin performed a backwards aerial as she evaded Joven's furious strike and landed just inside the door leading out of the library. "Maybe you should have paid better attention to your charge, barbarian." she taunted Joven as she slid back into the doorway. "Then you might have had the honor of dying before he-"

She was interrupted as something shot past her face, barely a finger's width from her nose to embed into the door hanging open beside her. Only years of practice saved her from flinching and as it passed by; her reflexes and experience told her what nearly took her nose off. A curved dagger, its handle and finger guard made from a single intact deer's antler. The blade sunk an inch into the solid wooden door, its handle quivering at the impact.

Her gaze slid to her left, towards the direction it came from. She looked towards the desk where her target had been eliminated. To her target she'd thought dead, who was standing next to his desk, his arm at the completion of a throw, and a scarlet stain down his neck and the front of his robes, as well as his forehead and nose where he had collapsed on the blood sprayed surface. His face was pale, but there was a glint of something dangerous in his eyes. He had a sister to the dagger he threw in his left hand, and though he leaned against the side of the desk, he was in a far better condition than the assassin had thought she had left him in.

The young man couldn't possibly be alive after that much blood loss, much less conscious. The barbarian's presence would make a direct assault to finish the job impossible. Her client had told her that the Spengur was only a man, nothing more. Their information was wrong.

Joven, also shocked at his murdered ally's revival, renewed his assault, charging after the elf with a battle cry that shook the books in their shelves. She snapped her attention back to him, rolling back into the hallway and dashing for the window at the end. Joven burst into the hall already having turned to chase her, his shoulder slamming into the wall and cracking the wood. The elf leapt, her hand flashing out in an arc. The wooden shutters exploded outwards, and she neatly dove through the opening.

Joven crashed into the windowsill, his thighs slamming into the table there and crushing it against the wall. He looked out, but could no longer see the elf. She must have disappeared into the shadows. He grabbed the shutters roughly and slammed them closed, bolting them in place again before rushing back to the library to check on his charge.

The young mage lay half across the floor, half up against the wall next to the desk. His chest rose and fell faintly, and there was a gurgling sound that told Joven he was at least breathing. Gullin hopped back and forth on the table overlooking the mage in worry. He knelt before the wizard, and felt a moment of panic. His experience as a warrior told him that a neck wound like that should have killed him already, and even if treated right away there's nothing someone could do to save the victim. The injury was also exactly the same kind that had killed the tribunal before. How long had the assassin been trailing them?

"Endrance, no..." he croaked, his throat tightening around his voice as grief shot through him. He reached out with a gauntleted hand to brush the young man's hair from his face as he watched the mage's weak breathing. "Why wasn't I there?" he asked. "I could have saved you!" he covered his face with his other hand in shame.

Endrance's head tilted up marginally, and his lips moved slightly. "That's what I want to know." he whispered hoarsely.

Joven blinked. "Endrance? You're awake! Gods!" he placed his hand gently on the young man's shoulder as the wizard opened his eyes and looked at him blearily. "You're alive! By the gods!" the barbarian exclaimed, surprise and joy on his voice. The mage bobbed his head slightly, wincing.

"Yep. Still alive." he whispered.

"I need to get you help!" he exclaimed.

Endrance grabbed his arm before the man could leave. "No." He said. "Don't go. They'll know."

"So?" Joven exclaimed angrily.

"If the people find out about this it would shake their confidence in me. And we both know who it was that attacked me."

"But you're injured!"

"I have a healing spell," Endrance whispered. "That was how I survived this. A little more of it and I should be safe enough."

Joven nodded. "What can I do to help you recover?" he asked, kneeling before him. Endrance smiled weakly at his bodyguard, as he pushed off his knees with his hands to stand. Joven stood as well, reaching out to steady the wizard as he wobbled.

"Let's get me something to eat." Endrance whispered.

The two of them walked out of the library, slowly as Endrance got his legs back under his own control. He looked back at the blood spattered desk and books. "Are my Draugnoa okay?" he asked, his query carrying as much concern as was physically possible in a whisper. "Is Selene okay?"

Joven looked down the hall, to see one of the Draugnoa stirring as the mist dissipated. "Yeah, they got knocked out with some kind of gas. They should be okay in a little while."

Endrance smiled faintly. "All right." he chuckled weakly as he wobbled down the hall, constantly forcing Joven to adjust the young man's angle so that he remained upright. "Oh man," he whispered.

"What?" Joven demanded.

"They are going to go crazy when they see the mess in the library." he responded.

Chapter 30

The interior of the entrance to the Tomb of Rothel was lightless and slightly damp. The faint *drip drip drip* of water echoed as it leaked through the circular entrance to the tomb. The walls were continuously damp from the water above. A small amount of the water pooled at a small depression in the entrance chamber before dribbling across a seam in the stones and down the steps into the tomb proper. It seemed to disappear somewhere along the line, but even so the stonework was very slick.

The air was stale, dank, and musty. The sounds of water moving above the tomb were muffled by several feet of earth and stone. Slowly the water above gurgled against the circular capstone that sealed the tomb away from the world, as if the whole place was afloat at sea. The continual dribble of water did little to prevent a buildup of moss and fungus in the entry chambers of the tomb. The smell of algae lurked in the pungent, stale air.

The reservoir above was dark as well; the deep cloudy night above it had dulled the water's mirror sheen to a surfaceless depth unnoticeable except to those who were carrying light. Endrance stood at the edge of the reservoir at almost the exact same spot he had stood before, except this time he was flanked on his right side by three women and the other by his personal bodyguard Joven. The collective group of them wore a cloak of thick fur to help shield them from the icy wind that poured down the mountainside from the snowy peak several hundred meters above even the eighth bowl of Balator. Gullin sat quietly perched on Endrance's shoulder, seemingly asleep.

Endrance glanced at Anna, Bridget, and Selene. They looked about themselves one last time, and finding no one near, nodded back at him one at a time. He looked to his left at Joven, who nodded and muttered. "Do it."

The young mage rubbed his neck before beginning. It had been three days since the almost successful assassination attempt and even though his wounds had healed and he had recovered his strength he still occasionally felt a twinge where his attacker's near-fatal garrote had struck. A very faint thin hairline scar ran across his neck, nearly invisible unless he was to call attention to it and point it out. He had to take great care with his voice until the wound had fully healed, or else he risked undoing the tenuous healing to his vocal cords. As it was, he has had to speak only in whispers and was not up to the task of casting spells at full power until today.

He adjusted the silk gloves on his hands. He wore heavier silk clothing when he was out at night, as well as one addition: a shirt made of very finely wrought metal links. Lighter than leather armors but still noticeably heavier than regular cloth, it provided more protection than his silk shirt could possibly grant. He wore it at everyone's insistence and the women made sure he wore it at all times except when he was in bed. It was an irritation to wear and felt restricting, but he knew he would rather wear it than have to deal with the four insistent barbarians over the matter.

Endrance went over the spell he had been working on for this specific task. He checked to make sure that all preparations were complete. Finding everything he had set up and ready, he went to work casting the spell. His hands moved about in front of him as he shaped the spell, and his arcane chant gave the magic power. For several minutes he labored over the spell, one of the most carefully worded and precisely designed spells he'd ever even attempted. He devoted half of his aura into the spell, a significant amount for any spellcaster.

He reached out both hands, and gathered energy between his hands, fingers clawed around a rapidly spinning ball of golden colored wind. He struggled to hold the winds in as he neared the completion of his spell. He released the formed spell as his arms fully extended, and he spoke the final command word. The golden wind roared from between his fingers. It swept out across the surface of the reservoir, and Endrance sagged as the sudden drain of energy left him light headed. Anna caught him up expertly and he leaned his head against her arm as they stood side by side, his hairline barely reaching her collarbone.

The water rippled in the darkness, and near the center of the reservoir a small ripple began to swell larger. The disturbance of the water swirled, and began to spiral up into the air, forming a waterspout. It was at first thin, but increased in width and speed as more of the reservoir's mass was drawn up into its power.

The waterspout carried up higher and higher, until it seemed to reach the limit of its growth. From there, the water that continued to pour up the spout started spilling out from the top, spreading across the air above the waterspout. As the water floating above filled out, the water of the reservoir emptied. The water swirled up, and it took only a few minutes until the only water that remained were from small puddles from the uneven surface of the reservoir floor.

The bottom of the waterspout, having run out of water to absorb sucked itself up into the airborne pool of water. From the shore of the reservoir, The little amounts of light the night sky cast was reflecting off a perfect sphere of hundreds of thousands of gallons of water hovering a few dozen yards in the air. In his mind, he heard Gullin ruffle his feathers as the bird looked up at the sphere of water in the sky.

Perfectly cast. Gullin observed. *I will remain above ground and monitor the spell's duration. Nonetheless, I would advise more haste than caution.*

Endrance tilted his head to Joven. "Go." At the command Joven nodded and tromped into the reservoir basin, his boots sinking several inches in the sediment on the bottom before he stepped out unhindered with a loud *Shhluuck shluuck* noise. The barbarian made his way carefully across the surface to the stone cap that lay in the center.

He examined the circular stone that marked Rothel's tomb. The markings and the seal of Rothel glittered faintly despite the lack of ambient light. Joven grabbed a torch he had strung on his belt and with quick practiced strokes of flint and steel, lit it. The light from the torch seemed a beacon in the dark night. The light illuminated the backs of the four outside the reservoir, as they had spread out to look for anything approaching.

They had chosen to come at night for several reasons. Endrance's reasoning was that they could get in, find the book, and get out. Then return the reservoir to normal while all the farmers who relied on this water source were asleep. That way they wouldn't be aware that he had been using magic on their reservoir. The last thing he wanted to deal with was complaints of 'cursed' water. The Draugnoa insisted that the tomb should remain secret, and they should do as much as possible to prevent others from finding the location of the tomb. Joven's reason was simple: The enemy uses the darkness to gain the advantage, why shouldn't he?

The torchlight illuminated a stone cap nearly a man and a half across, with three rings of ancient text encircling the seal of Rothel. Several black iron bolts rimmed the seal. They bore no rust from the centuries of immersion in water, and it was likely they had been treated by some method. The muck around the base of the seal had mostly been washed away from the water spout, and Joven now stood on somewhat grimy stone, the same quality as that which composed the outer walls of Balator. Joven noted each block of stone he could see had some kind of symbol carved in the center, though it was unreadable, being of the shifting language that Endrance's spellbooks bore.

He set the torch on the seal, and stripped off his gauntlets. With bare hands he felt along the damp surface of the seal. Surprisingly the stone had not accumulated even the smallest amount of moss or algae during its multi-century existence. He eventually found the inconsistencies that Endrance had instructed him about. The center seal of Rothel had several square grooves in its surface, each half a hand span square. The seal was five squares by five squares, making a grid of 25 evenly cut squares in the seal. Joven closed his eyes, thinking hard. Endrance had told him the sequence of buttons to push, but it had been very complicated, and he had to concentrate very hard to remember the first six steps.

Joven carefully pushed the stone tiles in a seemingly random order, at first confident but swiftly becoming hesitant as he found his memory trailing off no matter how hard he thought about it. He struggled through it, but came up short on the last button. He glanced back to see if Endrance was watching. The mage wasn't. He furrowed his brow, trying his hardest to remember. The wizard had been reluctant to grant the task to him, insisting that one of the Keepers would be better suited to trigger the opening, but Joven had asserted that he would be the one best able to handle anything that might come out of the tomb immediately upon opening.

Still drawing a blank, Joven growled in frustration, raising his fists as his irritation grew into anger. He slammed his arms down in a two fisted hammer strike, his muscles rippling in the torchlight. The stone seal hardly shuddered from the impact, and the torch barely rolled a finger width in response. He grunted, raising his arms and shaking out his hands. He would have to figure out the last button.

One square that had been struck under his fists as he let out his frustration clicked and depressed. The whole seal shuddered much more than when he had struck it and Joven quickly snatched up and put his gauntlets back on. Grabbing up the torch, he looked back out to the rim of the reservoir and whistled sharply. The four keeping watch gathered together as Joven turned to look back at the seal.

The outer rim's black iron rods started extending out, one at a time. They rose to just over a man's height and stopped. Joven could see now they were octagonal rods, and along their surface many ancient symbols had been carved upon them. He watched all of them rising and muttered, "What do they say?"

"They are tales of his deeds." Endrance replied, his voice right next to him. Joven jumped and whirled around. Somehow all four of them had already made it to the stone around the seal. Endrance continued saying, "There is one rod for each year of his reign, and each rod is inscribed with the summary of his deeds for that year."

Joven looked over the fifty-four rods total as the last one rose into place. He grunted in appreciation. "He led a full life." he concluded as the stone circle in the center, as well as the iron rods extending from it, slid aside noisily. The capstone grated aside, and rancid air *whooshed* out of the egress, causing everyone to hold their breath as fresh air rushed in. Years of bad air and pressure from above had made the air inside sickening, and the group had to wait several minutes before they felt it was safe enough to descend the water slick steps inside.

Endrance glanced at everyone. "Alright, we go in, get the book, and get out as fast as possible. The spell I cast uses power at a faster rate the more volume it is holding. If the spell collapses before we get out, the water will flood the tomb and drown us." He drew an affirmative nod from each person present. As if reminding them, the sphere of water above made a slight gurgling sound.

Joven stared at the water orb, and frowned. "That really bothers me." He stated. Bridget nodded silently, agreeing.

With Joven leading and the three Draugnoa following behind Endrance, the group cautiously went down the steps into the entry way of the tomb. Joven's torch illuminated only a short distance from his position making the dark seem a hungry beast, its jaws just waiting for the light to diminish so it could devour its prey. The floor under their feet glistened with a faint sheen of stagnant water.

"So..." the barbarian began. "What do we have to be careful of?" he asked, a short sword in his right hand and the torch in the left. A big ax or great sword like he preferred to use was far too unwieldy in tight stone quarters so he took weapons that would be dangerously effective in such an environment. Short swords, daggers, hand axes, cudgel, and a pick were strapped to his hardened leather armor. He even slipped the dangerously lethal punching spikes on, granting him weaponry even if he were to lose the rest of his weapons. He was prepared for almost any kind of indoors engagement.

Each of Endrance's Draugnoa bore their weapons as well, in order to support Joven in combat. Anna, by far the best trained of the three, wielded a short hafted spear, and a round shield on her off hand. Bridget carried a single curved blade in her hands, the blade was too wide to be a scimitar, and it had no point much like a cleaver and it was more than sharp enough to slice through a man's arm as easily as a stalk of wheat. Selene carried perhaps the most fearful of their weapons. It was a curved dagger, designed for reaping necks and not grain. The weapon was attached to a slender long chain, nearly twenty feet in length. The chain was coiled in her left hand, and from what Endrance had seen of their practice sessions with their weapons Selene definitely knew how to strike with the bladed head anywhere within the chain's reach.

Each of them wore their armor and their cloaks. Endrance wore his heavy silk robes, a cloak, and his soft leather boots. He had the chain shirt on, as well as a small silver dagger on his belt and the pair of antler-handled daggers Joven had crafted for him. He also had a cheap pair of cloth gloves on, a pair easily replaced. He was the lightest armed of the five of them, unless they considered his spells or the lightning upon his fingers.

Joven tromped down the stairs cautiously, moving the torch about and peering into funeral alcoves along the way as they descended. Coffins filled these spaces, all closed firmly and covered with fungus. Their ornate casings of detailed and molded black iron lent to the rumors that king Rothel's most faithful soldiers, upon their liege's death had buried themselves alive in his tomb to become the king's vanguard in the next life.

They came across a spiraling stair, heading further down. Every two flights Joven found a sparsely placed torch bracket with rotted splinters of wood left within it. Taking a moment to bracket the torch he brought in, he dug into his pack, producing a dozen more small torches. Shouldering his pack again, he lit the new torch and moved on down. At each bracket he replaced the crumbling torch from the bracket with the lit one he carried, lit a new one, and moved further down.

Several hundred steps down they emerged from the stairs to a long walkway where the dark was so oppressive and deep that Joven's torch could not pierce the darkness more than a few feet across. If there were walls, they were pitch black and did not reflect any torchlight. The group carefully advanced into the hall, and after a while Endrance felt a difference in the pressure of the air.

"Joven," he stated, and the barbarian stopped. "Hand me a torch, please." he asked, holding his hand out while peering out into the darkness.

Joven grumbled, but shuffled his short sword, current torch, and new one until he was able to safely light the second torch without setting his chin on fire. He placed the handle in the mage's hand, and Endrance swept the torch into the darkness. The torch passed though, visibly burning and shedding off light, but the light fell on nothing.

Endrance looked down at the floor. The light still cut off at exactly the same place as the torch Joven held. He dropped to a knee, and felt along the floor out over the black line. There was no floor beyond it. He ran his hand along the edge, and was able to determine they were standing on a stone walkway over nothing. He rocked back slowly, standing after finding his balance again. "Let's stay on the path we can see." he stated, shaking his head. "There's a long drop with an indeterminate stop if you walk out of the light."

Joven and the Keepers nodded, ushering Endrance back into the center of the path and following the bridge across the void. The expanse seemed to be endless on all sides, even though the young mage knew that they had only descended a few hundred feet under the earth. Their progress was slower than he had wished; they had to carefully advance across the bridge for fear of falling off.

After nearly five hundred feet the bridge fed into a wall, with a door of unbelievable proportions. Made entirely of Balator's black iron, the portal was over forty feet tall and fifteen wide. Across the surface of the door as if they had pushed their way out of the surface of the metal while it was still hot but remained forever coated in black iron, was dozens of twisted and contorted skeletons. Their postures were bent, their hands clawed, and mouths agape, lending the impression that they were in great torment when crafted. A chill ran down Endrance's spine as he looked up at the barrier.

The shifting light of the torches made every jumping shadow, every flicker of bright in the dark seem like movement across the door. Made it seem like perhaps, the people whose skeletons were trapped across its surface were still somehow alive, and twitched and twisted in pain whenever someone wasn't looking. The chill spread to the others, who also held their torches up to see the door. The three Keepers gathered closer to their husband, wary.

"This is definitely *not* what I was expecting down here." Endrance said. "I thought your people refused to use magic."

"We don't like it, generally." Joven grunted, the only one apparently not bothered by the door's decorations. Prodding one of the closer skeletal arms with his short sword, he was searching while the mage continued to stare up at the door. The metal on metal *clink* was satisfying enough for him, and he continued to search around the door. "There should be a way to open this, right?"

"So, I may ask" Endrance stated, "Why in the world does your legendary, heroic, barbarian king have a door that says 'I'm evil' so badly that I feel like running and crying in a corner?"

Joven shrugged. "Maybe he liked the style?"

"Likes." Endrance corrected. "It's becoming increasingly possible the correct term is 'likes'."

The barbarian turned to him and frowned, still poking the door with his left hand as he spoke. "What do you mean 'likes'? The guy's been dead for over a thousand years!" he knocked on the iron with his knuckle. "No way Rothel is still alive, everyone would know, right?"

Endrance sighed, his shoulders slumping. "There are ways you can be dead but still 'be' around, Joven." he held up a hand, closed except his forefinger which he held up. "First, there are incorporeal undead like ghosts, wraiths, et cetera," he held up another finger. "Then there are corporeal undead like zombies, vampires, ghouls, litchdom, revenants..." he trailed off, seeing that Joven understood his point.

"Okay, okay," Joven acquiesced. "I get it!" he folded his arms across his chest, twisting the sword around in his right hand and tapping the flat against his side as he spoke.

A close examination of the door proved fruitless, as the five of them spent several minutes running their hands and their scrutiny across its surface. The Draugnoa could offer no suggestions from lore, and Joven's favored option of just bashing it in seemed too impractical. Endrance knew no spells that could open the door, and even if he knew how to teleport like his master could, it wouldn't work if he could not see the end destination.

"Look for those secret switches in the door." he requested, looking along the door's frame. His gaze followed up one side of the portal. He did not have nearly the light to see anywhere more than a dozen feet above him, and he realized at that point the trigger may be as far up as the top.

He examined the face of the door again, this time trying to see any pattern to the way the sea of bodies rising from the surface was arranged. He began to pick out an odd pattern in the positions of the skeleton's hands. Despite being contorted and in poses best left to those who are dying an agonizing death, their limbs were arranged, or propped in such a way as to make a somewhat zig-zag path up the face. Quite literally 'hand' holds, they would allow someone to scale the face of the door with little difficulty.

Endrance turned to his Draugnoa. "Well, I think I figured it out." he stated flatly. "But I'm sure one of us is not going to like it."

They turned to look at him as he looked back at the wall and pointed at the lowest skeleton. "See how these skeletons are all bent in strange angles?" he asked, waggling a finger at the first one. The flickering light of the torches made it seem as if the skeleton's jaw was waggling back at him. "They are arranged in a back and forth pattern. By using their outstretched hands, you can climb up the face of the door, up to where the switch that opens the door is."

Joven nodded, sheathing his short sword. "All right." he said. "I'll go up."

Endrance held out a hand, stopping him. "Wait, Joven." he interjected. "You're both too big and too heavy. I think it would be safer if one of the more nimble people here took on this challenge."

Selene stepped forwards. "I'll go!" she volunteered, smiling at Endrance. He felt a slight warming of his cheeks as she beamed at him. "I'm light, and I can climb pretty quickly." Endrance nodded, and she clipped away her blade at her hip and tucked the chain into the folds of the sash around her waist. She walked right up to the door and looked up at the first skeleton.

Selene put up a brave face. She was frightened of the ominous metal portal and its deathly guardians, but she had promised herself she would be brave for the man she loved. The other women had noticed Endrance's tentatively building affection for her. Selene was certain that Endrance wouldn't want her to be afraid. Practicing with one's weapons in a training yard and with familiar opponents was one thing, but this was real, and she was terrified. Trying desperately not to give away her emotions, she reached up and grasped the hand of the closest skeleton to the ground.

The hand did not move, as she half expected it to. It was however strangely warm. As if the black iron never truly fully cooled. It wasn't hot, so she continued pulling herself up. Soon she was clambering up the second, and then the third. *Hey,* she thought, *this isn't all that bad. It's kind of like climbing a tree.*

She had made it up a quarter of the way when it became too dark to continue on. Looking down, she called out to her companions. "It's too dark from here on! Bring up some light!"

Joven went to toss the torch he held in his hand, and thought a second time about it. "Hey!' he called out. "How are you at catching flaming sticks?"

Selene shook her head. "Not that great." she replied. She was perched with one foot in the upheld arm of one skeleton, and the other in a hand twisted down below a higher up skeleton's body.

Endrance quietly chanted as he cast one of the more simple spells. Upon finishing he held up a fist and opened his hand, and the brilliant white light of his light spell flooded out from a seemingly infinitely small speck. He flicked his wrist and it flit up into the dark, to hover over her head just like he had done for the soldiers when he fought the goblins.

With the tiny beacon of light hovering over her head, Selene continued her ascent. She found that when she reached the center of the door there was a strange depression in the face of it, with a blood red gem the size of a person's head set in it. Around the rim was a ring of ancient script, and two fist sized yellow gems, one on either side of the large one. "I found something!" Selene called.

"What is it?" Endrance called.

"It's some kind of gemstone seal." Selene said, examining it. "I can't read it of course, but it seems simple." She relayed the symbols that she saw in order from the top around in a clockwise fashion.

"It says only someone who has the blood of Rothel can open this door unhindered." Endrance said at last, having done the translation in his head. "So, hopefully one of you has the blood of Rothel in you."

Joven shrugged. "Well, I might. My families' bloodline began during the years of Rothel's reign."

Anna and Bridget shook their heads. "Nay," Bridget said. My family came from Betton, two days ride north of Mount Balator. And Anna came from yet another border town."

"Well I still think you four are the best choice we have." he said. "If Joven's blood doesn't work, then one of yours might."

Anna raised a brow. "And if none of ours works?"

Endrance shrugged, while inclining his head towards the door. "Then we probably will have to come back again once I've figured out how to do that."

Joven raised a hand up. "So how are we getting our blood up there, and how much do we need to give?"

Endrance dug into his satchel and produced a piece of cloth which he tore into four strips. "We should just need enough for it to touch the sphere in the center. Here, take a strip and soak some of your blood in it. But it has to be enough to stay wet until it touches the sphere."

Joven frowned. "Why?"

Endrance handed him a strip. "It has to do with blood sacrifice. Fresh blood carries a small portion of you in it. A small portion of your magical energy as well. But as it dries, the easily attained essence of you also dries out, until it's pretty much worthless."

Joven pulled a dagger and used it to cut a slice into his palm. He held the strip wadded up in his hand as his blood trickled into the cloth. "If that's so, then why did you have all the stuff that had your dried blood on it burned, instead of just washed off after the assassination attempt?"

Endrance handed the other two strips to Anna and Bridget. "Because," he explained, "Even though it is dried out, blood still has power. A skilled enough necromancer can draw your essence out of the dried blood, and use it not only to cast spells on you that you cannot defend against, but it's even rumored that they can learn your darkest secrets, or even gain some of your power by consuming it."

"Necromancers?" Bridget asked, carefully nicking her hand against her weapon. "I never heard of them doing that before."

"Hope you never do!" the young mage exclaimed. "Necromancers perform all kinds of dark and illegal magic."

Joven frowned. "What makes necromancy so bad?"

Endrance shook his head. "It's pretty complicated. Magic is about potential, while necromancy is a form of stagnancy." The mage shuddered. "Necromancers use their magic to gain power, no matter what it costs them or more preferably, others. They perform dark rituals, sacrifice innocent lives, steal souls to power vile experiments, and some have even tried to steal power from the old gods."

Joven sighed, handing the bloodied rag to Endrance. The young mage collected the other two as Joven muttered. "Well, there's yet one *more* thing I have to figure out how to kill."

Endrance quickly cast the levitation spell, floating the first blood soaked rag to her.

"That's Joven's." he said.

She took the wadded bloody cloth, and wiped it across the crimson gem's smooth surface, smearing some of the barbarian's blood across it. The door rumbled, and one of the two yellow gems glowed with an inner fire. But the second did not light, nor did the door open. Selene looked down at Endrance, puzzled. "Maybe the bloodline's too diluted?" she asked.

Endrance frowned. "Well we have no choice but to try someone else blood. How about you Selene? What about your bloodline?"

Selene shook her head. "I don't know. I was orphaned when I was an infant. All they could trace back was my totem animal."

Endrance sighed, "Well, pick one of the others then, and hope it works!"

Selene looked at the two cloths, and then down at her fellow Keepers. They looked up at her expectantly. "Which one of us?" she asked.

Anna shrugged. "Why not yours?" she asked. "We know we aren't the right lineage, but you might be." She looked at Bridget, who nodded. "Give it a try." Bridget called.

Selene looked at them a moment more, then nodded, more to affirm it to herself than to acknowledge it. Carefully cutting her left hand with her blade, she hesitated a few seconds, her open palm hovering over the crimson gem.

"Go ahead, Selene." Endrance encouraged. "There's nothing wrong if it doesn't work."

Selene pressed her hand against the gem, hoping desperately that her blood was indeed the right lineage. She felt a strange sensation pass through her body, starting at the top of her head, and rushing down her body, through her arm and into her palm, but then it was gone.

At first it seemed that it had worked, for the second yellow gem lit up and the door started shuddering in its frame. Selene smiled for a moment, but that vanished the instant that the door stopped and the two yellow gems went dark. A dull, steadily beating red light pulsed through the gem in the center. Something warmer seemed to pulse through Selene's body as she stared into the red light.

The skeleton she was perched on twitched. Selene seemed not to notice as it started to creak. Several of the skeletons began to shift, and twist, and move of their own accord. Selene was thrown off her perch, and dropped only a few feet before she landed in the arms of a skeleton which had reached out and caught her. Her eyes stared blankly at the terror as it pulled her in, its mouth clattering.

A scream, as clear as a clarion rang through the dark depths.

Endrance saw the trap trigger, and knew he had to act fast or else Selene would be killed. He quickly started casting a spell, his chanting out of sync with the clattering of metal bones. He plucked the silver knife from his belt and released the spell, the magic propelling it like a shot. After having time to refine the spell, it was far more accurate than before; it didn't even backlash his hand as the knife spun through the air and impacted with the skull of the skeleton holding her. The knife recoiled, spinning off into the dark, with the tip chipped and the blade bent.

The skeleton silently recoiled, dropping Selene. She tumbled down the still struggling to move skeletons, and landed on the walkway with a hard thud. Bridget dashed over to her, grabbing her by the arm. Dragging the still limp girl away from the door, she readied her heavy blade. The two standing Keepers took position in front of Selene and Endrance and were ready for the attack.

The skeletons writhed in the door, and they watched in horror as the iron bones began pulling themselves out of its surface as if they had only been submerged in sand. The first skeleton landed on the stone walkway with a loud *Krang* of thick metal hitting stone, and the dread thing stood, its eyeless stare focused on the group of five before it. Several more of the things landed shortly afterward, easily numbering five to their one.

"Uh, Endrance?" Joven called. "I don't have a weapon that can cut steel!" he cried. "Stay back there! It's safer for you!"

The young mage watched as Joven struck the first skeleton with a hand ax, whose handle shattered under the force of the blow, barely knocking the iron horror back. "Shit!" he shouted. "These things are hard!"

Bridget and Anna worked together, a pair of beautiful warriors in action. Anna parried clumsy striking hands with her shield and knocked yet others out of the way with her short spear, while Bridget's weapon chopped in powerful arcs, thudding into skeletal iron and cracking limbs, severing some of the thinner bones. But the fight would not last long. Anna could only defend so long, and Bridget's weapon was already nicked and dinged badly from striking only a few of the attackers.

Joven resorted to wrestling maneuvers, grabbing a skeleton and trying to wrench it out over the edge of the walkway. His strength was the only advantage he had; even though he could toss one over the edge another would enter the space the prior had left behind.

Endrance had no spells strong enough to destroy that many creatures, and he wouldn't be much help if he joined into the melee himself. He drew his dagger, with one last desperate ploy. *Perhaps the magic in my blood is strong enough to confuse the trap.* He thought. *If they target only me, I buy them time to take Selene and retreat.* He quickly slashed at his palm, wincing as his knife dug deeper than necessary. His blood welled up in his palm, and he snapped his hand at the door as he cast the propulsion spell, flinging a spatter of his life's blood at the ruby gem.

The bloody spray splashed across the door, from yellow gem to yellow gem. The effect was almost immediate. The crimson gem went dull, and the two yellow gems lit up brighter than before, their flame burning at the inside of the gems like they were trying to escape.

The skeletons stopped in unison mid combat, one of which had a bony iron hand around Anna's neck. The iron sentinels of the portal shuddered as one, turning their backs to the defenders, and marching back to the door. One by one they walked right into the iron surface, and it accepted them as if it were a vertical wall of water.

The walkway was soon empty of all but the five on the walkway. The iron door's surface was smooth, unblemished. The yellow gems in the door shone brightly. The door began a slow, grinding descent as it sank into the floor. The door sank all the way out of sight, stopping as the lip of it lie flush with the floor. Darkness waited beyond the door, but it did not loom out from the opened portal nor did it disgorge more horrors for them to battle.

The young mage stooped to a knee and examined Selene, who was still lying limp on the stone. Her breathing was regular, but she stared directly ahead as if she were looking at something far away. Her hair spilled across the floor like a puddle, the gleam of the light spell giving her hair's black color an almost violet sheen. He stared into her eyes, calling her name as he held her. He wasn't sure what had happened to her from the fall, but something was wrong with her.

She didn't hit her head. He concluded, thinking back. Remembering those critical moments right before the fight began he realized that she had not fallen off because she had been shaken, but rather she had fallen off because she suddenly went slack. *Maybe the trap in the door did something to her.* He noticed then that in the light of the spell her black eyes also appeared to be red. No, her eyes were red, and her hair had in fact turned violet. It wasn't a trick of lighting. The pupils of her eyes were disturbingly square.

Selene murmured something as Endrance continued to call her name "Selene!" he whispered. "Selene! Come back to me! Selene!" He held her with both hands and wished that there was a better way to help her, but he could do nothing but call her name.

She blinked once, twice, and her eyes came into focus. They were black and round again. "Endrance!" she whispered faintly. "What happened?" she sat up, and her hair was its normal color.

Endrance shook his head, helping her to stand. "I don't know. I saw you touch the gem, and then right as the trap went off you just... fainted."

She held her head with a hand. She shook her head after a moment. "I don't know what happened," she began. "I felt this weird...energy flow out of me, and then suddenly it was if I wasn't even there with you all." she looked haunted. "There was this fire, and I felt very hot. And there was this horrible smell, and I think I heard someone laughing in the distance while dozens of other voices moaned."

Endrance looked at her quizzically. "Do you remember the smell? Was it like rotten eggs, or like rotted flesh?" he had a bad feeling that he knew the answer already. Things he had observed about her before were tumbling into place, and the information she just relayed was related to some of the research he had done while examining the summoning circle they had found.

She nodded, her face contorted as if she couldn't get the smell off her tongue. "Yes." she said. "It smelled kind of like rotten eggs, but worse and it burned at my nose."

Endrance hung his head with a sigh, his heart plummeting. "Well," he said. "I figured out what happened." he concluded morosely.

Selene looked at him until he lifted his head, and met his eyes. "What?" she asked.

"The door reacted to a presence it didn't want to get through it." Endrance stated. "There was something in your blood that made the enchantment on the door think you were an intruder."

She stared at him as he explained, not understanding. "I don't understand." She said weakly. "What is so different about me that it would do nothing for Joven but attack me?"

Endrance looked up at the other three who stood around the young man, and they were also paying attention to what he was saying. He closed his eyes and willed himself to state his theory.

"You feel agitated around me despite your feelings for me, you have an affinity for nighttime activities; you practice when you think we're asleep and won't notice. You have an unconscious allure that I can hardly resist. Your eyes and hair changed color during your vision. Have you ever been sick?" Endrance expounded.

Selene shook her head. "Not very often. Usually I only get sick for half a day if I do."

Endrance breathed deeply. "And have you ever been injured?"

Selene nodded. "Yes, of course. We train with real weapons as we get better as Keepers."

The young mage knew the next question to ask. "I can guess that you keep the bandages on longer than you really need to don't you? You get better faster than many of your sister Draugnoa?"

She frowned. "I..." she trailed off, looking up at her fellow Keepers. Anna and Bridget looked at her as if to say 'go on'. She gulped, but answered.

"Yes." She admitted. "I usually got better fast, but everyone else took a long time and I didn't want to stand out, so I pretended I was still hurt." She looked down at the ground. "Sometimes I would have to hurt myself again when the healers came to change my bandages."

The young mage ran his hands through his hair. He had finally put together the last pieces of the puzzle. Now her unconscious animosity towards him made sense. It wasn't her fault; it was just instinct. He didn't know how to tell her.

"I'm so sorry that you found out like this, Selene," Endrance stated, "You are a Nephilim."

"A what?" Selene exclaimed, glaring at Endrance.

Endrance, your spell is half-expired. Gullin advised him.

The young mage inclined his head to her, and turned to start walking to the open portal. "If we're going to discuss this we need to keep moving." The rest picked up their weapons and followed. He walked over the threshold as he spoke, his pace remaining clipped and quick.

"Nephilim is the term for someone who is descended from the pairing of a mortal and a being from another realm. Records say they can be half angel, demon, pretty much half any being that lives in another realm." He explained. "Your signs that you have shown point to demonic in origin."

Anna and Bridget flanked him, but Selene pushed past so she could look her Spengur in the face. "Half *demon*!" she shouted. "You're accusing me of being *half demon*! That's impossible!" her eyes flashed angrily, and for a split second Endrance could see the red in her eyes again. She walked backwards slowly as she stared him in the eyes.

Endrance looked her in the eye, his pace slowing only slightly. "Selene, I know the signs. I have seen the traces, and that is what you are. We really should save this discussion for later and finish what we're doing." his voice was gentle, but firm.

Selene's face screwed up, and she turned forwards again, and only the darkness could see the tears on her face as she stalked alongside Joven as the tunnel beyond the door got smaller. The stone looked smooth cut, polished at one point, and even had ornate torch brackets set into the walls, though the wood of said torches had long since corroded. The tunnel eventually shrank into a passage, just tall enough that Joven could reach up and touch the ceiling, and only wide enough for two people to walk side by side. Silence reigned between the group for moments as they moved further down.

"What I want to know is," Bridget commented as she fell behind Anna and Endrance, "Why on earth did they bother with such a huge door, if there only was a small passage beyond it?" She gestured with her free hand, which went unseen since she was in the rear. "Was it even necessary?"

Endrance shrugged. "I would guess ego." he said. "Though, I suppose the door behind us was a safeguard; perhaps a challenge as well. To protect the tomb from people who would take their possessions, just like us."

"Oh yeah!" Joven blurted, turning to Endrance and almost knocking Selene in the head with his torch as he pivoted. "How did you stop the trap? You couldn't have been of the right bloodline."

The young mage looked confused, holding up his hands and shrugging. "I have no idea. I hoped that my blood was magically charged enough to draw their attention away from you. Then I could have led them away while you figured out how to deal with them." he prodded Joven, and the barbarian resumed walking. "I didn't expect it to stop the trap entirely." Anna noticed the blood slash in his hand and grabbed it, tending to the wound as they walked. Endrance had almost forgotten the stinging pain, but it came back as she bound the injury.

Anna peered back down the tunnel they came. "Dear husband," she started, "the door appears to have remained open. I do not believe it will be closing anytime soon. Why are you rushing?"

The wizard grimaced, "Because Gullin just informed me that the spell is in its waning stage."

"Waning?" Anna frowned. "It's going away?"

"The spell is now past halfway done, and we haven't even gotten to the book yet."

Silently, the five of them pushed onwards as fast as they dared, and in minutes came out into a larger chamber. Roughly as wide as ten men laid out and just as long, the chamber was piled with gold, tapestries, and other riches. In the center of the tomb was a raised dais, three steps high. Upon its center lay a black iron coffin; its surface glinted with the light of their torches. Joven had noticed immediately that the coffin itself had several thick iron chains across its surface, all of which were anchored into the stone, solidly pinning the vessel onto the floor

"Alright," Endrance stated, tapping Selene on the shoulder and pointing to one corner. He directed the other three to respective corners of the tomb, and they began their search. Endrance took up a search around the dais, careful to never step on the stone steps. There was one book quickly found, but it proved to be a ledger of the king's last days.

The other four continued to search, while the young mage carefully paged through the book. He hoped earnestly, that the book here would say where the Journal of Lehtor was stored. He reached the end and read through the last few pages as quickly as possible. "The book of Lehtor was buried with the king." he muttered. "That's all it says. Not where in the tomb."

Anna glanced at Endrance. "Maybe they meant it literally." she said, turning her gaze to the coffin in the center. "But if that's true then how do we get the book out of that?"

Endrance sighed. "This is probably going to hurt." he said walking onto the dais, one step at a time. Nothing happened. He stood right next to the coffin, and looked about. "That's a relief." he exhaled, and then pondered the coffin. He had no way of getting the chains off in time, nor did they have a way of opening the coffin anyways. He could try some spells, but he never studied spells like the ones he would need to open the coffin cleanly.

Endrance sat upon the surface of the dais, and pondered a solution. He had studied one of his predecessor's spells; one that would let him consult with an ancestor spirit, but it was a ritual and took time. If he was going to use it, it would have to be now. He was running out of time.

The young wizard dug into the satchel he brought with him, and produced five white candles, thick but short. He set them in a circle around him, and then pulled a small silk sack from his satchel. Opening the end carefully, he meticulously poured a line of salt in a circle, making sure that the candles were equidistant from each other. He last took a fingertip and made an impression on the salt in the line in front of him, barely a dimple.

He took out the book he had kept the notes of the ritual in. He set the book on his lap and opened to the page he had marked in advance. He lit the candles and made sure he was ready to begin. He looked to his bodyguard, who indicated he was ready. Carefully, he recited the words of the ritual as he touched the inner edge of the circle, pouring a small amount of energy into it.

"*Ancient spirit, oh restful one in silent sleep.*" He intoned, following the ritual's requirements. "*Come back to me from the deep. Oh restful one in silent sleep. Trust in me your wisdom keep!*"

As he finished the ritual, he held the hand he had cut before over the line of salt. He squeezed his fist, and a drop of blood soaked into the silk dripped from his hand into the depression in the salt. The drop of red seemed to do nothing for a moment, and Endrance was uncertain if it had worked.

The spot of red seemed to leech through the ring of salt, drawing a line of red around the center of the white line. It filled in swiftly, and Endrance found he could not easily budge the hand he was touching the salt with. His magical energy slowly fed into the circle, and it could possibly drain him if he let the circle run unchecked. A trickle of sweat beaded at his brow. *Not again.* He thought.

A laugh echoed throughout the burial chamber, dry, raspy cackle. Endrance startled from where he was sitting as the sound emanated from under the coffin's lid, but couldn't move as his hand was still firmly anchored. He wouldn't be able to leave even if he wanted to. However the spell circle was supposed to protect him from the spirit he had awoken.

The other four froze shocked as a translucent, plate mailed hand rose through the iron lid, and used the sides of the coffin to help King Rothel sit up. The figure was an imposing one, even though it was nearly transparent. A hulking brute at seven feet solid, King Rothel was almost proportionally bigger than Joven in all ways. His body was covered in spectral black iron plates, though he wore no helmet. The head of the ghost was in fact intact, as if he were not dead, but in fact just an image of himself before death. His eyes, however, were white orbs, transparent and unreadable at the same time.

A preternatural chill swept through the room, and the torches guttered and dimmed. Only the light of the five candles remained bright, and though their bodies prickled with gooseflesh, no one moved to even warm themselves. Endrance could feel the power of the spirit that stood before him. It was almost too much for him to bear being so close to it. He knew the circle's properties, as well as his blood, was the only thing that would keep him safe from the apparition should it attack.

The spirit leaned towards the young mage, and seemed to sniff at him. He was not disturbing the air but he seemed to have picked something up. He smiled.

"So." The ghost's voice was distant but still potent. It was akin to hearing a general bark at his troops from the back of the formation. "I see one of my father's kin has come to pay his ancestor a visit. What is it that you want so badly, that you would dare to disturb my rest?"

Endrance was unsure what he was talking about, but he knew that it could be used to his advantage. "Lord Rothel," he began, "The prophesied time is upon us, but the details of the event are lost to time and memory. I seek the Journal of Lehtor."

Rothel smirked. "Which prophecy is it that you speak of?" he turned his head to take in the room. "There are so many within its pages."

"I speak of the great eclipse and the birth of the child who would change the world."

The Great Spirit nodded, looking through each of the young mage's companions as he surveyed the room. "And you are here for nothing else? Not to plunder?" he finished his turn, facing the wizard again.

"I am only here to find the book, great king." Endrance plied. "I do not seek any of your glorious treasure."

The king was silent, as he seemed to be weighing Endrance's words. He pointed to the coffin. "The Journal of Lehtor is within." he said. "But you have not the means to release it."

Endrance's hopes dropped. "Very well, great king." he responded, acceptance in his voice. "Can you share with us the means to possess it?"

The ancient king of old had not seemed to have even noticed the wizard's companions. He remained eerily still when he wasn't speaking, an unnerving trait that many undead things possessed. One didn't know it but the minute movements a living person makes is overlooked... until it was missing.

"I will offer you the knowledge you seek," the ghost said plainly.

"What do I need to do?" The wizard asked.

"Child, do you know the significance of that book?" he asked. "The Journal of Lehtor was gifted to me by the fates." His tone was reverent, almost fearful. "Its knowledge can only be passed on to one who has the inborn power to survive knowing it. You can know what is within its pages, but it may extract a cost of you, if you aren't strong enough."

The spirit stared at him, his sightless orbs unchanging. "When my brother left me I turned to the only source of power I had left. Upon gaining the Journal of Lehtor, I read through it once. By the time I was finished I was struck blind. The declarations of fate are not meant for mortal eyes to see or mortal ears to hear. You must be more than a man, if you want to handle the power within."

He paused, whether for effect or to ensure comprehension the young mage couldn't tell.

"You may be better prepared than I; you bear the mantle of Spengur. I will tell you of the prophecy you require."

The ghost seemed silent and motionless for a second. It was perfectly still; in a way no living creature could, without even the slightest tremble or shift in body. Endrance felt as more of his magic slipped away in a trickle, and forced his self to remain patient. He also knew time was running out topside.

Endrance didn't see any other way. He needed that knowledge, for without it King Kalenden would be able to get away with his plot. The real child of destiny would be overlooked, and the world would not be saved because the hero was not prepared. Even worse, the king's son could help bring about the world's destruction. This prophecy was starting to prove very dangerous indeed, and it had only just begun.

The spirit of King Rothel finally responded. "Then I will give it to you, so strengthen your mettle, kin. If you do not survive this, no one else may have it." the phantom king bore a grim smile, "Do not return here again, even should you perish. There is not enough room for two of us here." Endrance frowned. What was he talking about?

The king held a mighty spectral fist over the wizard's head, the mailed hand outspread. He opened his mouth and a tone that was much too deep and unnatural poured out from it, like an oversized bell tolling. As he did so he slowly clenched his fist, the flickering from Endrance's candles barely catching across the translucent surface of the gauntlet. Endrance felt a spike of panic. Rothel had pushed right through his protective circle without as much as a flicker of power. This ghost was beyond the ken of such a simple protection spell.

To Joven and the three keepers, it appeared as if nothing happened. To Endrance, the moment the ghost closed his hand over his head was the moment that time decided it was going to take a break from flowing at normal speed. A piercing pain shot through his head, and agony rolled from the top of his skull down his neck and back. Images flashed through his head, accompanied by an infinite multitude of sound. Things, places, people, all kinds of images, both still and moving passed through his mind, each one as quick as a thought, but as painful as a blow to the head.

More than images, the visions were full experiences that he felt as if he were there. It seemed to the wizard that the cycle would never end, until suddenly one of the images sprung fully into his senses, blurring the others out of his thoughts, they were still passing through, causing searing pain as they crossed his mind, but they seemed strangely muted by the vision before him.

Before him lay a battlefield, never ending in any direction. It seemed to go on forever in all directions. There he could see millions upon millions of the many races of the world fighting together against the forces of a great evil. Humans, elves, dwarves, wolfmen, and many others all bore the symbol of a white mountain across their armor and proudly across their banners. Their swords gleamed in the twin sunlight and though he could see they had been in many battles before this, the troops in battle fought with an unwearied vigor.

Their vigor was needed in this field of war, as their foes were terrible and mighty. Endrance saw stretched out to his right an endless sea of demons, side by side, packed in a tight formation as they swarmed the races of the world. He saw many kinds of demons, but there were some that he was certain never existed before, beasts of sweeping horn, spike growing from flesh as tough as stone, and wielding infernal bladed maces that they swung with two hands, massive enough to pierce through armor and crush the body beneath. Behind them were gigantic four-legged demonic beasts, many men tall and incredibly powerful. They had many tails coming from their sides, each more than long enough to reach the ground, where they flicked about dangerously, their tips frighteningly bladed and sharp.

The battle raged on, and the races of the earth fought bravely against the demonic host assailing them. Catapults and ballista hammered the large walkers, and archers in the back fired into the hordes indiscriminately, taking down many demons only to have them replaced by many more behind them. The ground had become stained red with blood, and cluttered with the broken bodies of both men and demon alike. Endrance could smell the bloody stench; hear every clang of metal striking metal or bone, and the screams of the injured.

A roar that shook the air around him made Endrance shift his gaze up, and he saw something in the air above him. As if moved by an unseen hand, the battle around him shot away from him, falling away as if he had been the one anchored in place and the world had been dropped. He was now standing in the sky, high above where the clouds would have been that sunny day. There he witnessed a scene that he would not ever forget.

In the air before him was a white dragon, larger than he could ever have imagined. Its body was easily several hundred feet long, and its wings spread out twice that, casting a shadow across the land below it. Its scales were pearl, and even the small ones of its sides were as big as the mage's hand. The large scales across its belly and along its spine were easily as large as houses. The scene had seemed to freeze in time, the dragon suspended in the air as it had swooped down onto the back of a great black dragon of nearly the same size, if not bigger.

Endrance saw that upon the backs of these great creatures was a single man each. The white dragon bore one of the most impressive men the young mage had ever seen. His muscles bulging, plate armor gleaming, the warrior looked to be as large as king Rothel had been. His back bore a cloak with the symbol the soldiers below him bore, and he seemed to be the commander, if not their leader. His face was contorted into a roaring battle cry, his long blond hair flowing in the wind, only held in check by a golden circlet across his brow. His cheek bore a mark looking like a red sword, a birthmark of some sort. The warrior's armor was obviously magical, as it gleamed with an unnatural brightness, and the warrior moved as if the armor was not even there.

To say the warrior wielded a sword would be an injustice. The weapon he clenched in his hand was a blade of pure crystal, translucent but iridescent, little colors shifting in the light as it moved. The rest of the blade was formed of thick golden wire, intertwined and forming the handle, guard, and pommel out of one piece as thick as a man's little finger. Set into the guard was a grand emerald, brilliant and perfect.

The black dragon was as impressive and frightening as the white, though the man that stood in the saddle on its back had the look of someone far more dangerous. Clad entirely in black plate armor, many blood coated spikes adorned it. The skulls of large creatures made up its paldrons, with a black spike protruding from each eye socket. Its helm incorporated the front of a demon's skull as the faceplate, black steel formed the rest, and a crown of spikes adorned its head. Endrance didn't know how or why, but he felt that even though the dragons were dangerous magical creatures unrivaled by any and without any true predators, they were not as dangerous as the man in the demon-bone helmet was.

In his hand was a bastard sword of black steel, the guard a twisted bar of metal, and the grip bore little spikes in it. The pommel was a grinning skull. The worst part however was the blade, which was crafted out of what looked like segments of flat bone, each part bearing a nasty barb on alternating sides of the blade. The edge of the weapon was wickedly sharp, and Endrance could see some kind of living eye set in the guard. Demonic power flowed out of this weapon, and he could see lines of blood across the blade's surface, as if it had veins.

The whole scene remained suspended in the air before him, and he could feel the image burning itself into his mind. The white dragon was swooping down on the black, its jaw open in a roar and claws extended to intercept the black, as it's foe rose up to do the same. The barbarian hero had his sword raised high in the air above him, his other hand grabbing the saddle he stood in, while his opponent held his demonic blade back as he built up strength for a sideways stroke.

Time picked up again, and the dragons clashed into each other with a crunch of claws and teeth impacting scale and bone. The two dragons collided, their claws and teeth finding each other and biting in. They began plummeting down to earth slashing at each other with their claws and even their tails, the white dragon's tail spiked while his foe's was bladed.

As the two twisted and writhed in battle, the two men upon them had begun to fight. Their swords clashed as they performed staggering feats of strength and agility, quite literally running or leaping across the dragons as they twisted, keeping the great beasts below them as they fought. Swords clashed, crystal struck bone, and they fought each other with everything they had. The two warriors fought across the bodies of the battling dragons, and in seconds it was over.

The black dragon got in a lucky hit, its bladed tail darting between scales and burying itself deep into the white dragon's chest. It roared in pain and clawed its enemy's eyes. Dragon blood rained down onto the swiftly approaching battlefield below. The demon-skull-faced warrior swung his sword, the segments of it seeming to wriggle as the blade bit deep into the hero's collar between his neck and left shoulder. The teeth of the sword ground, and blood sprayed into the air. The barbarian's eyes flickered, and it seemed he would drop, when his eyes snapped open with rage, and with a bloody roar, he grabbed the demon blade with his left hand, the teeth digging into his palm as he pulled the black armored foe closer to him, tearing his wound even deeper and spilling his blood into the air. The man in black armor struggled for a second and slid closer, neither of their footing good enough to let them resist. The hero plunged his sword into the man's chest, the crystal blade cutting into the black metal as easily as flesh, the tip erupting out the man's back, spraying dark blood into the air.

The ground rushed up to them, and before Endrance could do or say anything, the fighting dragons dropped past him, colliding with the earth below. He remained hovering in the sky, watching the combatants crushed and scattered on both sides by the impact of the dragons in their death throes. His vision turned up to the sky, and he found himself looking upon the twin suns. He watched as a great darkness swelled up from behind the first sun. Blackness in the shape of fingers wrapped around the sun and blotted out much of its light. The massive hand pulled the sun up into the sky, and Endrance felt his perspective dragged along with it, pulling him up into the sky. In the darkness above, he watched in fear as the light of the sun brightened when the hand squeezed harder and harder. The brightness grew so strong that Endrance was certain he would never see again when the sun itself exploded. He cried out and he felt himself falling again, the wind whistling through his ears, and he knew what lay below to arrest his fall.

He was back in the tomb of Rothel. The companions saw him suddenly convulse, then collapse onto the stone next to the coffin. The ancient king vanished as the circle was broken by his body crossing over the salt. As they rushed over to him, they could see foam on his lips, and every muscle in his body was clenched as his body seized up. His eyes however radiated a faint white light as he stared sightlessly into the ceiling above them. Selene cradled the Spengur's head, and for a split second she thought she heard the sounds of battle in the distance. The young mage could not scream, but his throat released a keening, wordless whine of pain.

Only seconds had passed before his body relaxed, and he went limp. It looked as if he was in a deep sleep. The Draugnoa decided to carry him out, one at his head, one at his feet, and the third at his side to keep him stable. Joven then took the lead, rushing the group back out of the tomb. They moved as fast as possible down the stone corridor, no longer concerned about traps or monsters within. They exited onto the bridge over the darkness, and as they escaped back the way they came the walkway rumbled as the great door behind them rose back into place again.

Selene looked back, and thought she saw King Rothel watching them sightlessly before the door's lip rose above her line of sight. She would be glad to be out of this horrible place. Too many bad things had been revealed here, and she didn't know how she was supposed to react to the revelations.

Taking the stairs up as fast as they safely could, Joven noticed an increase in the trickle of water flowing down the steps. They were almost out of time. They reached the top of the steps, and they carried Endrance out at a run, making it to the last set of steps out of the tomb. Water trickled over the lip of the entrance, and Joven fearlessly leapt out of the tomb, landing knee deep in water. Looking up, he saw the orb of water was raining steady trickles of water from its surface. If it collapsed now, they would be crushed and drowned before they could save the young man.

The three girls bearing the wizard emerged right afterward. The barbarian whirled around the outside of the portal into the tomb and came to the capstone seal. One single square of stone was raised above the rest in the grid where Joven had to first open the tomb, he reached between the iron bars and slammed his fist down on the stone.

The capstone ground slowly over the hole. The barbarian turned back to the women, but they had already begun slogging to the nearest shore of the reservoir. Joven followed suit, pushing as best he could through thigh-deep water and mud that clung to his boots. The spell holding the water was failing quickly now, water was cascading from the sky, and the water level was quickly rising to Joven's waist.

The Draugnoa had managed to get Endrance up on the shore, and were kneeling down at the edge, reaching out to give him a hand up. The reservoir was just deep enough that the barbarian could drown in it, weighed down with his armor like he was. He threw himself at the side of the reservoir and pulled himself up the ledge, his muscles bulging with effort. Bridget grabbed his shoulders and heaved, pulling him the rest of the way out of the reservoir just before the spell failed completely, The last half of the sphere's volume collapsed in one instant, creating a massive splash and spraying water over a hundred feet into the air, misting the air and raining thousands of gallons across the reservoir.

They watched the water levels equalize, until the water level was only a finger's length from the rim. The rain stopped, and as they looked about it seemed that no one had seen the event at all, save for the four conscious ones present. Selene kneeled next to their Spengur, patting his cheek with her hand.

She opened one of his eyes, and he stared up into the air unfocused, unseeing. His green eyes were brightly luminous, actually radiating green light. Checking his pulse, he was alive, but weak. He had survived a trial so far, and they needed to get him to the longhouse if they were to help him recover. She looked about for Gullin, but didn't see him in the sky. "Gullin?" she asked.

Anna shook her head. Bridget looked around on the ground, and saw a small lump on the ground a few dozen yards off. She trotted over, and found Gullin crashed into the grass, his wings still splayed, and his feathers ruffled. He appeared to be alive; his legs and head twitched spasmodically. "Found him." She declared.

"We need to go." Joven said. He put his fingers to his lips and whistled sharply. Moments later Joven's huge horse appeared out of the dark. It came up to him and nickered. The Draugnoa with Joven's help propped Endrance up onto the saddle, and the barbarian hopped on behind him holding the mage so he could ride hard.

The horse dashed off into the night, carrying the barbarian and his charge to the road towards the higher bowls of Balator. The three women went to their horses, but would not likely catch up to Joven's powerful steed. Their horses were not of the same sturdy breeding that the bodyguard had.

The sentries on watch that night had been instructed that the Spengur would be working late, and upon seeing him upon the horse with Joven, didn't even attempt to stop them as the two rode up the ramps that led to the next higher bowl. Even on horseback and unhindered, it took over an hour of riding to reach the seventh bowl, and the Spengur's longhouse. The entire time, Endrance did not stir, but hung limply, as if a dead man.

Joven carefully picked up the Spengur, and carried him to the doors of the longhouse. Outside, the guards who had been posted at Endrance's longhouse stood at ready upon seeing one of their superiors approach. Joven looked at the two, and scowled. "You!" he commanded, looking one of the two in the eye. The barbarian straightened up, clapping his hand over his breast. "Find a medicine man, tell them that their Spengur has been injured and they need to tend to him! Hurry!" Joven ordered, and the guard swiftly turned about and took off at a full run.

Joven pushed past the other guard, and entered the longhouse. He set the young mage upon the bed and made sure the fire was going by the time the medicine man arrived. The man tended to the wizard's injuries, but could not do very much as the man had been struck down by magic and not a sword. He could only suggest letting the man rest and he should awaken in time.

It was not the best news Joven could give the wizard's Draugnoa when they finally arrived at the longhouse.

Chapter 31

It was dark, but comfortable in the Spengur's bedroom. No candles were lit save one, held by a single woman who kept watch over her husband. The youngest, Selene had insisted on being there when he woke up. Her fellow Draugnoa understood her motivations; Endrance had many things he needed to explain to her. They had left her alone in the room when the unconscious mage's familiar Gullin had awoken and started dazedly composing itself. The other two knew that Selene and Endrance had been growing close those last few weeks, and they were uncertain what it meant that he labeled her 'Nephilim'.

Endrance was first aware that he was no longer in the cold, wet tomb of Rothel, but in a warm, comfortable bed. Prying open an eye, the dim light confirmed he was indeed home. He slowly sat himself up stopping suddenly and grabbing his head as he felt it throb anew, reminding him that he should never try powerful magical rituals without some kind of serious protective gear. He didn't want it to become a habit or anything.

The light shifted, and moved around the bed to the side. Endrance squinted at the light, as even though it was the only candle in the dark, it seemed unusually bright to him. He could make out the form of a woman behind it, and risked venturing a guess. "Eh... Anna?" he asked, unable to see clearly. The woman set the candle on the stand next to the bed, and he could see past the glare of the flame and to the person behind. "Oh!" he exclaimed, "Selene! I'm sorry." he apologized. "I could not see who you were." His night vision was slowly returning, and he could then tell that the two of them were alone in the room.

She sat on the edge of the bed, turning her head away from him. "I am starting to think," She whispered quietly, sadness carrying more clearly through the air than her voice, "That I cannot see who I am either. Or what I am."

Oh yes, Half Demon Nephilim. The young mage closed his eyes and recollected his thoughts. There was the tomb, the bridge, the door, and the ghostly king. He opened his eyes again, saddened. "Selene, I-" he began, but she interrupted him.

"What's going on with me?" she exclaimed in a harsh tone, just shy of shouting. "Now I'm some kind of demon? How can you say that?" Tears were running down her face, and Endrance didn't have the heart to tell her that he could see them clearly now in the dim light. "Why would you do that? They could stone me to death on your word alone!"

His head slumped, staring at his upturned palms as he sighed. "Selene, I did not call you a Nephilim to get you killed or out of some form of hate," he began, "I did not say those things because I wanted to punish you." he fought with himself about reaching out to try to comfort her, but decided against it. "You know I have an extensive education; I was taught a wealth of things other people could hardly imagine existed. I was taught by Kaelob about the Nephilim, and about how each side raises their children."

Selene half turned to look at him out of the corner of her eye. "Go on." she murmured, wiping at her face with her hands.

"Unlike the half angels, when a half demon is born one of two things happen. Either they are taken by their demonic parent into hell, where they would either die quickly or become one of the most dangerous of their soldiers. Or they end up with their human parent. Most of the times they either don't want to take care of the child because they had been raped, or they want to avoid the social stigma of having made one. They usually are thrown away to die or dropped off at orphanages under the cover of dark." he shrugged. "My master taught me how to identify one by signs of their heritage."

She sniffed. "How come?" she asked, unsure of his reasoning.

Her husband frowned. "For my safety, he said." Endrance admitted. "I would have to use magic specifically designed to kill them. Otherwise it would be exceedingly difficult to handle one."

Selene burst into tears again, crying into her hands. "Is-" she sobbed as she tried to talk, "is that -sniff- what you are going to do with me?" her whole body shuddered with sobs. "Kill me?"

Endrance shook his head vehemently, at this point reaching out and putting a hand on her shoulder. "Never!" he said, louder than he intended. "I would never even think about hurting you, Selene!"

"But!" she sobbed, "I'm half-demon! Everyone is supposed to hate me!"

He crawled to the edge of the bed and swung his legs out from under the sheets, sitting right next to her. He pulled her close to him and held her tightly, her head resting against the crook between shoulder and neck. "Selene, while your people may have decided that what a person is can be enough reason to kill them, I cannot abide by the same desire." he looked her in the eyes as she gazed up at him, her face puffy from having spent much time crying even before her husband had awoken. "I love you, Selene. I would never, ever hurt you. Not ever."

She stiffened upon hearing those words, and relaxed back into his arms. "Not ever?" she said, though she heard the sincerity in his voice the first time. It was relieving to hear him say it again.

"Never." he replied.

They both laughed then, wiping away the tears that had fallen. Endrance ran his hand across her upper back as they sat there, feeling for something. He looked at her quizzically. "Have you been feeling any kind of itching or scratchiness along your back?" he asked.

She shook her head. "No. It's been three days since the tomb. Am I supposed to?"

He nodded. "I wonder then, why did you start developing your demon half so late? You are already a year older than I, and from what I learned Nephilim develop the most of their abilities around puberty."

She shrugged, straightening the front of her dress. "I don't know, maybe it was something to do with my childhood like you said?"

"Well that's possible," the young mage said, thinking out loud. "Demons and more specifically half demons have a strong emotional bond with their abilities. If you had been raised to be a keeper since you were a child, then perhaps the lack of strong emotional stimulus could have done it."

She quirked an eyebrow at him. "Could that be because of you?" she asked.

He smiled. "The most likely reasoning would be that one of your parents was a tempter type of demon. It could be a succubus or incubus.

Then it would make sense that we inadvertently triggered your development when we had made love for the first time."

She nodded. "I had thought the spring had gotten a little too hot to be natural."

Endrance smirked. "And here I was certain it was just that good." he joked, getting elbowed in the ribs as a reward.

The door opened and Anna and Bridget entered, having heard enough laughter to know things had been settled. The two closed around the Spengur, climbing on the bed after they had lit some of the oil lamps in the room.

"Dear husband," Anna said with concern. "Are you well?" He could see the pattern of partially healed bruising around her neck, just the right shape for a skeletal hand.

He nodded, "Just a headache, I guess." he admitted, rubbing his temples. "I feel tired, but I have work I need to do. The information is in my head now, and I think we should be able to get prepared." An image passed through his head, of the great hero, in his full glory riding atop the white dragon. He shook his head, trying to clear it away. "Let's get to work."

The suns rose the day of the eclipse like any other, the only real difference from any other day was how close together they began. Nearly touching from the start, their path across the sky brought them closer together. Bridget could see from her chair outside the longhouse that the suns would be coming together in the hour before they would set. She also traced the path of the moons, and they would be crossing in front of the suns during the same hour they meet.

She got up from her chair, and relayed her estimations through the window leading into the Spengur's longhouse. After Anna left to relay the information to Endrance, she went back to her chair and sat back down. She heard someone walking on the rock rubble nearby. The boot steps passed, and she watched the patrol of guards passing the longhouse on their rounds. She waved at the youngest of the guards, who actually looked at her, and smirked when he hurriedly turned his eyes back to the patrol route.

She had been trying to figure out a way to get to spend more time with the Spengur. He had so little time to spend just with them, so the three were competing in one way or another to get some time with him. They had been making a competition out of it; who could steal away more time from the other without letting the mage catch on. While Selene's motivations may have been different than hers, they all had agreed on it.

Though, lately Selene had been getting the bulk of his time many days out of the week. Bridget mentally shrugged as she thought it over. They weren't even doing anything worth gossiping with Anna about. Most of it was talking something about demons, some kind of religious stuff. She figured that whatever it was going on with Selene gave her an edge in this game; he was interested in what made her different, she guessed.

She had started to recognize that the man had some likeable traits, despite his tragically scrawny build. She was glad to see he was still training with Joven, and had filled out a little, but at this point he was still far less than she would hope. Perhaps she could try talking Joven into increasing the man's training a little.

As the day marched towards noon the sky grew redder and redder as the celestial bodies began to overlap, until the sky over Balator became as vermilion. People scurried about, finding places to sit safely and watch. No one worked this day, instead taking this as a portent and took shelter within their homes. Those nearing childbirth were moved to the nearby temples, and several armored men kept watch over the proceeding.

Endrance stood within his longhouse in the main room near his chair. Every bit of furniture that could be removed had been, except for the chair in the back where he usually sat. The men working for him had managed to cram six beds into the room. They were going to fit twelve, but Anna reminded them that there needed to be room for the midwives to work. Any overflow would have to go into the two guest rooms in the longhouse.

Endrance rubbed his eyes as he awaited the eclipse. He had set up preparations in case of an emergency, as well as making sure the room was well stocked. He had instructed his Draugnoa in the major signs to look for, and insisted they act as midwives for any birthing happening in the longhouse. Selene was now busily bringing in water and other supplies needed to take care of the birth. Endrance had been up until a few hours before sunrise preparing for every eventuality he could think of.

Joven stood watch next to him, his brows furrowed as he scanned the room around him. Joven hadn't said anything to Endrance, but he had felt that something wasn't right. He had a nagging feeling in the back of his head that was both familiar and yet alarming at the same time. His experience told him that something didn't add up around Endrance. He looked down on his charge's head as the young wizard continued to observe the work being done, and knew it wasn't the wizard himself, but that whenever he was around him he felt uncomfortable. Like some kind of bad presence was following the young man around. He squinted at every nook and cranny he could find, probed every shadow that was cast, but could not find any proof to his gut feeling. Sighing, he took up watch over Endrance again, resolved that he could react to any threat towards the young man before they could do harm to him.

The Sha'hdi had found a safe perch up in the rafters above the main room. The longhouse had short walls built within, and many of the crossbeams that supported the roof ran through the entire house, allowing for an enterprising assassin to traverse the entire building unnoticed even if she didn't have the ability to meld into shadows. Humans almost never look up when trying to find someone and that fact would make her assignment an easy proposition. Already having mapped out her escape route and precisely who she would have to kill to escape, she sank into a predatory crouch, her muscles coiled like springs ready to release, patient and certain that her moment to strike would come.

While Joven looked on, and the women busied about, Endrance was feeling a growing sense of worry spread through him. What if he made a mistake? What would the king do when he disobeyed him like they planned to? What if something went wrong and he never found the child? He started to feel weak and uncertain. It must have shown on his face as he stood there, as he felt a large hand clap him on the back, nearly sending him flat on his face. He looked back at Joven's signature grin.

"Relax, Endrance!" he said, winking. "You'll do fine. This is what you were hired for, after all." he pointed at a white-dressed woman that walked past him, carrying an armful of towels. "Everyone here believes in you, and we will all stand by you, no matter what happens."

His reassurances got the young wizard to smile. Even if the worst came, he knew that he could make it with his friend's help. They had done the work, found the knowledge, did the research, and prepared for this moment. They were ready. Endrance nodded, and was about to speak when the double doors suddenly swung open.

A disheveled guardsman burst into the room. He looked around for a second, his eyes adjusting, seeing the Spengur he shouted, "The eclipse! It's starting! And that's not all! Suddenly four of the women's labor increased greatly!" He cleared out of the way as the first of the women were brought in.

More men in armor came carrying on wooden pallets the four women. Three of the women Endrance had never seen before. The first two were attended by their husbands, each in different stages of worry. The third carried by two men, nothing more. The fourth woman that was carried in was not on a wooden stretcher, but rather a cloth mattress carried by four strong men and followed by a smugly smiling King. Endrance's heart dropped as he saw them lay the queen on one of the beds. The king strode over to the wizard's position and stood before him, his armored hands resting on his hips.

"You are ready." he said it more of a statement than a question. When the young wizard nodded he smiled again. "Good, remember what we talked about." he said ominously, turning and walking back to his wife's bedside. The hem of his cape nearly whipped into the young man's face as he strode away. He wore lighter armor this day, fine chain reinforced with black steel plates over the shoulders, upper chest, forearms, and thighs. His boots landed heavily on the wooden planks of the longhouse. The king's sword lanced neatly through a gap in the cape and his back, sitting ominously in its minimal scabbard.

This time when he saw the king the anxiety he felt before was not present. Something was different, but what was it? He didn't have time to ponder the change, he couldn't afford to be distracted.

Endrance waved Anna over. She approached quickly. "So what does it look like?" He asked, partially aware of what she would say.

She looked over the scene. "These four went into labor exactly at the same time. They look to be ready to birth right away, and the eclipse will begin any minute now." she pursed her lips as she watched Bridget come inside to help with the birthing. "We should be able to handle everything here, just stay back unless we call for you."

He stepped back again and watched the midwives work. Walking to the doors, he peered outside and watched as the suns and the moons seemed to meld together. The eclipse was a beautiful dark orb with a corona of flickering multi-hued flames. Endrance saw colors flare that he never had seen in the daylight before, and forced himself to look away before he damaged his eyes. He then heard the four women groan almost in unison.

243

Attending midwives shooed the bearers out of the house, and hurriedly began working with the soon to be mothers.

He shut the doors and locked them, it was time and now he had to watch the births. It was an amazing and yet strangely disturbing thing to the young wizard to watch someone give birth. The women panting and pushing, the husbands standing by, holding their wives hands; even the king had taken off a glove to hold his wife. Endrance noticed that the king's wife was squeezing his hand so hard that his skin appeared to have a strange texture. When the blood was pushed out it looked entirely covered in scar tissue. He realized that the king must have a great deal of calluses from all the years spent fighting growing up. Shaking his head, he looked around again as the first of the four women finally yielded her child. The cord was cut, and Anna whisked the babe away from its mother to present the child to the Spengur.

He turned the babe over gingerly, careful not to harm the squealing newborn. Male, that was correct. However the babe had no birthmarks as the prophecy had predicted. Turning the baby back over to his mother, he declared that child was not the prophesied one. He noticed the king's smirk out of the corner of his eye, barely catching his gaze for a split second in the rush. Again, he remembered the king's threat.

He was unable to dwell on it as the second child was born only a few moments later, and again it was whisked away to be handed to the Answer-Seeker's slender hands. A careful examination of the child revealed a birthmark, but it was only shaped roughly like an acorn. The child was also female, and the prophesied one would be a man. He declared the child was not the prophesied one as well. The child was brought back to his loving parents. He sighed, turning to regard the remaining two mothers.

The queen screeched in pain, her face contorted in pain and agony. Bridget struggled to hold her down as she squirmed, and despite this she nearly threw her to the floor. A thin trickle of blood dripped from a corner of the twisted sheets onto the floor. Her eyes remained locked on her husband's eyes and he stared back with a steely gaze, seeming almost indifferent to her pain. Her free hand gripped the post of the bed, and he realized that the wood, while not of great quality, had compressed and splintered under her grip.

Barbarian women were scary, he thought while looking down at his own thin fingered hand. Someone like Bridget or Anna would utterly crush his poor hand in childbirth. He then realized he was thinking about himself having kids, and he shook the thoughts from his head, a hint of a blush rushing through his cheeks. This was no time for him to be thinking of that.

The remaining two women were having an incredibly rough time. Their bodies were covered in sweat, and the midwives were trying to stop them from bleeding too much. The King seemed a statue, staring solely into his wife's eyes. His intense concentration was so great he neither blinked nor did a single muscle twitch. His wife was staring back into his eyes, her face unsurprisingly in pain and anger.

The other woman was half sitting up in the bed, breathing hard as Selene tended to her. She was otherwise alone, her husband or family absent. Endrance noted that as the woman clasped Selene's hand that she wore a wedding band on her finger. She groaned in pain as a powerful contraction tore through her. She seemed to be much calmer than the queen, save for immediately during a contraction where pain forced its way across her face.

He leaned over and asked his vigilant guardian quietly. "Joven?" he asked.

Joven's eyes flicked to him and back out over the birthing. "Hmm?" he grunted, his massive arms crossed in front of him. Only Endrance from his vantage point of being slightly behind his bodyguard could see a trio of slender throwing knives Joven had palmed in his hand.

"You know what happened to her husband?" he asked, pointing towards the lone woman.

Joven shrugged. "Her husband's one of the King's generals and Balen's equal. He's currently mobilized with his army skirmishing against the wolfmen south of us. He couldn't break away to be here," he said. "Though I know him to be a good man, and that he served with my brother Balen. Would have been here if he could."

Endrance nodded. He had a strange feeling pass through him. His eyes closed as he thought back to the Journal and its prophecy. *The child would be of the nation, but forsaken by it.* He had to carefully contemplate the context of the text to understand, as the current verbal recitation of the prophecy did not have that information. *So, I don't think that the king would fors-*

Both pregnant women cried out at once, and the midwives moved to their feet. Endrance could not see all the activity through the blankets covering them, but he could tell that the time had indeed come. It was strangely disturbing to watch as he couldn't help but notice both sides of the birthing room were doing the exact same thing. The pregnant women cried out in unison, the midwives announced the same events during the birth, and even they both suffered unusual blood loss birthing their children. He glanced at Joven, who gave him an indifferent shrug as he peered up at the rafters.

Jalyin was perfectly still, her crouch in the shadows of the rafters above the proceedings undisturbed by the flicker of torches and braziers. She watched her mark's bodyguard, and knew he would be trouble. He had been slower and clumsier than her, but if he were to connect with a blow it would most assuredly take her down, at least long enough to prove fatal. And now he looked up into her area, scanning the ceiling for potential threats. She was confident that her abilities were more than sufficient to hide her, she had before stood in the shadows within a hand span of a mark and he never knew she was there till... well, he never knew she had been there while he lived. Now she watched him bemusedly. His eyes crossed over her area, and she felt a flicker of uncertainty as his eyes seemed to actually lock vision with her. After a tense moment of looking into his eyes, his vision shifted on to the rest of the shadows in the rafters. She settled again, realizing that he was just peering into the shadows, and only seemed to be looking her in the eyes.

Joven glanced down at his ward, who was practically wringing his hands he was so distressed. The young mage had a good heart, and a type of kind strength that would endear him to others easily, but his naiveté would let others take advantage of his good nature. Joven knew that if the young man lived long enough to get the experience he would need to grow up, the wizard would become a great man. The bodyguard's eyes flicked over the threats within the room and knew grimly that this night if any, would be the time he would be thrown into the fire to prove what he was made of. A smirk edged its way onto his face. He hoped he would survive long enough to give the man a chance to survive the flames. It was his life, his duty, to die before his charge. He knew it would be his destiny.

The sky outside went dark, and a great rumble echoed across the sky. The two mothers cried out once in unison, and the flames within the room flickered briefly and died out. The torches completely lost their fire, while within the brazier only a faint ember glowed. The two pregnant women went silent and still. A cry of alarm spread through the room, as the midwives had to finish working in the dark. Endrance felt his strength leave him. His muscles trembled, and his aura seemed to flood out of his body into the ground at his feet. The others in the chamber didn't seem affected, though he couldn't be sure as even his acute night vision had also become hazy. He felt like he had spent almost every possible drop of power he had.

In a panic he thought that the cause was the eclipse, but he remembered one of the key phrases of the journal of Lehtor: *And lo, the world went dim, and even the light of magic waned in reverence of the savior of the races of the earth.*

He felt a hand catch his arm before he fell to his knees, and Joven helped steady him. He could hardly see or move, but his bodyguard seemed entirely unaffected.

Elsewhere, Jalyin nearly fell from her perch. Only her natural litheness and decades of training kept her from collapsing and slipping off the rafter when the magic dimmed. Elves of any kind, having naturally more magic than humans to begin with, suffered greatly when they had no magical energy at all to exist on. She gritted her teeth, clenched the rafter's wood hard enough to stick a splinter through her gloved hands, and remained silent despite the pain and fear that coursed through her. She would endure this, as she had endured many torturous things, and take down her mark as her employer had paid her to.

The barbarians across Balator seemed none the wiser nor impeded at all by this sudden lessening of the world, and in the darkness and the ruckus of the Draugnoa trying to deliver two babies in the dark where no fire would light, no one noticed the change in the woman's appearance, nor did anyone see Anna take Selene's place as the young Keeper barely made it to a chair and sit down exhausted. The King's ever present smile faded into a scowl, but no one could tell in the dark if he was trembling.

In the dark two babes cried out for the first time. Almost as if their cry was a signal, the braziers burst into light again, and those who felt the fatigue of their energies being sapped could tell the draining effect had slackened, but not restored them. Jalyin felt herself sink back into the shadows again as magical effects returned into force. Endrance's vision and strength returned, and Selene shook her head as she pulled herself up to help again.

Anna and Bridget came up to him, and presented the babes to him. Both children were very healthy, and had strong lungs, crying out loudly as they were cradled. Examining their features, he found them to be similar. He had not seen which of the two the child of the king was, and which the child of the general was. He knew the other means to determine which was the one by birthmark. Directing the Draugnoa to flip the babies over, he saw that the first child had a mark on his left shoulder that looked like a dragon's head. He then saw that the second child had a distinctly different looking dragon's head on his left shoulder as well. The journal only said the child would have the mark of a dragon upon their shoulder. Perplexed, he looked for the only other identifier noted in the journal.

The journal had also identified that the child would have a mark 'like unto a scar' that would be in the shape of a sword. He examined the first child. There was no other mark on his body. . He turned the other child over onto his back, to examine his chest. This babe, crying loudly and healthy, had a black mark across his left breast, where his heart would be. The mark was blackened, looking as if it had been branded onto the skin, an impossible feature in a newborn. The mark looked like a skull.

He looked up at his Draugnoa, the look of fear on his face infecting theirs. The hairs on the back of his neck and arms rose as he realized that he had stepped into incredibly dangerous territory. This mark was a very bad sign.

"Tell me, whose child is this?" he asked quietly. The room was not yet silent as Selene was doing her best finishing up caring for the mothers.

Anna, who was holding the child who only bore the dragon's mark, said "This is the child of the general's wife."

Endrance nodded slowly. He knew then that the other child, the child of the king, was going to be trouble. The whole eclipse birthing was trouble, but the king's machinations only made the situation more dangerous for him.

As he sat there, he realized he had a chance. Here in his hands he held a babe who was destined to grow up to terrorize the world with darkness and evil. He could end the child's life now, and save the world from darkness later. He could even do it with a small amount of lightning, and the baby wouldn't even feel a thing.

He shuddered and almost shoved the baby back into Bridget's hands. No, he couldn't. He just couldn't take a life that was innocent, no matter how dirty it would become some day. There was only one thing he could think to do that would help. He touched the back of the babe's head with his left forefinger and whispered a single word of power, using one of the first spells he ever learned to sling. The meager amount of power he had recovered since the darkening drained, and nothing seemed to happen visibly.

Satisfied, he took a step back and looked over the two newborns. Their similarity was striking, and Endrance was starting to get a nagging suspicion.

As if he knew what Endrance was thinking, the King stood and walked towards the Spengur and his bodyguard. Joven didn't budge when the king approached, and received a stern scowl, but was more intent on his goal than protocol. "I take it you have examined the children?" he asked, a wicked smile of anticipation on his face.

Endrance nodded. "Yes I have your majesty." The hairs on his body hadn't relaxed, and he could feel the trickle of adrenaline in his system. He realized that something else made sense here, and he was just now figuring it out as he spoke to the king. Something he could not have realized until then.

The king frowned threateningly. "Well, what say you? Let's get this done with." He looked about the room dramatically. "Everyone is dying to hear who the child we have been waiting for is."

Endrance almost flinched when he said that. He was being threatening, but subtle. Endrance would have to admit the king was sly. He was a barbarian, but he was also clever and savvy.   "I have found some... unexpected results here. I believe I'll need a few minutes to find out what the signs mean." he said, hoping that it would give him time to think of a way out of this. He really didn't want the king to be mad at him, especially if he had to point out exactly *why* his wife's son is not the child of destiny.

The king's eyes narrowed. "No no," he dismissed the notion, waving a gauntlet covered hand, "Just tell us, and we can make the announcement together." he said, no one but the young mage was able to see the threatening glare in his eyes as he spoke. "You wouldn't want your king looking surprised before his people would you?"

Endrance nodded. "Very well then. I will state my findings now, before everyone here. Are you ready to hear it?" he asked.

The king stared down at the young mage. Endrance looked down at the floor as he realized that there was no way to avoid a confrontation. The king raised his hands up and exclaimed "Well?" in a barely concealed tone of irritation. Endrance was about to speak when Selene interrupted.

"Endrance!" she exclaimed, causing the young wizard to step to the side to see her past the king. "Come quick!"

Thank the gods! He thought in relief as he rushed past the king and over to Selene, who was crouched in between the legs of the General's wife. Her hands were soaked in blood. "She's bleeding too much!" she exclaimed, grimacing as the mother's breathing grew slower. "We need to get her to the healer fast!" she proclaimed.

Bridget also called out to him in panic, and he turned to them to see the queen's eyes roll back and to fall unconscious.

The king passively observed his wife. He had thought she was tougher than that. But at the rate things were going she would not survive to see her son become the destined hero. However the drain on magic could weaken the protections he put in place. Her death could ruin everything. The king rushed over to the queen, grasping one of her hands. He looked over at the Spengur and shouted. "What are you doing? Get over here and help your queen!" Endrance startled. He looked down at the dying mother as the king bellowed, "Get over here now!"

He looked up at Anna, who scowled and jerked her head towards the king, and Endrance nodded, crossing the floor quickly and scooping up some extra strips of clean cloth as he did so. Examining the woman, he could see that not only did she suffer unusually copious bleeding, but also seemed drained of her vitality. He realized then that she may have been magically able, and was amazed she had remained conscious as long as she did.

The king clamped a metal shod hand onto Endrance's shoulder. "Dammit! Don't you have a healing spell or something?" he demanded. "Help her!"

Endrance dropped to a knee, partially because he needed to get down to her level to treat her, and partially because the king's grip almost broke his collarbone.

He shook his head. "No, my king!" he exclaimed. "The eclipse had drained my energies! I cannot cast any spells until I have a chance to recover!" He shook a fist full of cloths as he spoke. "I will do what I can to help her."

If I had any energy left, any at all, I might be able to help them! He thought, hoping he remembered the information in the books he had studied properly. He was about to set the first stitch when he felt a ring hanging on the necklace he wore under his robes grow hot against his skin, stinging him. He felt a smidgen of magical energy return to him as the ring cooled. It was not much, but enough for at least a single casting of the healing spell he had researched.

Unknown to him, Anna had suddenly felt the silver ring on her finger become almost unbearably hot and nearly passed out on the other side of the room.

He glanced at the king as he set the needle aside. "I think I have the power for one healing spell. Please let go of my shoulder so I can move freely." The king released his grip, secretly surprised that the kid had already recovered enough power to cast a spell. He had a formidable power indeed. The king's own wife had not recovered from the drain of the eclipse, and would soon die if not helped.

Endrance said the simple word phrase and moved his hands in the swift gestures needed. He had chosen this spell among the other possible healing magic because it had been the best balance of speed and complexity of casting versus the injuries it could heal. While it may not fully heal the queen's injuries, it would definitely be enough to stop the bleeding, and perhaps mend some of the tearing.

The spell did its work quickly, and Endrance could see color return to the queen's cheeks. He still had some work to do, but he would manage. Something seemed a bit off, but Endrance was not able to tell what it was since there was too much going on around him and he had never performed surgery before, much less worked on that area of a woman's body.

He tended to the queen for another minute before he was certain that she would pull through alright. He stood, blood smeared on his bare hands, arms, and the front of his chest. He nodded at the king, and started to speak when he felt a soft hand on his shoulder. Turning he saw Selene looking into his eyes, her expression solemn. "The general's wife..." she began, closing her eyes and turning towards the bed opposite of the queen.

The figure in the bed was still, and the sheet had been pulled over her face. Endrance stared at it at first, not comprehending what lay before him. It dawned on him when Anna looked to him and shook her head sadly. His expression fell, and he felt something strange welling up in his heart, an aching pain that brought tears to his eyes. He stumbled over a tangle of bloody sheets that lay strewn between the beds, and fell to his knees at the base of the deceased woman's bed. A horrible wrenching sensation twisted up in his gut, and all he saw turned blurry as hot tears started running down his face.

He had been aware that people might die over the course of his career, but he had not expected it to happen so soon, especially not to someone under his direct care. His fists balled up against the sheets at her feet as grief ran through him. He didn't know how to cope with the pain of seeing another human being die. *I don't want her to die!* His thoughts raged through his mind. *I don't want anyone to die!* He slammed his fist into the bed, wishing he could do something more.

Something more happened. As he sobbed, a pale golden wind seemed to flow softly from the woman's still form. Not nearly as voluminous as the other times, it was still beautiful and still frightening to behold. The rest of the people in the room, except for Joven recoiled as the wind swirled around the wizard and spiraled into the Crystalphage on his left forearm. The midwives and the two families still present had the presence of mind to flee the longhouse, shouting and carrying their newborn children. That left him alone with the king and his wife; his men must have left during the eclipse, as the door was unlocked and open.

The energy he had gathered was likely not much compared to the spell bracer's total, but with it came a secret. It was a secret that confirmed his suspicions of the king. And part of him found this discovery funny, but tragic at the same time.

"The woman's dead." He heard the king speak the words, but they made no impact in his mind. "And I grieve for your loss, but you have at least done a great work saving my wife's life. There's nothing more you could do here." The king was standing nearly right behind the kneeling mage. "Stand, Spengur, and tell us the answer to the eclipse!" his commanding voice filled the room.

Endrance stood. His courage was fueled by his anger at himself for being powerless when he was most needed. He turned to King Kalenden, and looked him in the eye. "I have your answer, king!" he said firmly, his aggression tainting the tone of his voice. "Your son is in fact the child of destiny!" Endrance exclaimed loudly. "But your son is also the child of destruction!"

The king visibly thought through the mage's statement. "Wait," he said, "You said that my son was both the child of destiny and the child of destruction. Prophecy says that they will oppose each other. How can he be both?" The king did not look confused, if anything, he looked about to become angry.

Endrance smirked, realizing that this was the moment that he either gave in or stood strong. His heart told him to speak the truth, while his fear told him to just give in to the king's demands. "He cannot." Endrance said. "If you only had one son, but you should know most of all that both of the babes are your sons!"

"The general's wife bore your son, out of wedlock. The general was away at war far too often, yes?" Endrance stated, his eyes locked with the king's. "And that one is the child of destiny. The other, born of your wife, is the child of destruction."

Endrance chuckled, feeling a bit mad. "So either way, I have done what you wanted! Your son is the child of prophecy! But he will gain you no clout, nor honor!"

The king's face hardened and the wizard could see him trembling with anger. "Is that so?" the ruler asked with an even tone.

"Yes, King Kalenden." He said, having committed to the course.

The king's face twitched, but otherwise did not express his anger through his face. "So you say my child is the destroyer?" he queried. "And my illegitimate son is the hero?"

Endrance shrugged. "That is how it appears."

"Good." The king stated, pulling an orange crystal from his belt and holding it out.

It was Crystalphage. The gem dimmed in brilliance, and the wizard could feel a massive amount of power flow into the king. The crystal turned black, and Kalenden dropped it as he flung a hand out towards the doors and muttered a word. The twin doors slammed shut and locked of their own accord.

"It was you!" Endrance exclaimed, backing away from him. "You are the summoner!"

Kalenden laughed viciously, pointing a hand at his wife and chanting a few more words. The woman shrieked, combusting into flames, her silhouette having horns and wings for the brief moment before she was gone and the bed was empty and singed.

Endrance's senses pounded. His blood burned, and anger blasted through his head again. He clasped his hands to his head, unable to react to the current situation. His head hurt beyond his own ability to comprehend. He had finally found the one who had tied everything together, and it was the very man who had allowed him to be hired.

The summoner's laughter faded, and it looked the room over slowly, sure in its superiority. "Three women, a rebellious son of Daelen, and a wizard so young he's barely out of boy's clothes. This is just precious. I think I might cry." he mocked, bringing a powerful hand up in a mocking gesture of wiping a tear from his face. "No matter, I will simply have to kill the lot of you, and call some demons to take your forms until I have a reason to get rid of you publicly."

He smirked as he looked Joven in the eye. "It's time, Jalyin. Finish your assignment. You can kill the others too." he said.

Joven was about to rush to try to intercept the King when he caught a flicker of movement above. Reflexively he lurched to the left, throwing his body in between the motion and the young man who was still trying to compensate. A blackened steel knife seemed to blossom from his chest, just where his charge's head would have been. The blade only sank an inch through the armor plating into the meat of his right breast, a trivial wound in comparison to being knifed in the head.

Everyone seemed to move at once. The Sha'hdi seemed to materialize out of the darkness of the rafters itself, while Draugnoa leapt to the fight. Joven threw his daggers at the assassin as he pulled a pair of hand axes from his belt with the other hand.. The three keepers interposed themselves between the moon elf and their husband. Endrance staggered back, slowly collecting himself as the world came into focus for him. The Draugnoa had only their daggers, and he would have to help them.

Jalyin swung onto the side of the rafter she was perched on, the thrown knives Joven sent her way sailing just past the mark. Using her powerful legs, she propelled herself at the mage's guardians. They would keep stopping her from getting any direct strikes on him, and murdering them wouldn't affect her pay. She had been itching to kill these ignorant fools for some time, but she had to follow the orders of her client. Now she was free to slaughter them all.

The assassin spun as she flew at the blond haired keeper, black daggers seeming to appear into her hands as she swung them out in an arc, a precise scissor strike that should have sliced the barbarian's throat open neatly. Somehow, the woman jammed her dagger into the crossing blades, catching them where the two blades crossed, locking the two together for a brutal instant. Then in an instant the assassin was away, dodging the expert knife strike Bridget had aimed.

The elf easily performed a back handspring, simultaneously leaping over Selene's low strike, and sliding under Anna's throat slash. She landed perfectly, and spun to strike at the two at the same time. The two women expertly spun while falling back, catching each other's free hand and keeping the other stable as the assassin's daggers sliced through the air they previously occupied. Bridget almost caught her off guard, forcing the elf to spring out of the way as she kicked a nearby pan at her with a thundering crack. She skidded on her knees under the projectile, which clattered against the doors.

She popped up to her feet to have to block a piercing strike that Selene thrust, turning the blade away from her body as she whirled the other to counterstrike. That dagger was deflected by Anna's desperate block, and Bridget vaulted over the two Keeper's shoulders to strike downward with her knife. The assassin disengaged and slid backward faster than humanly possible, just barely avoiding Bridget's hammer strike, the blade of the knife just barely cutting down her right eyebrow as she faded out of reach. A drop of blood dropped from her eyebrow, and she lunged back into the fray, a scream of frustration escaping her lips as she brought her daggers to bear.

King Kalenden drew his sword and unhooked his cloak as Joven pulled the dagger from his chest and readied his axes. They were made for war, but the king's sword would be dangerous. The bodyguard was not as well armored as his opponent, and he was likely not quite as strong as the king was. Things were looking grim.

Joven took the offensive, lunging with a swipe with his left hand. The king indignantly batted the weapon out of the way. Joven swung his other axe as hard as he could. He wasn't aiming for the king, but his weapon. The two axes crossed the sword's blade, and the three weapons locked together. The king was smiling as Joven struggled to keep control of the bind.

"What's the matter, Joven?" Kalenden said mockingly. "Is the legendary strength of Daelen's brood not good enough?" he lifted his blade, hardly impeded by Joven's struggling. "You are a fool to think you can beat me on your own."

"Well, you know me." Joven replied, using the hooked axes to give him leverage as he delivered a powerful straight kick to Kalenden's abdomen. He slid back from Joven, and the sword slid free, carving deep notches into Joven's axes as sparks flew. "I'm not as dumb as I look."

Endrance opened a trunk they had stashed behind the chair he usually sat in when conducting business. They had set it there when preparing, knowing that it might be necessary. A large quantity of weapons was piled inside. He grabbed the bipennis battleaxe and hefted it. "Joven!" he shouted, heaving it towards the man. The barbarian threw both his axes at the king, whirling to catch the axe as it came close.

The king sidestepped one of the axes, and the second bounced off his shoulder cop, barely nicking the metal. He dashed towards Endrance's bodyguard, trying to get a shot off while his back was turned. Joven smoothly caught the axe as he spun and kept turning, using the momentum of the turn to make the first swing with his axe a powerful one.

Endrance turned to the fight with the assassin and his guardians. Their daggers flicked through the air, the four of them a whirl of motion and deadly steel. The assassin was more agile and skilled than any human woman could have been, but the three Keepers fought in unison, having been trained for years together. One could sacrifice their defense to make an attack on the shadow elf, knowing faithfully that another would be there to defend her. The three were making it impossible for the assassin to successfully hit any one of them.

He couldn't help in that fight at all, for interrupting the women's unison could be deadly. He didn't have the skill with his knives to fight on the assassin's level, and he didn't have the familiarity with the keepers to join into their dance of blades. He looked at the trunk of weapons, which contained the three's favored weapons. It seemed they would have to wait for now.

He saw that Kalenden had drained energy from the Crystalphage he had been carrying. It was even larger than the one in his bracer, but might not hold as much as the perfect star cut of his gem. He just needed to tap into it and draw upon its power to refill his aura. Up until that point he had been reluctant to do so; it had within it immeasurable power, and he had not been able to figure out the meaning behind the third circle of script. He didn't want a repeat of the prior time where a spell circle had run rampantly out of his control, but now he didn't have a choice.

Joven fought with king Kalenden on more level ground. The king was stronger, but he didn't have all of Joven's experience. Trained in multiple fighting styles, Joven was keeping Kalenden guessing as he rapidly changed his attack and defense patterns. He had managed to get a strike against the king's armor, but didn't do any real damage.

Endrance closed his eyes and concentrated on the well of power he wore on his arm. Immediately the script illuminated, golden light radiating from the engravings. He touched on the power contained within, and nearly staggered under the magnitude of what he felt. The gem contained nearly tenfold the power Endrance could currently hold within his aura, and the power pulsed, ready to be drawn upon.

He mentally pulled on the power, and the brilliant sparkle of the gem dimmed as he siphoned away some of its inner light. His aura blossomed with power, growing as full as it naturally came to. He didn't stop right away, instead dealing with the discomfort as he poured yet more power, bloating his aura with golden light.

He opened his eyes, so buoyantly full of power he felt fantastic. The pain, the aches he had before, none of it mattered. The weakness of his body was trivial compared to the power of his mind and spirit. He turned to the fighting pairs, and it seemed so much less threatening than it did before.

He reached out with both hands towards the king and spoke with joy on his voice. "Joven, please move."

The barbarian caught a glimpse of the young wizard out of the corner of his eye and with full force leapt away from the king. He crashed through one of the beds, collapsing it under his mass.

The king turned to him, surprised at the young wizard's seemingly miraculous recovery. He had fully recovered all his power in the few seconds they were fighting? "Impossible!" he shouted, throwing his left hand forward and pulling his sword up to his shoulder.

"*Ignatius.*"Endrance spoke, and from his hands fire raged. The sweep of fire slammed into the barbarian king, and he disappeared into the flames. The front of the longhouse disintegrated under the force of the fire, and the roof caught on fire.

"This is very unbecoming of you, your highness." Endrance said, his unflagging cheerfulness adding a pleasant tone to his voice. "I do not think this was a wise decision. The Spengur's word is irrefutable when it comes to magic!"

The flames and smoke cleared, leaving the edges of the blown out walls and ceiling burning. King Kalenden still stood, singed but shielded by some spell that he had thrown up to protect himself. "You wouldn't even be here if it wasn't for me, whelp!" He growled as he replied harshly. "I give you everything you could ever want, and this is what you give me in return? Betrayal?"

"No." Endrance said. "You seek to destroy everything. You put yourself here to prevent the prophesied hero from coming to fruition. I will not let you damn the world like this." The ceiling fire was spreading, and embers were drifting down from above.

The king snarled his face almost contorted into an inhuman mask. "I am going to kill you for this, Endrance!" he shouted.

"Maybe so," Endrance responded. "But not today."

"Take your child and go! But know that this is not over between us!" he shouted. He should kill the man, but he couldn't without the people of Balator seeing him as an assassin himself. He needed to find a way to bring the man's evil to light before his people.

The king scoffed, and glanced at his child, who lay wrapped in cloth at the foot of the bed. He turned away from Endrance and strode over to the bed, maintaining a grip on his barbed sword. He looked at Endrance one more time, and then picked up the bundled child in one hand.

"We aren't done yet, Spengur." He grunted, walking out the hole in the front as the roof above still burned. "We are going to finish this soon. Very soon."

The man was gone, but the assassin wasn't. She back flipped out of the way of a three point strike concerted by the Draugnoa, landing near the ruined doors.

"It looks like our little match is postponed." She teased. "I will be seeing you all in due time."

Endrance pointed at her with a gloved hand and said simply, "No, you won't."

Jalyin lurched backwards, trying to meld into the darkness, but the brilliance of the lightning spell abolished it before she could reach it.

Thunder shook the timbers of the burning longhouse, and the bolt of lightning struck her low in the gut, crashing her through the remains of an already devastated wall and out into the darkening sky. A thud was heard several dozen yards distant, but no other sounds came from outside.

Endrance chuckled. "I'm pretty sure I hit that time." He said with relief. His buoyancy faded as the energy he had expended from the two spells had drained him below his maximum, and the sense of invincibility disappeared in an instant. The elf was gone, leaving the five in a burning building unopposed. The keepers panted from fighting, and Joven quickly moved to his charge.

"We need to get out of here." He said, and Endrance lowered his bow. "The building is burning."

The young wizard looked around the room frantically. The only person who hadn't been evacuated when the fighting was over was the baby the General's wife had delivered minutes before.

The desire to protect life overrode his sense of self, and Endrance stumbled through the drifting embers and smoke to the baby while Joven and the women scrambled to retrieve what important items they could before the fire got to them.

He found the bundle of cloth was okay. Gullin had swept in while everyone was occupied, snatched up the baby by his swaddling clothes, and laboriously hauled him out of the line of danger. Even as Endrance approached, Gullin remained perched above the baby, using his outstretched wings to shield him from most of the falling embers.

Endrance carefully scooped up the child, who somehow, during the battle to the death, had stopped crying and was quietly watching the new events. He rushed with the child out of the longhouse, hoping the smoke hadn't damaged the poor infant's lungs. Exiting the building, he skidded to his knees and examined the baby for injuries.

Endrance felt a sudden shock of worry as he saw that a burning ember had landed on the baby's cheek despite Gullin's best attempts. He quickly wiped it away, and saw that though the babe's cheek had been burned he did not cry. He drew up the energy he needed, and carefully chanted out the healing spell he had used on the queen. It wasn't really meant to treat burns, but it was the only thing he had that would help.

He stared down at the child as the spell finished its work. The long finger thick burn drew in on itself, becoming a thin line. His hands trembled and his mind reeled as he couldn't believe what he saw. He looked down at the burn, which had healed so that all that remained was a reddish scar in the shape of a sword.

Inadvertently, the Spengur had given the hero the identifying mark, not found it.

Joven burst from the house, the smoke thick and the house visibly burning from the outside. He was dragging a pair of trunks, and had almost all of his weapons strapped to his person. Depositing them, he whistled for his horse which arrived almost as if it had been waiting nearby.

"We need to get out of here, Endrance!" Joven shouted. "I'll get us a small cart to pull our things!" and with that the big man rode down the path to the main road.

Endrance looked up, and the eclipse had begun to come apart, though they were still almost entirely merged. The people of Balator were still in their homes, and even the men on guard were nowhere to be seen. The king could have ordered them away, Endrance realized. No one would be coming to help them.

Anna came out the front doors, coughing and spitting. She carried a large bag haphazardly stuffed full of clothes and other essentials. Bridget was right behind her, carrying a large bundle of the kitchen's food supplies and dragging the trunk with their weapons behind her. Endrance walked up to the two as they deposited their collected things beside the trunks Joven hauled out.

"Selene?" he asked frantically. The fire had gotten to the point where almost the entire thing was burning.

Anna shook her head. "She was right behind us!" she coughed.

Endrance held the child out to her. "Take him! I have to find her!" he exclaimed, and deposited the child into the eldest woman's care.

He ran into the now burning longhouse, and immediately the heat and smoke burned his eyes, forcing him to squint as he stumbled around the falling timbers of the rafters towards the back of the longhouse.

"Selene!" he shouted, trying to tell where she was. Heading towards the wrong end of the house would be fatal for her and possibly him.

She didn't respond, but he thought he heard coughing from the bedroom. He charged over to the door, which was hanging loose on a single hinge and had flames dancing across the surface. He shouldered through it, and found Selene collapsed in the doorway between the storage room and the bedroom. He rushed over to her and knelt, touching her shoulder. She was still alive, and conscious.

"I'm sorry, my love." She whispered, cradling a rectangular bundle wrapped in the cloth of her cloak. "I went to get the books you wanted so badly." She coughed, and tried to stand. "It would be a shame if such old books were destroyed in the fire, right?"

He concentrated, and cast the strengthening spell on himself. He scooped the girl up, trying his best to not double over himself due to the smoke. He nodded to her, assuring her. "Yes, it would be very sad, you did good to find it." He said, looking about for an exit.

The house was falling apart rapidly, and fire was everywhere. He had one chance of escaping, and that was out the door in the back that led to the hot spring. He quickly worked his way across the room, carrying his wife across the bed to the door to the back. He didn't have the hands free, so instead kicked at the door. He nearly put his foot through it, but it didn't budge on his first try, coughing, he stepped back and delivered one more kick, his heel impacting with the door latch. This time the door flung open, and he barreled through into the cold night air, not stopping until they were near the water of the spring.

Selene looked up at him, her eyes watery and blurry. "Are we okay?" she asked.

Endrance nodded and looked over his shoulder. The roof of the building had collapsed in the center, and the rest would soon be following. "Yes, were clear of the fire." He assured her.

Selene smiled weakly. "Good." She whispered. "I'm going to fall asleep now, wake me up when it's all over." Her eyes drooped, and her form went limp in his arms. As things faded to black she could hear him calling out to her.

"Selene!" he cried, shaking her gently. "Selene, don't leave me! Selene!"

It felt like the last time he would hold her in his arms, but this time his voice accompanied her into the darkness.

Chapter 32

Her husband's voice echoed in her head as she fell into darkness. The descent was dark and frightening as wind rushed by her and her stomach plunged. She fell unimpeded by anything, and felt like she was plummeting forever. Above her somewhere she could hear her husband call her name, his voice echoing down to her from countless miles away. Air rushed through her hair and around her, whistling by at great speed.

Her descent slowed, and she felt her feet dip downwards as her head came up. Her feet felt something firm beneath her, and she almost fell over as gravity returned, setting her standing upon a surface as smooth and as cold as polished stone. All around her was an endless expanse of black. She could only see herself reflected in the surface she stood on. She looked around the darkness but she could not see anyone, or anything else. Only her own heartbeat pounded in her ears as panic started setting in.

She was wearing the simple white dress she had worn during the night of the sacrifice; the one she wore when her life in Balator ended and her life with Endrance began. She was barefoot, and she did not carry the knife on her arm as was her habit and tradition.

She took a step, and she did not fall through the darkness. That was good. She walked forwards, trying to get somewhere in the darkness. Her footsteps echoed faintly through the void, a delicate *pat pat pat*. She wasn't sure where she was, but she vaguely remembered being in Endrance's arms not a moment before. The thought was fleeting, and she could not keep a hold of it and it was soon gone.

She ran, and the darkness continued on as far as she could see. "Hello!" she shouted as she ran. "Is anyone out there?"

The undefined nature of the place prevented her from telling how far she had run, nor whether she was any closer to reaching anything resembling a destination. Her breath never became harsh, and her legs never grew tired no matter how long she ran. Her steps slowed, and eventually she drifted to a stop, losing the will to continue trying.

She sank to her knees, her despair rising as she realized that she would not find her way out. Tears welled in her eyes, and she cradled her face in her hands. She felt so entirely alone, and in the darkness she found only despair.

She cried for longer than she ever had before, but never did she start feeling better. Her tears fell upon the polished surface, pooling before her knees in little dancing balls of water. She could barely see through the film of tears in her eyes but something in her reflection caused her to pause and wipe the tears from her face.

The reflection put her hand against the smooth surface below her, as if only against a clear glass window. She scowled as she wiped her palm across the underside of the surface she'd been crying on. The tears pooled before her skittered away, as if her own hand had wiped them from the glass.

Selene leapt back to her feet, and would have left the floor entirely if it weren't the only surface to stand on. The sudden change in something she thought was normal startled her from her depression.

Her other did not move. She remained kneeling, and her eyes were narrowed as she glared at herself on the other side. Selene stared wide eyed as the woman who looked like her changed first subtly, then more dramatically.

Her eyes were different from her own; they were a deep red that seemed almost luminescent, with square pupils like a goat's. Her hair seemed to turn violet from the roots, and the color bled through her hair to the tips. Her lips twitched, and a sultry smirk grew on her face, an expression Selene had never used before.

The double dipped her head towards the surface, and her head passed through it. The world seemed to flip for her, and Selene took another step back as her duplicate now stood before her instead of below her.

The double looked down at her white dress and frowned. Looking back up at Selene with a smirk, she snapped her fingers on one hand. As if suddenly drenched in crimson blood, her dress turned from white to scarlet, bleeding from the shoulders down to the hem at her feet. As Selene stared, the back of her double's dress tore, and two reddish, webbed demonic wings rose behind her.

"So," the duplicate said. Her voice Selene's own, but somehow different. It had a confident tone that she didn't possess. "We finally meet, at last."

Selene took a defensive pose. She didn't have her weapons, but she was a capable hand to hand fighter, her hands would have to do. She gulped as she watched her darker self.

"Who are you?" she asked.

"Who am I?" the scarlet keeper asked, touching a hand to her chest. Her dress had somehow changed the cut and dimension, hugging her curves tightly, and the neckline plunged dangerously low to a point. The woman in red laughed prettily, but still conveyed a mocking tone. "Why, my pretty little thing. I am you."

Selene shook her head, denying what she saw before her. "No!" she exclaimed. "I can't be you!" She shrunk back as her opposite took a step towards her. "I don't want to be like you!"

"Oh?" the duplicate intoned, her eyebrow raised. "I think the truth is you *want* to be me, but you're too afraid to make. That. First. Step." Her words matched her steps as she came closer and closer to Selene. "It's not all that bad, being who I am. It just requires that you…" the crimson doppelganger looked up and out the corner of her eyes as if she were thinking of a word. She leveled her gaze upon the frightened keeper. "How do the humans say it? Open up a little."

"What do you mean?" the white clothed Selene asked, remembering to keep her guard up.

Her scarlet opposite smiled knowingly as she reached out and placed a fingertip on Selene's outermost fist. Almost delicately, she pushed her hands out of the way as she came into Selene's personal space. The smell of spring rain permeated the air around her, and still somehow Selene couldn't resist as her opposite placed her hands on her shoulder and waist, as if they were about to dance.

"It's really simple, my sweet self." The demonic duplicate explained, reaching down and setting Selene's hands on her own waist. Her skin was surprisingly warm in the dress, and she was surprised that the crimson fabric was dry after all. She half expected it to actually be soaked in blood.

"I am the demonic half of you." She said sweetly, pulling her in close and wrapping her arms around her. "I am what you will grow into. Even if you resist, eventually you will be the one on the other side of the looking glass reflecting back at who you are now." The smell of rain was everywhere, and Selene couldn't help but breathe it in. It seemed to be almost intoxicating, and she couldn't move of her own accord.

Her scarlet self pulled her in close, and she could feel the heat of her body pressed against hers. "I am very certain things would be better if you just accepted me… into you. Then you would be able to stand strong against what's going on… out there."

She looked her double in the eyes, her alien gaze disturbing but also alluring. "You would even be able to stand next to your husband, and not feel as you have before. You could be as strong as him, even stronger." She inclined her head towards her other's, her lips just a hair from Selene's ear. Selene shuddered as her duplicate spoke, whether out of fear or rising attraction she couldn't tell.

"So what do you say," she whispered. "Let me in?"

Selene was paralyzed as thoughts ran through her head. Was she feeling turned on by herself? Was that just a demonic ability? The other version of her was confident, strong, and powerful. She had wings, and with them she could fly, and would have the strength to carry her husband with her.

But what about her husband? What would he think? She struggled to remember Endrance's discussions with her about her heritage. Somehow she was unable to even think past the moment, her thoughts drifting away on rain-scented wind.

"I…" she started, finding resistance impossible. She opened her mouth to accept, and she felt a warm hand touch her shoulder.

"I think you should let her decide this on her own terms." A familiar voice came from behind her. "Besides, seducing yourself? Even among demons, that has to be odd behavior."

She looked over her shoulder and felt relief as her husband stood behind her. However he looked different than he usually did. He wore only a simple pair of pants, and soft leather shoes. The most unusual part of his appearance was his upper body. The arcane tattoos that normally lay nearly unnoticeable on his skin glowed golden, hovering an inch off of his skin. Every inch of his exposed body was covered in geometric arcane patterns. Behind his head hovered a glowing ring of a spell circle that looked almost like a halo of golden light. As she saw into his emerald eyes, she saw even his irises were scribed with golden arcane script.

The scarlet Selene released her hold on her white-dressed self, and eyed the newcomer hungrily. "Well, she's taking so long to come about it herself." She said defensively. "I am only giving her a little push, that's all."

The woman crossed her arms, pushing together an impressive amount of cleavage as she shifted her posture. "She's all alone in here without me anyways. Alone in the emptiness of her own heart." She pouted, pursing her lips.

Endrance smiled, touching the white-clothed Selene's shoulder reassuringly.

"She will never be alone," he stated surely, waving his hand up over his head. As he did, the darkness above became alight with thousands of specks of light. "When the darkness becomes too deep for her, I will cast stars into it, to light her way. When she feels lonely, I will whisper in her ear that I am near. When she cries, I will turn her tears to roses." His emerald eyes shone as he stood confidently before her demonic half. "So there is no rush, you see? She will always have me."

The other half of Selene scowled. "Fine, I will step back... for now." The complete version of her started to sink into the polished floor, her feet being absorbed by the reflective surface. "But know this, Selene. You cannot avoid the truth. You are half demon. The sooner you accept this the better off you will be in the long run."

And as her other vanished, Selene looked down to see her reflection had returned. As she looked at her own face, it winked at her, and returned to normal.

She turned to her husband, who stood before her. "How?" she started to ask. "How did you get here? I thought I was all alone in here."

Endrance embraced her, smiling lovingly. "I will always be with you, my love." The young mage winked. "When you feel alone remember that I love you, and know that I'm always by your side." He stepped away from her, and she saw his appearance was becoming slightly transparent.

"Please, wake up when you get the chance to, okay?" he asked, his body slowly fading. "Don't keep us waiting!"

He faded from view, his tattoos being the last to disappear. They were both right. She was going to have to accept that she was a half-demon, and live with it. But unlike many of her kind, she had a man who loved and cared for her to help her go through the process. He was someone who had the knowledge and experience to actually help her. She closed her eyes, and knew it was time to wake up. With effort she focused on opening her eyes to the real world.

Her eyes fluttered open, and she realized she was tucked into a small bed heaped with furs. Her body was incredibly hot, and she shifted under the covers, wincing as freezing cold mountain air snuck in under the furs and danced across her naked side. She looked around the room, and found herself in a cave of some sort. A small fire pit in the center of the cave was burnt out, the cinders long since cooled.

Scattered throughout the room were several travel packs, the trunks that Joven had retrieved from the longhouse, and several of the bodyguard's weapons were leaning against the stone of the wall. A large sack was near the exit to the chamber, and Selene could see several white furs folded up within.

She rummaged through the pack until she found one of the white fur coats her fellow Keepers wore when they couldn't tolerate the cold. Their training included working in the cold, as their traditional garb was only the white linen dress, and the cold practically ignored the thin layer of cloth. Still, having a higher cold tolerance did not make her immune to freezing, so she pulled on the coat, and slipped into heavy winter boots.

She looked down the cave corridor, but didn't see anyone. No one was around, and she wondered how Endrance had been in her dream a minute before but had left her bed so quickly. He probably used some kind of spell to be in her dream, and he had left her to recover.

Walking cautiously down the cave corridor, she found several other rooms of varying sizes. Some of them had simple furniture in them as well as the biggest one which had a rug across the stone to help keep feet warm. She still didn't find anyone, but could hear some faint noises in the distance. Following the tunnel, it came out to a cave opening to the exterior.

The cave opened up to a mountainous area somewhere in the barbarian territories, as far as Selene could see. Snow was everywhere, and though the sky was clear and the sun out, it didn't look about to thaw anytime soon. The area was a relatively flat space about fifty feet across, one side mountain and rock, the other winter pines and sharp slopes. The air was thin, and she figured they were up the mountain a ways at least.

Anna and Bridget were sitting on a fur covered chair nearby, but hadn't noticed her approach. They also wore heavy boots and winter coats, as well as gloves that helped keep their fingers warm. Selene hadn't seen any more when she dressed, so they may not have had enough for all three. Gullin sat on top of a small fire surrounded by stones, enjoying the warmth in a way only those immune to fire could afford.

Selene blinked at the sunlight reflecting off the snow, and when her vision refocused, she couldn't help but stare as she spotted her husband.

Endrance skidded backwards in the snow, both daggers drawn and held defensively, blade reversed in his hands. He was breathing hard, but seemed to be concentrating very hard. He wore the armor they had given him, as well as his heavy winter clothes. His hair was bound back behind his head, and the hood of his coat flopped uselessly on his back, likely having fallen off in the fighting.

His opponent was Joven, which was more surprising than Selene would have expected. The big man strode towards his charge, his face a mask of determination. The barbarian wore heavy furs and hardened steel armor. In his hands was a pair of long daggers, sturdy and likely sharp. He lunged into Endrance's space, slashing with his right blade.

The young mage didn't dodge as Selene expected, but stepped forwards and deflected Joven's arm with his left forearm. Hooking the back of his dagger against Joven's arm, he pulled the barbarian towards him while slicing at his ribs with his right blade. Joven, an expert fighter, was able to deflect Endrance's strike with his left and counter with the same blade. The young mage ducked and twisted under Joven's extended right arm, sliding away and leaving a shining new cut across the steel plate on his opponent's thigh armor in passing.

Selene walked up beside the two Draugnoa standing watch. "What's going on?" she asked.

Anna and Bridget looked up at her surprised. "Selene!" Anna exclaimed. "You're awake!" The two stood and embraced their sister.

Bridget tilted her head towards the two fighting in the snow outside. "I'm being impressed by Endrance's knife fighting skills. The man's been keeping even with Joven for almost ten minutes of constant fighting."

Anna settled back down on the fur, rolling her eyes. "It's almost like neither of them are willing to admit they're getting tired."

Bridget pulled Selene down to sit on the fur with her. The woman picked a comb up from a nearby box and started brushing Selene's hair. The young woman hadn't even thought to check on her hair, which had been treated badly by the fire and nights of unconscious nightmares.

"To be honest," Bridget said quietly. "Endrance has the advantage in this fight. While Joven's much more skilled than him, the man's smaller, lighter on his feet, and much nimbler. I think he would be able to win, if he wasn't worried about hurting his bodyguard."

Selene half shrugged, wincing as a particularly hard to loosen knot in her hair was tugged painfully by the brush. "He should know the first rule by now, right?"

Anna nodded, reciting the rule even though the three all knew many combat rules by heart. "First rule of fighting with knives, expect to get cut."

The barbarian and the mage moved in a manner that almost seemed like a performance. Their strikes, blocks, and counterstrikes flowed into one another, and their weapon's effectiveness was reduced to causing nicks and scratches across armor or clothing. Their movement remained fluid, and the snow was trampled in a large area as they fought.

Selene smiled slightly as she watched the look of concentration on her husband's face. Maybe they hadn't realized it yet, but from her perspective she saw that he was concentrating so hard not on the fight itself, but on avoiding inflicting wounds on his opponent. Joven's armor had too many scratches across vital areas for it to be coincidence. The big barbarian had stamina, but this fight would have been over quickly against someone trying to kill him. All they had to do was slip in, cut the bodyguard in a few vital places, and use their superior agility and speed to avoid the man until he bled out or at least weakened enough to finish off.

"I don't know…" Selene said, "I think he might be trying to avoid that rule."

The young mage must have heard her voice or seen her out of the corner of his eye, because his 'flow' faltered for a split second. Joven took advantage of this, hooking his dagger against one of Endrance's and sending it flying. Endrance tried to leap back out of the way, but Joven caught him upside the head with his elbow and forearm. The young mage spilled across the snow, his lost dagger landing into the snow several feet away with a *piff* as snow was displaced.

Joven stopped advancing, and waited for the young man to recover from the blow. "You see there, that's what I'm saying is your problem!" he exclaimed. "You lose concentration on the fight for even a second, and your enemy is going to be all over you like soldiers jump on free ale."

Endrance sat up in the snow, wiping the pain and flakes of white from his face. He sighed, pulling himself to his feet and retrieving his other dagger. Tucking them into his belt, he shrugged as he turned back to face Joven.

"I still held my own for several minutes." He began. "In a close quarters battle like that minutes might as well be an eternity."

Joven shook his head. "The purpose of teaching you this is not to teach you to 'hold your own' for any amount of time. You need to be able to win quickly when you engage an enemy with your knife! The longer the fight gets, the more chances your enemy has of killing you!"

Endrance nodded his head and held up his hands in a gesture of appeasement. "I understand, I understand. But I was distracted."

Joven scowled. "Another thing you can't allow! Distracted by what?"

Endrance inclined his head towards the cave entrance and pointed with a finger. "It seems Selene has awoken?"

Selene watched the two approach her, and stood to hug her husband strongly as he reached her. She heard his breath rush out as she squeezed, and lessened her hold. He took a breath and coughed slightly as she let him go.

"You've gotten stronger." He observed, his hand on her shoulder was assuring.

"Really?" she asked, uncertain. Endrance wasn't very physically strong, so he could be guessing.

"Yes, really." He replied with a wheeze, "I should let you run through burning buildings more often. Soon enough you'd be beating Hydras in arm wrestling contests."

She frowned at him, but couldn't get angry. She had long since learned to tell when he was joking and being serious, though sometimes he didn't convey it clearly.

Bridget held up a brush with a few dark tangled hairs. "Her hair wasn't violet." She observed. "She doesn't need to change to use her strength, Endrance."

"How long were you out here?" Selene asked. "When did you come visit me last?" she asked.

He shrugged. "I've been out here all day sparring with Joven and practicing my spells. I slept next to you every night since the fire, though Anna and Bridget have been checking on you almost every hour I'm not there."

Her eyebrows wrinkled up as she tried to make sense of his statement. "But I saw you in my dreams, right before I woke up. How would you have been out there, but also in my dreams?" Her vision became unfocused as she remembered her dream, which haunted vividly in her mind.

Endrance blinked at her, puzzled. "I don't know." He admitted. "I did dream about you while I slept the last few nights, so maybe somehow my thoughts reached you from where you had gone to."

Selene sighed. "I guess it wasn't you after all."

Reaching out to her, the young mage comforted her. "Now, Selene, it might have been me in your dream, or you could have dreamed *of* me. You know, like when you dream of other places or people."

She nodded. "It just seemed so real." She sniffled. "It was also about my demonic half. And you were... different."

"Oh?" he stated, wrapping an arm around her shoulder and walking with her towards the tunnel in the cave. "Tell me about it."

"I think I'm not ready to talk about it; Maybe later?" she asked.

He nodded, glancing back at the trio behind. "Well, then we can talk about our plan then. Come on everyone."

The five of them met back in the largest of the cave chambers. Finding suitable places to sit down, they sat comfortably while they began to discuss their next moves.

"So where is this place anyway?" Selene asked. "Are we still in the kingdom?"

Joven spoke up. "This is a cave my father showed me a long time ago when I was still a young'n. We used to rest here on extended hunting trips around the mountain." He shrugged. "We needed a place to go to that the king wouldn't find."

"But Balen works for the king. If Kalenden asked him for places we could be-"

"Balen doesn't know about this place. You see, my brother was a military blockhead since before he had teeth. By consequence he never went hunting with his father like I did."

"Oh." She admitted. "What about your other brother?"

Joven narrowed his eyes at her. "He hasn't been seen in a decade."

"Oh." She repeated again, feeling awkward.

Endrance watched the exchange silently, but chose to change the subject then. "So!" he began. "We managed to escape from King Kalenden and his men. Joven led us through a hidden path up the other side of the mountain where we are for the moment safe. While Selene recovered from the fire, I've been intensely practicing my fighting skills so I can help for the next stage of the battle."

He looked each of the Keepers in the eye, and ended by staring into Joven's. "We're going to take the fight to King Kalenden."

"Initially we were going to remain behind, and search for a way to expose his corruption, but he's already taken that option from us. Our last observation shows that he has declared we died in the longhouse fire, a tragic accident. But before I died, I confessed to him his son was the chosen hero. I cannot let this stand. We know the truth, and we can't let him lead the world to destruction without a fight. I didn't want to be an assassin of a king, but I would rather be considered a killer than let evil like this be perpetrated because I let it remain."

"We have brought the babe to Anna's family in Betton, and they are taking care of him as their own. He will be safe, so long as we move quickly before the king starts searching the outlying towns for us. We need to act soon, any longer risks chance of either our or the baby's discovery."

"And," Bridget chimed in, "If we go on the offensive while he thinks we're running…"

"Exactly!" Endrance agreed. "He won't be expecting us to strike at him directly when he is supposed to be chasing us down. Right now the best way to discredit him would be to make a public appearance."

Selene raised her hand. "But he's the king. And he's the demon summoner who had been manipulating things for who knows how long."

Anna shrugged. "This is a valid point. Even if we arrive publicly, decrying the king's proclamation can still be turned to his advantage. He has to have some demons at his disposal, as well as his royal guard. He himself is one of the best warriors in Balator, and he's got powers he's gained from his traffic infernal."

Endrance clenched his fists as he focused on the discussion. "I understand. As it is we may have to remove him from the throne and hope we can find the proof after the fact. But don't worry; I have a plan."

Joven grinned. "Oh, I love this plan."

Selene watched the big man grinning foolishly. "Let me guess." She began. "It involved you hitting something." She stated.

"Yep." Joven agreed, nodding. "Hitting things really hard."

"Oh yes, that reminds me!" Endrance exclaimed, digging through a belt pouch. "I have prepared a few spells for each of you to use."

Endrance held up a metal brooch, like the ones used for a heavy cloak or fur cape. Joven's totem, the bear, was etched into the surface. The wizard flipped the brooch over, and the women could see the inside had arcane script carved into the lip of the metal.

"Bridget, you remember the strength that I had the day we sorted things out?" he asked.

"Yes." Bridget admitted. "Hard not to remember being kicked through a door."

"Well, the spell was designed to grant someone the commensurate strength and toughness of a bear. It takes what strength you have and amplifies it. I have crafted this brooch for Joven that will allow him to use that spell for exactly fifteen minutes." Endrance shook his head. "It's the best I could do, and it will only work once." He flipped the brooch to Joven. "You activate it by touching your blood to it. It will start working immediately."

He produced three armbands, made of white leather and with decorative silver coins punched into the leather. From tightly braided cords hung three crimson feathers, which looked to have been donated by Gullin. He handed one to each of his Draugnoa.

"These you wear on your main arm, opposite arm and position from the traditional knives you wear. I have prepared three castings of my healing spell on each, and can be activated by breaking the threads holding one of the feathers. They should not be too hard to snap by pulling, but they shouldn't just come loose either. Pull hard."

As the four around him donned the items that Endrance gave them, Selene looked at the wizard as he stood waiting. "What about you, Endrance? Did you make anything to help you in this battle?"

The young wizard only grinned. "Of course."

"What did you make?" she asked.

"I…" Endrance's voice trailed off as he thought about it. "I couldn't explain it in a way that would make sense easily. Just be confident that I have taken much time and effort into ensuring my hide comes out of this intact."

Joven adjusted the drape of his winter cloak as it settled upon his shoulders. "Well whatever you did, I am impressed. I didn't even know you could make things with magic in them."

Endrance shrugged. "I didn't really do that."

"Then what are the things you gave us?" Joven asked.

"Well," The young mage began. "For your object, it has a spell inscribed in silver, which can conduct power into a spell. The only thing you don't have is the ability to channel your own power into a spell. But you may remember my statements that blood sacrifices give some of the person's power up when performed."

"Ah." Joven exclaimed. "So if I smear my blood on it…"

"You will empower the spell and make it work." Endrance concluded.

He turned and gestured at one of the Fjallar-feathered armbands. "These are a little different. Gullin was kind enough to give me nine of his feathers. The Fjallar are very much entwined with magic and particularly the powers of fire and time. The spells for those have already been cast; they lie dormant in the cords I wove. The feathers allow me to keep the power needed to cast each spell; breaking the cords releases the power and heals you."

"Why couldn't we use the blood thing like Joven would?" Bridget asked. "I mean, if we need healing we'd be bleeding already anyways, right?"

"Ah. That would be the case." Endrance said. "But the efficacy-"

"The what?" More than one voice asked.

"The… strength of the healing spell is dependent on the power put into it. I wanted it to heal as much as possible, so I devised this method so I could provide the power for the spells. Using your own blood may very well not even be enough to heal the injury that bled you in the first place."

"Oh."

"These should be sufficient for now." Endrance concluded. "The point being that I haven't made a truly enchanted item like the bracer I'm wearing."

"So for the moment we wait until the king has his next big public event, so that we can appear before him in front of the largest audience we can manage." Endrance explained. "Then we challenge his attempt at breaking barbarian tradition, and hopefully damage the people's trust in him enough that they won't act until we've taken care of the king."

"If we can prove he deals with demons, we won't have to do a thing; the people of Balator will tear him apart. It would show that the ruler was corrupt and breaking the worst taboo… Knowing magic." Anna clarified.

"What do they do to people they catch practicing magic who isn't the Spengur?" Endrance asked.

Joven shrugged. "Usually a crowd of people will gather and stone them before any official execution could be arranged."

"Oh." Endrance said. "That's pretty… horrible."

"Yeah." Bridget agreed. "They can be so impatient."

"Bridget!" Anna exclaimed. "That's not what he meant!"

The middle Draugnoa smirked. "I know."

Joven rolled his shoulders and unhooked the cloak. "I'll have to have better weaponry if I am going to end up fighting Kalenden. I'll need the family axe."

Endrance sighed. "All right. Where is it? Please tell me it's not buried at the bottom of some family tomb or was lost in a dragon's den years ago or something."

Joven looked at the mage incredulously. "What? No!" he exclaimed. "It's at my mother's house. She's kept it since the death of my father Daelen." The barbarian shrugged. "I don't know about your people, but an heirloom weapon does not make much of an heirloom if you bury it with the family members that died carrying it."

"You're right." Endrance said. "I'm sorry. How hard would it be for you to get it?"

Joven grinned. "It's my ma's place. I'll know how to get it, and you've met her, so you should know that she would let me use it if it meant preserving our family's honor."

"So…" Endrance began. "You could go get it on the way and meet us at the castle bowl?"

Joven nodded.

"Fine. We will take only a few more days to prepare while we wait for an opportunity to move. If in a few days we do not see one in the near future, we make one. Understood?" The wizard detailed. Everyone nodded or spoke up in assent. "Good. Anna, Bridget, please help Selene with whatever else she needs to get prepared; she's had less time than we have."

The five split up then, each to prepare for the upcoming conflict in their own way. Joven maintained his best armor and weapons, familiarizing himself with their grips and weights as he practiced with each. Anna and Bridget checked Selene over, and as a trio they trained with their favored weapons until they felt they were in their best form. Only then did they begin sparring with each other in earnest, their egos set aside for the sake of becoming as prepared as possible to protect the Spengur whom they had come to love.

Endrance's preparations were all the more arcane. While the bodyguard prepared his equipment, the Draugnoa prepared their bodies; the mage had only to prepare his mind. He sat cross-legged in a room in the back of the caves, nestled away from the myriad distractions the other four would cause to his concentration. His eyes closed, he retreated into the safest place he'd ever been; inside his head.

Within his thoughts he touched upon his aura, the knowledge he had gathered over years of study and practice, and the experiences he'd had in the few months he had been away from home. He also felt the tattooed lines that marked his meridians, the magically reactive inks that had been apparently tattooed upon his body since before he could remember. As he expanded his senses, he began to include the intricacies and potent power behind the bracer on his left forearm. During the process, his aura lit up anew with faint golden light, visible and audible but not brilliant, like a faint visible wind washing up around the meditating mage.

He had learned more in these few months out on his own than he had in a year studying under his old master Kaelob. While he had great respect and admiration for the man, he knew that this was a critical stage of a wizard's advancement. Without the life or death struggles, the battles with both his foes and his self, he would never have found out so acutely what kind of man he was.

Only by being faced with what he was capable of, and the magnitude of effect even the slightest of his decisions had, was he able to see in himself both a great hero and a terrible monster. It was analogous to the prophecy that had ended him exiled in a cave, seeking to overthrow a kingdom. He had within himself a great savior and a great destroyer, for magic was the thing that let him do things that only the gods could best him at.

He pictured himself in a great library, where the shelves within stored all of the things he knew or remembered. There were shelves stacked with book after book on a subject. There were shelves in the back, out of the way places that were filled with dusty recollections of older times. There were a great deal of shelves he pictured empty, devoid of all but a few pages of his limited understanding of the subject. In the center of the library was a circular reflecting pool, a pure white marble pool only an inch deep where the water reflected his state of mind.

The mage walked out into the reflecting pool, standing on the surface of the pool and causing concentric ripples to flow across the surface. From the center he held out his arms and took a breath. He concentrated on the things he would need to do and the magic he should need to handle the threat.

From all over the library, books lifted from the shelves and floated over to the mage, entering into a gently wobbling orbit around the circumference of the pool. He held out his hands and splayed the fingers of his hands as two books floated in front of them. The books pulled closer to him, coming out of their orbit and flipping open under his fingertips. The information he was seeking was recalled, and he gathered what he needed before flicking his fingers and sending them back into orbit. He repeated the action several times, gathering his memory and ordering it how he would need.

Spell formulas danced at his fingertips, words of power pulsed in his ears. He was surrounded with the trappings of his craft. The mage took the information he had gathered and he made himself ready. In this trance he was unaware of the outside world in its entirety, but the world within his mind was infinite and under his complete control.

He opened his eyes to the world several hours later. He had reminded himself of the little intricacies of every spell he had learned or devised. Each tiny part of the spell was needed to be known perfectly, or else the spell could cost many times more power than was really needed to use it. Having gathered his thoughts, he would be far less likely to make little mistakes during spell casting in the next few days. While he didn't look forward to the sensations he would be feeling next, he knew the grave nature of the task before him mandated its necessity.

Gullin? He called his familiar. *I need you now. It's time.*

The bird fluttered into the room. *They're concerned for you, you know.* He told the mage. *You've not eaten since yesterday.* The crimson bird perched on his shoulder.

Is that so? I'll have time to eat after I'm done with this one. It's going to be a big one. Endrance replied.

You said that about the last ones you've done. The familiar replied, pecking at his cheek.

Hush you.

The mage concentrated on the spell form he would need, and focused on the meridians of the inside of his right forearm. "Here we go." He muttered.

By the time he was done half an hour later, he was hunched over his arm, his clothes soaked with sweat. Perspiration dripped from his brow, and his eyelids fluttered as he struggled to remain conscious. The lap of his robes had been stained in sweat and spatters of blood. Electric tingles of pain shot up and down his arm in spasms, and Endrance could taste blood in his mouth. He must have bitten his tongue again.

Oh dear. Gullin scolded. *However would you heal those kinds of injuries if I wasn't around to help?*

Are… are you making a joke? Endrance asked, the oddity of Gullin's behavior distracting him from his pain.

Indeed. Let me handle the words, you form the rest. The familiar instructed.

Endrance formed the hand symbols and gathered up the energy needed for the healing spell. While perched on his shoulder, Gullin crooned a strangely melodious and complicated sounding birdsong in his tripartite voice, and the spell took effect. The gash across his tongue and the general pain of his strained body eased, but didn't disappear entirely.

So I think I figured out how you do that. Endrance stated.

Oh? Let's see if you get it right this time. Gullin replied amusedly. They had been using the familiar's abilities as a springboard for advancing Endrance's education, and so the Fjallar had refused to explain how he had helped Endrance heal his damaged throat.

You are in fact providing the words of power. Endrance stated. *Another fact is that the spells work, and while I can't say for sure, they seem to be very strong for the amount of power I put into it. This would lead me to believe that you are using the words of power in your natural language.*

That is mostly correct. Gullin responded, chirping happily. *To be more accurate, our songs are a language of power of their own right. And you noticed that spells are more powerful because our language is closer to the true language of power than yours is.*

True language? Endrance asked.

Another lesson, another time. Gullin stated, fluffing his feathers up. *Let's go to the fire and eat!*

Endrance picked himself up and went to eat after changing into a different set of robes. He had sweat more preparing himself for true war magic than he had when engaging in live knife combat practice with a barbarian warrior. His arm would be sore, but he covered over the forearm with the sleeve of his robe. He didn't need to call unnecessary attention to the work. They would think he was just injuring himself.

He ate, rested a while, and returned to the meditation room to continue working. He would be prepared for when they got the chance to move. They all would be. The fate of Balator, maybe even the world, depended on their actions in the next few days.

Chapter 33

Their opportunity came the day when their latest incursion into Balator revealed that later that evening King Kalenden was going to hold a feast celebrating his son's birth and great future. A large gathering of commoners and nobility alike was allowed to visit, so all may see the child and witness the chosen hero. This was the best opportunity they could hope for, and they slipped into the kingdom proper under the guise of hooded cloaks, hiding among the crowds of commoners. Nearly invisible against the background of milling crowds of barbarians yearning to see the child, they were able to move with the throngs until the whole of them made it to the seventh bowl where the feast was to be held.

It was an outdoors feast, with the tables laid across the expanse of grass and dirt that made up the empty space between the road and the Spengur's hut. Endrance suppressed a twinge of irritation, as he wasn't able to pick out the remains of his home in the yard anymore. It seems that men had been clearing the burnt timbers out of the site since it was safe enough to approach.

The king and his wife, alongside his newborn child and his eldest son, had their table set up in the newly cleared spot that had once been Endrance's meeting hall, where less than a week before he had helped deliver four babies and set about a chain of events that dazzled his mind just thinking about it.

The other tables present were along the sides, and the main of the expanse held hundreds of milling people. It appeared that this was to be a standing affair, where after coming up and viewing the child, one could grab a handful of food and enjoy their king's benevolence. Endrance found it hard to keep his head down, he was so agitated. He didn't feel that strange irritated and hostile sensation he had before though. Perhaps there was something in the throne room, not the king himself that had affected him?

As the suns neared the horizon, the crowds of people had formed a crowded line of people, hoping to get a good look before it got dark. Endrance and the others gathered together as the line coalesced near the king's table. They kept their weapons and faces hidden as they approached.

For this day, Endrance wore not robes, but sturdy pants and boots. On his chest he wore a simple vest underneath the chain shirt he had been given, and over that he wore his Blood Tiger Hide coat. Since he had not worn it since clothes had been provided when he arrived in Balator, the coat had been waiting for him in his travel pack when they fled the kingdom. He was not concerned the king would identify him prematurely because of it.

Anna, Bridget, and Selene wore different sets of armor and clothing. Anna had light fur armor with winter gear over it, and a hooded cloak. Bridget wore heavier fur layered armor and a similar cloak. Selene hadn't worn armor at all, instead wearing a simple tunic and breeches under her winter gear and cloak. Her combat style required her to be as unhindered as possible, and armor just got in her way.

Joven wore his heaviest armor, and was better armed than four barbarians. He concealed most of it under his cloak, and tried not to move too much or give away his battle ready state. Fortunately for them, it was perfectly normal to carry weapons and wear armor even to formal events; it was just part of their ways.

All too soon they were at the king's table. Perhaps it was Endrance's heightened senses due to alertness, but he saw that the queen that was sitting at the table with Kalenden was not the same woman that he had helped birth the baby. She looked exactly the same, but there were subtle differences that he just couldn't identify. Perhaps it was just his senses trying to pierce through whatever magical disguises Succubi wore when they took on human guise.

The group came to a complete halt in front of the table, forcing commoners to move around them to see the baby that was seated on display between the king and queen. The king looked up from his meal and at the group before him. His expression hardened as he realized who they must be.

"Good evening, your highness!" Endrance called out aloud, projecting his voice. People who had been passing by or wandering away from the table turned back to look at him. "Your Spengur has returned!" With that he threw the hood of his cloak back dramatically. This part of the confrontation was a show, for all the people of Balator to see. In unison the four framing him also shed their hoods.

The crowds burst out into quiet confused muttering. From what Endrance had been able to glean during their trip up the bowls was that the Spengur, Joven and the Draugnoa died in the fire. There had even been bodies that had been returned to their families, except for the Spengur. His body had supposedly been incinerated. Now they had returned, even though the families of the Draugnoa had burnt bodies delivered to them and Joven's childhood room held his coffin.

The king jumped to his feet, and several of the royal guard near the table hustled to bring their weapons to bear. Disturbingly, the queen did not move or change her expression, and most disturbing of all made not one move to protect her newborn child as weapons were brandished all around her.

"So I hear you told everyone I was dead!" Endrance declared. "And that I told you that your son there was going to become the hero of prophecy!" he swept his hand out to the people gathered around him. "As they can see I am in fact quite alive, I'm sure they wonder then how wrong you are about your other claims."

"Yes." Kalenden growled. "A problem I intend on fixing."

Endrance smiled. Though frightened, his nervous energy was giving his mouth the volume he needed. "Oh I'm sure you could, but it's too late now. I've already done the damage I intended on doing here. Now they doubt you, and I've thrown suspicion over everything you did that day."

The king's eyes narrowed. "That's not all you're doing here, or you wouldn't have come dressed for war."

Endrance shrugged. "Oh, yes." He said aloud. "Your Spengur has returned to tell you, people of Balator, of a great evil he had discovered in your kingdom!"

As he spoke he walked away from the table into the crowds of people, who scattered several feet away from him out of fear. One of the royal guard tried lunging at the mage with a spear, but Joven caught the haft with a gauntleted hand and shook his head disapprovingly before shoving him back. Gullin descended from his spot in the sky to land on the wizard's extended arm.

"I'm here to tell you of something involving magic!" Endrance continued. King Kalenden's fist tightened, cracking the wooden arm of his chair as he shoved it away from him. "And it is most grave news indeed! I have discovered someone has been trafficking in demons in your kingdom!"

A collective assortment of shock and disgust echoed back from the crowd of commoners. Whispers carried the news back farther, and soon everything he was saying was being carried on hushed lips beyond the crowd into the temples nearby. King Kalenden trembled with rage, his face reddening and the veins on his neck bulging as he was doing everything he could to keep from throwing the whole table out of the way and strangling the scrawny mage on the spot.

"I did not declare King Kalenden's son to be the child of prophecy, and for it he tried to have me killed! He then told you all that I and my servants had died in a fire!" Endrance exclaimed loudly.

The wizard turned and pointed an accusatory finger at the king. He paused just long enough to allow the people of Balator to see clearly who he was pointing at before he spoke.

"There is the user of magic!" He exclaimed. "There is the one who has summoned demons and is using spells, other than I, your chosen Spengur!"

"Lies!" The king roared. His men began advancing on the young mage. "You try to shake my people's faith in me?"

"I need not!" Endrance responded. "Here is your proof!"

The mage pulled from his pocket a small stick of wood, six inches long and one wide, hardly a quarter inch thick. On the flat face of it was carved sigils of arcane script. Endrance held the object in both hands over his head, and with deliberate action, broke it in two. It was similar to the crystal sphere that his master Kaelob had used long ago during his final tests in that it was a one use object containing a spell. A pulse of invisible power burst out from that point, washing out in an expanding sphere of influence.

He felt the magic of the object he created take hold as the spell swept over the area. It was an old trick of magic, something that the first Spengur had known and shared in his book but had been lost to generations since. It was specifically meant to reset wildly fluctuating power in an area, basically smooth out rumples in a weave of cloth. This effect was relatively unnoticeable to anyone who didn't have any magical talent, since it was something only the initiated could sense. However another mage would be almost immediately aware of the secondary property the spell had. In stabilizing the flows of power, it canceled out working magic.

The effect didn't work on objects infused with magic, like the tattoos on his skin or the bracer on his arm, but it did work on illusions or other spells that had to be 'maintained' by the caster. As the pulse passed by, the world seemed untouched. Where in Ironsoul, someone's makeup might have vanished, a straight nose would have bent again, or the color of a woman's hair would have returned to its original hue, here the people were entirely unaffected by the spell's effect.

When the spell washed over the king and his entourage, a profoundly noticeable change struck. Like a cloud of smoke being blown away by the breeze, the illusions were stripped away from the queen and the entirety of the royal guards. Fair skin and dark hair fluttered away to reveal pebbled skin with a deep red undertone and violet locks with jutting horns that swept a foot into the air above the queen's head. Red square pupil eyes replaced brown soulful ones, and clean straight white teeth stripped away to reveal fanged ones framing a forked tongue. Webbed wings projected from her back, folded closely to her form.

The royal guards had been similarly transformed, but not in so nearly a dramatic a fashion. Their hair and eyes shifted, becoming similar to the demoness in color and quality, but remained otherwise unchanged. Selene had been similarly affected, but the people were already in such a panic over the appearance of the demoness that the commoners near her didn't notice.

Kalenden blinked several times as the pulse lashed away the half dozen spells he had put up to protect himself before making this appearance. The move was something he hadn't even known was possible. The demons who had taught him had never even hinted at the possibility of such broad counter-spell. His shock registered on his face before he could grab control of his emotions again. The brat had more power to him than even the Sha'hdi had deigned to mention.

"You see!" Endrance cried out, Gullin hopping into the air again as he flung his arms out in exclamation. "Your king carried a terrible secret! He called up demons, and even made one his bride!" He pointed to the demoness, who had finally been motivated to stand menacingly, her wings spreading while the nails of her fingers lengthened into talons.

The commoners proved themselves to Endrance that moment. Where he expected they would flee out of fear and some did, the bulk of them rallied, becoming enraged. Their people being led not only by someone who used magic but made deals with demons? It was unacceptable to them. Endrance saw some of the very men who had been proud to serve the king draw their weapons and shout. Hundreds of barbarians were quickly forming into a mob.

The king had just had his people taken from him. The very thing he had spent years making preparations for had not only been dashed, but had also brought all of his dirty secrets into the light. He strained to contain his rage as he stared at the young man who had turned everything on its head. He had underestimated the student of Kaelob. No, he had accounted for the brat's training; even his demonic tutors had assured him of that. There was something about him that was different.

The king spotted something that he had not noticed before, and it finally made sense. The king puffed his chest up and bellowed as loudly as he could. "ENOUGH!"

The advancing mob hesitated, and Kalenden took the moment to grab the succubus by the arm and haul her and the baby towards the castle approach. The royal guard, though outnumbered, jumped in between the king and his people. Over their heads rocks sailed through the air as people behind the front lines pushed the whole forward.

Endrance and his companions watched as the king beat a retreat towards the castle. Every royal guard under his command filled in the pass to the eighth bowl, fortifying it against attack as the king passed. He looked his friends over, and finally saw the change that had been made in Selene.

"Selene, you've changed as well." He said, taking her hand. "Do not panic, it is a little thing."

Selene grasped a few strands of her hair and held it before her. "The spell revealed my real form?" She asked.

"It stripped away whatever natural magic was being used to conceal it, for now." Endrance replied. The mob had all but forgotten about them, and for the moment that was what the mage wanted. "You will learn how to hide and reveal that part of your heritage as you become aware of it."

"The rest of the royal guard," She said. "They were Nephilim like me."

"Yes." Endrance said. "It seems the king had been collecting them. Maybe even breeding them."

"Do you think I'm one of those?" She asked. "One that had been bred?"

"If you were, would that change anything?" The young mage asked. "If you were you still ended up here, beside me. I wouldn't have you anywhere else."

She realized as he held her against his side that she no longer felt the aggression or anxiety she had experienced in his presence before. It had vanished sometime since the day she woke up from the fire. She leaned her head against his, and felt a moment of peace she had not in months since the Spengur had arrived in Balator.

The five of them stood and watched as the people rallied against their once king, having seen him for what he really was. At first the mob seemed to make headway, but the approach to the eighth bowl was made so that armies could be held off with only a few men at the turns and twists of the passes. The king's army had turned on him in moments, but he still had his royal guard, whom had fallen back on the king's tail, guarding him as he retreated to the castle.

"I don't get it." Endrance said after a few minutes of watching the masses of men and women assembling to try to batter down the first of many gates up the pass.

"What?" Joven asked, whistling in appreciation as dozens more gathered. People were pouring in from lower levels of the city as word spread faster than a flash fire.

"Why did he retreat up to the castle?" Endrance asked.

"Well it's the best defended structure." Joven explained. "The design of the passes-"

"That's not it." Endrance interrupted. "He has nowhere to go. He could hold off the people for a few days, or a month. But he would eventually run out of food. They would eventually overpower the guards or outlast them and get in. He put himself in a bad position."

Joven shrugged. "People make mistakes when cornered."

"No it can't be that easy." Endrance said, shaking his head. "Kalenden is a shrewd and clever man. He wouldn't have gone up there unless it gave him some advantage."

"Do you think he's going to use magic to run?" Anna asked. The mage shook his head in response.

"He wouldn't give up on all he has here that easily." Joven agreed.

Endrance thought as hard and as fast as he ever had before. Something was wrong here, and he was the only one who could put it all together. The king retreated to the castle. He didn't prefer to fight an extended battle in Endrance's home terrain. He has to have some advantage in the castle.

And then it clicked in his head. The last few pieces fell into place, forming a picture that made him realize it may be too late.

"We need to get up there immediately!" Endrance exclaimed, shock registering on his face. "I just figured it out!"

"What?" Joven asked.

"No time!" Endrance shouted, rushing forward towards the front of the mob. "We need to get there before it is too late!"

The four caught up to the young man quickly, and together they rushed up to the front of the crowd as they prepared a renewed assault against the gates. They were shouldering a battering ram made of a stone pillar they must have torn down from somewhere. Endrance skid in front of them, his hands held out to stop them.

"Wait!" he shouted as loud as he could. The roar of the mob was too loud, and they started to move forward, most of them haven't even seen the mage.

Joven stepped in front, thrust a hand against the front of the ram, and with a deep breath bellowed at the top of his lungs. "WAIT!"

This time, the people of Balator stopped. The mob wasn't broken, but enough in front heard him and stopped, causing the rest to gradually subside as they realized nothing was happening.

"The Spengur wants to address you." Joven continued, stepping aside. Endrance took a breath and shouted to be heard over the masses of people milling before him.

"People of Balator!" Endrance called. "I am your Spengur, am I not?" He was met with shouts saying that he was more or less correct. "Then you have tasked me with the job of handling problems involving magic, have you not?" Again, those who could hear him agreed. Word quickly started filtering backwards through the ranks of the mob.

"Then I ask you, why are you trying to do my job for me?" He asked, provoking mixed responses from the crowds. "Let me handle the king, and protect you all against this magic user whom you used to trust!" The crowd seemed unsure, but Endrance was unable to tell more than what the people a few dozen feet in front of him were feeling about his speech.

"Let me go ahead of you, if in an hour's time I haven't solved the problem, come and finish the task. But at least let me open the way for you." He pleaded.

The men and women of Balator looked down at the scrawny whelp of a man, someone whom nearly any of their own stood well over and outweighed by several pounds. If they were not able to force their way past the royal guard, what was he able to do? Their puzzlement was obvious on their faces.

The wizard sighed, and turned to Joven. "Please watch my back." He said with resignation. The bodyguard interposed himself between Endrance and the crowds of barbarians. He approached within a hundred feet of the gates. He could hear the rattle of several crossbows being levered and brought to bear against him.

Endrance looked over the walls and could count several crossbowman ready to fire upon him. While the wall was over a hundred feet away, the sky was clear and the wind was low, they would be able to hit him quite easily with their training. He smiled, for the conditions were perfect.

The wizard waved his left hand in a sweep in front of him from right to left as he slung a spell. *"Peltaeus!"*

The snow at the mage's feet drew up as more crystallized from the air around him, forming a transparent shield of ice a centimeter thick. The ice thickened as the crossbowmen unleashed the bolts in their crossbows. The lethal bolts cracked through the air, and embedded into the ice shield, punching into but not entirely through the barrier. Cracks shot through the ice in a web like pattern.

The royal guard paused, surprised by the power of the spell. Endrance noted that he had to use far less energy than he had to use than during the trial he had fought to earn his title. He wondered for a brief moment if that trial had been in fact meant to prepare him for this day. He held up his right hand and touched the creaking and crackling curve of ice before him.

Without an active thought, he drew in power from his aura, formed the spell within his mind, and spoke the final word of power. *"Cularus."* He spoke, his voice resonant with power.

The unseen force of his launching spell built up for a split second in his chest, and rocketed down his arm, sweeping out his palm and into the ice. Instead of shattering the fine webbing of broken ice, its force swept up the ice and bolts alike flinging them back at the archers like a thousand tiny flechettes made of slivers of glass.

The men ducked too late, and all but a few were caught in the spray of wickedly sharp ammunition. While it didn't have enough force to kill someone as tough as the Nephilim at the gates, it was quite strong enough to blind or incapacitate enough that he could approach closer. He reached the gates themselves unhindered by any further crossbow bolts.

Now too close to use bolts, it would be a perfect time to use boiling tar or hot oil of some sort. But the gates had just locked up less than a half hour before; even if someone had thought to put some cauldrons of oil to boil, it wouldn't be hot enough to do any damage yet. Endrance pushed hard at the gate once, testing it. Heavy iron banded wooden doors a foot thick barred his passage.

He couldn't see through the crack between the doors, but Gullin could. The bird circled in the sky above him, providing him with more information than he would normally be able to acquire.

The bar is a foot thick, three feet off the ground. It appears to be dropped into place. Gullin reported, sailing up in the wintry air.

Is there a bar lock? Endrance asked.

Yes.

Then I'll have to blow the door down.

May I suggest allowing the barbarians to do the hard work for that part? You should save your strength for the king.

Endrance turned to the mob that waited impatiently for him. He waved to the men holding the pillar. "Go ahead." He said.

The fourteen men hefting the massive pillar made of a single piece of carved stone rushed forward, charging at full speed and strength. Their charge met the barred door, and wood cracked and splintered. The door bowed in, but didn't cave under the initial blow. It took the men a moment to reset their grip, but they resumed battering the door with a steady pace. Minutes later, the door finally broke open, splintered and bent as the barbarians broke through.

Men poured through the gates around Endrance, their own weapons from their service in the military, and several of them were still in their service armor. Joven kept an eye on his charge, just in case any of the men would rather take a swing at the only magic user they were supposed to allow in their kingdom. They seemed instead more interested in finishing off the royal guard at this stage of the switchback.

It took an hour of fighting to get through to the castle courtyard. There the mob was repelled by the black iron portcullis and the assembled fighting force of the rest of Kalenden's guard. Endrance and Joven could not see a way past this without doing significant damage to the castle and risking tiring the mage out.

The fighting degraded into a stalemate, where the men inside with their pikes and crossbows could keep the mob away for hours. It seemed that Endrance would have to seriously hurt or kill all these men just to get inside, when a familiar form on the other side came into view.

"Balen!" Joven called out, moving out to the front of the mob. The general shoved some of his own men aside and strode up to the gate. "Joven!" he called back.

Joven moved until he was just on the other side of the portcullis from his brother. "Balen!" he exclaimed. "You have to let us pass!"

Balen shook his head. "I can't let you do that brother. Stop this madness, and give up. I cannot let you attack the king, even if he was wrong about your death!"

"What?" Joven asked.

"The king said you faked your deaths. Why?" Balen asked. "Were you trying to make an opening to take the throne?"

Joven shook his head, confused. "What?" he repeated. "The king tried to kill us! And he's summoning demons using magic!"

Balen frowned at him. "What nonsense are you speaking of? I heard that your Spengur there cursed the queen into that hideous form."

Joven sputtered. "Of course he would tell you that! Endrance revealed the queen's true form, not cursed her! Of all people, you would think a child of Daelin would side with the word of the Spengur!"

Balen slammed a palm against the iron bars. "Damn you Joven! You know that the Spengur is an old rite, and has no place in this place! We can make it just fine without a magic man to 'fix' things!"

Joven and Balen were almost nose to nose, their argument grew so heated. "You fool!" Joven exclaimed. "Your damned insistence on ignoring magic is how a mage managed to remain king all these years without you noticing! You were closer to him than anyone else!"

"Fool!" Balen roared, his hands wringing the iron bars of the portcullis. "I dare you to say that again!"

Joven grinned, his expression mocking. "Or you'll what? Stay inside some more? You foolishly locked yourself into a situation you can't get out of!" He took a step back and laughed. "I'll tell you what, you let just me and the Spengur and his women in, and we'll sort this out between us with a fight, like civilized people."

Balen surged away from the gates and strode to the center. "Open the gates!" He commanded. "Shoot anyone but the Spengur or his people!"

Endrance and the Draugnoa picked through the mob, crossing the empty space to Joven. The assorted men and women seemed to be itching to move forward, but wouldn't unless they could see an opening. The mage viewed the number of royal guard who remained inside the courtyard, and grimaced at Joven. "Are you sure about this?" he asked. "I can't protect us from that many bolts and arrows if they decide to just execute us."

"Trust me." Joven growled. "They will listen to Balen."

"Are you sure you can win?" Endrance asked. "You've said he's better than you."

"Yeah." Joven admitted. "But I've had practice since then, and now I have the axe."

"I won't be able to heal you if you get badly injured during the fight if I have to press onward." Endrance said. "You'll only have the one chance at this."

"I know." Joven said; his expression was grim. "Endrance… If I don't make it, I'm glad to have served you."

"You better make it." Endrance said with a faked chuckle. "Or else I'll have no one to complain to or drink with when the girls start driving me crazy."

Joven laughed at that, patting the man on the shoulder as the gates rose. "You'll be just fine, man. You'll do just fine."

The five walked into the courtyard, and the portcullis dropped back into place almost instantly on their heels.

Surrounded on either side by Nephilim with loaded crossbows, Balen waited.

Chapter 34

Endrance and the Draugnoa stood to the side, while the two sons of Daelen squared off in the center of the castle courtyard. The royal guard had cleared a circle of stone over a dozen yards across for them to fight in. Though loyal to the king, it appeared that they respected the general enough to allow him this demand. In a way, Balen had already helped them. Beyond this point, there were no physical barriers to circumvent; it was only the king and his men waiting for him.

There had to be very little of his guard left, Endrance realized. They had killed or incapacitated eight of them at the first switch, and four more at the other two leading to the castle proper. This meant that the twelve men keeping the mob at bay would be the last remaining of the men loyal to the king, other than general Balen.

Balen was wearing a heavy armor breastplate of black steel, with gold trim and detailing across the front and back. The shoulder cops and bracers were of a similar makeup. From his back he wore a deep red cloak of thick cloth, trimmed in gold threads. The man wore only a two handed greatsword on his back, similar in design to the one that Joven usually wore. A long knife was strapped to his belt, but all of his equipment seemed of extraordinary quality. Even the furs he wore under the armor were of the finest quality buckskin.

"Poor Joven." Balen taunted, as the two circled each other, neither having drawn a weapon yet. "You still think that having more weapons makes you a better warrior."

"Wrong, brother!" Joven exchanged. "I believe there is a time and a place for every weapon."

Balen pulled his greatsword free. The blade was of black steel, expertly crafted with etched knot work all down the blade on both sides instead of a groove. He spun the sword around experimentally, showing his skill with the blade. "You are the one who is wrong, brother!" he returned. "If you can kill something with one blade or the other, it is a waste of time to change your tools."

Joven unbuckled the belt holding the haft of the axe under his cloak. "If you're so set on staying the course, then why are you disobeying the word of the Spengur?"

"The Spengur is an expired habit!" Balen shouted. "He is no longer needed in our kingdom!" He raised the greatsword menacingly. "And when he has been cut out, this time there will be no others. We will finally be free of their magic."

Joven closed his eyes a second as the axe on his back dropped to the ground, the points on its head biting into the stone and sticking straight up. He took a step to the right, and placed a hand on the pommel of the axe of his family line. The wood was dark, stained so deeply red that it almost appeared black. The leather straps wrapping the handle were scratched in ancient script, and the head of the axe was formed of a milky white form of steel foreign to Balator. One side of the axe head was carved in a relief of a hundred warriors at the ready, while the other bore the same one hundred warriors slain. A white steel spike topped the axe, its point glittering with the remaining light of the day.

"Father disagrees." Joven said evenly, opening his eyes.

Balen's eyes widened as he realized what his brother was holding. "How did you get that..."

"Was at home." Joven said loudly "When we told mother what happened, she was eager to give it to me. She hoped that seeing it would remind you of your first and foremost duty as one of the guardians of the Spengur."

Balen blinked away his confusion, tightening his grip on his weapon. "It doesn't matter." He reasoned. "The king has given me a new duty now. If you weren't so hard headed you would stand aside brother!"

The general rushed forward, his greatsword soaking up the late day's light. Joven gripped the axe of Daelin and brought it up to counter his brother's stroke. Sparks flew, and the clash of their steel hurt Endrance's ears as he watched the fight progress. Balen was stronger than his younger brother, older and more practiced in real combat. Joven was a little faster, and the difference in experience was by such a small margin that the fight could drag on for a long time. They pressed in at each other, the edge of their blades scraping against each other for a moment before disengaging.

Balen thrust the greatsword forward, baiting his brother with a feint. Joven batted the point of the blade away with the pommel of the axe, and stepped into the greatsword's range. His higher up grip on the haft of the axe meant that he could use it effectively much closer than Balen could use his weapon. He brought the axe down, but Balen deftly hopped back out of range, swiping with his sword as he evaded Joven's strike. The sword's edge crossed Joven's chest and biceps in a line, cutting through fur cloak and striking sparks from the protective plates that saved the bodyguard's life. The axe of Daelin struck a flagstone of the courtyard, and it cracked under the force of his strike.

Balen went to take a step in to finish off his brother before he could recover from the strike, but instead of pulling up the axe with both hands, Joven let go with his left and hurled a knife. The narrow triangular blade scythed through the air like an arrow. Balen jerked to the side as a reflex, and the blade punched through the steel plate into the meat of his chest near his right shoulder cop. Joven pulled the axe free from the stone; Balen yanked the blade out and threw it to the ground in rage. Joven raised his axe, the empty scabbard of one of his throwing knife sheaths visible through the slash in his cloak.

Maybe Joven had always held back before or Balen wasn't really committed to killing his brother, but so far the two were fighting on equal footing. As Endrance looked around, he saw that the royal guard were either too occupied with the mob teeming at the portcullis, or the fight with their leader to pay too much attention to them. Now would be the perfect time to slip inside.

As steel clashed with steel, and the two strongest brothers he had ever seen fought to the death, he tapped the Draugnoa on the shoulders as he moved towards the doors in. "Let's go." He said. "I'll have to trust Joven here." The three women seemed reluctant to abandon their friend and comrade, but there was nothing they could do to interfere with the fight and not draw attention from the remaining men. Endrance looked up to the sky, and Gullin dropped down to alight upon his arm.

Joven had caught sight of his charge moving quietly towards the doors into the castle, and knew he had to draw more attention away from the doors. He skipped back, avoiding a swing meant to disembowel him as he brought his axe up for a downward chop.

"This is foolish, Balen!" He shouted, his voice louder than he would normally have if it were just the two of them fighting. "We are brothers! Fighting like this just mocks our family's name!" He reversed his swing at the last moment, coming up under his opponent's guard, causing a shower of sparks as the spike on the axe head drew a line across the stone.

"You are the fool!" Balen cried, sidestepping the swing and thrusting with his greatsword. Joven barely managed to deflect the stab before he was run through. "Picking a fight with me, when you've never won a single sparring match with me!"

Joven whirled around the second thrust, bringing the axe of Daelen in a low strike at his thigh. Balen danced backwards, redirecting his strike to disrupt the flow of Joven's attacks. The brother's weapons locked for a moment and they strained against each other, trying to force the other to fall back. Muscles bulged and leather creaked as the two pitted their strength against each other.

Up close, Joven saw something wrong with Balen's eyes. Where before they had been clear and intense when they had sparred, there was something in his eyes that seemed to be missing. It was as if the edge in his gaze had been dulled or he was drunk on something. Joven then realized that something had been done to Balen that was slowing his reflexes and skill. If the man had been affected by magic, maybe it wasn't his desire to fight him.

He did not get a chance to think further, as in his realization he faltered his pressure upon Balen's blade. The general pulled his head back and delivered a powerful head butt. Joven reeled back, blood streaming from his newly re-broken nose. He was only barely able to defend himself from the next several attacks as his brother battered at his defenses. Whatever it was that dulled his mind, it hadn't dulled his combat sense in any significant way.

He bested a strong horizontal swing and nearly took off Balen's arm with the counterattack, forcing the man to give him some room to breathe. Joven used a free hand to wipe some of the blood from his nose. "I get it now." He said. "Please, stop this! Don't let Kalenden control you any further!"

"No more talking!" Balen cried angrily, resetting his grip on the sword. "Fight me!"

"I'm sorry for this, brother." Joven muttered, and he wiped his bloody fingers across the bear emblem clasp. The fresh blood mingled in the grooves and channels of the etched symbol, and the spell designed in the brooch found both the power to activate the spell and the target to affect with it. The barbarian felt the most peculiar sensation he'd ever had. He felt some kind of drain on him, but it wasn't a physical one. It felt more like he had spent all day thinking of difficult things.

Physically, a euphoric rush of power blossomed out from his heart and spread throughout his body. The heat and vigor rushed through tiring limbs, washing away aches, pains, and fatigue while also filling him with strength. His eyes and ears sharpened into focus again, and he felt as if he were actually filled with too much strength for his body to handle. The feeling was exhilarating, and he grinned as he grabbed the axe with both hands again.

The two clashed their weapons again, but the results were drastically different. Balen's sword was repelled in the instant the two weapons clashed, the extraordinarily durable black steel blade nicked a centimeter deep. Joven didn't even lose momentum, whirling his axe back around with one hand and striking again, the smile on his face brightening as he saw just how much more powerful he was. His next strike was parried, but it forced Balen back several more feet as the man didn't have the strength to block such a powerful blow.

Balen deflected the third strike, but at the cost of another nick in his weapon's edge. The bodyguard was relentless, his strokes coming in just slow enough that Balen could defend, but with so much force that he could do nothing but recover from the hit before he struck again. The weapon Balen wielded was tough, but under the stress of Joven's enhanced might could not stand long.

Joven brought the weapon down with as much strength as he could. The axe head sheared through the blade at the guard, shattering the blade. The spike cleaved through part of the breastplate of Balen's armor, and the whole head hit the flagstones at their feet with so much leftover force that the stones buckled, sending an explosion of stone chips and fragments into the air. Blood spattered from the gash carved into Balen's chest as stone fragments rained down around them.

Disarmed and injured, Balen dropped to his knees. He looked up at his brother, who stood before him, the light of the declining suns casting him in silhouette before their blaze. He closed his eyes and dropped the broken handle. The man had somehow overpowered him.

"You've gotten strong, Joven." Balen said, defeated. "Finish this. I am no longer worthy to lead."

Joven lifted the axe of Daelen again. The axe of his father, no, their father. Would he want the next person's blood spilled upon the blade since his death to be one of his son's? Joven hesitated, and sighed. He got the feeling that no matter what had happened this day, his father would be disappointed in them.

"Kill me." Balen said, laboring to breathe. "And take command of my men. Only then it will be finished."

"No brother." Joven said at last. "It is not finished." He swung the axe. The wooden pommel was not capped in metal or carved to make it lethal, so it served his need. Careful to hold back his magically titanic strength, the heavy *thunk* of the wood hitting bone was still heard through the courtyard as Joven knocked his brother unconscious.

Joven sincerely hoped that Endrance would be able to undo whatever magic was affecting his brother. But before that, he would have to make sure the mage survived. He looked up from his prone opponent when he saw one and then more of the royal guards lift their crossbows towards him. Soon more men were aiming at him than at the mob trying to get into the gates.

"I don't suppose you guys will follow my orders now, will you?" Joven asked tentatively. The men sighted down their quarrels at him. "I guess not." He said.

He looked at the odds before him. Not good, but he did still feel the massive rush of strength and power from the spell Endrance gave him. "What the hell." Joven said. "I might as well help clean up the table scraps."

The barbarian leapt towards the nearest grouping of Nephilim. The twang of crossbow bolts releasing cut into the night air.

The foyer into the great hall held no more defenses. Looking down the side halls, Endrance saw no one of any sort walked the halls. Already, the anxiety he felt before was building up again, faster now that he was aware of the reason.

I sense no one, Endrance. Gullin advised. *That may be due to interference.*

Yes I figured as much. Endrance replied. *I was only partially aware of what lies here the first few times I was here, but now I am certain of it.*

Be careful, Endrance. This place makes me uneasy.

"All right." Endrance said aloud. "This is it. You three, cover me from any kind of fighters that may be in there, and I will have to handle Kalenden's magic. If his demoness shows up, hit her as hard as you can with everything you've got. True demons are far more powerful than your average man."

The women nodded, unclasping their cloaks and letting them fall to the floor. Ready, they looked to the doors, took a readying breath, and shoved them open, rushing out over the great hall's polished stone floors. The three Draugnoa led, with Endrance at the back of the vanguard.

The great throne room was distressingly dark. The only light in the chamber was from a pair of candelabra flanking the throne in the back of the room. With the single torch light of the room behind them, and the candles far off, the great hall was as dark as the blackest night. The doors swung closed as they came in, leaving them in darkness.

The king sat upon the throne, leaning his head on one hand while he tapped the pommel of his sword with the other. The dark stone of the throne room, as the reflective sheen of the polished stone floor, gave the room the appearance that the throne and king were afloat in a sea of stars. He watched them with a carefully blank expression, the earlier rage and confusion he had visited upon having been banished.

Selene blinked several times, trying to shake the feeling of abject fear she felt. The darkness of the expansive hall, the sheen of the polished floor, the stillness of the room that left only the pounding of her heart in her ears left her shaking in fear. It was like she really was back in the realm of her mind, where she was confronted with the truth of what she really was. The chain of her weapon rattled almost imperceptibly as she trembled.

Anna took the lead, with Bridget on the left and Selene on the right. So far, they could only see the king. Even Endrance's slightly better night vision saw no one else. It was a good thing he had killed that moon elf assassin, or else this would be practically a perfect killing ground for her. Gullin shuddered, but didn't cry out or take flight. As Endrance walked forward, his hands clenched in fists, the familiar walked up his arm and huddled down on the mage's shoulder.

Endrance was terrified. What was he thinking, casting doubt upon the king's rule and even coming here to what, kill him? He had known somewhere that the man would never willingly give up what was his. He'd rather have it all burn down around him than give it up. He took a steadying breath, and tried to take control of his shaking. It had to be done. If he didn't stop the man, Endrance would have only a pyrrhic victory.

The four of them stopped only ten yards from the king, their weapons at hand and their senses straining to pick up any sign of ambush. Anna moved behind the Spengur, shielding his back from attack while he confronted the king.

"I see you cower behind your wives' skirts as usual." Kalenden said; his voice surprisingly without emotion. His voice carried throughout the darkness of the room, echoing off the unseen stone walls around them.

Endrance shook his head. "I'm here for you, Kalenden. The Draugnoa are here to handle anything else you would have distract me."

Kalenden arched a brow. "Oh?" he asked. "I don't need anything to distract you. After all, you were so thoughtful as to bring your own."

The king remained immobile, though the hand tapping the pommel of his sword never ceased moving, the rhythm of his gloved fingers tapping black steel with an even and steady pace.

"Perhaps I should explain." Kalenden said. "Have you gotten attached to any of those bitches you brought with you? It's a shame that one of your women belong to me."

Selene balked, filled with the realization that she was the one he was referring to.

"Come Selene." Kalenden said playfully. "Come, serve your lord. Serve… your father."

The girl's eyes widened, terrified. Bridget and Anna exchanged glances with Endrance.

"Now it is not really that much of a surprise is it?" Kalenden said, his fingers still drumming on the sword. "After all, I can summon as many breeders as I need, and I couldn't trust anyone else to help me populate my personal retinue of Nephilim, now could I?" His eyes searched the expressions of the four before continuing. "I've been breeding the things since I was old enough to do the summoning circles properly."

Selene was shocked. She finally found out who her father was, and it was the very man she needed to kill. The man had just… bred her, like someone would a horse. She felt the demonic half of her boiling in her blood, just begging to be released. She could almost imagine the demonic image she had seen in her dreams pushing her to let her out.

Endrance stepped in front of her, as if he were shielding her from the awful truth with his arms outstretched. She saw the muscles of his back tensed as he addressed her newly discovered father. It had a strangely calming effect for her, just like the action did in her dreams. Maybe he hadn't visited her with a spell, but he had been there.

"I already knew that." Endrance said, angry. "We've already recognized her heritage. Stop trying to play mind games. It's over Kalenden! I'll give you one more chance. Surrender!"

Kalenden still watched impassively. "Hmm, then I accept your surrender."

Endrance shook his head, flexing his fingers. "No. It is your time to yield."

Kalenden still did not change his expression, but the tapping of his fingers slowed. "Why would I surrender when I'm the one in control?" he asked, his voice was as calm as a frozen lake.

Endrance looked around. "I see nothing here you have any control over. Your people have turned against you, and your Nephilim have been scattered. You have nothing."

"I have nothing." The king stated. "We both know that is wrong."

His hand stopped tapping and grasped the pommel of the sword, silencing the beat of his fingers on the metal. In the echoes of the silence a breeze washed through the hall. The candles upon their candelabra were extinguished, plunging them into darkness.

Endrance heard the twang of something hitting metal, and felt Anna stumble up against his back. He could see nothing, but heard her gasp, followed by the distinct sound of liquid spattering upon stone. He whirled grabbing at her in the dark to keep her steady. He felt hot blood on his hands, and she was struggling to breathe.

The other two crouched low with them, but only the single attack had struck out.

"We need light!" Bridget cried. She immediately shifted in the dark, and heard something whistle past her ear in the darkness.

Endrance nearly lost his composure. They knew they were walking into an ambush, but the king was too prepared for him to overcome. He shook his head. No, as long as he still lived or could carry words with his lips, he would not stop until the man was defeated. It had to be done.

He drew up the reserves of his power, focused it into the light spell he had used so effectively before in dark situations. Its brilliant light would be more than sufficient to blind anyone who was firing at them in the dark, and let them see enough to fight back. Endrance formed the mudra with his hands, and was chanting the word needed to sling the spell when something impacted with the side of his head.

The impact was enough to throw off his spell, but not enough to ruin it entirely. The word of power he was saying was misspoken as he was jarred, and the spell fragmented before backfiring. The extremely brilliant speck of pure white light exploded into hundreds of weaker versions of itself, scattering throughout the room in a cascade of unfading sparks. The specks of light hung scattered through the air, their faint light blanketing the room in dim illumination. The dimensions of the room could be barely seen, and the light was reflected off the sheen of the polished stone floor.

Now they were almost literally battling within a sea of stars. Endrance shook his head and touched the spot where he was struck; not feeling any pain. His hand came away bloody, with strands of hair stuck to his gloves. He had been hit with something sharp, another throwing knife.

He turned back to Anna, and saw she was still weakly struggling, a knife having hit her high in the chest, near her heart. She was grasping at the feathered armband Endrance had given her, but her blood slicked fingers didn't have enough of a grip to pull one of them free. Endrance reached down and yanked one off before she lost consciousness. The cord snapped, and the power invested in it was released. There was no light, but the wound in her chest started healing immediately, the knife working out of her body as it did so.

Endrance left her to get back into the fight on her own. He surveyed the room as the stars drifted lazily around him, but he could only see king Kalenden standing up from his throne. A shiver of realization came upon him. The only one who would be skilled enough to use knives in the dark like this had to be the Sha'hdi. But he had killed her, hadn't he?

Laughter, feminine like the assassin had, but harsher and scratchy echoed through the chamber.

"You almost had me that time, mage." Her voice echoed through the hall. "But you are not the only one with a miraculous recovery up your sleeve."

There was a whistle of something streaking through the air, and Endrance didn't have time to duck as the knife came at him. The knife clattered against the face of Anna's shield as she surged up from the ground, interposing it between the mage and the deadly blade.

"Thanks." Anna whispered. She looked very pale in the starlight, and she was already breathing hard. "We'll keep you covered, just expose her."

Gullin! Endrance thought desperately. *I need to make more light than this!*

Gullin had been grasping desperately to his shoulder using his wings to try to keep stable. *Cast it again?* He offered.

She'll strike when I do that! He replied. *I have to amplify the one we already have out!*

I can help with that, Gullin replied, *but it will leave me vulnerable.*

Gullin, please! He desperately asked of his familiar. *We are all vulnerable now!*

The bird took to the air, flying up to the top of the hall. In the starlight, Endrance saw a dark shadow flit past the bird as it bobbed erratically through the air, a thrown weapon that missed its mark. He had to try to draw attention from the assassin long enough to pull off the desperate gamble.

He stood up straight and threw his hand out towards Kalenden. "*Ignatius!*" He cried out loudly. Again, fire washed out from his outstretched palm. The room temporarily brightened under the flames, and the assassin was temporarily revealed, crouched by one of the pillars near Selene. Even as she was revealed, she flung one last dart, which clipped Gullin across the breast as he ascended. The familiar faltered, but did not give up his attempt.

The assassin leapt back, but Selene had caught a glimpse of her. The blade on its chain whipped forward like the sting of a scorpion, and the assassin was rewarded with a slash across the outside of her left arm as she tumbled out of the way. Selene rushed in, her eyes wide and her breath steady, already being drawn into the trance of battle. Jalyin acrobatically dodged out of the way of her next strike, but was finding it much harder to avoid the woman now she was armed with a weapon she was an expert at.

Gullin cried out a tripartite call, and some of Endrance's power went through his connection to the bird and into the fragmented spell. Half of the specks of light winked out, but the other half increased in brightness threefold, illuminating the room from wall to wall better than it likely ever could under normal conditions. His work completed, the bird found no more strength for flying, and fell to the stones below. Endrance did not hear an impact through the din of battle.

Bridget rushed in on the tail of Endrance's fire spell, knowing that the king had resisted such a spell before. As the flames died down the King stood, taking up his weapon and entirely unharmed. Bridget leapt into the air, her curved sword slicing an arc through the glimmering stars. A battle cry on her lips, she brought the weapon down with all her strength.

Anna sank to her knees. While the healing spell had healed most of the damage, something was wrong. Her head swam and her vision faded in and out as her pulse dulled. Her spear rolled out of her numb fingers, her shield slipped from her arm. The spot where she had been stabbed burned and itched.

"Poison!" She managed to choke out, "She used poison!"

Endrance turned his head to see her collapse to the floor again, this time without much struggle. He dropped down to her and yanked off a second feather, trying to help fight off the damage the poison was causing. The spell worked what it could, but it was not meant to heal such forms of injury. Endrance was helpless to watch as she faded.

"Anna!" he shouted. "Stay with me, Anna!" He cried out, unable to turn away despite the sounds of the other Draugnoa battling without him. Bridget was barely able to force Kalenden to fight back, while Selene seemed evenly matched against the assassin at the moment. They needed his help, but so did Anna.

Anna looked up at him with a weak smile. "Don't fear for me, husband. I just need to rest a little." She said. "Go. Help the others before it's too late."

He watched helplessly as she went still before him. He didn't see her breathing anymore. A thin, keening wail escaped his throat. He bowed his head as grief overwhelmed him, touching his forehead to hers. He felt despair grasp it's icy fingers around his heart.

One of the rings on the chain he wore around his neck turned icy cold and blackened as it deeply tarnished in seconds. Somehow it slipped off the links and hit the stone, bouncing once before rolling to a stop against Anna's still hand. The sister ring she wore was tarnished and cold, the two rings touching.

A woman's scream echoed out through the hall, and he turned in time to see Bridget stumble back from Kalenden with the king's sword stabbed deep into her leg. She dropped, unable to support her weight. Valiantly she tried to raise her weapon as the king bore down on her. His swing battered her blocking sword down and the barbed blade of the king's sword bit into her collar. She screamed out, blood spattering from the wound as she was held in place by blade and barb. The king tugged at the blade, digging the barbs deeper and evoking another shrill cry from Bridget.

Kalenden looked over at Endrance, and for the first time since they arrived, he smiled. He was showing the mage that he had won, that he had nothing to fear from him.

The mage's clothes rustled, and he looked down to see a trickle of golden light seep from Anna's still form and swirl dutifully into his bracer. It wasn't a lot of power, but with it came memories, impressions, and a sense of sadness that cut him to the quick. She was gone, wholly and truly gone.

There, he felt something stir deep within him. Something he'd never felt before with such intensity or depth. A rage, no, a wrath poured through him, and all the uncertainties he had didn't matter anymore. The icy fingers of despair were evaporated in an instant as this wrath swept through him. Nothing else mattered anymore, than the destruction of this fiend who manipulated him and hurt him deeper than anyone ever had. The king was wrong; he had *everything* to fear from him.

He stood, the wail in his throat turning into a hoarse shout as he turned on Kalenden. He thrust out his right hand, pouring energy through the spell scribed there without taking care for the amount he used. The power flowed through his arm, rippling the sleeve of his clothes. As the energy ignited the spell tattooed on his fingers, the lightning burned away the fingers of his glove as white hot lines rippled the air with heat and static charge. The sleeve of his shirt started smoking as more of his scribed spells came to light and burned at his clothing.

The king raised his left hand in defense, the palm towards him. "*Infernus.*" The king shouted, slinging a spell of his own. Angry green flames blasted out from his palm, the fire malevolent and concentrated in a line of flames.

Endrance released the power of his spell, and the throne room was lit as bright as the hearts of the suns. The lightning struck dead center of the incoming pillar of hellish fire, and blasted it outwards as it drilled through the force of Kalenden's spell. The king had as much if not more power than Endrance in this place, but the young mage had fury and skill beyond Kalenden. While the king had spent years learning from demonic tutors, siphoning away power during his reign, he could not have spent as much time practicing magic as this young man who had dedicated his whole life to the art.

And Kalenden was not even close to as angry as Endrance was.

The lightning dispersed the green flames as it powered through the king's spell, and touched the palm of his hand. There was a crack of thunder and the smell of singed flesh. Kalenden flinched back, his hand scorched even through the protective spells he had already laid in place, his gauntlet blasted into fragments from his burnt flesh. He let go of his sword, and Bridget fell the rest of the way, taking the blade down with her.

Selene was having a hard time fighting the assassin. The elf woman was skilled, talented in the art, and superhumanly nimble. While she had range and a weapon that was hard to predict, the assassin, had years of training and practice. The chain dagger was versatile, but she couldn't put her full strength behind the strikes without breaking the chain or shattering the blade with the supernatural strength she had. While she didn't have the muscle mass that Bridget did, she would guess she was likely as strong as Joven was.

It was just one part of being Nephilim, it seemed. On the other hand, her reflexes had improved since she realized what she really was. It was as if the demonic side of her was trying to prove its usefulness to her, to convince her to let her take control. Trying to show how much easier it would be to kill.

A scream echoed through the throne room, and her fighting rhythm was thrown off. Bridget! She saw her drop to her knees, and the king bringing his sword down on her, the Draugnoa vainly raising her curved chopping blade to defend.

289

In her moment of distraction, the assassin flung the last handful of her knives at the girl. The three blades, their edges seeping poison, found their mark. The blades caught her in her gut, her right shoulder, and left forearm as the Draugnoa flinched from the attack. Jalyin smiled. The fight was over. The barbarian outside might have been able to shake off one of her poisoned daggers like that day of the eclipse, but the eldest of the three Draugnoa succumbed to only one. This girl who hadn't even developed her abilities as Nephilim wouldn't stand a chance of fighting off three doses, alongside the injuries the knives gave her.

Selene looked back at the assassin, and as her vision blurred, she found the elf's smug smirk very irritating. Sinking to the ground, she felt a coldness seep through her, though her wounds burned terribly with poison. Her heartbeat faltered, and darkness swept over her.

I...I'm sorry, my love. She thought as her thoughts started fading. *I don't think I'm going to make it.*

The assassin watched a second longer as the woman admirably fought the poison before losing the battle. The room ignited in brilliant fire and lightning, and the assassin saw that Kalenden would need more assistance. That brat was going to be more trouble than it was worth. The jagged scars radiating from her abdomen where the mage's lightning had hit her ached sharply as she watched the man use the spell on Kalenden. If he had hit her with a spell of that potency, there wouldn't have been enough of her left to heal, much less gather with a broom.

Up from the darkness in Selene's mind, she heard her own voice laughing at her. The demonic side of her was still there, still vital and potent.

"You fool." She said. "Now we are going to die, and you could have stopped this, had you left me in control."

Selene had hardly the consciousness to respond, but in desperation replied. "Can you do anything now?"

"Not as we are." She said. "Please," her other half actually pleaded with her. "I don't want to die any more than you. Let me take control. I will wrest victory from this defeat."

Selene was nearly gone, and she decided then that it wouldn't matter either way. If she did or did not give up control, she would be lost. "Fine." She replied wearily. "You have control... of everything."

The demonic half of her didn't speak to her, but she felt like warm hands grasped her heart. The warmth grew into heat, and that heat grew... into hellfire.

Jalyin was considering how best to retrieve one of her throwing knives without getting caught in the crossfire between wizard and summoner, when a strange organic sound caught her attention. Looking back at the body of the last Draugnoa, she saw the body convulse and shudder. The Draugnoa must not quite have died from the poison.

"Oh, still alive?" she asked, drawing her long daggers. "I'll have to remedy that."

The assassin's approach halted almost immediately as the woman's head snapped up, her face in the rictus of a snarl. Selene's eyeteeth had elongated to fangs, and the back of her dress boiled as she pulled her feet under her and rose. Steam poured from the wounds on her body, and the three knives wiggled their way free of her body, clattering on the stone. Her square-pupil eyes glowed through the shadows cast by her hair. She held up a clenched fist and released of all things a trio of crumpled red feathers.

The back of the dress burst with the sound of flesh tearing as two bat-webbed wings erupted from her. Blood sprayed the pillar behind her, but the woman seemed beyond caring. The demon had finally risen to the surface.

Jalyin backflipped away, trying to gain some distance from the Nephilim, but the half demon was faster than she could have expected. The red eyed woman, her violet hair streaming behind her in the arcane starlight and trailing speckles of blood from unhealed injuries slammed into her face with a clenched fist. The world flipped end over end as the assassin was rocked half a dozen yards back, crashing to the ground in a daze.

Kalenden growled as he squared his shoulders to the mage, whose fingers still smoked from his spell. "You will have to do better than that to best me, whelp." He grated, raising his hands. Though the king tried to seem unsurprised, Endrance could see the tremble in the king's exposed hand.

Endrance raised his as well, his rage making the feeling that his hand was on fire trivial and unimportant. The next exchange of spells would be the most important battle of his life, and he wanted the man dead. Pain was something he had shrugged aside.

The first few seconds was a blur of motion, magic, and chaos. Elements were thrown at each other; the air trembled and crackled with power. Whenever one threw fire, the other rebounded with ice or water. Chunks of the stone floor rose to catch lightning flung, and whirlwinds swatted stone fragments out of their paths. In this place, the king had access to an enormous amount of power, but the mage was not without his tricks.

Scattered across his body, the lines of his meridians glowed with arcane power. Traces of golden light shined through the cloth of his clothes, and the wizard's own protective magic soundly defended against the powers the king threw at him. The young mage had woven a powerful spell into his left forearm that trailed up the meridians and formed a hypnotic spiral in the palm of his hand. As long as Endrance gave the spell power, he was able to safely touch elemental forces with that hand and redirect them somewhere safer. Already the sleeve of his shirt had disintegrated under the heat of the hellfire he batted out of the way, and his bracer gleamed with the light of the dozens of small stars hanging in the darkness.

As the two battled, Jalyin unsteadily pulled herself to her feet. While she had been able to roll with the hit, the blow had still caught her off guard. Selene appeared in the air above her, diving down with her hands formed into claws. The assassin evaded, and saw up close her nails had actually become talons, her fingertips bloody from the forced transformation.

The Nephilim was caught up in the throes of her otherworldly heritage, something that she would have been taught to protect against, if she had not slipped through Kalenden's fingers. It was poor planning on his part. A berserk half demon was sometimes more dangerous than a full breed. At least a full demon could know when to retreat, or when to stop fighting.

Jalyin dived back into the fray, slicing at the woman with her daggers. More often than not, her blades struck home, cutting into Selene's skin, and slicing away parts of her dress and clothes. The Draugnoa paid no mind, instead slashing at the assassin with her hands in primal fury. Leather was flayed, and the assassin was cut as badly as the woman was. The elf got leverage on one of Selene's arms, and threw her over her shoulder, trying to get some room to think.

The woman's wings snapped open to catch her in mid air, and she righted herself as she landed on her feet. Scarlet eyes burned angrily as every nerve of her being trembled with the desire to do great violence to Jalyin. The assassin, bleeding and battered, felt a flutter of fear for the first time in decades.

With a roar that was as much feral animal as it was human, Selene rushed towards the assassin, her bloody talons gleaming in the starlight.

Endrance was exhausted, but he couldn't give up the fight. A lot of his power had been spent battling king Kalenden, but that initial volley was the most damage he had managed to inflict on him. The king had put up too many warding and protective spells while the mage had been working his way up to the castle, and stripping those away would take too much time to do him any good.

Panting, he eyed the king. The man seemed at long last to be tiring, but did not look nearly as worn out as the wizard was feeling. The wizard couldn't beat the man in his own house at his own game. It was time to do something different.

"Those are some wards you've got." Endrance stated. "Did your demons teach you those?" He threw out a low powered lightning bolt, which scattered in the air a foot from the king's face.

"Yes." Kalenden said, seeing weakness in his opponent and taking the opportunity to lord it over him. "They taught me how to defend against everything that could harm me." The king flung another volley of stone shrapnel at Endrance, forcing him to dive out of the way. His redirecting spell couldn't move physical objects. "They are the only ones who could teach me real power."

Endrance's mind raced. He knew he had a solution here, but what was it? He racked his brain, trying to figure it out. He remembered everything he had read through the studies he had made of demons after finding that first circle. Then, the answer came to him.

He stood up straight, his hands dropping to their side as the spell light faded from their tattoos. "The demons may have taught you much," Endrance admitted, "But you did not take into account something."

The king with his confidence unfaltering, scoffed. "And what would that be, whelp?" he asked, his voice dripping with scorn. The summoner called up a ball of hellfire and held it, ready to finish Endrance off.

Endrance raised his hands, and prepared to sling a spell he had thought he had forgotten. But as he attempted to remember it, the spell came looming to the forefront of his mind, fresh as the night he had accidently learned it. The intricacies of the spell rocketed through his mind and the he need only speak the final word of power to bring it to life.

"Demons don't have souls." He said. He thrust his hands out, fingers splayed, poured every last drop of power he had left into the spell and called out the final word of power.

"*Animorbus!*"

The soul lance had no visual component, but a thundering sound erupted from his outstretched hands. A shockwave of spiritual energy lanced out from his palms, crumbling the remains of his gloves to dust. The ripple of power washed through the air, extinguishing the few specks of light unlucky enough to be caught in its wake. Though spiritual in nature, the air between the two blasted in all directions, whipping Endrance's loose hair back.

Kalenden raised his hand to shield himself, but his eyes registered shock for the split second between him realizing his wards weren't working and the spell impacting him in the chest. The armored man rocked backwards, slamming into the throne and snapping the back clean off as he crashed to the ground. Dust flew up around him, and he did not rise again.

Endrance rushed up to the throne, and looked down at the body of the man he struck. King Kalenden lay dead, his soul shattered from his instantly lifeless body. The black armor of his breastplate crumbled to dust as he watched. The man was finally gone, his skin graying even in the pure white light of the multitude of stars.

Jalyin was able to misdirect Selene's attacks long enough to disappear around a pillar. As she took a steadying breath, she saw the king was slain. She grimaced part from pain and part from distaste. There went one of her compatriots. Now she would have to report back alone, and injured. If she wasn't careful she wouldn't survive leaving the room, much less meeting with her client.

The elf silently stooped, picking up a fragment of shattered stone, and flicked it towards the mages direction. As she expected of Selene in her berserk state, the Nephilim went after the noise. Now the mage would have to deal with her. As the enraged woman half ran, half flew towards the wizard she excused herself out one of the servants passages. It was not her job to die for her client, and she was going to have to be as clever as she ever had been if she wanted to survive reporting back.

Endrance turned from the body of the king as he heard a growling sound coming from behind him. He blinked in confusion as he saw what looked like Selene, but wasn't Selene rushing towards him, fingers slick with blood and webbed wings upon her back. The wildness of her flying hair gave him the split second impression of horns before she slammed into him with a full force tackle.

The woman hit him hard, and knocked the wind out of him. Dazed, with little energy left, and physically exhausted to begin with, he was unable to stop her from pinning him as they landed several feet from the body of the king. He looked up at her in panic, realizing that she had lost control of her demonic blood. Now she may very well kill him.

"Selene!" he wheezed out, trying to breathe. He opened his mouth to speak when she kissed him hard and rough. He froze in shock as he felt her tongue shove deep into his mouth and her hips started gyrating as she straddled him. The scent of fresh rainwater filled his nostrils, but there was a barely noticeable acrid scent to it, like a touch of sulfur. The fangs in her mouth cut into his lips as she savagely kissed him.

Ah... Damn. He thought. *Succubus.*

He was unable to hold her off until she finally released her liplock on him. "Selene!" he blurted. "What are you doi-"

"Sex or death?" Selene asked, her voice drawn out in a breathy hiss. "Which do you want first?"

"Ah, I don't have time for this!" Endrance cried out, thrusting his hand up against her chest. "*Cularis!*"

The force of the spell flung her into the air with a yelp that sounded remarkably more like Selene than he had expected. She flared her wings, halting her ascent, and glared at him angrily. He had to get her to calm down so he could put his attention to saving as many lives as he could.

"Selene!" Endrance shouted. "Do not give up, shake this off! You are not alone!"

For the first time since she had awoken, the other half of her remembered those words from her dream. Her eyes wide, she saw for the first time that the darkness was alight with stars. Just like he had promised. As she looked down at him, she saw that many of those symbols and arcane marks glowed upon his person just like his dreams. It wasn't exactly the same; they were duller and they didn't cover his whole body, but they were there.

You see? Selene said to her demonic half. *He's there for us. I don't want to kill him, and I think you don't really want to either. Let's come back to him… together.*

Endrance wasn't sure what exactly changed, but Selene's face softened as she glided down to the stone. Her wings folded up against her back, taking up much less space than Endrance thought they would. Her eyes retained their demonic appearance, but finally he could see the human side of her had returned. She took a half step towards him, hesitant.

"Selene?" he asked tentatively.

She smiled; the fangs she had before were gone. She spread her hands, and he could see that her talons had returned to normal fingernails. "It's me." She said, her voice was normal, if not a little scratchy. She grimaced, rubbing at her throat. "I have to stop screeching like that." She admitted.

"Oh thank the gods." He exhaled, relieved. "We need to tend to Anna and Brid-"

He halted in speech as the air in the throne room started to stir. Golden light flared up from the bracer at his wrist. He looked down at it, and over at the corpse of the now deposed king, and paled as he realized the mistake he made. "Oh no!" he exclaimed, trying to scramble far enough away. "Not him!"

Too late, he realized that he had been close enough to the death of the strongest spellcaster he had fought since he sparred with his master so long ago. The bracer would capture the energy that fled Kalenden's aura, but with it would come knowledge. Endrance could not know for certain if he would only learn a little from the transfer, like he did with the goblin shaman, or if he would be overwhelmed with the subject's ego, like with the blood tiger. No matter which happened, he did not desire to learn any of the man's demonic magic.

The golden wind rushed up into the air from Kalenden's body, scattering specks of light in its passing. The power rushed to Endrance despite his efforts to escape and siphoned down into the gemstone. The gem returned to its full brilliance as it gathered the remaining power of his aura.

Endrance lost the ability to run mid-stride, falling to his knees, and slowly collapsing to his side clutching his head. Images, memories, vile knowledge sifted through his mind. The only thing that kept him conscious was that it was not the first time his mind had been bombarded so, and this was only a single stream of memories, not an endless torrent like before. As the power flowed into his bracer, and the memories flowed into his head, he was able to gather his concentration, focus his mind, and put the incoming information into perspective.

Inside the library of his mind, the reflecting pool of water in the center shivered, and as he stood upon it, he looked to the ground around it. The pool rose up on a pillar of stone, steps falling naturally as the column rose to the center point of the room. From there, he waved a hand at one far wall and at his command, everything regardless of memory or knowledge he was gathering from the king was shelved there in books.

He was not sure if it was the nature of the knowledge he was sorting, or that somewhere in his mind he desired it to be so, but the shelves turned black as coal as the demonic red and black bound books flew into its spaces. As the trickle of information faded away, Endrance clenched the hand pointing at the shelves. Iron bars and chains sprang into existence, locking him out from the knowledge, but also locking it in.

As he was about to return his focus to the world around him, he caught the flutter of a single memory he missed. Reaching out, the speck of sound and light that hadn't even formed into a page came to rest on his palm. A single, short memory.

Kalenden growled in frustration as he read through the correspondence he had been handed. He looked up at the deliverer with a scowl. Jalyin merely shrugged in the face of his frustration.

"What do you mean, she won't send any more assistance?" he demanded the letter crumpling in his clenched fist. "I've fulfilled my part of the bargain! She has not given me what she promised!"

Jalyin shrugged again, eyeing him with the amusement of a predatory cat. "I think she has. She taught you how to better use those demons you were summoning."

"Fifteen years ago!" he shouted, standing. "And I had already learned how to summon them before she showed up!"

Jalyin scoffed, her black leather armor soaking in the light from the fire in the room. "You were summoning whores, your majesty. She showed you that they had more to teach than just bedroom antics."

"I swear to you…" Kalenden growled. "If that whelp manages to interfere in my plans-"

"Oh, do try to have some sense." Jalyin retorted. "You gave her all the Crystalphage she asked for, what leverage do you have left, oh great king? You have me and nothing else." She narrowed her eyes at him. "And you may not even have that much if you don't change your tone."

A tense moment passed. Kalenden sighed, dropping back into his chair. "Fine." He said with resignation. "Any news on the search?"

"Not yet." Jalyin reported. "He managed to escape the fire without leaving any traces." She touched her abdomen as she spoke. "And the eclipse kept everyone who could have seen them in their houses. We may have to consider they left the city entirely."

Kalenden leaned back, rubbing his neck. "That may do us some good. I have to show my son to the people this afternoon, and I don't want any unexpected surprises."

"You know I can't make public appearances." Jahyin responded. "But if something goes wrong, come back here. I'll help however I can."

"At least you are." He admitted. "I wish I could say the same for Valeria."

Endrance blinked, coming out of his trance. Selene was shaking his shoulder and calling his name, but he couldn't hear her for a moment as the words of Kalenden's memory echoed through his head.

"I wish I could say the same for Valeria."

Valeria was the name of the prior Archmagus of Ironsoul, the woman who had centuries before trained his master, Kaelob, when she was just a wizard. She was also believed dead, having died alongside two wizards in an experiment gone wrong around the time he was born. This was too much information for him to deal with at the moment; he filed it away along the rest of his memories.

Endrance picked himself up with Selene's assistance. Somehow she had returned to her completely human appearance. As he stood, the doors across the hall slammed open, shedding more torchlight into the hall. Joven burst into the hall, dripping blood and breathing hard. Almost a dozen crossbow bolts stuck from his armor and body, and Endrance would have been surprised he was standing at all, if he hadn't known the man.

Behind his bodyguard were dozens of men and women with torches and weapons. They had finally gotten through the gates and came to deal with the traitor-king.

Endrance waved weakly. "Hey." He said, his voice carrying across the great hall. "A little help here?"

Chapter 35

Endrance stood on the trampled and packed dirt where once his longhouse stood. Wrapped in heavy winter furs, he watched the construction crew as they worked. Men dug foundations, and workers chiseled at the stone wall that the longhouse had been built up against. As he watched, a mason measured the pass back to the hot springs, shouting orders to the men working under him.

Joven stood nearby, the both of them grim faced in the gray morning light. It had been one month since the kingdom had risen up to overthrow their king, and while it was still in political turmoil, the regular people, the ones who served in the military, worked the farms, or built homes, had returned to a relative normal in the face of the coming winter. The month had been the hardest Endrance had ever experienced.

"General Balen says they found no sign of the child or the demoness Kalenden had posing as his wife." Joven reported. "They did find a skeleton of a woman in the dungeons; Balen says it's probably his real wife."

The mage nodded. "I figured that was what had happened. She probably escaped with the child within the hour we defeated Kalenden."

Another silence passed. Endrance watched but not paid attention to the work building a new, stone structure longhouse. He had consulted directly with the masons in the redesign, and in time it would be better than before.

"Selene said she was going to stay with Bridget a while longer." Joven said, placing a hand on Endrance's shoulder. "She's having trouble adapting to using her left."

Endrance sighed, fogging the air in front of him. He couldn't let himself cry, his tears would freeze in his eyes. Now, like his physical body, his heart ached. "I did what I could."

"I know," Joven said comfortingly, "No one else could have saved her life. She's glad she lost only the arm, even if she won't admit it to you."

"I know. I know." The mage muttered. He returned to silence, staring at the work crews but not watching them. Tears threatened to fall as the wintry winds picked up.

A few moments passed uncomfortably before Joven looked back at him. "You know… Anna was a great woman. I'm certain she is glad to see you moving forward."

Endrance glanced back at his bodyguard. In addition to the normal weaponry he carried, a short spear and metal shield had been added. He shut his eyes, filtering through the pain that clenched at his heart. "It hurts like this every time, doesn't it?" he asked. "Every time you lose someone."

"Yes."

"I don't suppose the pain goes away, does it?"

"No. It just… becomes easier to bear, I guess."

"And I have to do this again, won't I?"

"For as long as you live, my friend."

Endrance stood watching for a while longer. The king's body had been thrown aside, and the pillar carved with his deeds was being defaced in the light of his deeds. There was talk of some of the other barbarian tribes making their way to Balator with intent on claiming the throne for their own. Endrance knew not what kind of effect it would have on the people here, but he guessed one lord's rule would be just as bad as the other.

A man on a light horse rode up to the two of them. Joven's hands touched the axe of his father, which he now carried with him at all times. "What is it?" he demanded of the messenger.

"General Balen sends you a message!" the rider called. After Kalenden's death, the magic he had used to corrupt Balen's mind had faded, and the general was appalled at his behavior. Since then he had been doing everything in his power to keep the military in line and maintain the peace within the walls. Word had been sent to the armies abroad to return to the city.

"General Rohl is returning with twenty thousand men. The remaining ten thousand will be fortifying our borders." The runner relayed. "He says that there's trouble coming from the southwest."

"Trouble?" Joven asked. "Our southwest borders end on the icy shores of the ocean."

"I'm just relaying what he told me." The runner admitted, wheeling his horse. "Last, there is a visitor here to see the Spengur."

"A visitor? Here?" Joven asked.

"We kept him at the front gates." The runner answered. "He comes from Ironsoul."

Endrance's attention perked. "I haven't heard any message from my homeland since I arrived here." He stated. "I'd like to hear what this man has to say."

An hour later, they rode up to the grand gates of Balator. There, a man rode upon a black horse, wearing heavy fur clothing against the snow and still his teeth chattered. Escorting him were six men in the winter armor of Ironsoul's military. They didn't look any more comfortable than their emissary did.

"I apologize for the delay, but it takes time to ride up and down a mountain." Endrance said, riding up near the man in furs. Joven eyed the six men and scowled. "Please, do you have a message for me?"

"You are Endrance from Wayrest? The... Spengur of Balator?" the man asked, looking at the lean man who sat before him.

"Yes. Yes I am." Endrance admitted, feeling more certain of who he was now than when he had set out nearly a year before. "I am Endrance, the Spengur of Balator and Wizard of the Circle of Magi."

The man nodded, pulling a thin scroll case and holding it out to the mage. "It took us some time to find you, and request allowance through the circle, but we are finally here." The man spoke in an officious tone.

Endrance opened the case, retrieved the scroll, and read through it. With surprise on his face, he looked up at the man before him. "What is the meaning of this?" he demanded.

The man drew himself up, giving a declaration. "By order of High King Mastadon, and with approval of the Arch Magus of the Circle, for the murder of a regional magistrate and four soldiers of the royal army, Endrance of Wayrest is to be put under arrest and brought back to the capitol for judgment."

End of Book One.

Look out for the continuation of Endrance's story in the next Spellscribed book!

6896124R00178

Printed in Great Britain
by Amazon.co.uk, Ltd.,
Marston Gate.